I0535336

SKY HORSE

SKY HORSE

Kate Andrus

Copyright © 2016 Kate Andrus
All rights reserved.

ISBN: 0692776273
ISBN 13: 9780692776278

This is a work of fiction. Names, characters, places, and incidents are either the product of the author's imagination or used fictitiously. Any resemblance to actual persons, living or dead, business establishments, events or locales is entirely coincidental.

This book is dedicated to the memory of our dear friend Noel Twyman. Your love of the land and the sport of foxhunting came alive for me with every story you told. I hope I was able to do justice to them on these pages.
We miss you, friend.

PROLOGUE

———

THE HARSH SQUEAL OF BRAKES and a hot rush of air were all that he felt before the sickening crash that threw his world into chaos. The vehicle bucked and spun, twisting violently before tumbling, tumbling, tumbling. He held tightly to the wheel, unbelieving, as his body rode the movement of the truck. And then suddenly, the world stopped. He perceived lights, red and blue and white, coming toward him through the fog and smoke. A crumpled mass of metal in the ditch ahead of him.

His ears were filled with the sound of the screaming horse. He climbed through the wreckage, glass and twisted metal tearing at his skin. The screaming intensified, threatening to swallow him whole. He crawled and crawled, but he made no headway. He knew he had to get there. He knew only he could save it.

He finally saw the horse. It stood near the wreckage, steam rising from its body. It no longer screamed. The horse flicked its head at the sight of the man and walked to him with its head down. The man felt its breath as the horse leaned over him and whispered a muffled nicker. Thank god, he whispered, throwing his arms around the big colt's neck. Thank god.

Suddenly, his arms were ripped away. Blood drenched the sleeves of his shirt. The horse was gone. The scream of the man replaced that of the horse. It ripped through his body, threatening to break him apart. The sound punctured through the shroud of darkness and echoed across the night.

The sound of his own voice wakened him from the dream and he sat up with a start. He got out of bed, sheets and t-shirt drenched in sweat. He brought his hands to his face and rubbed it as he stumbled to the sofa. It was still dark, he noted, but nothing could induce him to go back to sleep. Not with the horse there waiting for him.

———————

CHAPTER 1

THE WOMAN DREAMED OF HORSES.

The drum of a thousand hoof beats punctuated her sleep. She turned her head toward the sound and felt the force of their power reverberate across the convex surface of the frozen landscape. Black and bay and chestnut and gray they came, powerful legs plundering the ground, feet striking and rising in unison. As they passed, she felt the hot swirl of breath and heated bodies combine, and she caught the fragrant scent of sweat and salt and something else she could not name. She wondered whether she should be afraid. But no, she smiled in her sleep. That other scent was pure joy.

Her heart choked with loss as she watched them disappear over the horizon. She scanned the ridgeline, holding her breath until she saw what she was looking for.

The white horse. He stopped and looked back at her, pawing the ground and tossing his head. Steam rose from his body, cloaking him in a mist that glistened in the reflected light of the starry sky. She was meant to follow, she knew. She held out her hand and stepped tentatively toward him....

As he stretched his long neck toward her, a ray of light broke through the clouds and shone warm on her face. She turned away, unconsciously brushing the heat from her eyes. The sudden move startled the horse, and she knew before she saw that he had bolted.

———————

The harsh blare of a trucker's horn out on the highway tore Annie from her sleep. "The horse!" She bolted awake as the horse's whinny faded into the air. "He's calling me. Where did he...." She opened her eyes to scan the horizon. But only the stark white of her bedroom walls met her eyes.

"A dream," she muttered. "Damn, it was only a dream." She collapsed back into her pillows and gave herself over to the comfort of her bed, snuggling deeper under the down comforter. If she kept her eyes tightly shut, she thought, perhaps she could call back the vision of the horse.

But it was no use. The insistent hum of cars speeding along Interstate 95 outside her apartment tugged urgently at her for the day to begin. She rolled over, listening now to the sounds of morning in a busy city. She heard the mumble of a television; neighbors watching the morning news. Somewhere nearby a dog was protesting its fate. Why on earth, she wondered, did people get animals that were bred to live in packs, and then leave them alone in three hundred square feet of unnatural materials, to live most of their lives alone and lonely?

Annie opened her eyes and stared at the ceiling. The stark white of the apartment walls had a cold quality that was not softened by the warmth of the morning light. If it weren't for the luxurious bedding, the room would have all the charm of a jail cell. In reality, it wasn't much bigger. She stretched her arms out wide; a small and dubious luxury made ordinary by her solitary presence in the bed. Reluctantly, she tossed the blankets aside and got up.

She turned on the shower and paused to examine her hair in the mirror. She ran her fingers through the mass of red curls that, as always, had turned into a tangled frenzy during the night. The steady march of white strands was unmistakable. She peered more closely. Her mother's green eyes, complete with crow's feet, stared back at her. She sighed. Probably time to make an appointment with the hairdresser.

As she showered, Annie thought about the horse. The dream felt like a powerful message, a warning to her that something missing was about to return. Annie leaned her head back and closed her eyes as the water ran over her wet mass of curls and down her back. She ran a bar of soap over her skin and felt a ripple of satisfaction at its smoothness. If only the rest of her body wasn't losing its battle to aging.

She turned off the water and reached for a towel, chuckling to herself. *Powerful token horses coming to give her a message?* she thought. *Ridiculous.* She rolled her eyes at her own foolishness. *The dream probably had something to do with sex.* She would have to remember to ask Elliot what he thought.

Annie was startled from her reverie by the insistent chirping of her cell phone. She grabbed her hair and twisted it into a neat pile, quickly knotting it at the back of her neck. Smiling, she wrapped herself in the towel and reached for the phone.

Annie glanced at the clock and nodded to herself. Elliot always called at seven.

"Good morning," she said. She heard over the scuffle and bark of dogs in the background. She smiled and waited, knowing that at that moment he was doling out scraps of his peanut butter toast to their mob of French hounds, a particularly cute breed recognized by the American Kennel Club as the Petit Basset Griffon Vendeen, or PBGV for short.

"Hey!" he finally said. "Sorry, there's a bit of a ruckus here."

"Sounds like you are doing the morning feeding," she said, imagining him surrounded by their pack of scruffy hounds, all clamoring for their share. Annie shed the wet towel onto the bedroom floor and shrugged herself into a robe. In the kitchen, the auto-setting on her coffee pot had done its magic. She gratefully poured herself a cup.

"Breakfast is done," he replied. She heard him shush the pack into temporary order. "These scoundrels are just trying for some of mine."

"Your own fault," Annie laughed. "You're the one who gave them a taste for peanut butter."

"Yeah, yeah," he answered. He tried to sound gruff, but Annie heard the smile he was trying to suppress.

"Before I forget," Annie said, "you need to take Dodie over to Sam's by 2 o'clock on Friday. Sam is doing the Pennsylvania and North Carolina dog show circuits and has Dodie entered for a couple week run. She thinks she can finish her this round."

"Ok," Elliot said. "Hang on." Annie heard him shuffling to find a pen. Sam, their dog handler, was fussy about the dog's needs out on the road. "I'll pack Dodie's food and toys, but it looks like she's due for her Bordetella shot."

Annie sat down at the counter and clicked open her laptop. "Hmmm. Okay." Her eyes wandered to the email in front of her. She made a few hasty keystrokes to compose a reply.

"Can you call him?"

"Call who?" She took her eyes off the screen. "Wait, say that again?"

"You never listen," Elliot said.

"I was listening." She swiveled in her chair, putting the computer screen to her back.

"I said Dodie needs her Bordetella vaccine before she goes out."

Annie sighed. "Ok, swing by Doctor John's and get it done. I'll call him after I get off with you."

"What time will you be home on Friday?"

She hit a key to bring up her calendar, and quickly scanned the contents of the week. "My last meeting is at 3."

"We have the Jordan's at 6:30, remember. It's a two-hour drive home so you should just make it if you don't dally."

"I'll get there."

"And I was hoping to plow under the garden later this week."

Annie glanced up at the bedside clock. It told her she had to get going. "Are the Brussels sprouts all out?" She gathered up the pile of marketing analysis that she had meant to look over the night before, shoving them unread into her briefcase.

"Yes, everything is out. I want to get the peas in as early as I can this spring, so I'd like to have the soil ready."

Peas. That reminded her. The new book. She sighed again. "I have a million things to do this weekend, and I need to work on that new recipe." She made a mental note to stop at the grocery store on the way home on Friday. Or even better, maybe Elliot could get them. "When I get home tonight, I need to make a grocery list…."

"That's not your home."

"What?" She picked up the discarded towel and hung it in the bathroom, then quickly chose an outfit from her closet.

"I said that apartment is not your home. This is your home."

Annie caught her reflection in the hallway mirror as she fumbled into her clothing, phone tucked under her chin. God, I look lumpy, she thought. She straightened up and brushed her hand over the place in her skirt that should have been smooth.

"Did you hear me?"

"What?"

"I said this is your…."

Annie sighed and rolled her eyes. "I know that. It's just easy to say." She hated to admit that the work apartment, as she and Elliot called it, was more likely to qualify as her home these days. She saw her real home much less often.

"Well, don't forget it. I'm holding our life together all week long. I don't want you to lose sight of your real focus."

"Okay, okay, sorry." She glanced at her watch again.

"I'll let you go. I know you are antsy."

"I'm running late. I'll call you later." She paused and added, "I love you." She hung up the phone and grabbed her briefcase. Another awkward goodbye, she thought. There had been too many of them recently. And she had forgotten to ask him about white horses.

Elliot and Annie had moved to Charlottesville not long after college. Her first real job had brought her there, and she had immediately fallen in love with the rolling mountains, the soft, hot summers and the fields full of grazing animals. After years of saving money and mooning over the area's beautiful farms, they had finally bought a place just outside of town. Twin Oaks was a few acres of pasture and woodland with the Rivanna River running through it. It had been the perfect place to raise their four children. Their daughters Emily and Bella were grown and out of the house now, and the twin boys Jake and Galen were in college. The place was probably too big, Annie thought, as she imagined Elliot rattling around the house by himself.

The region around Charlottesville held every kind of pleasure for them, from the vineyards and Sunday afternoon polo matches to the vibrant downtown district. It was rich in history too, more than enough for both Revolutionary and Civil war buffs. Another bonus was The University of Virginia, Thomas Jefferson's magnificent university, where they could buy their children a good education at a reasonable price. And of course, it had the foxhunting community.

The problem, she thought, was that she was too busy to enjoy any of it these days. Although she hated to admit it, her job was taking a toll—on her health, on her enjoyment, and on her marriage. She knew Elliot was lonely, and she was too.

She sighed. He was lucky. His freelance strategic planning work gave him the power to pick and choose. He could go out with the hunt club on a crisp winter morning or take the dogs for long rambles in the woods.

By contrast, Annie spent her life desk-bound from morning to night. That is, she thought, when she wasn't on a plane or rushing from meeting to meeting. She had always loved working in marketing. Her latest job, as VP of Marketing for DenseLogic, was to establish the little tech start-up firm into a power player. They had taken a mundane concept—what is consumer behavior—and revolutionized it so that that companies could practically see into people's kitchens and bedrooms. For someone with an old-school marketing background, Annie found the work particularly rewarding. Her tried and true marketing methods were invaluable in establishing customer awareness and relationships, but she also enjoyed being stretched by the newer generation of marketing kids coming out of grad school. She loved the energy and creativity of her young staff.

She came home on weekends to whatever activities Elliot had planned, but often found that she was too tired and out of shape to participate in them fully. She cherished the image of her "real life" in Charlottesville, but more and more, she was struggling to actually live it.

And then there were the cookbooks. Annie's passion for cooking was just a hobby, she told herself, but she and Elliot had managed to combine their talents for writing and photography into a few interesting and attractive books. Now and then, her editor even asked her to write on other topics. Over the years, Annie had several published titles to her credit. People often asked her how she found the time, and she answered honestly that she had never known a minute that couldn't be put to use. Some people watched TV or knitted or—god forbid—took naps in their free time. Annie wrote. Even when the kids were little, she had gone to work all day, and then squeezed in several hours of writing early in the morning and late into the night.

Most of her books hadn't sold all that well. Still, they were satisfying in their own way. The book she had written last year, Potatoes Galore, had apparently filled a hole in her publisher's list. Such a silly title, she thought, but against all logic, that one seemed to be doing pretty well.

Her publisher in New York had become a good friend over the years. Dorothy Traver of Halcyon Days Publishing was even the namesake of their newest puppy. She dismissed Annie's excuses that she was too busy to write books when she worked so much. "Bullshit," she had said. "You have even more time than you used to. What else is there for you to do at night, sitting in that apartment by yourself?"

Dodie had a point. Life away from home was a lonely place after work, and Annie found solace in the routine of researching, writing and refining recipes late into the evening. She cooked evenings and weekends, and Elliot worked with a food stylist to re-test and photograph the food during the week. It was a good system.

On Friday afternoon, Annie navigated Route 29 south, away from Northern Virginia and its frenetic pace. Subdivisions and shopping centers eventually gave way to rolling hills and pastures. As always, she allowed herself a deep sigh when she got her first good glimpse of the Blue Ridge Mountains, just as she neared the village of Warrenton. The sight of the mountain told her it was time to release the problems of the office. She gave an involuntary shudder as she shifted her thoughts toward home.

She thought again of the white horse and glanced at the dashboard clock. There was just enough time for a quick stop at Horse Country, the beautiful tack shop nestled into a quaint corner of the town. A new pair of breeches would be a good idea, she thought. Unfortunately, they would have to be a larger size than anything she had at home. She sighed, questioning the logic of stopping at the store. She hadn't ridden in a long time, and there was no immediate need to go shopping. Still, something compelled her to take the exit and follow the winding road to the little shop at the end of the Alexandria Turnpike.

Annie wandered the aisles of the store, looking for something in her size. She finally found a pair of stretchy black breeches that did not cut off the circulation to her thighs. That odious task accomplished; she browsed a little and found an irresistible Baker plaid dog coat. Aideen, the slim Irish woman who helped her at the counter, admired the jacket and asked what breed it was for.

"PBGV," Annie answered, eyeing the shiny fox pins in the store's glass display case.

Aideen raised her eyebrows. "I thought those dogs had rough coats. Hunting dogs, aren't they?"

Annie blushed unaccountably. "Well, it is for an elderly dog that we keep clipped," she answered, suddenly embarrassed. *It's just a cute coat,* she thought. *Why am I making excuses?*

Aideen wrapped the breeches and tucked them into a bag. Annie felt sure that the tag with the XL size emblazoned on it was noticed by the other customers waiting at the counter. She grabbed the bag and hurried away with her purchase. Country girl she might be, she told herself, but she suddenly felt like a fraud—buying breeches in a size no horse should have to carry, and buying a jacket for a dog that didn't need it. When she got home, she thought, she would quickly slip the breeches into her bottom drawer so she wouldn't have to explain her purchase to Elliot. She could just imagine herself telling him, "I bought new riding breeches because of a dream." He would think she was cracking up. Well, maybe she was.

———

Annie stretched and smiled, extending her hand to the other side of the bed where Elliot lay. He rolled towards her, reaching out to gather her into a sleepy embrace.

Annie sighed and curled into his arms. "I can't believe it's already Monday," she whispered into his neck.

"Sshh…just a few more minutes." He stroked his hand over her back, lulling her back toward sleep. "You'll wake the dogs."

But it was too late, they both knew. Already the pack, alerted by their movement, were patrolling the edge of the bed, waiting for the sign to start the day.

Annie stretched again and rolled out of bed, snatching up her robe. "It seems like the weekends go by faster and faster," she said.

Elliot nodded, sitting on the edge of the bed and tousling dog heads as they popped up to greet him. "I'm exhausted," he said, "Too much company, too many outings. Maybe we could have a quiet weekend one of these days."

Annie nodded absently. She picked up the overnight bag she used for weekday travel and carried it into the bathroom.

Elliot shrugged and got out of bed. The dogs immediately gathered at his feet. "Come on, monsters," he said mildly. "Time to go outside." He opened the bedroom door to allow the stream of noisy fur to escape and called over his shoulder, "going to put on the coffee." He saw Annie wave her agreement as she reached for her toothbrush.

———

"So what's going on this week?" Elliot asked as he poured her a cup of coffee.

"The office shouldn't be too crazy, and I'll have to get right into the car Friday afternoon and head up to Philly for the dog show. I'm meeting

Sam at the hotel." Their long-time handler was a striking blonde who always smelled of cigarettes and dog talc, but who really knew her way around the show ring.

"Ok," Elliot said, sighing. "I hate it when you are away on weekends."

Annie grimaced. "You could come too."

"I know, but I promised I would go fly fishing with Jeff on Saturday, and I'm taking pictures of the hunt trials on Sunday."

She reached for his hand and squeezed it. "Your life is so much more fun than mine."

"Right," he said. "You love your work."

Annie sighed. "It's true, I do." She glanced at her watch. "Gotta go." She gave Elliot a quick kiss and headed to her car for the two-hour drive to the office.

The office complex where Annie worked had a pleasant, youthful vibe. There were all the traditional perks of the millennial work environment—ping pong tables, organic lunches, video games and an outdoor Zen garden. Annie's favorite place, though, was the nice pond-side path behind the complex. After her round of Monday morning meetings, she skipped the tofu and kale tacos being offered in the company's cafe.

"John, I'm going for a walk," she called over her shoulder as she passed her assistant's desk.

"Your afternoon is full," he called back. "Gene has the investors here and...."

"I won't be long."

Annie set a quick pace around the two-mile path. She hoped the exercise might pump some blood back into her brain after the morning's mind-numbing meetings. Instead, it seemed to drain the last of her energy.

"It's the humidity," she told the ducks who skittered to the water's edge in hope of a handout. She hadn't brought anything to share so they did not stay to listen to her excuses.

She sat down on the bank, heedless of the grass stains that she would surely find when she got up. The exodus of the ducks suddenly made her feel lonely.

The most natural thing in the world would be to call Elliot and admit that she was feeling stagnant, that this life wasn't working for her anymore. He would soothe and sympathize. But she knew this was something she had to fix herself.

Annie's weight had skyrocketed in recent years to a number she couldn't admit, even to herself. She was out of shape, out of touch, and her home life was just a story she told people. Her work had always defined her, but somehow that definition seemed inadequate to her these days. Maybe it was her recent birthday, she thought. Or maybe it was those damned gray hairs in the mirror.

Her cell phone vibrated to life. She reached into her pocket and glanced at the screen. "Meeting in 10 minutes!" John's text was accompanied by an anxious-faced emoticon.

Annie stood up and brushed off the back of her pants, silently commanding herself to dismiss the gloomy thoughts. There was no room in her life for this kind of reflection. She just had to carry on. And that was what she was going to do.

CHAPTER 2

———————

"THANK GOODNESS YOU'RE HERE!" SAM tossed Annie a leash as she walked into the hotel room, already blue with cigarette smoke. "Take Dodie out to pee, would you? I have got to get this Havanese clean. He's on first thing in the morning."

Annie watched her carry the struggling ball of fur into the bathroom where the water was already running. Dodie stood on her hind feet and scratched furiously at Annie's leg, demanding her attention. She reached down and scratched the dog's ears, noting with approval the dog's immaculately trimmed coat.

"She looks great, Sam!" Annie called into the bathroom. She didn't wait for a reply, knowing that she wouldn't be heard over the sound of splashing dog.

Annie sat on the bed and looked around the room. Show clothing was strewn across the bed and floor, and there were stacks of show catalogs, paperwork and dog food stacked on the side table. Everywhere, there was dog hair. She shook her head as she clipped the leash to Dodie's collar and led her into the hall. No wonder hotels hated dog people.

Annie enjoyed the atmosphere of the dog show world, with its beautiful canine stars and the odd assortment of humans who served them. She was at ringside to see her dogs as often as possible. After her champion Micah had died, some of the joy had gone out of showing her perfect and perpetually funny dogs. Still, the National Dog Show in Philly was one of her favorites and she tried not to miss it, whether she had a dog entered or not. And now with Dodie, the beautiful little bitch that she and Elliot had acquired from friends in Finland, she had a renewed desire to be there.

———

Dodie won her class on Saturday and Sunday, bringing her point total to ten, well on her way to her title.

"Nice job," Annie said as Sam left the ring. Sam thrust the blue ribbon into her hand, along with Dodie's leash.

"Good bitch," said Sam, in her professional "don't mess with me" mode. Annie got out of her way as Sam sent her assistant into the ring with another dog. "Take this and fix her head," Sam said, tossing a brush in Annie's direction. "I will be right back."

Annie rolled her eyes but bent down obediently to smooth Dodie's tousled hair. Despite the fact that Sam needed to go back into the ring for Best of Breed, she knew nothing was going to stop her from going outside for a quick cigarette.

After the breed judging was over, Sam found Annie back in the benching area. "You staying for Groups? The Havanese won his breed so we'll be in there."

"No, I can't get back home so late today. I have work in the morning."

"When the hell are you going to get off that merry-go-round?" Sam demanded.

"When we don't have to eat, I guess," Annie muttered. She looked up and met Sam's concerned eyes. "I mean; retirement is a little way off yet."

Sam shrugged and pointed to the little white Havanese that was dozing patiently on the grooming table. "Well, don't worry about me," she said. "That one's got a future. He ought to keep me going for the foreseeable future." She swept her hand toward the kennels of snoozing show dogs that lined her space. "Business has been picking up lately. People are coming back since the recession eased."

Annie nodded. "Looks like it. Good for you."

Sam scooped up a pile of ribbons. "Anyway, your dog's almost finished." She deposited Dodie's ribbons into Annie's hands. "Not bad, huh?" Annie looked down at what amounted to a very expensive handful of satin. She shook her head and sighed.

Sam raised her eyebrows. "You sigh a lot, have you ever noticed that?"
Annie chuckled. "Yeah, I've heard."
"You okay?"
"Yeah, just tired. Lots going on at work." She ruffled Dodie's head and gratefully accepted a couple of kisses before leaving the wriggling little dog in the arms of the handler.

Annie's thoughts took a depressing turn on the drive back to northern Virginia. She loved showing dogs and that new little bitch was certainly worth the effort, she thought, but a persistent voice in her head repeated, what is all this for? And if I love it so much, why aren't I doing it myself, instead of standing around watching?

Annie stopped for coffee at one of those giant service areas off of Interstate 95. She ordered a latte, and as an afterthought, added a cinnamon scone, remembering only after the first bite that she didn't like the taste of cinnamon. She stuffed it back into the bag and tossed it into the back seat.

She didn't want to go back to the apartment. Or more accurately, she thought, she didn't want to go back to the office. She picked up her phone and hit speed dial. Elliot's voicemail message answered cheerily. Annie sighed and clicked off without leaving a message. She tossed the phone on the passenger seat and stared at the road ahead, ignoring the insistent ring of his returned call.

CHAPTER 3

———

"ANN, DID YOU SEE THE dog show on TV this weekend?" John asked, popping out of his office as soon as he saw her bouncing red curls pass by the top of his cubicle wall.

"Yes, I was there," Annie replied.

"Oh, of course you were. I forget how fabulous your life is." John glowed. "I should have known."

"Yes, well…I don't know about that."

"Are you kidding, honey? Us city folk never do anything good. Your life is so…. interesting."

Annie smiled and excused herself. My pretend life, she thought. She sat down at her desk and unpacked her laptop. She always had troubling when she re-docked, and today was no exception. She stared into space while the computer did some kind of scan.

"Got a sec?" Her boss popped his head into the office, catching her off-guard and a little embarrassed.

"Sure, Frank. What's up?" Annie sat up and nodded at the computer screen. "Just waiting for this thing to decide what it needs to do."

He nodded, averting his eyes in a way that caught her attention. "What's up?" she asked again. "I thought you were traveling this week."

"Something came up," he said. "Can you meet me at ten?"

"Sure." Annie paused. "Anything wrong?"

"No, I'll see you then."

Just before the appointed time, Annie got up and walked over to Frank's office. The tech guys had been called to do whatever it was the computer wanted, so she went and poured a cup of coffee before heading over to the other side of the building. She was surprised to see Gene Ladden, the president of the company, in Frank's office. She assumed their meeting was running late.

"Sorry, I'll come back," she said, poking her head into the office. "Just call me when you are free."

"No, no, come in." Frank waved her in and gestured to a chair. "We're ready for you."

Gene began. "Annie, you know we're selling a chunk of the company to DataChurn."

"Yes, of course." The deal had been the buzz of the office for months.

"Well, I find that…" He hesitated again, glancing at Frank and then back again. "We have to re-allocate personnel…"

"Of course," she smiled. "With our growth this year, change is inevitable. Marcus is ready to move up now, I think."

He looked down at his notepad, tapping it with his pen. "Yes, that's my point. Marcus is ready." He looked up, still avoiding her gaze. "We'd like to put him in charge of the northern Virginia operation."

Annie felt a ball start to form in the pit of her stomach. "But, what about…"

"You know; we have always appreciated your work. I know that a lot of our success is due to the team you have built. Last quarter's figures alone were…."

Annie nodded, tuning out his words as she tried to collect herself. She felt the sting of tears behind her eyes. She looked at Gene and realized that his mouth was moving but she had no idea what he was saying. She willed her voice steady. "You're firing me?" she asked.

"No, no," the president said quickly, finally turning to look at her. "It's just that…"

She looked at him squarely, daring him to avert his eyes. He put his head down and stared at his notepad. For such a smart guy, she thought, he was terrible at confrontation. "What is it then?"

His eyes stayed down, the thrum of the pen in his hands betraying his nerves. "We'd like you to move to Dayton," he said finally.

"What?"

Gene glanced at Frank. "I know it would be a big change for you, but we thought it would be best now. The new investors are…."

"Young?" she asked mildly. "Hip? Cool?" She paused. "Under 40?"

"You know we have always valued…"

"Yeah, so you said." She raised her eyebrows. "At least you could have had the balls to actually fire me, Gene, instead of asking me to move to Siberia."

"We knew you might see it this way," he said. "But the Dayton operation is new and it would benefit from your experience." He looked up. "And I know how hard your current commute is, trying to keep your house in Charlottesville."

"Are you telling me I've taken my eye off the ball?"

"Well, not exactly. But even you can see how much investment things are taking these days. The next chapter of the company's future will require a lot of energy…"

"More energy than someone my age can muster?"

"Annie, don't take it this way."

Annie stood up and smoothed her skirt. She knew she was playing into their hands. They had called her in for one thing and they all knew it. Part of her wished she could deny it to them. She would go to Dayton, she thought, and blow them all away with her managerial skill. But she knew the truth as surely as they did. She was not going anywhere, at least not with them.

Her core vibrated with an energy that was neither anger nor joy. A strange sensation, she noted, that was nearer ecstasy than rage. She swallowed hard and leaned over the desk to steady her shaking legs. She looked from one of them to the other.

Annie had known these guys for five years. She'd questioned Gene's ability to grow the company, and had serious doubts about his management skills. But she had always liked him. He was only thirty-two, about the same age as her daughter Emily. Her maternal side actually felt proud of Gene's accomplishments, and she genuinely enjoyed helping him succeed. But for as much time as she spent teaching her own people leadership skills, the top of the company was hopelessly clueless. They were nothing more than boys with fancy algorithms.

"I quit," she said. She saw the two make brief eye contact as Gene reached for the folder that was on the desk in front of him.

"I was afraid you might feel that way," he said. "So I put together some papers...."

Annie turned her back and walked to the door. "Annie, wait," he said.

She turned and looked at the two of them one more time, then cast her gaze squarely at Gene.

"I'm ashamed of you," she said as she closed the door.

———

CHAPTER 4

ANNIE COULDN'T SLEEP. SHE TOSSED and turned, causing Elliot to threaten to sleep on the sofa. She knew he wouldn't, of course. Now that she was home full-time, he could not bear to be away from their warm bed.

She tried to lie as still as possible, feeling trapped under the layers of percale, fleece and down. When she did drift off, during the darkest and most depressing hours before dawn, the insistent buzz of questions woke her, opening her mind once again to the stream of what-ifs.

Annie glanced over at Elliot, frowning at his knack for easy sleep. She pretended to doze, all the while watching the bedside clock tick away the minutes. She was waiting for a number that expressed itself as morning, testing Elliot's patience for early rising. 5:42? No, that was too early, she thought. He groaned and rolled over, grumbling to himself.

When the clock strikes six, she thought. Even Elliot would have to admit that 6am was morning, and she could finally throw back the blankets and make her escape.

"What's wrong?" Elliot rolled over and opened one eye, sleepily surveying the tangle of sheets around Annie.

"What do you mean, what's wrong?" she whispered incredulously, rolling over to look into his eyes. "I still can't believe what I did."

"It's over," he said, closing his eyes again. "Go back to sleep."

Annie sighed and turned to stare at the ceiling, unaware of the fistful of blanket she had balled into her tensed hands. *You left the office on the spot,* her inner voice raged at her. *It felt good at the time,* she shot back.

Unprofessional, it answered, tsk-tsking back at her. *Oh shut up,* she said, rolling over and pulling the blanket over her head.

Her little voice was right though, she thought. That feeling of ecstasy was short-lived; now all she felt was remorse, and a little terror.

She glanced at the clock again. 5:59. Good enough, she thought. Annie threw the covers back and got out of bed. "Stay in bed," she said over her shoulder. "I'm going to make coffee." She heard the creak of the bed and knew Elliot would follow her, reluctant as he was to get up.

She turned on the coffee pot and pulled the butter and jam out of the cupboard. What's really bad, she thought, as she slid a slice of bread into the toaster, was the nagging sense that it was really over this time. She wasn't sure she could bounce back again and start over with a new firm.

Annie sighed and made a mental note to make some fresh strawberry jam. She frowned as she read the label. When had they started using this store-bought crap?

Annie tucked herself into the wingback chair and tried to conjure the image of the white horse. She suspected her problems had started with him. After all, wasn't he the one who made her start questioning her life?

It seemed he had deserted her too. If only she could sleep long enough for him to return, maybe he would have an answer.

———

While Annie could not tame her unsettled mind, she could at least try to keep busy.

"I'm running up to the apartment today," she said. "I have the movers coming at 1:00."

"You know, you have a couple of months left on your lease," Elliot said. "There's no rush." He bent down to kiss her forehead. "Christmas is coming. Maybe we could catch some concerts in DC. It might be handy to still have it."

Annie shook her head emphatically. "I want out of there as soon as possible. If I never see northern Virginia again, it will be too soon."

———

With the apartment taken care of, Annie turned her attention to her house. She ravaged every closet, cupboard and cabinet, cleaning each one out and replacing all the shelf paper. Now she bent over the old walnut floors in the great room, rubbing wax into the wood in wide circles.

"Slow down, would you?" Elliot said, watching her push sweaty wisps of hair off her damp forehead.

Annie sat back and shook her head. "No, it feels good," she said, gesturing to the floors. Her eyes took in the dusty shelves and dulled cherry paneling. "This room's been neglected. I'm going to touch everything before I'm done."

Elliot shook his head. "Knock yourself out." He stood at the door and looked back. "Anything I can do?"

"Stay out of my way."

When the floors were done, Annie cleaned out the fireplace and carried the ashes to the backyard. Elliot grumbled when he saw her put down the buckets and bend down to the pile of firewood that was his special project, but he just moved over and let her join him. They worked together silently, stacking a mountain of firewood.

After a couple of hours, Annie stood up and stretched her lower back.

Elliot stopped too, taking a sip from his water bottle and offering it to her. "Thanks for the help," he said.

Annie shook her head at the water and looked around. "Guess this will keep us for a bit," she said, standing back to admire the neat stacks of wood. "I'll just haul some in the house and lay a fire."

Elliot waved her off. "No, no, I'll do it," he said. "You know how I like my fires."

She shrugged. "Okay, it's time to put up Christmas trees anyway. I'll start on that."

Elliot rolled his eyes. There was one artificial tree for every room with a fireplace, as well as the foyer and the kitchen. It was the one thing he didn't want to help with, but he knew he would be roped into putting them up, especially the taller ones. "Okay," he said sullenly. "But I draw the line at decorating. That's up to you."

Annie nodded. She knew the rules. She tried to make the project of decorating the house cheerful, stirring up a batch of cookies and turning on Michael Buble singing Christmas tunes. One batch turned into dozens though, until Elliot finally declared enough was enough.

"I thought you were done," he said, eying the variety of cookies and fudge that covered the counter. "What are these?" He bent down to sniff a sheet of cookies that had just come out of the oven. He picked one up and held it to his nose. "Oatmeal?"

"Dog," Annie replied.

Elliot pulled the cookie back and examined it closer. "Dog?" he asked, puzzled.

"For the dogs. Their Christmas cookies." She turned and looked at his perplexed face as she deposited another tray on the counter. "You're right though, they' are oatmeal-based. And I'm sure you'd love the liver powder I added."

"Hmm," he said, putting down the cookie. "Guess I'll pass." He looked around the kitchen. "You about done?"

Annie nodded and opened the lid to a pot that was steaming on the stove. Elliot leaned it to take a whiff and wrinkled his nose. "What on earth is that?"

"Suet."

"Suet," he repeated. "Of course."

"For the birds. I stocked up the feeders, I noticed they needed suet."

"I'm sure I have some. It's a buck a block at the feed store."

Annie shook her head dismissively. "This is more natural."

"And a lot messier," he said, taking another look into the pot. "It sort of kills the cinnamon and spice vibe of the kitchen."

"Well, if you are looking for good smells, you might want to make yourself scarce. I'm bathing the dogs this afternoon."

"All of them?" Elliot asked skeptically, imagining the mass of wet dogs and hot blow dryers the mudroom would be subjected to.

"All of them." She looked over at Socks, sunning herself on the windowsill. "Even her," she said, pointing to the unsuspecting cat.

"Well that's just cruel." Elliot held up his hands. "I surrender. I'm going for a hike. You sure you don't want to come?"

Annie shook her head, bending down to peek into the oven. "No, if there's time. I need to go Christmas shopping.""

"Aren't you done?" he asked, folding his arms and glancing toward the pile of shopping bags heaped up on the dining room table.

"Yes," she said, following his gaze. "No." She shrugged and shook her head. "I don't know. I just need to take one more spin through the stores."

Elliot rolled his eyes and grabbed a cookie. "Okay," he said, grabbing his coat and a handful of cookies. "I'll be photographing birds down by the lake."

After he left, Annie leaned against the counter and surveyed the piles of cookies. Who the hell is going to eat all those? She thought. She picked up a snickerdoodle and nibbled at the edges. She could always pack them up and take them to the food bank, she guessed, but maybe what she needed to do was throw a party.

That's it, she thought. I will throw a Christmas party. She glanced out the window at Elliot's receding back. He will probably be annoyed, she thought. But a little party planning was just what she needed right now. Anything that would distract her from the loss of her job and the coming bleakness of January.

She put on a brave face, and planned a large and noisy party for family and neighbors to announce her retirement from the rat race of the big city.

She was exhausted. She was terrified. But she was home.

CHAPTER 5

⎯⎯◆⎯⎯

ELLIOT FOUND ANNIE CURLED UP in the den. "Come on," he said. "We're going for a walk." He swung his field coat over his shoulder and held out his hand to help Annie up from the sofa.

"No, I don't want to," Annie said, snuggling deeper under the fleece throw. She turned her head back to the book she was reading.

Elliot reached out and took the book from her hands. "It's time you got on with your life. This..." he said, lifting the book over her head, "isn't good for you."

Annie grabbed for the book. "Since when is reading bad for you?"

Elliot shook his head. "You know what I mean. You made a bold move when you left your job, but what do you have to show for it?" He looked down at the jacket cover. "Another day on the sofa reading Jane Austen?"

The truth was, Annie had no idea how to fill the hours that suddenly had become available. She had answered the question by burying herself in books. "I'm in recovery mode," she said. She pulled back her book. "Just a little longer."

"What you need is some fresh air and exercise. Look around at the world." He dropped his hands at his side. "Is this what you quit work for?"

Annie looked up from the book. "Yes," she said, "I quit work so I could do whatever I please."

He put on his coat and grabbed his camera bag. "Fine. I'll see you later."

She sighed and tossed the throw off her lap. "Hang on," she said. "Where are we going?"

Elliot turned and smiled. "We're going foxhunting." He looked down at her slipper-clad feet. "You probably want to put on some boots."

Annie scrambled into her jeans and boots, and found her long-neglected field coat in the back of the closet. Soon they were in the car and headed down a dusty country road.

Annie and Elliot had been introduced to the sport of Virginia foxhunting soon after they arrived in Charlottesville. Their daughters had taken riding lessons and Emily had enthusiastically pursued foxhunting with her junior club. It wasn't long before Elliot and Annie started following the field on foot.

Annie had never ridden to hounds herself. Her old quarter horse had not been up to that kind of pace, so she had been content to occasionally follow the course of the riders from a distance. Since Emily had gone off to college and then started her new job out West, Annie had gone out only once or twice a year. Elliot, whose passion for photographing the action had not ended with his daughter's exit, continued to go out as often as he could, and it was he who had maintained the friendships they had with members of the foxhunting community.

Elliot pulled the Jeep to a halt. The scarlet coat of the huntsman immediately caught Annie's eye. They stepped out of the car, and Annie pulled her scarf close to buffer the sharp wind that swept across the open meadow.

An air of urgency suffused the field, as riders quickly tacked their horses and swung on board, anxious to respond to the call of "riders up." Hurried announcements were followed by the formal call for the hounds. Annie smiled. This was no place for the clichéd call to "release the hounds." Here instead was the more refined "Mr. Garrison, may we have the hounds please."

Annie watched as the hounds set across the field, moving in unison toward an unseen goal. Horses and riders dashed across the expanse of rolling hills in their wake, the steam of heated horses and shouted voices rising over the cold air. And there was the added romance of the clothing, Annie thought. The fancy coats and breeches, the tall riding boots and handmade leather crops added elegance to the mad dash. She wondered if the clothing itself was what originally captured the imagination of those early artists who painted pictures of the chase. She could hardly imagine the same hunting portraits of men sporting dungarees and field coats.

It was those very clothes that caused foxhunting to be seen, by the few people who bother to think about it, as a sport for rich people—one that exploits the animal for mere pleasure. It was ironic, she thought, that it had even been banned in the United Kingdom, the setting for the sport's most iconic images. The reality was that foxhunting had begun for the purpose of eliminating the pests that damaged barnyards and killed livestock.

As Elliot trotted off across the field, Annie looked around for a comfortable vantage point. She knew she couldn't keep up with his sure-footed pace, but she could still enjoy the spectacle. She settled onto an outcropping of rock that gave her a view of the rolling country and the river bottom in the distance, and thought about what she knew about the sport.

In the United States, she remembered, foxhunting would more appropriately be called fox chasing. The organizing body for American foxhunting, the Masters of Foxhounds Association, strictly forbade intentional killing of the fox. She knew that it was pretty rare for a fox to be killed, even unintentionally, during a hunt. With the fox's speed and agility, virtually all go safely to ground before their lives are endangered. Still, the occasional fox does die, just as the occasional rider tumbles off and bumps his head, the occasional hound is struck by a car, and the occasional horse steps into a groundhog hole and breaks a leg. It is not a sport for the faint-hearted. It is bold and it is wild, and its members are a passionate bunch.

Annie knew that the members of the local hunt club added a lot of value to the local culture. The people who make up the foxhunting community are strong conservationists, working hard to protect the expanses of farmland from development, protesting extensive use of pesticides, and noting detrimental changes in the wildlife population. They love their horses, they love their hounds, and above all, they love their foxes. In these modern times, when most people's days are filled with cars and office buildings and pollution, the mere viewing of a fox careening across the field is celebrated. The hunters watch the hounds pick up the scent and pursue it with wild abandon.

And everyone in the field is cheering for the fox.

CHAPTER 6

—————

ANNIE SCRAMBLED INTO THE HOUSE at the sound of the ringing phone. She dumped her purse, along with the groceries she was carrying, and lunged at the receiver of their one landline, an old-fashioned phone that was installed on their kitchen wall.

"I want to go to the hunt on Wednesday," Cobie said when she picked up the ringing phone.

Annie smiled. Their friend Cobie was not one to spend time on niceties such as "hello" and "goodbye." He generally jumped right into the heart of the matter. "Of course you do," she said. "It's Boxing Day. You'd never miss that."

"Yeah, but I'm thinking I won't ride," Cobie said. He continued before she asked the question that was on the tip of her tongue. "Knee's acting up." Annie nodded her acceptance of the excuse, but she was a little surprised. Nothing ever stopped this man from the field.

"I thought me and Elliot could take out the Jeep," he said. "You too, of course."

"Absolutely." Annie pulled the fixture card from the top desk drawer. The hunt club sent out this card detailing the schedule for the season. It showed the date and time of each hunt. Annie knew that The Meryton Club hunted every Monday, Wednesday and Saturday from November to mid-March, always starting promptly at 10 am. So the main purpose of the card was to say where each hunt would begin. The fixtures, as they were referred to, were an assemblage of farms and properties that Monty, as Master of the Hounds, had negotiated permission to hunt.

"Perfect choice for the Jeep," said Annie, nodding her approval. "It's Watley." There were long expanses of open space at Watley. The old farm, which encompassed over 1,200 acres, was a cattle operation, mostly used for grazing. This meant there would be few plowed fields, other than some acres of winter wheat, to interfere with the Jeep. There was little in the way of stream or forest to impede their progress. And even better, Watley belonged to one of the hunt club's members, so there would be no one to fuss about tire tracks, especially if the vehicle was carrying Cobie. With some hunts, car followers had to stay to the roads, hoping to get a glimpse of the field from a distance. But at Watley, they could do some good four-wheeling. The ground was pretty dry right now, so going would be good.

"Fancy breakfast, of course," Cobie reminded her.

How could he think Annie would forget? Every hunt had what was referred to as a breakfast, often just sandwiches and cookies for the riders to tuck into after a long, cold morning. These were generally very informal affairs, set up haphazardly on the tailgate of someone's truck. People were always grateful for the chance to eat something, particularly if the food was warm. It gave them a chance to compare notes on the day, chat with the huntsman, and catch up on gossip.

But some days, like the Boxing Day hunt, which was held the day after Christmas, called for something more. Whether one rode or not, it was an event that no one cared to miss. It was a great opportunity to catch up with people you hardly ever saw outside of the hunt community. The non-riding property owners were invited, giving them a chance to rub elbows with the romantic group of folks that they occasionally saw dashing across their property.

"Great," said Annie. "We will pick you up at 9:30." She chuckled when she realized that the connection had gone dead and Cobie was already gone.

———————

On the day after Christmas, Annie and Elliot bundled equipment and gear into the car and headed to Cobie's. They carried a thermos of hot coffee, laced with a bit of Irish whiskey, as well as a tray of cookies for the breakfast's hostess. Before they left, they tried to rouse some interest in the adult children who were scattered all over the house, but they soon realized that no one was budging from their warm beds.

"I may come and catch the breakfast," said Emily, sniffling as she pulled the blanket over herself. "I want to see Sara." Even though Emily lived in Colorado now, she often tried to ride with the hunt when she came home. She and Sara had grown up together, taking lessons in the same barn and staying over at each other's houses throughout their middle school and high school years. They found it harder to stay in touch after they went off to different colleges, but they both looked forward to Emily's visits home.

"I'm surprised you haven't called her yet," Annie said.

"I know, but this cold is making me feel awful…. just not home long enough…" she mumbled into her pillow.

Annie leaned down and ran a maternal hand across Emily's forehead. At least there's no fever, she thought. "Ok, we'll see you if we see you," Annie called as she headed out the door. "Otherwise, we should be home by 4."

The day had dawned crisp and cold, and the projection was for temperatures to reach 35 by noon. The sky held a high cloud cover, and there was a mild, polite breeze blowing out of the west. Perfect conditions for photos, Elliot told her as they drove north. They picked up Cobie promptly at 9:30 and took the short drive to Watley, pulling in and sidling the Jeep right next to Sara's trailer.

When Sara saw Annie, she waved her over. "You should have told me you were coming," she said, greeting her with a hug. "When I heard that you finally left that job of yours, I promised Emily I would get you back in the saddle." She turned to finish tightening the girth on her own horse, a big paint she called Mosey. "You got the present yesterday, right? Now that you have some time, she wants me to help you get the dust off."

Annie nodded, thinking of the gift certificate under the tree from Sara's stable, along with the soft calfskin riding gloves.

Sara turned to look at Annie. "I thought I'd see Emily out here today."

"I couldn't get her out of bed." Annie smiled. "She's got the sniffles. But I'm sure she'll come to the breakfast."

Sara nodded and gestured to the big chestnut tied to the side of the trailer. "I could have given you Dude today."

She saw Annie raise an eyebrow. "I know he's tall but gentle as a lamb," Sara said. She nodded toward the little girl standing at his side. Annie knew the girl must be at least 12, but she looked like she was about 7. "Of course, Candy has him today. But call me next week and we'll talk."

Sara knew that the sight of the little girl would shame Annie, just a little, and she was right. Annie nodded to the girl, and promised Sara that she would call. Then she walked off, leaving Sara to wrangle the junior riders into their final preparations.

"Morning," shouted Gray when he saw Cobie. "What are you thinking, man? Where's your horse?"

"Never mind that," Cobie replied. "Talk to me about your plans today."

As she walked past, she heard Gray and Cobie debate the first draw.

"Wind's coming from the west. I say we head straight to Mason' Creek." Gray said, waving his hand toward the near woods.

Cobie folded his arms and shook his head. "Naw, that will keep for later. Best start up the hill and head straight to Lawson's."

"I want to get to that dog fox who lives near the water."

Cobie kicked the ground and waved his hands in the other direction. "He won't be there this time of day. Better push him back later on from the other side of the mountain."

Elliot stood at a discreet distance to listen to the debate, knowing that their path by Jeep would have to follow the hunt carefully so they wouldn't foul the hounds' scent. Annie saw him smile as Monty approached. Monty would be the one to settle things.

Annie wandered the trailers, saying hi and patting horses, keeping a watchful eye out for the tray of sherry she knew would appear. Formal days began with mounted riders served a bit of sherry and a "hand cake," often a bite of fruitcake or nut bread. In the old days, sherry would be served in a stirrup cup; an elaborate pewter cup fashioned with the head of an animal at its base. Given that a big hunt may have as many as a hundred riders, the stirrup cup was replaced these days with a smaller, and safer, plastic cup. This humble plastic cup was still offered up on a sterling silver tray. When Annie saw a group of riders clustered together around an anonymous form, she knew she had found what she was looking for.

Annie saw Barbara, the hostess, in the midst of the assembled horses, holding her silver tray high above her head to allow the mounted riders to help themselves. She smiled when she saw Annie. "Glad to see you!" She offered Annie a cup. "I don't think I have seen you since last season!"

Annie accepted the thimble full of sherry, which she downed quickly. "Here, let me help you with that." She took the tray from Barbara's hands.

"Thanks," Barbara released the tray and helped herself to a drink. She looked toward the barn. "I should really go find my horse anyway. There are some other folks passing drinks."

"I can pass the rest of these."

"Wonderful! I appreciate it."

"Did you make ham biscuits today?" Annie asked. She loved those delicate biscuits that held a thin strip of intensely salty Virginia ham.

"Couldn't have a hunt breakfast without them," replied Barbara brightly, turning at the sound of the junior riders who were descending on the tray. "No, no dear," she said to one of them. "Not that cup. Take one of these sparkling ciders."

Barbara smiled and nodded at Annie, then turned to the barn to get her horse. "Thanks again," she called over her shoulder as Annie was engulfed by the youngsters. "I'll catch up with you back at the house."

This was one of the things Annie loved about the hunt. Among the riders, there were rich and poor, working and retired, young and old. No one thought to ask about her job. Hunt day was all about the horses, the hounds, the weather, the field. The rest of people's lives were mere noise, and on a day like this, no one wished to bother with such trivia. Today, no explanations were required.

At ten o'clock, the hounds were called for and the field assembled. Monty gave a couple of announcements, including a reminder about the breakfast, something that no one in the group was likely to have forgotten. Then the field was off.

For three hours, they followed at an exhilarating pace. The clouds closed in a bit, and huge snowflakes fell. The snow was not enough to cause slippery footing, Annie thought, but certainly added to the romance of the day. Annie drove the Jeep most of the time, Elliot too impatient to sit when he could run across the field for a closer view. Sometimes Cobie got out too, but Annie was surprised that he seemed to be content in shotgun position for most of the day.

It was a luxury to be out this way with Cobie, Annie thought. Under no other circumstances could she have so free access to the knowledge of what was taking place in the field. Talking was frowned upon in the hunt field, so even if she had ridden by his side, she would have been left to her own devices to try to understand the actions of the huntsman and his hounds.

In the cozy confines of the Jeep, Cobie could chat away without bothering anyone. He described the draw that the hounds made, why they had taken a certain line, and the meaning behind the various noises they were making. His descriptions were over her head much of the time, and Annie realized how little she understood about the actual process. She particularly enjoyed his comments on the individual hounds they came upon. As a long-time member of the club, he knew each one well and spoke knowledgeably about their skills, their conditioning and their various talents.

"See that one there?" He pointed to a small bitch that was lagging behind the field. "That there's Tika." He watched her progress, nose to the ground. "One of the best bitches in the kennel. Gotta remember to tell Gray she's tired today. Good to know."

"Why is that?" Annie asked, watching as the bitch stopped to look up and scan the horizon, trying to catch sight of the field. She was an easy one to identify, even for Annie. She had one large spot on her left side that formed the shape of a heart.

"Because it probably means she's in whelp."

Annie nodded, smiling. She watched the strong little dog, cold, wet and muddy, working the scent with all her might, and tried to imagine herself laden with the seed of as many as fifteen puppies.

The day was turning chillier, now that the clouds had covered the horizon in earnest and the wind had risen over the wide plateau.

"Will Gray call for home soon?" Annie asked, turning the Jeep's heater up a notch.

"There it is," Cobie said, pointing toward the sound of Gray's horn. "Gone home." The long, slow wavering blast had a deep, mournful quality to it, and signaled the end of the day's hunting. "Show off," Cobie commented drily, as the horn continued extravagantly. Gray's skill on the horn was well known, though he used it judiciously in the field. "That lad's in fine form today."

Elliot had heard the horn too, and they saw him lope across the field, making his way toward them. He jumped into the backseat.

"I think we've earned our breakfast," he said, pulling off his top layer of clothing to reach for the small flask that rested in his vest pocket.

"Well, you did, at least. You must have walked seven miles this morning." Her husband always ran with the field, impressing everyone with his ability to predict the direction the draw might take, and being in just the right place when the fox made his appearance, pursued by the pack. Annie looked over the field, watching as first flight walked for home. She caught sight of Tika too, now trotting proudly alongside Gray's horse. She would have to remember to seek out the little hound and congratulate her.

"Onward," said Cobie, pointing toward a large white manor house that had stood gracefully at the top of the crest since Jefferson's time. "I need a drink."

CHAPTER 7

———

AT MERYTON, THE FOUR HIGH Holy Days of hunting were celebrated in the proper way with a formal hunt breakfast. These days are the Opening Hunt, Thanksgiving Hunt, Christmas Hunt and New Year's Hunt. This year's Christmas Hunt fell on Boxing Day, the 26th of December.

Barbara had outdone herself, Annie thought, as she walked through the dining room to the den where a lavish bar was laid out. She eyed the white tablecloths and silver candlesticks appreciatively, noting the massive arrangements of local holly, pine and dried berries cascading out of oversized trophies. Sideboards groaned with platters of smoked salmon, ham biscuits, and deviled eggs. She paused to peek into one of the many chafing dishes.

"That one has sautéed scallops," Elliot whispered, sidling up to her. "This one here is beef tenderloin."

"Hand me one of those ham biscuits," she nudged Elliot and pointed to a large tray in the center of the table.

Elliot reached over and picked up two. "Napkins are over there," he gestured with his free hand.

"Thanks, I am going to get a drink. Do you want something?"

Elliot lifted his glass of white wine in a mock toast. "Barbara had this in my hand by the time I got to the door. She made me promise to try it with the oyster stew." Elliot grinned. "So that..." pointing to his nearby bowl, "is what I am doing."

Annie nodded and kissed him on top of his head, already bent back to his stew, before moving on to the bar herself.

As she made her way through the crowd, she picked up snippets of gossip about the condition of someone's marriage and the fitness of someone else's bulls. She paused for a moment to hear the whisper about Davis, the handsome young whipper-in, and the woman who just bought Tanglewood Farm.

Annie ordered a bourbon on the rocks, as she waited for the beleaguered bartender, she greeted Jack and Elise, a couple of retired members. They were anxious to hear all about the hunt, reliving the thrills that they have had to forgo as age and infirmity had set in.

"Annie, did you ride today?" Jack asked.

Annie shook her head, gesturing to her jeans and tweed coat. "Hi Jack, Elise. No, I was a road warrior today. Cobie and I went out…."

Jack nodded vaguely and turned to scan the crowd. "Ah Barrett!" he called out. "How was the day?" He was rewarded with a grin and the start of a long-winded description of the chase down Mountaintop Road.

Elise patted her on the arm. "You're no competition for the horses, I'm afraid."

Annie nodded as she accepted her glass from the barman. She turned to answer Elise, but she saw that she had wandered off to the buffet.

Annie nibbled her ham biscuit, and meandered just on the edge of the party, a little shy of imposing herself into conversations already in full swing. On the back porch, Gray stood in a cluster of men sharing jokes and raunchy stories. Barrages of laughter burst from the men and heads turned at the sound. The bartender on the porch was busy too, paying no attention to who he poured for. Annie watched as Barbara tried to monitor excesses. But this is the hunt crowd, Annie chuckled to herself as she sipped on her drink. They have an enormous capacity for food and drink. She knew Barbara would just have to hope that the consumption of both was adequate to balance things out.

The running joke about foxhunters and their liquor, Annie thought, is all too true. They drink before a hunt to make the jumps seem smaller. And they drink after the hunt to make the jumps sound bigger.

Cobie was with the rowdies on the porch for a little while, but then Annie noticed him find his daughter Lindsay in the crowd. He whispered something in her ear. Then he walked around, tousled the heads of the little kids, and chatted up the junior riders. She heard him agree to go take a look at a pony that had thrown a shoe, and others clambered to have him come and admire their own mounts. Soon Annie saw him wander back outside toward the trailers with a small stream of youngsters in his wake.

CHAPTER 8

———

ANNIE'S PHONE RUNG FOR THE third time in an hour. And for the third time, she looked at the number and sighed. She had avoided talking to her editor the entire month of December. Annie hadn't called to wish Dodie a merry Christmas; she hadn't even told her about work. But she knew that Dodie wasn't going to give up easily this time. She picked up the phone.

"Hi," Annie said, in as cheerful a voice as she could muster.

"How's Garden Fresh coming?" Dodie said brightly, as way of greeting.

"Hi Dodie. Happy New Year to you too." Annie took a deep breath, bracing herself to tell her friend the whole story.

"I thought I'd better check. It's due in March and I know how busy you get."

"Actually, not that busy." Annie's voice broke. "Dodie, I.... I quit my job."

She heard Dodie's sharp intake of breath, expecting the gasp of surprise, but realizing in the same moment that it was just Dodie tugging on her cigarette.

But Dodie's voice stayed neutral. "What happened?"

Annie crumpled into the red leather chair near the fireplace. "I don't know where to begin. Nothing happened. Everything was great. I mean, I was tired, I was too busy, I was traveling too much…"

"Yeah, that sounds great."

"You know what I mean. Work was going well."

"And then?"

"And then it wasn't. I don't know what the hell I was thinking."

"Fuck 'em."

"But Dodie, work is all I have ever done…"

"Too much, I always thought." Dodie's tone was disdainful.

"That's the way I do things. You know that. Work is more enjoyable when you are passionate…"

"And it makes you more susceptible to disappointment when the passion is gone."

"Give me a break, Dodie. I think I'm still in shock. I keep asking myself why on earth I did it."

"Let me repeat, fuck 'em."

Annie got up and strode to the window. She wanted someone to listen to her. She hadn't been able to talk to anyone about her concerns about her future, not even Elliot. "Dodie, seriously," she said. "I'm miserable."

She felt Dodie bristle. "Annie, do you think you are the first person ever to be unemployed?"

Annie felt a quick shudder of resentment. "Well, it's never happened to me."

"Be that as it may, do you have any regrets?"

"What do you mean?" She paused, thinking. "I regret quitting."

"Do you really?"

"Well," Annie said, biting her lip. "Maybe I don't. That's what is eating at me. I'm glad I'm not there. I just don't know what to do next. It seems like I should be doing something…. important."

"Was analyzing the personal lives of consumers so important?"

"No, but…" Annie paused again, tears stinging her eyes. She hadn't cried at all, but talking about it brought her feelings to the surface. "At least I was making money."

"I will say it again, Annie. At the risk of being crude, fuck 'em."

Annie chuckled in spite of herself. "Dodie, you passed crude ten miles ago."

Dodie inhaled, and Annie could imagine the cigarette smoke swirling around her friend's head. She could almost smell it.

"You say you're bored," Dodie said. "Annie, that's an incredible waste of time."

"But...."

"You made a decision, in my opinion a very good one. You have nothing to regret." She paused, and Annie could imagine that she was tamping out her butt.

"I have a hard time accepting that. I was too...hasty."

"Maybe. But what are you going to do? Let it eat you up forever?" She paused for effect. "Happiness is the best revenge."

"I'm afraid that happy is too lofty a goal right now. I just need to get through January without going crazy. I have already cleaned this house to within an inch of its life." She looked around the room at the polished silver and gleaming floors. "I'm accustomed to having every moment scheduled. I look at my phone a thousand times a day, expecting it to burst into life the way it used to. I don't know what to do with myself."

"How's the book?"

Annie paused.

"You haven't worked on it," Dodie accused.

"I needed to get my life back together."

"And now?"

"I'll get to it," Annie huffed. "Don't worry. Have I ever missed a deadline?"

"Okay, but when this book is done, I want you to write what you want to write."

"What the hell would that be?"

Dodie sniffed. "Oh, I don't know. You used to be pretty interesting."

"Humph." That was probably true, Annie thought, but right now she couldn't see it. Her head had been so full of management and leadership and mentoring for the past thirty years, she didn't know what else might be in her head.

"Some kind of business book?" Annie hesitated. "I don't know, Dodie. I think I need another job."

Dodie snorted, and then sighed dramatically. "Do you really? You said your stock options were impressive."

"But I support so many people…. you know that. The dogs and the kids in college." Annie sighed too. "It's just so much. And at my age, it has occurred to me that I may never be able to find another job." She looked around the spacious house. "This place isn't cheap, you know."

"If you say all this crap to me again in a few months, we can talk about it. But seriously, get your head back on Earth first." Annie thought about this as she heard Dodie light up another cigarette and take a deep drag. "What's that thing that Emily used to do? Foxhunting? You have always talked about doing that. Have you gone horseback riding?"

"No, I have been making excuses." Annie hesitated. "It's been a long while since I rode a horse, not since Dexter died. And now I'm too fat to get into a riding coat."

"Well, that's a project for you then."

"What?"

"Killing foxes."

Annie sighed. "Dodie," she said. "They don't kill foxes. They just…. chase them."

"Hmmm," replied Dodie. "Kill them, chase them. None of it makes any sense to me."

"Well, neither does catch-and-release trout fishing, if you think about it," said Annie, referring to Elliot's favorite pastime.

"I try not to think about it," said Dodie. "Or any of those other country things you people do."

"Anyway, I would have to get in better shape before I ride."

"Listen to yourself," said Dodie. "Annie, I have known you for how many years? Twenty? And you have been horse crazy all that time. But you complain you don't have time, you don't feel good, your pants don't fit…"

"The coat," Annie smiled, in spite of herself.

"What?"

"I said the coat doesn't fit." Annie paused. "I bought new breeches."

Dodie paused to tamp out her cigarette. Annie knew this pause meant another change in the conversation. Whenever Dodie wanted to change the subject, she lit a cigarette. Sometimes she even stubbed out the one she was smoking just to light a new one and start in on a new topic. "By the way," she said. "How's my godchild? The Divine Miss T?

Annie laughed. The new puppy's registered name was RabbitRun's The Divine Miss T, but Dodie had quickly adopted her as her own.

"She's with the handler."

"Why don't you show her yourself? You have time now."

"Sam will do it faster than I could."

"Excuses, excuses," Dodie said between puffs.

Annie pursed her lips, biting back a reply. Sometimes it just wasn't worth having someone who knew you as well as Dodie knew her. What she needed right now was to get off the phone. And maybe have a brownie. "You should quit smoking," she said.

"And you should lose weight."

"Dodie!"

"Look, I couldn't care less how you look. And I know that man of yours would love you if you were an elephant." She paused. "All the years I have known you, it's been 'dogs this and horses that'. I'm New York born and bred, so I never really got it, but I have always liked the idea of your life." She paused for effect. "If you can't do the things you love, then your life is seriously out of balance."

Annie nodded, silent. She agreed; she had always liked the idea of her life too. Dodie took her silence as a cue to end the call, promising to call her the following week.

Annie hung up the phone, thoughtful now. Dodie was right, about many things. Her lack of emotion about the decision, her cut-and-dried attitude, was actually good to hear from her old friend. Annie was only hurting herself with her self-pity and doubt. She needed to set this aside and move on. It wouldn't be easy. She had to figure out a new career, pay the bills, lose weight, and get her life back.

Right now it all seemed like a bit too much. But what did she have but time?

CHAPTER 9

———

"Maybe I can work for a non-profit."

"Hmmm? What?" said Elliot.

Annie peered at the list of job postings on her computer screen. "A non-profit, you know? Something charitable. Something where I could do good."

"You mean like cancer and hospitals and stuff?"

Annie spun her chair around and thought about it. "I don't think so." She mentally ticked off her current involvements. Animal welfare, historical projects and conservation were their main charities. "Maybe Nature Conservancy or something like that."

"Whatever you think," said Elliot, absently turning the pages of the latest photo magazine.

She stood up from her desk and looked over his shoulder at the photo essay of the Italian countryside. "Maybe we should travel," she said. "You know, like that." She pointed to a picture of a couple hiking along the cliff overlooking the Mediterranean.

Elliot raised his head and looked at her. "I think it's a little late to become a travel writer, especially since we don't really like to travel."

It was true. They had both travelled so much during the course of their careers that the idea of far-off places left them both a bit cold. Annie shrugged. It was good to look at all the possibilities.

In fact, Annie was trying on possibilities the way that one might try on hats. Her newfound freedom seemed to afford her the chance to try almost anything, but she couldn't quiet her mind enough to follow one train of thought to its conclusion. She considered and rejected Dodie's advice again and again. Could she write something good? Could she get back to her horses and dogs? Could she lose weight? Every night, tossing in her bed, she thought that maybe she would start these things the next day. But in the light of the cold mornings, she rejected the ideas again. No, she concluded. It had been insane to quit her job. She had to go back to work. Every morning found her, with a cup of coffee and a pastry, scanning the want ads for work.

"You know, no one talks to anyone anymore," she said to Elliot, sitting back down at the desk. She clicked a few keys to send yet another resume off into the ozone.

He looked up from his magazine and turned to her. "What?"

"Applying for a job used to have some personal element," she said. "Now you just throw your resume out into some netherworld, and never hear anything again." She swiveled in her desk chair. "Did you know humans hardly even look at these applications anymore? At least not the first round. Keywords are scanned, and if there's a match, then, and only then, your resume might be looked at. And the average human resources person looks at a resume for less than twenty seconds. The reality is, I could never get a job at a non-profit. My resume would never get me looked at."

"Like on-line dating," Elliot said. "Glad we aren't trying to meet each other these days." He smiled up at her. "I can just see the ad you would have written thirty years ago. "Barrel-racing cowgirl seeks guy who absolutely does not fly fish or take pictures." Pretty sure we would have missed each other."

"Thank goodness for bars, then," she chuckled. "You had the legs of a cowboy, muscular and a little bow-legged."

"Yeah, too bad I didn't know one end of a horse from the other back then."

"Oh, I think it's worked out okay."

Elliot got up and kissed her. Then he went off to make a pot of coffee.

"Stir that lentil soup while you are in the kitchen, would you? It should almost be done, and I need to finalize that recipe today."

"Got it," he said as he left the room.

Annie went back to scanning the job boards. The stock cash-out had been substantial, comfortably in the six figures. But no matter the amount, she couldn't escape the nagging feeling that she was going to have to make it last the rest of her life. This end-of-the-world frame of mind had a reasonable foundation. After all, she was fifty-five, and now it felt like the corporate world was going to pass her by. She could not even imagine where to start looking for a new job. And if she were honest with herself, she didn't really want to.

"Sunsetter," she knew her type was called. People "of a certain age" who had already proven themselves in the job world, who were at an age where ambition and titles were not enough anymore. Most companies just weren't interested in people like her. In fact, Annie had just read an article that quoted staffing people (average age thirty-two) who said they were suspicious of any applicants over age thirty-nine.

Elliot reminded her that he had an income too. Of course, she knew that was true, but that kind of consulting money came in fits and starts, and one never knew from quarter to quarter what to expect. And health insurance costs were through the roof. That alone was reason to find steady employment again.

As she did every day, Annie sat down at her desk and ran the numbers. Pay off the credit cards, re-finance the house? Could she do that without any income? How were her royalties looking anyway? After the initial advance, they never amounted to much that you could depend on. But that book on motherhood always did well in May, and the potato book had been well reviewed. She made a mental note to check those accounts.

Her own house, she had noticed while scrubbing it from end to end, needed some maintenance too. There were squirrels in the crawlspace above the garage. They had created a hole to get in and out, so the siding needed repair too. The roof shingles were getting old. She eyed the old window near her desk. It had been painted shut years ago. All the windows should probably be replaced, she thought. The yard needed tree work, and her arborist, a guy they had used for all of the years they had been here, did not come cheap. Could she afford any of this?

She sighed again. Probably not.

———

CHAPTER 10

"Maybe I can be a greeter. You know? One of those people who stand in front of the Wal-Mart and say hi to people?" Annie called out as she heard the back door swing open. Elliot entered, a swirl of leaves blowing in behind him. The PBGVs followed too, a small tornado of fur, each carrying fallen leaves or dried twigs in their messy beards.

Elliot walked into the kitchen and took off his hat. "Oh, that wouldn't be a waste of your time."

"Hey!" she said, swatting him with the wooden spoon she held. "Watch the sarcasm."

Elliot dropped his camera bag on the counter and walked over to the stove. "You don't even shop at Wal-Mart."

"Well, no. But I could start." She thought of their bank balance. "I probably should start."

Annie scooped a spoonful of sauce and held it up. "Taste this."

"Not enough salt," he said. "Maybe a bit more garlic."

She nodded, reaching for a pinch from the salt cellar that sat next to the big old Aga that was the centerpiece of their kitchen. She tasted again. "You're right." She wiped her hands and grabbed a pen to make a quick note.

"Cobie is sick."

Annie turned suddenly, her raised spoon dripping sauce onto the floor. "What?"

"Cobie," Elliot said again. "He's sick."

"Define sick," Annie said as she leaned down to wipe up the spot before the dogs got to it. She stood up and looked him in the eye. She suspected that he was not talking about a winter cold.

"I don't know. I was shooting the hunt at Sidwell's Reach this morning, and at the hunt breakfast, I noticed Cobie sitting up against a truck tire. Didn't seem like him." Elliot took a pitcher of water out of the refrigerator and poured a glass. "So I asked how he was doing."

"What did he say?"

"It was what he didn't say that concerned me. He just gave me a look, then turned away and said 'we'll see.'" Elliot took a swallow of the cold water. "I asked Red later what that was all about. He said Cobie hadn't been feeling well and had gone in for some tests."

Annie nodded. Red was Cobie's next door neighbor and would be sure to know the facts. "Well, maybe it's nothing."

Elliot scratched his chin. "Yeah, let's hope." He put down his glass and peered into the pot that she was stirring. "You should have come out today. It was a great day. Foxes everywhere and the hounds were in full cry."

"I know. I'll come out next time."

"That's what you keep saying."

"I know. It's just that…. you take off and roam the fields so fast. I mean, you can put on miles and miles following the riders on foot. I can never keep up." Annie hated to admit that she didn't like to go anywhere with him when he had the camera. When Elliot looked through his viewfinder, the rest of the world disappeared. He became completely engrossed. She appreciated his stunning photographs. She just didn't want to be there when he shot them.

Elliot shrugged. "Sara said to say hi."

Another gentle dig, she thought. Annie had not called Sara as she had promised on Boxing Day. The new riding breeches, still in the Horse Country bag in the bedroom, were witness to that. Annie wasn't even sure when the "I would ride but…" excuses had started. Maybe it was when she injured her knee years ago. Maybe it was when the weight starting piling on. Maybe it was just because she did not own a horse right now, having put off replacing Dexter when he died, in favor of showing the dogs.

She knew that her mind lived squarely in two camps where this subject was concerned. Of course, she was a rider. It had always been a part of her identity, from the moment her grandfather sat her atop his retired racehorse when she was three years old. She had ridden throughout childhood, competed throughout high school, even went to college at Oklahoma State just because they had a barrel racing team. And when she had kids, she got them on horseback as soon as they could walk.

But another part of her held back. The thoroughbreds in the hunt field seemed too tall. The ground where she might fall seemed too hard. Her skills were rusty. She was more of a Western rider. Foxhunting could be intense. She was getting old. The list went on and on. The reality was that Annie had lost her nerve.

Annie felt this failing on her part deeply, especially now that she had time to dwell on it. It was so easy to live in her head when she worked. Her head was a very comfortable place to be when there were business strategies to create and problems to solve. But it was a decidedly inhospitable environment with too much spare time to fret and mope and worry. An active mind had always kept her in a happy place. Now all that excess energy needed a new place to go. Annie knew that the only thing that would keep her sane was work.

But maybe.... Annie breathed deeply, afraid to think the thought that had been hovering around the edges of her mind since her talk with Dodie. Maybe there was another definition of work, one that used more than her head for business.

She was afraid to say the words out loud. The white horse had begun to appear in her dreams again, now stamping its hoof on the ground and tossing his head. She still had no idea what he wanted, but on the edges of sleep, fragments were crystallizing to form a new image of who she might once again be.

She wouldn't say anything to Elliot, she thought. She wouldn't say anything to Dodie. And she wasn't ready to call Sara. But in the silence of her heart, she now resolved two things. "I'll get this weight off," she thought. "And I'll ride to hounds by fall." But she kept all of this to herself. Chances were good she would fail so it was probably best to not put it out there.

"I'll drop by and see Cobie next week," she said, pointedly ignoring the mention of Sara. "He promised to lend me a book last time I saw him." She took the pitcher off the counter and poured a glass of water for herself before putting it back in the refrigerator. She hated water, but wasn't that one of the big weight loss things? Drink a lot of water? She took a big sip. Yes, she confirmed to herself as she swallowed; she hated water. She turned to Elliot and smiled. "Don't worry, I'll get the scoop."

CHAPTER 11

———

ANNIE TOOK THE BACK ROADS toward an area of Orange County called Radiant, turning onto a country lane just shy of the town of Orange itself. There she found herself transported to the real Virginia; that of pretty farms, country gentlemen, fine horses, fields of soybeans and tobacco. And always, good whiskey, she added to herself, nodding at the sign that led to the local landscape's latest addition, a boutique distillery. Some might believe the part of Virginia that Cobie belonged to was a thing of the past. In fact, nothing was further from the truth. You just had to know where to look.

She had baked Cobie a blueberry cake. She hoped that it might make it a little easier to ask for a favor. But was it a good enough trade, she wondered, for what she wanted to ask?

She thought about him as she drove. Cobie Grainger was one of the most interesting men she had ever met. An unprepossessing figure in jeans and plaid shirt, his aw-shucks country boy routine hid a wealth of talent and a history of accomplishment. If she thought too much about all the things that he had done in his sixty-three years, she would probably have been too intimidated to get to know him. She certainly wouldn't have the nerve to ask for riding lessons.

But he had warm blue eyes that looked at you with a beguiling frankness. His friendly smile crinkled his entire face into some kind of inside joke that set everyone, even strangers, immediately at ease.

He was small in stature, small enough in fact to have spent his early career as a jockey on the steeplechase circuit. An expert on everything equine, Cobie was as comfortable in the hunt field as he was in the show ring, as comfortable at the race track as he was in the home of some wealthy client with too much money and not enough sense.

"Nice!" said Lindsay, eyeing the cake as she swung open the kitchen door. Annie stepped inside and set the cake on the counter. "Mom's in town, but she should be back soon. I'll make a pot of coffee to go with that." She nodded to the open door off the kitchen. "Dad's in the den."

Annie peeked in, but immediately saw that he was on the phone. She tried to back out quickly, but he caught her eye and waved her in, pointing to a big leather chair set off to the side of the desk. While she waited, Annie studied the many photos and trophies that lined his study. The wall told more stories than she could ever imagine one person having time to live. Cobie as a child, jumping a massive hunter over a coop in the fields behind his own backyard. Cobie in the winner's circle. Cobie at the Kentucky Derby, standing next to the famous trainer Clem Danson for whom he had chosen the brilliant colt Wayward. Cobie at Madison Square Garden, leaping over a seven-foot fence, the picture of calm astride an enormous white giant who seemed to be astonished at what he and the man were doing.

Annie loved the sound of Cobie's voice, and soon found herself listening to his call, in spite of her attempt to tune it out. His voice, pure authentic Virginia country, was not something one heard much anymore, particularly in and around Charlottesville, a city that had long ago succumbed to the imports who stayed to create their own version of Virginia for themselves. She realized that Cobie was talking to a doctor.

"The pancreas, huh? And that means what?" he asked. He nodded thoughtfully. "And how long will that take?" He paused and listened, leaning back in his chair. Then he shook his head. "No, no. None of that for me."

A few more questions, a few more answers, and he hung up the phone. Cobie nodded to the door, gesturing for Annie to close out the sound of grinding coffee beans. Annie jumped up and closed it as quietly as she could, not wanting to catch Lindsay's attention. Then she turned expectantly to Cobie.

"Calvin says six months," he said simply.

Annie nodded, biting her lip. He couldn't really be saying he only had six months to live, she thought. He's only sixty-three.

She felt her heart shudder as she gripped the arms of the chair. She gulped and blinked back the tears that stung her eyes before lifting her head to look at him. How the hell, she thought, as she met his clear blue eyes, could Cobie be so stoic? And what the hell am I doing here?

Annie wanted to say that doctors don't give such definitive deadlines anymore, especially over the phone. But Dr. Calvin Leonard was an old friend and probably knew that Cobie would want straight talk. She wanted to ask about a course of treatment and whether the cancer had spread. But they were none of her business. She just nodded. Her own reason for today's visit had flown from her head. She simply said, "What can I do?

"Get me some cake," he said.

CHAPTER 12

———

THE NEWS OF COBIE'S CANCER struck the foxhunting community hard. Word spread quickly at the hunt meets and cast a pall over the rest of the season. Cobie was no longer out on horseback, but tried to follow the field by car as often as he could. He liked to go out in the Jeep with Elliot and Annie, so they made an effort to get out every day.

It was hard for him, Annie saw, to ignore the surreptitious glances and sidelong whispers that were inevitable when he showed up. Harder still were the awkward conversations with those who offered well-intentioned, but to his mind, premature, condolences. Gray and Monty tried to maintain a feeling of normalcy around him, and included him in the discussions of the first draw at every meet.

When Cobie called on Tuesday morning two weeks later, Annie glanced at the number and handed it to Elliot. They often touched base to check the departure plan for the next day's hunt.

"He wants you," Elliot smiled, handing her back the phone.

"Hey Cobie," she said lightly. "What's up?"

"I need your help on something," he said. "A project."

"What sort of project?" Annie asked.

"Aw, I'd rather talk about it in person," he demurred. "Might be a foolish idea." He hesitated, and Annie sensed embarrassment in his silence. "Still, I'd like to see what might be done," he continued. "Could you come today?

Annie looked down at her clothes. She was already dressed for her interview with a local tech firm, the first she had landed in a month of sending resumes. She had dressed carefully in a sleek skirt and short jacket, adding a bright pink blouse that she hoped would conjure the right balance of energy and experience. She had hoped that today was the re-start of her career. She held the phone in her hand, considering. She could go to the interview now and then go to Cobie's later in the afternoon.

"You have some free time these days, don't you?" he asked, interrupting her thoughts.

Annie started to mention the interview, but stopped herself short. If she got a job, she wouldn't have any free time. "Oh, yes," she answered. "Lots of time."

"Good," he said. "I thought so. I think there's something we can do together."

Something about his tone drew her in. "You know," Annie said, nodding to herself decisively. "I am free. I can come out this morning."

She hung up the phone and looked at Elliot guiltily. "What do you suppose he wants?"

Elliot shrugged. "Maybe he wants some help with the club books."

"No, it seemed more urgent than that."

"Well," he said. "Better go find out."

Annie looked down at her clothes again, smoothing her skirt thoughtfully. Elliot raised his eyebrows, divining her thoughts. "You know; I didn't think that company was right for you. I heard the president is a hothead."

Annie grinned. "My thought exactly," she said. She walked down the hall to the bedroom, peeling off her suit as she went. She came back in jeans, already dialing the number of the human resources director to cancel the interview.

She drove the half hour to Radiant, thinking how insane it was to throw over all her plans over a simple phone call. But it was Cobie, she argued to herself. She knew that he did not ask for favors casually. She was intrigued. And if truth be told, she thought ruefully, she was grateful for an excuse to cancel that interview. The thought of going back to work had sickened her.

As the sign bearing the image of the winged white horse came into view, Annie slowed the Jeep and hesitated. PEGASUS FARM, the sign read. She shivered at the sight of the white horse, unconsciously turning the heat in the car to High. She leaned on the steering wheel, allowing the wave of hot air to hit her face. It was not her place to be here, she thought. She was not one of Cobie's closest friends. There were easily hundreds of people who knew him better, and for much longer than she did. She was not much more than a passing acquaintance of his wife. What could he possibly want from her? She shook her head and took a deep breath. There was only one way to find out. She shifted the car into gear and pulled into the long, winding driveway that led to the large white farmhouse.

———

Annie sat across the desk from him, just as she had done weeks before, on the day that he had gotten the news. She looked at him expectantly.

"I want to write a book," Cobie said.

Annie nodded, silent.

Cobie continued. "I have no idea how to do that. But I know you do." He leaned forward. "I can't put words on paper. But I can talk." He paused, thoughtful now. "And I can't help but feel I've got something to say...about foxhunting, about the hounds, about this way of life.

"I want the young folks, particularly them, to understand the value of what they learn in the field. Too many kids get a kick out of horses. They like the riding and the ribbons and the fun. And there's a lot to like. But I want them to understand the real world and their place in it. You know, this lifestyle, the lessons of nature, taking care of the environment, that sort of thing." He stopped, self-consciously looking down at his hands. He looked back up at her, his blue eyes shone sincere and questioning. "What do you think?"

"I...I don't think I'm the one to help you," she stuttered. "Sure, I am a writer, but you know, cookbooks and things. I'm not sure I'm the kind of writer you need. Barrett would be a better choice." Barrett Lynch, a Virginia-man's Virginia man, knew Cobie intimately. And he knew Cobie's world better than she ever could. Besides, he was also a writer.

"No," Cobie growled. "Not Barrett. Then it would be Barrett's story. I want it to be my story."

Annie sat back in the chair. "You just want your stories put on paper," she mused. "Not so hard, really. I guess I can transcribe and organize your ideas."

"That's what I was thinkin'," he replied. "Just get me going."

"Okay," she smiled, nodding her encouragement for his idea. "Let's get started."

———

Annie brought a tape recorder and showed Cobie how to use it, setting up a comfortable spot in the den where he could talk and jot down notes. At first, he was inclined to ramble, jumping from idea to idea without much thread to string together his thoughts. He started with some enthusiasm, quickly compiling a handful of tapes talking about the horses of his youth, the "old ways" as he called them, the things he thought people should remember. Annie drove to the farm to listen to his stories, to jot down her own thoughts, and to ask questions. They spent several pleasant afternoons this way.

But Cobie soon tired of this solitary pursuit. He didn't like listening to the sound of his own voice, which he considered high and reedy, disputing Annie's description of it as rich and melodic. Annie soon realized that if she were to create a story out of his myriad ideas, she would need him to stay on one topic long enough for her to understand it. She suggested they create an outline.

"No," he said. "I need an audience." He thought for a moment. "I want to just sit around and shoot the breeze with my friends and record that." He looked at Annie. "Would that work?"

Annie laughed out loud and gestured to the famous faces on his wall. "You mean folks like Taylor Admundson? Or Drake Hayes? Or.... Jaycee Mansfield?"

He gave her a quizzical look. "Yeah, like them," he said, nodding at the framed photos. "And of course, Barrett, Monty and all. The regulars."

Annie laughed again and shook her head. Cobie's friends were some of the brightest, the most talented, and in some cases, the most eccentric people that Virginia had to offer. The names she had mentioned were the CEO of one of the country's biggest tech firms, a legendary horse-woman who had recently won the Rolex event in Lexington, Kentucky, and an irascible character who bred racehorses, and whose family had settled next door to Thomas Jefferson. And she knew that was only the beginning of his list of best friends.

"Yes, Cobie," she smiled. "I think that could work."

They worked up a list of names and Annie gently suggested again that they assign topics for each get-together to cover. Cobie agreed, and chose a handful of people to discuss the history of the foxhound pedigree in central Virginia, and another group who would talk about the early days of foxhunting. Still another group would talk Thoroughbred bloodlines. Finally, he made a list of his closest friends—those nights would be for pure story-telling.

Annie and Lindsay laid out a schedule for these meetings, all to take place at the farm and all, by Cobie's request, as quickly as possible. Dorothy refused to be involved. Instead of mobilizing her, Cobie's illness had driven her into herself. Red came to take Cobie to most of his doctor's appointments, and Lindsay seemed to be in charge of general food and comfort, walking over from her own home on the property to the big farmhouse every day. Annie rarely saw Dorothy on any of her visits to the farm. Lindsay made excuses for her. "Mom's having a hard time with this," she would say. But Dorothy's absence was striking.

"But dad, there's time," Lindsay said, glancing over the month of March. "See?" She held up the farm bureau calendar that normally hung on the kitchen wall. "There are several good weekends here. Of course, we have to get past hunting season," she said, tapping her long finger on the middle week of the month, when fox hunting season ended for most clubs. She flipped to April. "And then we have to skip Easter and I think the point-to-point races will take up some people's schedules."

Point-to-points, which Virginia carried on in the tradition of the Irish steeplechase, were an exciting series of races over fence, hurdles and flats. Virginia boasted a springtime schedule of eighteen of these events, the most anywhere else in the country. These were sponsored by the hunt clubs across the state.

"No," he said firmly. "Just get them here." He turned to Annie. "Afternoons would be best. That's when I have the most energy." He flipped the calendar back to February and pointed to several days. "Here," he said, "and here. Skip Wednesdays. That's usually doctor's appointments in town. Just get them here."

And they came, without exception. They dropped everything, and they just came.

If the people on the list wondered who Annie was or why she was arranging the meetings, why she poured coffee and brought them trays of food, they didn't say. Nor did they object when she walked around with the whiskey bottle, lacing their coffees with a bracing dose. They just came. And they talked.

CHAPTER 13

———

ANNIE ARRIVED AT THE FARM just as a group of Cobie's friends were leaving the barn.

"These are the really old friends," Cobie smiled, gesturing to the half dozen men. "The neighbors, you know. Let me introduce you." He looked around at the assembled men and rubbed the stubble on his chin. "Hmmm," he said. "Some of them you already know. The ones who have the sense to hunt." Annie raised her hand to Archie and Barrett.

"Anyway, fellas, this is Annie. The one I told you about. She'll be arranging a horse talking night for all y'all." The men all nodded. She was glad to know that Cobie had already explained his plan to them.

Annie recognized several of their names and tried to match the neighboring farms to each of them. She knew that the history of the farm families who settled this part of Virginia was long and deep. History being what it was in this part of the world, she thought, it wasn't a surprise that many of them identified themselves with the land and with one another's families.

"Bet you didn't know he's my cousin," Archie said, gesturing to Cobie.

"Now don't start that again." Cobie grinned, punching Archie playfully on the arm. "This character has been claiming kinship for years. Seems that there were rumors of a...relationship, shall we say, with the neighbor's wife, back in the early 1800's."

Archie leaned against the barn and folded his hands good-naturedly over his ample belly. "That's right. When that kid came out looking for all the world like a Grainger, the mama hightailed it next door and offered to trade it for the neighbor's new calf."

Annie rolled her eyes. "That's not true!" she exclaimed, glancing sidelong at Cobie.

"True as heaven," Archie smiled. "Might have worked too, if the baby had been a girl. But the husband saw value in keeping a boy, whoever's it was."

"How many other cousins, un-intentional and unacknowledged, do we have here?" said Barrett, raising his hand. "I can make a claim or two, I think. You know, In Madison's day, when…."

Cobie waved his hand and shushed him. "We're here to talk horses, not some damn fool ancestors. Now come look at this mare here in the near paddock. She's going to foal any day now."

Annie's mind wandered as she watched the group walked toward the paddock. She saw them argue and laugh, continuing to rib each other about parentage and their own bloodlines. The collective memories of the group ran deep. The large tracts of land that were settled early had to be farmed, and whether the family was said to be rich or poor was only a small matter of interest. They had the land in common.

Cobie looked back and gestured her to the fence. Annie stood beside him and admired the mare, heavy with foal. She sighed and looked around. "What a beautiful place to be born," she said, referring to the coming foal.

"Yeah, it were," Cobie said, looking around. "Of course, my folks were poor as dirt," Cobie said. "My granddad couldn't get by farming his own property, so he managed tracts of land for the neighboring landowner, a politician who spent most of his time away."

"Ah hell," said Charlie. "We always ran in a pack of kids who didn't know one way or the other who had money and who didn't. All we cared about was the courage of our horses and the nose of our hounds."

"Pretty poetic, Charlie," Cobie sniffed, "for a family who sold all its land."

Annie felt Charlie stiffen. She remembered meeting him now. He still hunted now and then, but she recalled it was a sore point every time the club hunted the southern line of the Blue Ridge, only to have to veer east and away from the subdivisions that blotted the landscape.

"Now, now," Barrett interjected. "We all do what we gotta do. Fortunately…"

"Lord help us, Barrett," Cobie interjected. "No more history lessons."

Barrett raised his hands in surrender. "I was just going to mention the Virginia Land Conservation Tax Credit. If they had it in those days, Charlie might still have his land. Protection of farm lands started to take hold when that legislation passed."

"How does that work exactly?" Annie asked.

"The landowner creates an open space easement that limits property development rights in perpetuity," Barrett explained. "You go right on living on the property. You can pass it on to future generations. You can even sell it. But it can only be used for its traditional purposes. The property's natural or open space values are protected, assuring that the land would remain available for agriculture and forestry."

Barrett nodded toward Charlie. "For the families who own these nice tracts of land, it provides a good tax credit. But the most important thing is that it protects all this." He swept his arm across the rolling landscape. He turned to Annie and winked. "And of course, it protects our fox hunting lands."

Annie looked across the lush fields that rose softly toward the mountains. What would other Virginians think, she thought, the ones packed into the suburbs of DC, if they knew these places existed? Would they be resentful? Or would they be grateful that they were safe from development?

Hidden Virginia, she thought. Not the ostentatious farmland of Middleburg, where financiers and politicians laid down piles of cash to rub elbows with famous horsemen and claim rights to a prestigious address. But the quiet and spectacular counties of Orange and Madison and Albemarle, places you drive past on Route 29, getting just a tiny glimpse of the possibilities hidden there.

The men had already turned to the driveway and their waiting trucks, rousing Annie from her reverie. "I should go too," she said to Cobie. "You look tired."

Cobie took her by the elbow. "Naw, I'm fine," he whispered, leaning on her slightly as they went to join the others. "Wait a minute. Let me get these boys out a here." She watched as he said his goodbyes, noting that he leaned against Archie's truck for a moment to catch his breath before returning to the barn.

"I'm going to put this land into conservation," he confided when he returned. He picked up a halter that had slipped from its hook and replaced it neatly, smoothing the curl of the lead into place. "That Archie was never neat with the tack," he grumbled. He scanned the barn to make sure all was in order. Then he turned to her. "The lawyer is stopping by this afternoon. I was hoping you could be witness to the signing of papers."

"Have you told Dorothy?" Annie asked, hesitant. "Maybe she should sign."

"Not making a big deal of it," he said, waving away her concern. "No one needs to know. The farm passed directly from my father to me. The news will just come out in the will."

He saw the concerned look on Annie's face and turned away. "I was always planning to do it," he said. "Just seemed there would be plenty of time to get around to it. Guess I'm running out of that." He glanced sidelong at her frowning face. "Come on, I'll show you."

She followed him into his den. Cobie sat down at his desk and reached into the bottom drawer for a folder. He opened it and spread a map out on the table. She leaned in and followed the movement of his fingers as he outlined the plot of the land, and pointed out the boundaries of field, forest and stream.

Cobie looked up at Annie, seeming to read her thoughts. "Believe me, Dorothy don't care. I wouldn't be surprised if she moved into a condo in Orange after I'm gone. Lindsay will understand. Only to her advantage really, since she already lives on the property. She has her own deeded five acres of pastureland." He hesitated. "Of course, then there's Trace…"

"Trace?"

Cobie passed his hand over the grayed stubble on top of his head. "My son. Trace. He left the farm some years back. Never looked back, I guess. He'd probably find the sale of the farm pretty appealing."

"But where…."

Cobie waved off her question. "Okay by me, if that's what the family wants. But this way, neither my son nor any future owners of Pegasus Farm can ever sub-divide or develop it."

Annie nodded her support of the idea, wondering why she had never heard of Trace. She wondered where he lived, whether he knew about his father's illness. Had Lindsay called him? Or maybe Dorothy? She made a mental note to find out.

Cobie smoothed out the map. "It's only a small piece of property, in the grand scheme of things," he said. "Two hundred fifty acres. Well, two-forty-five without Lindsay's piece. But it contains some of the best views in Orange County." He pointed out a spot on the topographic map outlined by a series of circular contour lines indicating elevation. "That hill's called Lost Legend. You can see it right out the back door, off there in the distance." He gestured out the window. "You've been up there, or at least I know Elliot has. It butts up along Gladys' property, over here." He pointed to another tract on the map.

"Why is it called Lost Legend?"

Cobie shrugged. "A story for another time," he said. His finger followed a dotted line along the western boundary. "Gladys got over six hundred acres of prime farmland and river bottom that's already in easement. Together, they'll make a nice stretch of open land." Cobie nodded happily at the thought. Annie could imagine him riding those lands in his mind as he peered at the map, dotted with notations on elevations, water lines and forested sections. The thought made her melancholy.

Cobie looked up and noticed the look on her face. "Today is a good day," he said firmly. "In fact, it's a day to celebrate. I get to give something back, to my family, to my people. Hell, to the foxes." He gave her a wink. "After the lawyer is out of here, we're gonna break out the whiskey."

CHAPTER 14

———

"You asleep?" Cobie leaned over the wicker chair and peered down at her.

"Oh gosh no!" Annie stretched and rubbed her eyes, luxuriating in the rays of sun streaming into the porch. "You know I love your stories. You were talking about…" she furrowed her brow, trying to summon his last words, "a favorite hunting dog." She smiled triumphantly, knowing she has passed the test.

"And I sure appreciate you listening to them," he grinned and leaned back in his chair. "Even when you do it with your eyes closed."

Annie scrunched up her face and sat up. "Okay, well maybe I closed them for a second…." Annie turned at the sound of the squeaking screen door.

"Sounds like my wife's home," Cobie said, his face set in a grimace. "She don't much like my little project here."

Annie nodded and glanced toward the door again, sinking a little deeper into the deep wicker chair. Dorothy had told already her that she was fed up with the stories and with the friends that streamed in and out day and night. "It's always been all about Cobie," she had muttered when Annie had asked her advice on some photos.

Dorothy poked her head into the porch, noted the two of them, her eyes pausing on the pitcher of iced tea and cookies set between the two of them. She turned without comment back into the kitchen. Soon they heard the sound of her car pulling out of the driveway.

"Guess she went to the store," Cobie said mildly, leaning back in his chair and picking up his glass.

Annie nodded uncertainly. She thought it might be time to make an excuse to leave when she saw Lindsay walking across the lawn toward them. Annie stood up and waved.

Unlike her mother, Lindsay appreciated her dad's stories, but told Annie that she couldn't take the time to listen to them. After all, she laughed, she was pretty sure she had heard them all. With Cobie sick, her daughter to chase after, and her husband John away on deployment in Afghanistan, Lindsay had taken on the self-appointed role of general manager to the farm.

"Where you been, girl? Cobie said mildly.

"I went to check on the barn and look in on the new foal." Lindsay crossed her arms and leaned against the post. "She's looking real nice. Have you called the vet to take a look?"

Cobie nodded. "The stablemen know what to do. Quit worrying. I told 'em, just keep things going, fellas. No need to bother yourself."

Lindsay knew he still got out to the barn every day to see for himself that things were running smoothly. She straightened up and nodded, reaching for the door handle. "No harm in my checking in too," she shrugged awkwardly. "Well, I guess I'll just leave the two of you to your work."

Annie tilted her head at Cobie and nodded toward Lindsay's retreating back. Cobie watched her for a moment. "Hold up there, girl," he called. "Sure ain't nothing wrong with checking in now and then." He struggled to his feet, waving Lindsay off as she quickly turned to assist him. "Come to think of it, I haven't looked in on her all day. Why don't we go look at the little bit together?"

———————

"It's funny, isn't it?" Annie mused as she sipped her coffee. She smiled across the counter at Elliot's sleepy face. "There's tension over there for sure, at least between Cobie and Dorothy. Whatever the reason, Cobie seems to find my presence comforting. Even with Lindsay nearby, a lot of days he seems to only want me around." She put down her cup. "It can be damned awkward."

"Why do you suppose that is?" Elliot asked.

"I think maybe it's because of our lack of history together," she answered. "Maybe it's easier for him to have someone around who was not overly solicitous to him." She grinned. "Someone who he can feel free to let loose on."

Elliot nodded thoughtfully, scratching the stubble of his unshaven face. "And someone whose grief he doesn't have to feel responsible for."

"You're probably right," she said softly. Annie stood up and put her arms around him, burying her head in the warmth of his neck.

CHAPTER 15

THE LATE WINTER SNOWS HAD receded into the red Virginia clay, but the explosion of green that heralded the true beginning of spring had not yet begun. Still, the sunlight that streamed into the window had a different angle these days, Annie thought. Too nice to be indoors today.

She set aside her papers and looked over at Cobie. He was fidgeting restlessly with the stack of photos on his desk. Their eyes met and he smiled, following her glance out the window. He stood up and tossed a handful of photos onto the pile.

"Come on," he said, grabbing his barn coat from a nearby hook. "I've had enough of indoors. Let's go out. I want to show you something."

They drove the Gator, the farm's old four-wheeler, to the back field just below Lost Legend. He pointed to a hillside where a smudge of red clay stood out from the monotone of the cropped corn field.

"Look there," he said, pointing.

Annie recognized the telltale signs of a fox den. She scanned the ground carefully, finally seeing what he was pointing at, a vixen asleep in the sun outside her den.

Cobie leaned against the steering wheel and watched the fox intently. "She is relaxed," he said. "She knows that the horses and the hounds have retired for the season so that she can raise her babies in peace."

He climbed slowly out of the Gator and took a few steps up the hill. "There's always been a den there," he whispered back to Annie. "This vixen inherited this spot from her momma." He pointed out the wide oval front porch where the vixen lay. "That spot's perfect for napping in the sun. She's got a hidden back door too."

Annie got out and tiptoed to where he stood. "I see," she said, nodding happily.

Cobie grinned and folded his arms over his chest, satisfied. "A good spot to raise her kits," he said. "There's the stream nearby and of course, the cut-down corn field. Perfect for hunting field mice."

Annie knew there would be several dens in the territory. Some of them were just small holes, barely big enough to contain a fox. Sometimes a fox on the run would even borrow a groundhog hole to duck into. But she had never seen a cubbing den this close. "I thought she'd be inside," she whispered.

Cobie shrugged. "Naw, she's just like us, wantin' to take advantage of a nice day." He watched her for a moment, his eyes taking in the area around the den.

"Really, most of the year, she prefers to be above ground," Cobie explained. "She likes to rest in the cool of the cornfields during the heat of a summer day and spends her evenings out hunting for food. But now she's settled down to raise her family."

Annie nodded. "I think I understand the basics. Mating season for the foxes starts in the winter when traveling dog foxes come through the territory. That's when the foxes run like crazy and the hunters have their best sport." She looked up expectantly. "Right?"

"You got it," Cobie said, resting his hand on her shoulder. "Everyone's in high spirits then. The fox are running wild and the foxhunters are helping them along, moving those restless dogs to new territories to find available mates."

His voice grew gentle as he gestured to the sleeping fox. "But now, spring, this is the vixen's time. Look at her." The vixen had a coat of burnished red, with only small accents of white on her underside and the tip of her tail.

"She's a small one, isn't she?" Annie whispered.

"Can't be much more than ten pounds. Probably her first year."

Annie admired the lustrous brush that curled around her body. It gave her slight frame a more substantial appearance.

"She's in good shape," Cobie said with satisfaction.

"They eat almost anything, don't they?" Annie asked.

"Yeah, lucky for her she is not too picky about her food. She likes mice of course, but she'll eat snails, chicken, crayfish, berries, even corn." Cobie chuckled. "Hell, I have even seen the occasional fox come along after the hunter's tailgate breakfast to snack on dropped bread and other leftovers."

The vixen raised her head to look at them, but she did not move. "She's sticking close to home," Cobie said. "Must be close to having them babies."

A large dog fox trotted up and dropped something at the vixen's feet.

"Look at that," Annie said. "He's feeding her."

"Yeah, them old dogs don't help much, but they do provide food when she needs it." Cobie watched as the dog fox moved off and laid down at some distance from the den. "He'll pretty much leave the rest to her."

"How many will she have?"

Cobie removed his hat and scratched his head. "Oh, maybe three or four. They'll stay right around here all summer while she teaches them to hunt. Foxes hunt by sound, you know."

Annie shook her head. "I figured they were big on scent, like the hounds," she replied.

Cobie shrugged. "They have a great sense of smell, of course. Eyesight's not that sharp, but they can hear just about anything. They listen for the grass to rustle, and they pounce straight up and right onto that unsuspecting mouse. The youngsters imitate her." He chuckled. "It's quite a sight, watching them launch themselves into the air like an army of small cats. They pounce and miss their target over and over. Finally, one catches something. It's a proud moment, let me tell you." He laughed out loud.

Annie saw the dog fox sit up and regard them with interest.

"I think he's telling us we're bothering them," Cobie said. "We'd better move off. Don't want her upset." He looked back over his shoulder. "We'll have to come back and watch their progress throughout the summer."

"So, what happens next?" Annie asked. She paused to watch Cobie climb gingerly into the driver's seat before going around pulling herself into the passenger side.

"Oh, the babies will stay with their mama until fall," Cobie answered, leaning over the wheel and looking off at the distant hills. Annie saw his shoulders slump just a bit. "The sons set off and go out into the world. They'll run long distances to find a place to call their own."

Annie put her hand on his shoulder. He glanced at her and smiled. "The way of the world." Cobie stepped on the clutch and turned the key. The old Gator sprung to life, its energetic grumble momentarily drowning out their voices.

Cobie slowed the vehicle and turned toward home, taking a moment to survey the greening fields that swept toward the distant mountains. "Gray and his hounds will be out here again before you know it," he said.

Annie frowned and put her hand on Cobie's back. She wondered if he would ever again see the familiar sight of horses and hounds careening across his own fields. She glanced sideways at him, knowing that he was having the same thought. He reached out to squeeze her arm but she caught his hand and held it tight. Together they watched as the ghosts of last season's field galloped by.

Cobie gave Annie's hand one last squeeze and let it go. He downshifted the Gator and turned for home. "No worries," he said, winking at her. "Gray will help those little boys disperse into new territories to call their own."

Annie turned her head and wiped away a tear. And with him or without him, she thought, foxhunting season would begin again.

CHAPTER 16

ANNIE WATCHED COBIE AS HE paused to take a look at himself in the mirror. He was thinner, she thought. He glanced up and caught her eye. She chuckled and shook her head.

"Still a little vain, I guess," he said, smoothing out his stubble of hair.

Annie reached up and straightened his collar, noting the flush of red in his cheek. "You look just fine," she smiled. They both turned at the sound of knocking on the kitchen door.

"Who is it?" Cobie said, peeking over her shoulder.

"Relax Cobie, these are just your friends." Annie said, turning to put a reassuring hand on his arm. "You just invited club staff, right?"

"Yeah, that's the problem. Some of 'em haven't seen me in a while." He glanced back in the mirror. "Don't say it," he said. "I know I'm thin." He stood up a little straighter for the mirror. "Bound to scare 'em half to death."

Annie shook her head and opened the door to Barrett, who stood there smiling, bottle of wine in hand, with Archie. Cobie walked to the door to greet them.

Excellent, Annie thought. Reinforcements. The two close friends already knew what he looked like; they were here every other day. She peeked out to the driveway to see if anyone else was pulling in. Satisfied that there was no flash of headlights coming up the lane, she turned and closed the door.

"What's tonight's topic?" asked Barrett briskly, rubbing his hands together and shrugging out of his Barbour jacket.

Cobie eyed him for a moment. "Foxhunting," he said simply.

Barrett furrowed his brow. "Haven't we been....?"

"Sure, we been telling stories, but I want to make sure we document the whole thing. The jobs, the etiquette and all."

Barrett frowned. "Didn't Richardson do that in the beginning of the century? The Complete Foxhunter, wasn't it?

"Bah, that's ancient history," Cobie said, turning to lead the way into the den. "I'm talking present day America, and specifically, the way we do it at Meryton."

"Got it," Barrett said, giving Annie a wink. "We'll tell it your way."

"Well, Annie?" Archie said. "You got the recorder on. What do you need to know?"

Annie looked back at the door. "Shouldn't we wait for the others?" she asked. "I think I hear a car now."

"I'll go," said Cobie. "Turn that thing on and get started."

Archie looked out the window. "I think that's Monty," he said. "Red Tahoe, right?"

Barrett nodded. "Right then. That's a good place to start." He began. "You know that Monty is the Master of Foxhounds, right?" He waited for Annie to nod, pausing as she checked that the recorder was working.

"So Monty is kind of like the executive of the group. He's in complete command." He wiggled his eyebrows at Archie who stifled a laugh. Barrett turned back to Annie and shook his head apologetically. "Monty's an old pal, so we'll always be giving him some crap" he said. "But he is responsible for some important stuff. He has to negotiate with landowners for the fixtures we hunt on, and has to safeguard the interests of those holdings. That's a big deal, and not all that easy."

Archie nodded. "The Master is responsible for the health of the club; from its staff and its facilities to its hounds and the sport which is provided to the field. He decides the schedule of fixtures, called off the hunt for poor conditions—all that kind of stuff." Archie shook his head. "Glad it's not me."

Barrett grinned. "Aren't we all!" He eyed his friend affectionately and turned to Annie. "Archie would sooner punch a difficult landowner as look at 'em."

"Yeah, well, you only say that because of that one time…"

He was interrupted by Monty walking into the room, accompanied by Gray and Davis.

"Evening, Master," Archie said mildly. Monty nodded and smiled.

Annie raised her eyebrows as Archie explained. "We call him "Master" at all times, Annie. We make sure to thank him and wish him a good evening at the end of the hunt day." He saluted toward the men. "Don't we, Monty?"

"Bah," Monty answered, going over to the bar to pour a drink before seating himself near the fireplace.

Gray took off his tweed cap and smoothed his thick hair, taking a quick peek into the mirror as he passed. "Archie's just having a bit of fun, Annie," Gray said, his thick Irish accent rolling Annie's name into a sigh. "But the formality is not artificial in the field. The welfare of many creatures, both of the two footed and four footed varieties is at stake, so the Master is the final word. The respect of the field ensures that authority."

Gray reached into the refrigerator and turned back to Archie. "Where's your beer, man?" he asked. Archie nodded as Gray pulled a second beer out and handed it to him. Davis reached for a beer and Annie noticed that Gray silently shook his head. Davis immediately withdrew his hand.

"Would you prefer a Coke, Davis?" Annie asked.

"Yes, ma'am, that would be nice," Davis said, adding "thank you" before turning to greet Cobie.

Cobie eyed the young man nervously. Davis had been a student for years before the club gave him a trial as whipper-in. The young man looked up to Cobie, and Annie knew he wanted to appear strong for him. Davis smiled and extended his hand in greeting. "So glad to see you, sir. You are looking well."

"So Davis," she said brightly, drawing his attention away from Cobie. "You are the whipper-in. What does that mean?"

The young man glanced around nervously as the older men turned their complete attention to him. "Well, ma'am," he began. "My job is to help the huntsman." He nodded toward Gray. "I work to always keep the hounds between me and him. I count the couples to make sure that none has been lost, and I double-back to find any that have gone astray. And I guard the perimeter in front of the road or train tracks to make sure that the hounds are kept safe."

"Wow," said Annie. "I've seen you out there all by yourself. I assumed you were just having a nice day of hunting like everyone else." She chuckled as Davis blushed and ducked his head.

Barrett laughed. "I whip for the club too, of course not in a paid capacity like Davis here." He nodded toward the young man. "But I'll tell you, much of our day is actually spent in a continuous state of tension. You gotta be on alert all the time. A whip's horse is on duty too. He has to be sensible, sound and durable. The whippers-in are the eyes and the ears of the huntsman. We are there so Gray can cover a lot of ground in relative confidence. He trusts us to take care of his hounds, keep the field in the right place, and stay out of the way to avoid foiling the line."

"We track and signal fox sightings too," Davis added, warming to the topic. "I listen for instructions that come in the form of a horn blast from Gray. Later, it's my job to give the huntsman my observations about the pack."

"And that's why you must never, ever talk to him in the hunt field," Gray said, giving Davis a quick nod. "I expect them to note any superior performances that I may not have seen, as well as any problems in the order of the pack. They can't do all that if they are stopping to chat."

Barrett laughed. "Well, I admit, I might like a bit of a chat in the field. But since we are talking ideals, it is considered bad form to sidle up and chat with the whipper-in. We have a lot on our minds, or we should have."

"Including why you are standing between me and the field," Davis added boldly.

Cobie smiled at the boy. "The whip should be listening to the babble of hounds, scanning the sky for birds that may indicate fox activity and keeping tabs on the field as a whole." He nodded at Davis. "It's a good job, isn't it, boy?"

Davis beamed. "Yes sir, it is."

"Most of the time," Barrett added, "depending on the "intelligence of the field." Davis raised his hand to his mouth to hide a grin. The old men nodded and considered.

"What does that mean?" Annie asked. The men chuckled.

"There are folks in the field," Cobie said, "and there always have been, who just come to be on horseback, to get some fresh air and to see friends. Many of the youngsters are that way—coming for some high-spirited fun." He smiled at Annie and held up his hands. "There is nothing wrong with that, of course. But sometimes…." Cobie raised his eyebrows at the other men. "Folks just don't have a real connection to the land. They don't have an instinct for the hunt, an understanding of the draw and the cast, the interplay of fox to hound."

"Scenery," Barrett said drily. "Nothing but scenery to them."

"He's right about some of them," Monty said, rubbing his jaw. "We got more members from the city than we used to. Them, and their kids, can be a bit of a pain." He paused to consider. "Not that we aren't grateful for their financial support."

"Those kids are our future," Cobie declared. "But how many," he wondered out loud, "can hear the birds whisper the location of the fox? Or notice crows mobbing, or know that the direction of the fox's gaze is a surer indication of his path than the one he is running." He shook his head, placing a hand over his heart. "It pains me deeply to think what they're missing."

Cobie dropped his head. "The hunt has so many lessons to teach—about the earth, about stewardship of the land, about man's small place in the larger world. I'm just afraid there are precious few who understand."

He looked around at the assembled me. "Without this structure, without understanding the significance of the experience," he said quietly, "Who's going to safeguard the sport?"

"He's right, of course," said Charlie. "Sometimes I feel like I'm doing nothing more than leading a glorified trail ride."

"We aren't out there to take them on a nature walk, Cobie," said Barrett. "We're there to hunt."

"Ah hell, Barrett," Archie chuckled. "When I was a kid, I just hunted to ride too. I wanted the speed, the big jumps. Just wanted to show off." He raised his eyebrows. "Cobie, you were the same way."

Cobie shook his head. "We worked hard at those hunts," he argued. "Up early to do our chores. Hell, we had to hack to the fixture; no traileringgoing on then. We'd hunt all day, into evening." He shook his head. "Man, we'd come back after dark, starved out of our minds. And daddy would make us clean up and take care of the horses before we got a bite to eat."

"God, you're right. He'd inspect every piece of tack." Archie shook his head, remembering. "I still hate cleaning tack."

Charlie nodded. "We grew up with the old ways. We had dads who taught us what was right." He considered for a moment. "Other than us dumb kids, the whole field was filled with intelligence back then."

Barrett said to Cobie, "But we raised our kids that way. Zane and…. Trace. They worked hard too. Really knew what they were about."

The other men nodded, thoughtful. It was true; those two boys would have been the future of the hunt. But Zane had died in Iraq, and Trace…. well, Trace wasn't here.

"Nothing is the same now," Archie said. "Remember we could hunt a red fox for miles in those days? Now you're lucky to get a good run going at all. Damned groundhog holes everywhere. Like a Super 8 on every street corner for a fox looking to go to ground."

"Ain't that the truth," Charlie said. "And you can't go far anyway, what with the roads and the subdivisions."

"And whose fault is that?" asked Barrett, pointedly. Charlie colored slightly but didn't respond.

Cobie lifted his hands with a shrug. "I still think there's time to help the next generation have a taste of what we had."

"That's a lot to ask, Cobie. Most of these kids we have today aren't farm kids. This generation is accustomed to things being done for them. Unless they have a strong figure at their barn, nobody's making them do anything they don't want to do."

"We have had a couple of junior hunts," said Monty. "They're well attended. The kids mean well enough, and so do most of the parents. They just don't know any better."

"Can we do more?" said Cobie. "Organize the kids around walking out the puppies. There's more time for teaching them."

"Maybe Saturday classes outside of the season. Goodness knows the parents would be happy to drop the kids off for a couple hours. And the horse crazy kids would be glad to come."

"Make them work in the kennels with Billy," smiled Gray.

"Woowee," said Billy, poking his head in the back door. "I was just out checking on that little beagle you got out there in the barn." He looked around suspiciously. "Did I just hear my name used in vain?" He refused Lindsay's offer to come in, citing muddy boots, but accepted a glass of iced tea. "Having a bunch of kids underfoot helping me take care of the hounds? That would surely be more trouble than it's worth."

"Still," said Barrett. "It's something to think about."

Cobie nodded with satisfaction. "Some good thoughts there. Monty, can we ask Deborah to join us one evening to discuss it further? Maybe Sara too. She's got that barn full of youngsters that she brings to the hunt."

Monty nodded his assent. The other men gave each other knowing glances. They understood what Cobie wanted. But they also knew that the old days, and Trace, were gone, and it didn't look like they were coming back.

Cobie slapped his hands to his legs. "Now fellas, there's a new mare in the barn I'd like ya'll to take a look at." The men rose, thanking Annie and Lindsay as they headed out the door.

Cobie turned. "Where's Daisy? Where's my shadow?"

Lindsay looked at her watch. "She should be getting off the bus soon, Daddy."

"Don't know why that child goes to school so young."

"She's already four. It's good for her to be around other kids," Lindsay replied patiently, repeating an old argument.

"I still say she'd be better off here at the farm. Plenty to learn here."

"I know Daddy." Lindsay answered smoothly, walking over to make sure he navigated the porch step safely. "I'll send her along as soon as she gets here."

"You tell her Blondie needs some exercise." Blondie was Daisy's pony, a gift from her grandpa on her third birthday." He gestured to the pony in the paddock. "Most of her riding been on lead, but I hoped to get her on her own soon." He scratched the stubble on his chin. "I planned to get her out on the lead myself next foxhunting season, but..." He raised his brow at Lindsay as his voice trailed off.

Lindsay rolled her eyes and nodded her understanding. More than the stories, more than the reminiscences, she knew this was what Cobie wanted most. Her dad figured she was hopeless. But with Trace gone, he wanted to know that the knowledge would not die with him and his generation. He wanted to make sure it was passed on. And he had his eye on Daisy.

CHAPTER 17

IT WAS STORY NIGHT.

"Lindsay, you got any more beer in the frig?"

Lindsay laughed. "I got it all, Daddy, anything they want." She reached into the frig and picked up two bottles, but Cobie had already headed back toward the back porch. Lindsay rolled her eyes and placed the bottles into Annie's outstretched hands. "I just stopped in to pick up Mom," she said. "We are going to see a movie in Charlottesville." She raised her eyebrows at the laughter already emanating from the backyard. "You sure you don't want to come with us?"

Annie shook her head. She enjoyed story nights, although she found the stories sometimes flowed better when she stayed out of the way. "Don't worry," she said when she saw Lindsay pull out a tray of cheese. "Let me deliver these beers and then I'll come back and take care of the food."

Lindsay nodded gratefully. "Good luck with them," she called as she headed out the front door. Annie turned as she heard Monty's voice rise above the others.

"Every single person who starts foxhunting does it for the love of horses," Monty said emphatically.

"You think?" Charlie said, considering.

Monty nodded. "I'm saying that's how they start. They think it looks pretty, and they want to try out their horse. You always see folks like that come out a couple times every season."

"Risking life and limb galloping and jumping big fences is an adrenaline rush for sure," Charlie said. "But for me, it's always been about the actual hunting. I started out as a kid on foot with a pack of beagles."

Cobie nodded. "That's what separates those weekenders from the real hunters. If they start coming more and more, on weekdays and in bad weather, you know you've got 'em hooked. That's because they get bitten by the hunting bug. The hounds, their music, the view of a fox—if that's what turns them on, you've got 'em for life."

"No question about that," Monty agreed.

Barrett considered. "You know; I have always considered myself more of a hound person." He looked around the room for agreement. "I mean, after all, it is their party. The humans come for fun, and the horses come because we bring them. But there ain't no hunt without those hounds." Gray nodded emphatically.

"I suppose you could say the same thing about the fox," Charlie said.

"Point taken."

Wynn chuckled. "I never was interested in horses or hounds or foxes. Daddy ran a cattle farm, and I just never thought about it. Then I got involved with a girl."

Everyone laughed. Wynn's history with the ladies was long and complex. It made perfect sense that his start in foxhunting would begin with a girl.

"That girl took me out a couple times on western saddles, and I thought it weren't too bad. So then she asked me to go foxhunting with her. Hell, I didn't even know what that was."

"Wynn, why doesn't this surprise me?" Barrett asked.

"You hush now." Wynn continued. "So I went over there to Leland's farm, and I told Lee there, I need me a fox hunting horse and all the gear. So he got me up a horse; Topher was his name. Remember him? He ended up being a good horse. And he gave me an old Stubben saddle and bridle, all for $300."

Everyone laughed. "I remembered that horse," said Cobie. "And I think that old saddle ended up at Sara's place for the school ponies."

"I believe it did." Wynn agreed. "Anyway, I got there with Topher on my cattle trailer. Must have looked like a complete fool. But I got tacked up and said to the girl, "Now we ain't gonna jump any fences, right?"

Chuckles rippled through the room; the assembled group seemed to know where this story was going. Everyone fell now and then. Wynn continued. "I fell fourteen times that day."

The room exploded with laughter. "Fourteen times!" Deborah exclaimed.

"And all for a girl," Barrett added.

"I'm starting to regret this story," Wynn said ruefully. "But yeah, I fell on every jump. But damn it, I got back on and did it again." He paused to let the laughter die down. "Twenty-nine years later, I think I got it about right."

The group back in order, he continued. "I went on to learn about the hounds and I've been a whipper-in for the past twenty years. Hell, my life these days is about nothing other than foxhunting. I have something to do with it every day of the year."

"It is addictive," said Monty.

"So Wynn," Deborah said. "What happened to the girl?"

Wynn thought for a moment. "I have no earthly idea."

The room erupted again.

CHAPTER 18

———————◆———————

ANNIE GOT TO THE FARMHOUSE, her arms loaded with rhubarb crisp and chicken soup. She knocked at the door, finally pushing it open with her elbow so she could relieve herself of the bundles before she lost them on the steps of the house. She called out for Lindsay, for Dorothy, for Cobie, but no one answered.

She put the crisp on the counter and made room in the refrigerator for the soup. She noted how full it had become. She needed to stop bringing food. As word of Cobie's illness had spread, friends and neighbors had taken up the effort, and now there was every kind of casserole, soup and cookie at the family's disposal. A silly custom, when you thought about it. The family had no greater need for food right now than they had before Cobie's illness. But it gave people a way to express their love for the family. Annie told herself to talk to Lindsay about the food. Maybe they could get some of it packaged up and put into the freezer for later use. Or maybe the church could use it.

She went out the screen door, releasing it behind her as she went, just for the fun of hearing it bang shut. Screen doors in springtime, what was better than that? Annie raised her hand to shield her eyes from the bright sun, scanning the path to Lindsay's house for sign of someone. Seeing no one, she decided to walk out to the barn and see who she could find.

Cobie was there, leaning on the side of a stall, looking in at a litter of beagle puppies. "Look here," he said, nodding when he saw her round the corner. "Look what Wanda's gone and done."

Annie looked over the gate, noting Wanda's tail cautiously thumping a nervous beat as yet another visitor came to view her new brood. "Aw..."

"Daisy's going to love them pups," Cobie said. "Wait 'til she gets home from school and sees that." He smiled with pride, although whether at the thought of his grand-daughter or the little bitch who had been the de facto ruler of the barn for all of her five-year life, Annie wasn't sure.

Even though the puppies were a little too new to do much more than squeal and wiggle, it was easy to kill nearly thirty minutes watching Wanda clean each one, nudging them to her teats to eat.

"Look at that little feller right there," Cobie pointed to the little one on the right. "His nose is working like crazy. He's knows where his bread is buttered."

"I like the little bitch there," Annie said, gesturing to the little girl on the left. "Lovely head."

"No doubt they'll all have their place," Cobie said. "We'll just have to wait and see." Annie nodded. It was enough to just enjoy them, nestled as they were, in their bed of straw.

Cobie caught the attention of one of the barn workers. "Joe, bring the bitch some water, would you? And maybe grab a blanket out of the tack room. She might prefer that to the straw." Joe, one member of the large family who had worked for the Grainger's for many years, nodded and went to get the requested items.

Cobie watched Joe place the water near Wanda and then move the wriggling puppies onto the blanket. Wanda eyed him nervously but with goodwill. She had known Joe her whole life and trusted, as much as she could trust anyone with her new brood, the assistance he provided. While she settled down again, Cobie thanked Joe, and then asked him in a low voice, and in Spanish, for one more favor.

Annie's Spanish was pretty rusty, but she thought that Cobie had asked for a horse to be saddled. This seemed to be confirmed when she saw Joe headed to the front paddock and put a halter on Warrior, Cobie's veteran hunter.

"Are you going riding, Cobie?" she asked, worry in her voice.

Recently, the doctor had suggested that he could implant a morphine drip for Cobie's pain. He had refused, citing the fact that its presence might prevent him from riding. The doctor had gently asked, "Are you going to ride, Cobie?" knowing that the man's bones were growing weaker and more brittle with every passing day.

And Cobie had said, "Well maybe not. But I'm not ready to give up on the possibility." Annie knew this, not because she had heard it herself, but because Red had told her about it after the recent doctor's appointment in Charlottesville. She had found him sitting in his truck after dropping Cobie off at the house. The big man dissolved into a puddle of tears, and she had quickly left him there to regain his composure, knowing her sympathy would just make things worse. She had heard the truck start up and pull out of the driveway, spraying gravel as it went. She felt for him. These big tough farmers just didn't know how to cope with the death of a friend. Much as they knew about the cycles of life and death, much as they lived it every day on their farms, this was not one they had an easy time accepting.

Annie watched as Warrior walked into the barn, noting the ripple of muscles that ran down his shoulders as he walked, and the grace and power of his hindquarters. Warrior was a tall gray horse, almost white, with small patterns of black that played across his rump. They almost looked like stars, Annie mused, as she reached up to stroke the horse as he walked by.

Warrior was always a striking sight in the hunt field, head and shoulders above the others. It was always easy to find and identify the two of them, especially when Cobie sported the huntsman's scarlet coat.

Joe brushed him now, picking the mud out of his feet and combing out the long tail. He placed first one, and then a second pad on the horse's back, and then turned to reach for the saddle. Warrior's liquid brown eyes turned toward Cobie then, a hint of excitement in the toss of his head. Cobie walked up to the old gelding and scratched his ears, reaching high to find the right spot. Warrior dropped his head and leaned into the man, helping him get the angle just right. He nudged Cobie with his head, as though pushing him to go. *Let's go,* the old horse seemed to say. *Let's go to the fields, to the hounds, to the foxes.*

Annie watched the two of them together, eyes blinking back tears for the partners that had hunted the Virginia fields together for so many years. She knew from the stories that Warrior had been born right here in this barn twenty years ago, a racetrack prospect born to a well-known mare. Cobie had said that he just wasn't mature enough at age two to be raced, and was soon consigned to the owner's list of failed breedings. But Cobie knew talent when he saw it, and brought along Warrior as his own, jumping the young horse and training him in the ways of the Virginia foxhunter.

Joe finished saddling Warrior and bridled him, the horse willingly taking the bit into his mouth. Then he turned and handed the reins to Cobie, who walked the horse out into the sunshine to the mounting block. Annie's heart caught in her throat, but she said nothing. If Cobie wanted to ride, well then, damn it, Cobie should ride.

But Cobie didn't get on the horse. He turned toward her, his eyes shining. "Come on over here, girl," he said, gesturing to the mounting block.

Annie blanched and stepped back. "But Cobie, I'm in jeans and sneakers. I can't ride right now. It's a great thought, really. I...appreciate it," she said, eying the gentle giant standing quietly at his side. "Maybe next week."

Cobie's eyes turned steely gray, the color of the sky when a cloud passed over a brilliant patch of blue. "Annie," he said. "Get on the damned horse."

As so she did.

CHAPTER 18

———

ANNIE BLUSHED TO THINK OF her first forays back in the saddle. Cobie saw right away that she was trying too hard to be correct, to present a graceful post, to look somehow competent, when she knew what she looked like—a fat girl on a big horse. Warrior tried to understand what she wanted, putting his ears back in a questioning gesture. He did his best to guess where she wanted to go while she fussed with the reins. She wasn't sure where to put her hands or how to make her jelly legs communicate with the horse. "Sorry, buddy," she whispered into his ear. "I'm trying here."

But Cobie was patient with her. "Don't you worry; it will come back fast. You'll see. All the years you had in the saddle, your body remembers." She had serious doubts about that, but glowed self-consciously when he praised her natural seat. He repeated over and over, "Ride with your eyes, Annie. Ride with your eyes."

And finally she lifted her head, directing her focus where she wanted the horse to go. And miraculously, Warrior responded. Her body began to remember too, the grip of the legs, the tilt of the heel, and the set of her head. And before long, everything was better.

Cobie coaxed her into canters, repeating figure eights and serpentines across the ring. Within a week, he had Joe set up small jumps, making her first walk Warrior over them, and then coaching her into making the small bunny hops that Warrior must have thought they were. Annie had done some jumping when she was younger, but had never believed she would do it again. How could she have forgotten? That rush of all feet off the ground, just for a few moments, was exhilarating. The rhythm of the jump beat in her head. Approach, take-off, flight, landing, getaway. 1-2-3-4-5. 1-2-3-4-5. Tiny jumps, so she had to count fast, but jumps nevertheless.

After a couple of weeks of daily riding, Annie saw that Warrior was starting to enjoy himself. Their movements together were becoming synchronized, communication improving with every ride.

"That there horse is enjoying himself," Cobie said. Annie smiled happily, relieved that maybe it was true. "He needs to get out. He has been in the pasture since November. He needs a job." Cobie paused thoughtfully. "Looks like maybe he's got one."

Cobie insisted that she go out every day, and refused to talk about the book until she did so. He did not excuse rainy days or cold weather. Neither did he accept excuses that she was too busy, or one of their appointments would soon arrive. She brought Warrior in from the paddock and saddled him herself now, before presenting herself to Cobie in the backyard of the house, where he positioned himself on sunny afternoons. She luxuriated in the smell of the barn; of the leather and the manure and the sweet mash.

Soon, Cobie pushed her to go out into the field by herself. "Go, go," he encouraged her. "Get out there. Let Warrior teach you. He knows the ways. It's never too late to learn. I can go on and on right here, but that horse and Mother Nature can teach you anything you need to know."

At first, she hugged the fence line, afraid to do more than ride the perimeter of the near pasture, knowing that Cobie was watching her progress closely. But soon she realized that he was right. Outside of the ring, she began to find her rhythm, to feel the instincts spring back to life that had been lying dormant for so long. No techniques, no patterns, no witnesses, just her on a horse, moving together as one. Warrior seemed happier out here too, his gait free and his movements smooth and catlike.

And then one day, she just did it. She and Warrior were trotting the far edge of the field, passing the same coop that they passed every day. The coop, an inverted v-shaped wooden jump that was built into the fence line, allowed hunters to easily traverse fields without having to open and close gates. She paused, circling once and then again, eyeing the small gate that was installed alongside the jump. She turned the horse and walked away from the fence. Then she turned and requested an easy canter from him, focusing her gaze on the other side of the fence just as Cobie had taught her. 1-2-3-4-5, she said to herself. Warrior understood immediately and sailed over the coop with ease. Annie caught herself as they landed, a little askew but still in her tack. She laughed and looked back at the fence.

"We'll probably use the gate on the way home," she told him, patting his shoulder. Then she turned to the next field. "Let's go, buddy," she said. They were free.

Soon they were making their way together through the fields and the forests surrounding the farm. They raised herds of deer, dozens of them that skittered across their path as they went. Warrior took an interest; ears pricked up but never spooking. Turkeys pecked their way along the valley floor, an occasional one flapping awkwardly to perch in the branch of a tree and gaze down at them. She caught sight of the occasional fox, bunny, or coyote. She noted the signs of every den, and got to know the neighborhoods where the foxes frequented. Warrior showed her where to cross streams, and she gave him his head so that he could choose the right footing up and down steep embankments.

It wasn't long before her rides, which had started as nervous fifteen or twenty minute turns around the paddock, stretched to an hour, and then two. The afternoon visits to Cobie now started first thing in the morning, where she headed straight to the barn to spend the morning with Warrior.

She didn't always go out. Sometimes she just hung out with the old gelding, leaning against a tree, watching him and his paddock mate nibble the new grasses that were beginning to green the surface of the earth. All around her, life was waking. Buds were forming, birds were chirping, puppies and foals and lambs were being born.

Even Cobie seemed to be feeling better. He was eating well and hadn't complained much of pain. He came out to the barn more often, and spent long afternoons chatting and recording conversations with his friends. Sometimes Annie would hear howls of laughter coming from the backyard as she put up the horse, Cobie's afternoon gab sessions already underway. She would lean back and listen, happy for a moment to just experience the sound of the men's voices. Sometimes in the evening, when she listened to the day's recordings and transcribed the stories, it was all she could do to find the words beneath the sound of all that laughter. It seemed that this must be the best antidote for Cobie. How could someone resist being healed, surrounded by the laughter and camaraderie of that band of brothers?

For the moment, life was good. Annie could even imagine that the doctors were wrong. That there was no death sentence; that her friend could actually beat this dreaded disease.

Annie felt like a kid again. She felt competent. She felt whole. She felt real. She felt like the country girl she was meant to be. And astride Warrior, she felt like she had wings.

CHAPTER 19

THE BOYS WERE IN FULL cry today, thought Annie. They had broken out the whiskey, part of Cobie's collection of extraordinary Kentucky bourbons. He wasn't much of a drinker himself, but his work with Thoroughbreds had caused a lot of bottles to be gifted to him over the years. His pals were only too happy to help him with reducing the inventory.

The subject had turned to the hounds, and they talked rapidly and with enthusiasm, trading stories of favorite dogs, hard-driving dogs, and dogs that they found no favor with.

In Virginia, the American foxhound is king. Bloodlines going back to Washington and Jefferson still influence these lines. Of course, those original hounds were of the English variety. When the Marquis de Lafayette came to America to visit, he brought along a French hound as a gift for George Washington, the Grand Bleu de Gascogne. The Grand Bleu looked more like a coonhound, and it brought greater durability, a stronger voice and a better nose to the bloodline. This combined breeding produced the American foxhound as we know it today. Taller and generally a bit lighter than their English cousin, the American is known for its hard-charging tireless runs, its highly refined nose and its determination in the field.

The huntsmen are anxious to know one another's packs, hoping to find just the right hound to influence their own program. Pairings are often arranged to create new out-crosses, a practice that keeps the breed genetically healthy and vigorous. Much like in any other sport, huntsmen often draft hounds from other packs to round out their own line, trading with each other to balance age, speed, skill set and attitude.

Litter mates are all named with the same first letter, the huntsman progressing through the alphabet over the years, allowing them to identify age and sequence within the pack. Annie knew that Elliot, Ellie, Echo and Evan were all from the same family.

The records of these hounds rival those of the Daughters of the American Revolution for its level of detail and complexity. The Foxhound Kennel Studbook, along with the requisite Keeper of the Stud Book, records pedigrees for all hounds in every club, along with the entire kennel list for each club. At least three certified generations must be represented, and all these predecessors must also have been certified hunters. Formal names are given using the following protocol: the name of the hunt (or its prefix), the dog's given name, and the year of its entry into the field. A dog named Blitz, for example, will be entered into the roles as "Meryton Blitz '09".

Talk eventually turned to the creation of the perfect hound. Everyone agreed that it was by no means an exact science and that there was a lot of trial and error involved.

"Take Tillie," Gray said. "That bitch was probably one of the best hounds I ever had. She liked to work at the head of the pack, taking the lead in all she did."

He paused to consider. "I thought I might breed her to Racer until the day I hunted them together. I saw the two of them were so much alike, always out in front and advanced. Puppies from a litter like that would run the field so fast and so wide, no one would be able to chase them down. So instead, Tillie got Winston, an exceptional hunter with a beautiful voice. He was slower and more deliberate, a better complement to Tillie's strengths. I saved Racer for a slower and sweeter bitch that was a strong team player, and not as inclined to think for herself."

"Did those breedings work?" Annie asked. "Did you get what you expected?" The men chuckled and shook their heads. Gray shrugged.

"Did I get a star out of those matches?" he said. "Not necessarily. But if I keep making those kinds of decisions, the overall strength of the pack continues to improve, and we keep getting better hunting."

Cobie picked up his glass and took a sip of lemonade. "My dad came from the tradition of solitary hunts on foot with just one hound. The hounds that were bred for that job were strong, independent-minded dogs. They relied on no one but themselves on a scent. That attitude brought a kind of star quality to the lines that were being developed for the pack, but that had both its good and bad points."

Cobie leaned back and nodded toward the huntsman. "When Gray came along, he sought out the pride that these old dogs had provided, along with their brilliant noses. But he also valued a level of eagerness to please—biddability, as he called it. When he identifies a big star, one of those brilliant hounds that regularly outshine others in the field, he often trades them to hunts looking for a leader."

Barrett smiled. "A good pack can only have so many leaders. And Gray's hounds worship the ground he walks on. They get the best of everything, and he knows each of them intimately. He's done a fine job of building the pack."

"How do you establish that kind of relationship?" Annie asked.

"Well, I'll admit that I wail on them now and then," Gray said. "Especially if they are doing something that might put them in danger." He thought for a moment. "But they always know when they have pleased me, and they work for that." His eyes twinkled. "And we play a lot."

Archie chimed in. "Have you seen that pack at the hunt? If Gray dismounts, those dogs will sit right down and wait, every eye shining upon him. When he re-mounts, it is like God himself has gotten on the horse."

Gray chuckled. "I think it comes down to mutual respect, that's all. They want nothing in the world more than to do their job, and I want nothing more than to care for them so they can. We want the same thing. And when we get it, it's magic."

CHAPTER 20

—◆—

"YOU'VE LOST WEIGHT," ELLIOT SAID sleepily, tossing an arm over her as he rolled onto his side.

"Unlikely," said Annie. "This cookbook is killing me. Who ever heard of a cookbook writer losing weight?"

The cookbook was almost done. She just had to finalize those zucchini crown rolls and photograph them, and then she could get the manuscript off to Dodie. She had overshot the deadline, but not by much.

Annie had slowly begun to let go of her obsession with finding a job. In the hectic weeks right after Cobie's diagnosis, she hadn't even called back the tech company to re-schedule the interview. And she had begun to call herself a writer. Not a high-paying job, maybe. Sometimes not a paying job at all. But it felt honest, it felt true. In fact, much of her life felt true these days. They might still run out of money, but at least Annie was starting to have an idea who she was again.

She climbed out of bed, swearing softly as she tripped over one of the dogs who slept on her side of the bed. "Remember, we're taking the dogs out to Cobie's today."

Elliot rolled over and stared up at the ceiling. "Are you sure that's a good idea? The thought of this pack of city dogs running at will is a little scary."

Annie chuckled. She agreed whole-heartedly, wondering how she had come to agree to this scheme. It had started the day she and Cobie were discussing a list of well-known and talented foxhounds. Annie mentioned their own little hound had just come home from the show circuit.

Cobie rubbed his scratchy face. "Never quite got the deal with those shows," he said. "Of course, we have no choice but to have Gray take some of the better-looking dogs to that show up in Leesburg." He considered for a moment. "But that's some professional dogs there." He paused to consider. "Still, I'd rather have me an ugly hound that hunts like a demon than something that's plenty pretty, but not a brain in her head."

Annie nodded, understanding his meaning. She had been to the foxhound show, where serious handlers and huntsmen vied for foxhound perfection. Cobie was right; there was something authentic to those shows, probably more in keeping with what the original idea of dog showing had been, when it first began in England in the 1800s. Sporting men bringing their best sporting dogs to a gentlemanly competition. She chuckled to herself. Yeah, dog shows have come a long way.

"Why do you have that old pack of hounds anyway?"

Annie felt the sting of criticism behind Cobie's bland question. She knew that Cobie firmly believed in the value of an animal's work, and couldn't abide the idea of dogs as ornament. He was even okay with the idea of a dog as a pure companion, but he couldn't see the sense of eight hounds hanging out together in a house.

"We like the breed. They're clever, and they're funny," Annie wrinkled her nose. "They're cute, okay?" she said defensively.

"Well, cute or otherwise, you have yourself a pack of scent hounds and you should let them do their job."

"They chase things in our yard, if that's what you mean."

"A pack's joy comes from working together. Sure, there are some in the group with more talent, a better nose, and sharper instincts. But they get their satisfaction from doing it together." He thought for a moment. "Bring 'em out here. I'd like to see them in action."

"Oh geez, I don't know, Cobie. That might not be a good idea."

Cobie rubbed his cheek, thinking. "Yes sir, I'd like to see that. Don't know much about the breed, of course. But a hound's a hound."

"Their recall isn't great. I'm afraid we'll lose them if they are free to run."

Cobie gazed out the window. "I hunted a pack of terriers on foot when I was a kid. Some of the most fun hunting of my life," Cobie said. He turned back to her. "You just let those dogs follow their instincts and see what they are made of."

She had agreed to bring her hounds over a week from Saturday.

"Cobie has an area that he says is adequately fenced to contain them, at least mostly." Annie slipped on her jeans, noticing that maybe they were just a bit looser. "He says we have no earthly idea what we have here in this hound pack, and that he is going to show us."

Elliot got up and scratched the head of the nearest dog, which just happened to be Dodie, back from her tour of duty, and complete with a new title. "I'm sure he is right. The PBGV club does those hunting instinct tests in North Carolina every year, but we have never had time to get down there with them." He looked at the sleeping fur that covered the floor of the bedroom. "Still I'm not sure this is a natural pack of hunters."

"Well, we'll see. There is that pack in Pennsylvania with a club that hunts on foot. Cobie says it's not fair to these guys not to give them a chance to do their job."

"I thought their job was to eat, chase squirrels, visit unspeakable acts upon squeaky toys and just be amusing."

"Me too," she said wryly. She watched as one of the hounds stood on his hind legs to check the contents of a glass that had been left on the side table.

Annie wasn't ignorant when it came to dogs. She understood genetics, and had done thorough and thoughtful research every time she bred a dog. Her primary concern was for healthy stock, knowing that careless breeding could cause families to develop a propensity for epilepsy, bad hips or worse. She knew too that many breeders were so obsessed with looks that they quickly overcame these scruples in pursuit of a nice head carriage or superior angulation.

Of course, they hadn't had a litter for over five years now; since work had really taken over her life. A couple of their dogs were old veterans and a couple had been kept from favorite litters. Then there were the two they had been taken in through the Rescue Foundation. Annie could not remember a time when they didn't have at least six dogs around. Now whenever she missed the sweet scent of puppy breath, she talked Elliot into buying a new addition to the pack. Even though she wasn't always home to take care of them, Elliot didn't seem to mind. With that many dogs, the pack itself helped raise the youngsters.

The history of the breed was based on hunting, of course. PBGVs were built long and low, with rough coats that could protect them from thick brambles. Developed in France, the packs worked as hunting and tracking dogs for sportsmen who followed them on foot. PBGVs work together to flush and track small game, primarily rabbits, sending them into the open where the hunter can get a clear shot at them. The pack uses their voices to alert each other to the presence of a rabbit, or to the scent of a rabbit down a trail. Their long erect tails, known as Saber tails, helped the hunter catch sight of their dogs, often in the brambles, with only the flag of their tail visible.

Annie gave a short whistle, and the piles of fur rose as one. She led them out of the bedroom and let them out the back door, watching as the young ones screeched past her in anticipation of waiting squirrels. The older ones trotted out reluctantly, pausing to note temperature and precipitation before proceeding.

"This ought to be interesting," she said out loud, to no one in particular. But the oldest bitch, Maya, the grand dame of the household and ruler of the pack, looked up and held her gaze for just a moment. *"Don't you know it,"* she thought she heard the dog say.

CHAPTER 21

———

Joe was waiting for Elliot and Annie when they pulled up to the barn with their dogs. Elliot had insisted on crating them, not being accustomed to driving with all eight at once. That had been a wise decision, because the moment they arrived, every one of them was wild to get out and to explore a place with so many new smells. Annie opened the hatch of the Jeep, pausing to admire the expectant faces. They were certainly attentive, she thought. She only hoped that they would listen, once she set them loose.

Cobie came out the back door. Annie noticed a decided limp this morning, and whispered to Elliot that they should take the Gator out to the field instead of letting Cobie try to navigate it on foot. Cobie did not fuss as much at the suggestion as she expected, only giving a short nod to Joe to go and drive it around to the front of the barn.

Cobie paused to admire the dogs in their crates, asking the name and age of each one, nodding at the commentary Annie made on the personality of each. Joe brought the Gator up, and Cobie got aboard. He turned formally now, nodding at the parked Jeep. "The hounds, please," he said, Master of the field on this day.

Annie took a good look at the pasture they planned to use. Solid horse fencing surrounded the front portion, and thick shrubs grew along much of the boundary. It would be a determined dog that could find his way out. Still, she thought, shaking her head, one never knew when hounds got on a scent. Annie sighed and gave Cobie a formal nod, and then she and Elliot opened the crates, watching as each dog bound down and began sniffing.

Joe pulled off in the Gator, and Annie was surprised to see the hounds follow as a unit. Elliot ran ahead to open the gate, breathing a small sigh of relief as each of the hounds entered the relatively enclosed space. At least now there was something between them and the road.

The dogs seemed to start exploring randomly, each engrossed in its own sensations, and all conscious of the novelty of being at complete liberty. They watched in silence as the dogs sniffed the ground expectantly. Many minutes passed in this way, and then the group, Joe and Cobie in the Gator, Annie and Elliot on foot, started across the field. The dogs, noses to the ground, feathered, their whole rear ends wagging furiously. They fanned out around them, staying within thirty feet of the walkers.

Suddenly Freddie, her senior dog, put his head up and paused, taking in the wind that was running north to south across the center of the field. Then he put his nose down and started yipping, a decidedly more purposeful sound than any of them had made to that point, and moved in the direction of a covert that grew alongside a small stream near the center of the field. The thick brambles there had been the humans' objective, and Annie was pleased to see that the dogs had identified it too.

She was surprised to see the hounds cast themselves into a relatively organized unit, running ahead of them now and following the faint outline of a driving path. A couple of the younger dogs stayed up with Freddie, while the second group fanned left and right, uncertain what all the fuss was about. Two of the older dogs followed at a safe distance behind, glancing occasionally back at the walkers. Only one of the dogs, a sweet-faced bitch named Chanel, kept running back to the group, undecided whether to follow the pack or come back to her humans. Annie knew that her inclination would have been to stay with her people, and possibly even ride aboard the Gator with them. Annie watched with interest as the dog struggled between competing instincts.

She caught Elliot's eye as they followed behind. He was grinning from ear to ear, swinging the long lens of his camera to follow their movements. The babbling began in earnest now, some of the older dogs signaling their intent, the younger ones making noise out of sheer exuberance. It was musical to the ears, but Annie could not read her own dogs well enough to know whether their actions were informed or mere excitement. Cobie, however, instinctively read their intentions, and signaled with his hand for her to walk left, and come around to the side of the covert. This tickled her; she had just been designated whipper-in to the field. She headed to the side of the thicket where she could get a good view of the covert and signal a tally-ho or a gone away.

The rabbit burst from the back of the covert before the first dog even reached it. Freddie stood on his hind legs, trying to see over the brambles, and then threw himself headlong into the thicket. Soon all the dogs were inside, yipping furiously, their noses working every square inch of ground. Another bunny burst from the thicket, running furiously across the field. When the hounds emerged from the other side, they chased all the way to the fence where they were stopped in frustration. Annie walked through the pack, praising them furiously, and doing her best to lift them. Fortunately, Elliot had come along to her side of the covert, and they were able to draw the pack westward. Freddie once again caught an interesting scent, this one leading them to the right, away from the woods behind the pasture, and soon they were back to work.

It didn't seem possible to surprise any living creature in the field at this point, so Annie chuckled when she saw them on another line. The surprised bunny flew out of the tall grass, running in a frantic zigzag pattern. It too ducked through the horse fencing and out of danger, leaving the hounds once again barking in frustration.

"Enough, enough!" she called, red-faced from exertion. She smiled at Elliot as he turned to come back to where she stood, catching her breath. "Pretty good, huh?"

"Yes, good I would say," Elliot said proudly. "I think most of them could have picked up points today." He chuckled as Chanel walked up, sitting proudly on his feet. "Well, maybe not this one."

"She would have surprised me if she had," Annie said. "But Dodie did okay."

"She did. A little confused, but I think she could get the hang of it." He pointed to the hounds, many of which were still sniffing around the edge of the fence line. "That Freddie, he's a natural."

Joe and Cobie drove up, Cobie beaming ear to ear. "What did I tell ya? They have the makings of a good pack."

"I would accuse you of planting those bunnies there for them, but I knew there was a good chance they'd be there," said Annie.

"Well, you wouldn't want them skunked on their first time out." Cobie got out of the Gator and walked over, addressing the pack with lavish praise, speaking all manner of nonsense, and reaching down to pat Freddie. "Pretty good for a bunch of city dogs."

"They love you," she said.

"They just recognize a fellow hunter when they see one." He gestured back to the field. "And you're a decent pack leader. I saw how they paid attention to you out there."

"Yeah, well I don't know about that. I've got to figure out how to get them back to the barn and their crates," Annie said. "I have never trained them to a whistle or anything."

Cobie looked over the hounds. "I think they'll listen. They have a new idea in their heads now. They had a purpose today, a reason to work together. That goes a long way."

Elliot reached into his pocket, pulling out a zipped bag of dried liver. "Yes, but just in case, we can always use the international language of dogs. "

Cobie held up his hand. "A good pack leader shouldn't have to bribe his pack with treats."

Elliot put the bag back in his pocket and nodded. "We'll give it a try." He gave a sharp whistle.

And that was all it took. Chanel jumped into the back of the Gator with Annie for the trip back to the barn, while the others followed closely on Elliot's heels. It looked like a loyal and obedient pack, but Annie was pretty sure that they had detected what was in Elliot's pocket, the smell of liver now the only scent they cared to chase.

CHAPTER 22

ANNIE FLIPPED THROUGH THE PAGES of the book on hounds that Cobie lent her.

"What is honoring?" she asked.

Cobie stood up and looked over her shoulder. "See there," he said, tracing a line of hounds across the old pen and ink hunting sketch she was studying. His finger stopped on one particular hound. "In a pack, a hound "honors" when he gives tongue on a line which another hound has been hunting. You've seen that lots of times in the field, though maybe you didn't know it. One dog expresses interest in a scent he has found; another dog comes over, agrees, and says so. It looks like a simple act of cooperation, but there's a bit more to it than that."

"Remember those superstars we talked about the other day?" Annie nodded. "Those dogs with the biggest personalities, they hog the food at the trough, insist on being first for anything, setting another dog on its heels with a quick snap of his jaw. Talented, but insecure."

"Like that one." Cobie gestured to a photo of a large red hound. "Tartan. He was a beauty. Won the Hound Show up there in Middleburg. But he was bossy. He was prideful, he was bullying. His intention looked very subtle to the human eye. But he made the other dogs feel embarrassed or jealous or worried."

Annie raised her eyebrows and tilted her head. Cobie chuckled. "I know some people don't take to the idea of giving dogs human emotions but that's all the words I got for it."

"So are pack members willing to honor a superstar dog in the field?"

Cobie shrugged. "What is star-like quality in the front of the field is not necessarily the same as what is needed mid-field, or at the back of the pack. But it is the front-of-the-pack hounds where superstar quality can become a problem."

"But wasn't Loki a superstar?" she asked, thinking about the old dog that had just been retired last year. He now lived in the house with Gray and Betsy, a rare promotion for a pack hound.

"You are confusing superstar with leader again," Cobie said. "Loki was a superstar in that he had it all—brains, nose, pride, eagerness. But he also had leadership qualities. A calm assurance, a quiet competence," he said. "He works like a demon, but doesn't raise his head to say 'hey, look at me.'" Cobie thought some more. "He is never first at the trough, but when he does come, others willingly make room for him. He's quick to honor another's line. Not sure how to put it into words, but you just know he wants what is best for the pack. And the others know it too."

"So the bossy, showy, know-it-all hound you are referring to," said Annie, curious now. Her eyes went back to Tartan. "Won't the other dogs leave behind the jealousies they had in the kennel when they see him on a line?"

"You know; you would think so. In the heat of the moment, everyone out there is anxious to find the line and get on with it." Cobie smiled. "I always noticed that there was more willingness to go see what Loki found, to honor the line that he had identified. But when Tartan got on something, sometimes the other dogs would just take up their own lie even more aggressively, and only going to his when they have exhausted their own path. Of course, the youngsters don't know any better, so Tartan would find some support in the pack. At least some of them will go straight to the one making the noise. But the veterans can be more reluctant." He shrugged. "Jealous, don't want him to look good. No other way to say it than that."

Annie gazed at the photo of the handsome hound. "What happened to Tartan?"

"His pride just got in the way of greatness. He was challenged by other hounds in the field and couldn't put aside his resentment." Cobie shook his head. "Gray drafted him to the Lorrymore Hunt after only his second season."

CHAPTER 23

—•—

THE SUN BEAMED DOWN IN the pleasant and surprising way that it did when spring finally arrives. Lucky too, since the late April snowstorm had dumped a couple of inches on them the night before. This time of year, the sun would get rid of it all by afternoon.

Annie drove out to the barn, happily splashing through the puddles that accumulated on the roadway. She would not ride today; the footing was too sloppy for that, and she was pretty sure that Cobie had gone off to the doctors for a round of appointments.

Annie's object today was Lindsay. She knew Daisy would be at school, and she wanted some one-on-one time to ask her about Trace.

Trace's name had come up now and then when the men talked about young riders. He had apparently been a bold and talented boy, seeming to follow in his father's footsteps. Cobie never mentioned him, although he smiled and nodded if someone else did, never adding to the conversation. Annie had not had the nerve to ask Cobie about him directly, but she sensed there was a lot of sadness there.

Annie had assumed that the young man, who must be in his thirties, had been told about his father's illness. She assumed that he would come to pay a visit. But that visit never materialized. And with the weeks ticking down to the six-month deadline, Annie felt it was time to get to the bottom of things.

When she got to the barn, she grabbed two carrots and immediately walked over to the paddock. Warrior greeted her readily, and was already munching happily when his paddock mate trotted up to get his share. She patted both horses, and then turned to the small fieldstone cottage behind the barn, where Lindsay lived with Daisy, and John, of course, when he was home.

Lindsay caught sight of her from the kitchen window, and was at the back door by the time Annie arrived on the porch. "Come in, come in," she said, smiling. She looked at Annie's empty hands. "What, no food today?"

"I thought I had better stop. The refrigerator at the house is bulging."

"Oh, I know. Mom and I sorted, threw out and froze things yesterday." She gestured for Annie to sit at the pretty farm table in the center of the kitchen. "It's amazing the things people make. There was a bright red chicken dish, maybe it was pomegranate, I don't know. But the meat was positively scary." She shrugged. "Frank liked it." Frank was Lindsay's big black lab, whose primary job seemed to be that of lawn ornament. Annie had never seen him walk anywhere.

"Yes, well, I don't want to add to the problem."

"Dad seems to like your food best," Lindsay said. She set a cup of coffee on the placemat in front of Annie.

"Well, novelty and all." Annie stirred in a spoonful of sugar. "And I think he enjoys giving me advice on the recipes. He always has a comment." She smiled, and Lindsay nodded in agreement.

"Dad likes to give his opinion."

"He does that. But I notice he's more inclined to milder foods these days."

Lindsay nodded. "He is. Mom has been making mashed potatoes, chicken soup, things like that. So far that's been okay." She set a plate of cookies on the table.

"Compliments of that lady who lives in the cottage next to Red's." She picked one up and dunked it into her own coffee. "Pretty good."

Annie broke off half a cookie. "He'll like these. He still has a sweet tooth."

"I have been making him these protein shakes in the morning. He complains like crazy, but I notice he is getting them down."

"Have you heard from Trace?"

"Trace?" Lindsay said, frowning.

"I kind of thought that, with the illness and all, he would be coming for a visit."

Lindsay shook her head. "Don't hold your breath. Mom said she would tell him, but I don't think she has."

"Why not?"

Lindsay exhaled sharply. "Long story."

"Sorry, I don't want to pry. I just hear his name come up when the guys are talking, and I wondered."

"They talk about Trace?"

"Just when someone starts telling a story about the young riders. His name comes up." Annie set down her cup. "It sounds like he was a heck of a rider."

"Best I ever saw, for sure," said Lindsay. "But I'm his sister, so I guess I would think that."

"Where is he now?"

Lindsay shrugged. "Not sure, really. I heard he was working at Keeneland during the yearling sale. But beyond that, I don't know."

"Don't you think he should know?"

Lindsay nodded, looking off into space. "Not sure I want to get in the middle of it."

"In the middle of what?"

"I mean, it's okay for Mom to do it, but there may be hell to pay if Dad knows I did it." She hesitated. "Still, you may be right."

"Is there anything I can do?" Annie said.

Lindsay shook her head. "Believe me, you don't want a part of this." She thought for a moment. "Tell you what. I'll check with Mom. If she hasn't called him, I will."

"I think that would be good."

"Don't expect much though. I would be very surprised if he talked to me, much less come for a visit."

Annie nodded. "Still, it would be a shame to wait until it is too late."

"I'll see what I can do," she promised.

———

Lindsay called early the next morning. Annie rolled over and grabbed the phone on her bedside table, squinting to see the number displayed on her phone.

Elliot rolled over. "Who is it?" he muttered. "Who'd call this early?"

"I don't know, hang on." Annie fumbled for the button. "Hello?"

The dogs were now all up, watching as they did for any sign of life from the two people slumbering in their big bed. Elliot rolled over and got up. "Come on guys," he said. He opened the bedroom door, and a sea of fur followed him.

"Annie, it's Lindsay. Sorry to call so early."

"No problem. We were up, more or less."

"It's Dad. He's in the hospital."

Annie sat up straight now. "Where?"

"UVA. He was complaining of shortness of breath. I tried to get him to go during the night, but he refused. Finally, about 5, he relented."

"Okay," said Annie. "Do you want me to come down? Can I bring you some breakfast?"

"No, we're fine. I just came down to the cafeteria for some coffee. Mom is waiting upstairs. Dr. Landers stopped by to see her. They are chatting."

"Doctor Landers?" Annie asked.

"You know Leigh and Andrew Landers, right? Members of the club? They are both doctors on staff. Daddy trains their daughter Fiona sometimes."

"I'm not sure I've met them." Annie reached for a pen. "Is he in a room?"

"Not yet. He is still being evaluated. Might be an infection, I'll let you know."

"Okay."

She felt Lindsay hesitate. "Can I ask you a favor though?"

"Sure. What do you need?"

"Would you call Trace?"

Annie felt her heart sink. "Oh Lindsay, I don't know. I had never even heard of him until a couple of weeks ago. He will have no idea who I am."

"I know. That's the point. Mom says he doesn't pick up when she calls. And I don't think he'll pick up for me. This was her idea. She thinks maybe you can get to him."

Annie hesitated. It didn't seem like her place to make such an important call.

"Couldn't you call where he works?"

"We don't know where that is." Lindsay felt Annie's reluctance. "Annie, I'm scared. It didn't seem all that real to me until now. I mean, sure, Dad was sick sometimes. But he didn't seem so bad. He never lets it show. I didn't think…I mean; I have never seen him like this…" Her voice trailed off.

Annie understood. She picked up the fallen cup and reached for her pen again. "What's his number?"

"This is the most recent number Mom has, so hopefully it will work. Ready?"

"Yes."

"It's 859-555-6122."

"Where is that?"

"Kentucky."

"Okay." She glanced at the clock. Only 6:42. "I'll wait a bit to call."

"Okay, but he probably goes to work early. That is if he's working in a barn or at the track."

"Okay." She thought for a moment. "Any advice?"

"Just tell him…." Lindsay's voice quavered, and she paused. "Just tell him that we need him."

CHAPTER 24

ANNIE TRIED ALL DAY TO reach Trace by phone. She wasn't sure she had the right number because he didn't use it in his message. Just a curt "Leave a message." Annie tried to detect something of his dad in the voice, but if the Virginia drawl had ever been there, it was gone now. In fact, his voice had a hard edge. She left one message, and then two. In the first, she just identified herself and said she was a friend of his parents, and asked him to call. The second message was a little more direct. "Your father is very ill," she told the machine. "Please call." She didn't feel that telling him everything in a voicemail was appropriate, but she thought it might encourage him to call if he had more context. When she didn't hear from him by late afternoon, she called Sara.

"Sara, did you hear? Cobie's in the hospital."

"No, no one's called me. I have been in lessons, but there are no messages. Is everything okay?"

"For the moment, I think." Annie hesitated. "But I need some advice."

"Sure. What's up?"

"Lindsay asked me to call her brother Trace, and I haven't been able to reach him. I wanted to go to the hospital, but I was hoping to reach him first."

Sara's voice dropped. "You are trying to call Trace?"

"Yes. Dorothy and Lindsay asked me to try to reach him." Annie paused. "Did you know him?"

She heard Sara take a deep breath and exhale it slowly. "Look," she said. "I'm filthy. Let me jump in the shower. I can be at your house in forty-five minutes. We need to talk."

Annie nodded, forgetting to speak.

"Annie?"

"Yes, sorry. I'm here," she said. "Absolutely."

"Open the wine," Sara said. "I'll be there soon."

While Annie waited for Sara, she kept herself busy. She got out the wine and started some pasta sauce. She called and talked to Lindsay. Cobie was "resting comfortably" with some oxygen and intravenous antibiotics. He was sleeping, and she and Dorothy had decided to walk down to the local pub to grab some real food.

"Would you like me to come?" said Annie.

"There's no point," Lindsay replied. "Dad's asleep and we're just sitting around." She took a deep sigh, sounding bone weary. "This whole thing is just starting, Annie. We'll need you soon enough as back-up."

"Okay." She was slightly relieved. She had more questions than answers right now, and she didn't want to be face-to-face with the family until she understood a little better.

She heard Lindsay hesitate. "Did you talk to Trace?"

"No, but I left a message. He's probably at work. I hope to talk to him tonight."

Lindsay sighed. "You were so right. He needs to be here. I don't know what I was thinking the other day. Some things just need to be forgotten..."

Now did not seem to be the time to ask questions. Annie decided not to tell her that she had talked to Sara. But now she wondered. Would Sara have the answers?

———

Annie heard the crunch of Sara's tires and was at the door before she heard her slam the truck's door. Sara wore clean jeans and cowboy boots and her long blond hair was still wet. Annie handed her a glass of wine. "Come on in. I've made a fire."

Sara took a sip of the wine and peered around Annie into the kitchen. "Where's Elliot?"

"Oh, out tramping around somewhere, behind that camera of his." Annie glanced up at the clock. "I expect him back in an hour or two."

"Good. Then we will have time to talk."

They settled into the old plaid wingback chairs near the fire. "So... how was your day?" Annie began.

Sara chuckled and shook her head. "It's okay, Annie. No need for polite chat. You invited me over to tell a story and I came to tell you one." She took another sip of wine and leaned back in her chair. "Trace was always a sensitive guy."

Annie nodded, silent.

"From the moment he could walk, he was with the animals." Sara smiled, remembering the stories about Trace as a little boy. "This is the stuff of family lore. I've heard these stories more than once, believe me. Anyway, that's why they called him Trace. One minute he was there. And then suddenly he was gone without a trace." She chuckled. "Cobie would put the old terrier on his scent, and they would trace him, always back to the barn, or a field with a new calf or something."

"Trace loved those animals. He hunted his own little pack of terriers on foot. He loved the way they worked together, and he was proud of the way they did their job. But then he cried if they caught and killed anything.

"Everything that lived on the farm was his. There was not a lamb or a foal or a puppy that came into this world that didn't fall straight into his hands." She looked off for a moment, imagining the little boy that he had been.

"Cobie had a big brood mare, one of a line of racehorse royalty. Gretel was her name, a really nice mare. I actually remember her myself. By the time I met her, she was retired, pushing thirty years old.

"Late one night, Trace was about twelve, I guess, one of the barn workers banged on the door, waking up the whole household. Cobie hurried down to the door, Trace hot on his heels. It was the mare. She was in labor, and she was struggling.

"Cobie headed to the barn, ordering Trace to go back to bed. By now the mare was in serious pain. It was a big foal, and he was stuck. They called the vet. The wait was agonizing for everyone. Trace, of course, had snuck down to the barn and watched it all. He saw Cobie try to reach in and straighten the foal's legs to help get it out. But his hands were too big to do any good.

"Well, the mare was whinnying with pain, Trace stepped out of the shadows. "I can do it Daddy," he said. "My hands are smaller than yours."

Cobie told him to stay away. Told him Gretel was in too much pain and might hurt him. Said they just needed to wait for the vet."

"Well, of course, Trace started to cry. He watched as Gretel threw her head back again, the ineffective contractions convulsing her whole body.

Cobie told him, come on then and let me show you what to do." Cobie showed Trace how to reach in and feel for the foal's leg, and to see if he could reach its hoof and straighten it out. It was slow work, but that was one brave little boy. I can just imagine him, his arm all the way up that mare, working at it until he had both legs in place...""

Sara eyes shone and she sat forward in the chair. "The mare gave a big push, throwing the foal out and landing directly on top of Trace. The big foal was bigger than he was—had to be 150 pounds, according to Cobie."

Sara took a big sip of wine and sat back. "Anyway, that's the story of how Curly came to be. Cobie named the big bay foal after his son's big head of curls. After that, they were inseparable. Gretel was exhausted and had a hard time with her milk. Trace took care of her, and took care of that baby, like they were his own family. I knew Curly too, and that horse followed Trace around like a puppy until the day he died." Sara's eyes darkened now.

"So I am guessing Curly would have been over twenty now. What happened to him?"

Sara closed her eyes. "Trace was such a good guy. He really was."

She sat forward again, shaking herself and making eye contact with Annie. "Trace competed like a demon, and he brought that big boy to the top of the show jumping circuit. What a show they put on. You've never seen such a connection between horse and rider."

"Sara...."

Sara held up her hand. "No, it's okay. Lindsay has gotten you involved, and I want you to know everything." She continued. "Trace tended to play as hard as he worked. One night after a show, he went out partying. He was what? Twenty-two, twenty-three years old? Of course, he had too much to drink. Normally, that wouldn't have been a big deal. He could have slept it off in the sleeping cab in the trailer. But he had promised Cobie to be back early to take one of the young Thoroughbreds down to Lexington. So he took off."

Sara glanced up and saw the pained look on Annie's face. "I'm sure you can imagine the rest. The truck went off the road and struck a tree. Trace wasn't wearing a seat belt and got thrown clear. But Curly, along with the other horse that had traveled to the show, were killed.

"The police told Cobie later that they had to pull the sobbing boy, drenched in Curly's blood, from the trailer. He just wouldn't let go of that horse. He had his arms wrapped around him the same way he had held that foal on the day he was born."

Tears filled her eyes. "Trace was never the same after that. It might as well have been his own child that died. The police only charged him with reckless driving and DUI. I guess it's not a crime to kill a horse. But he felt like he had committed vehicular homicide. He couldn't forgive himself, and he couldn't look anyone in the eye again. Particularly not his daddy. They had argued about his hard partying before. Right after the accident, they fought. Trace was in a fury.

"After the initial shock, Cobie tried to be understanding. He really did. He could see that Trace was punishing himself more than anyone else ever could. But to Trace, every look Cobie gave him seemed like the world's biggest I-told-you-so."

Annie sat back in her chair, her own wine untouched. She thought of the curly haired boy and his beautiful horse. "I've never seen pictures of them," she said thoughtfully, thinking of all the memorabilia strewn throughout the large farmhouse.

"Trace got drunk one night and went around and smashed every one of them," said Sara. "He couldn't bear to see Curly, or to remember what they were to each other." Sara sighed. "Everything went downhill from there. Trace would go into rages, followed by weeks of sullen silence. Then one day he was just gone."

Something had occurred to Annie as she listened to the young woman speak. "Sara, you seemed to know Trace well. Were you good friends?"

"Oh Annie," she sighed, putting down her glass. She stared at the fire for a few minutes then rubbed her hands over her face. "Yes, I knew him well. Trace and I were engaged to be married."

Annie sat up with a start. "But...I mean, I remember you got engaged just after college, and I knew it was someone with an equestrian background. But with work and all, and Emily moving, I never got to meet him and then I heard it just hadn't worked out. I am so sorry, Sara. I can't believe I didn't realize. I thought your fiancé's name was..."

Sara waved off her discomfort. "It's okay. I know how wrapped up in work you were, and Emily and I went to different colleges. I understand."

"Still, I should have put it together. Oh Sara, I'm so sorry."

"Yeah," she shrugged. "Me too."

CHAPTER 25

———

LATE THE NEXT EVENING AFTER visiting Cobie in the hospital, Annie took a tape off the shelf to transcribe it. It had been made a couple of months before, and she just hadn't gotten to it. In fact, a number of Cobie's solitary musings were still untouched.

Cobie wanted to talk about jumping. He had jumped in every possible venue—from stadium jumping and eventing to steeplechase to, of course, foxhunting. And he had taught many young people to do the same. But he found that many youngsters, even those who were well-trained riders, were ill-prepared for what they would find in the field. Arena jumping is not at all the same as jumping in first flight, and he didn't feel that there was a good understanding of what it took to be there. Sure, you could let the kid just give it a try and get thrown now and then. They would eventually pick it up, or back down to the second field. But he wanted to try to provide a bit of perspective.

"One of the real thrills of the hunt is the jumping," he started. "But it takes a certain kind of person to ride first flight. First flight travels right behind the hounds. Jumps are frequent, sometimes sudden. Lots of awkward angles too, poor sight lines and god-knows-what kind of footing on the other side. Riders in this field require a strong partner, which is why those horses that carry them need to be ready to be there. They should be at least as strong, smart and brave, if not more so, than the rider on their backs. Of course, even in first flight, there are differences. Some horses will boldly lead. Others willingly jump coops that they have seen other horses jump. Still others, perhaps talented but green, require a bit of coaxing.

"Jumping in the field requires some order. Riders cannot go willy-nilly. They need to approach a jump single file, and leave plenty of room so you can turn away if the rider in front falls, or the horse refuses.

"A refusal can be dangerous, both to the horse and to the human partner, especially if it causes you to fly over his head and eat dirt. If your horse refuses a jump, you gotta just go to the back of the line and try again. You can't slow down the progress of the field by staying at the fence.

"If he's green, maybe he just ain't ready for that kind of jumping. There is a lot going on in the field, and while he may pretty sensible in the arena, he may have sensory overload out in the open. You can bet too, that he noticed what the other horses were doing. If he saw one horse acting up, he may get the hint that it's okay to act up too.

"Most refusals are the rider's fault, not the horse. You got to look to yourself first, check your own balance. Are you willing yourself over the jump before he is in the right place to go with you?

"Get your own head on straight before you demand something of him. And then stick with him, however green or stupid he may be. Maybe he just doesn't understand what you are asking. It'll probably feel mighty awkward, but if you hold on and follow him through, you'll both get to the other side in one piece.

"But if he can't do it, never punish him. That'll only make things worse." Annie heard Cobie stop and sigh. "If neither of you is ready, there is no shame in dropping back until it feels safe to tackle the fences again."

Here Cobie paused, and Annie thought that the tape had come to an end. But it kept ticking off, so she continued to play it to make sure there was nothing else.

She heard a small rustle, and then she heard the distinct sound of Cobie dialing his cell phone. She listened to the ring at the other end, and then heard the muffled recorded greeting that answered.

"Trace, son," said Cobie. "This is your dad. I...just wanted to say hi."
He hesitated. "I love you son. Give me a call, if you get a chance." Annie
heard him click off the call, and the sound of him getting up and leaving the room. She clicked the stop button, leaned back and took a deep
sigh.

CHAPTER 26

———

A BIT OF GOOD NEWS had come from the hospital stay. Cobie's original tumor had not grown much, and while they already knew it had metastasized, it did not seem to be spreading quickly. The infection was a symptom of a slipping resistance, so Lindsay and Dorothy were doing everything they could to strengthen his system. For now, this included no visitors. And a plan to get Trace home.

Sara called Trace herself multiple times. He never answered his phone, but apparently it rang so often, that someone in the barn finally picked it up one day while he was out in the arena. Sara had found out where Trace worked, and cajoled the young kid on the other end of the line to keep their talk a secret. Then she called Annie and told her to meet her at the hospital.

Annie and Sara sat with Lindsay and Dorothy, drinking coffee in the lounge at the end of the hall.

"I'm going," said Sara.

"Oh Sara," said Dorothy, reaching out to lay her hand on the young woman's arm. "Are you sure you should?"

Sara nodded, her eyes fierce. "I should never have let him leave. I should have fought it then. I should have gone and gotten him back." She nodded intently, her resolve growing. "But it's not too late. I can do it now. "

She saw the sad sympathy in Dorothy's eyes. "Don't think I feel like I can bring him back to me, Dorothy. Don't worry, I'm okay with that."

Lindsay and Dorothy gave each other a knowing glance. Sara didn't notice it, but Annie did.

"But I think if there is anyone he will listen to, it's me."

Lindsay nodded. "I hate to do this to you Sara. But I think you might be right. When will you leave?"

"Right now. I'm already packed. I figured since I was in Charlottesville; I was already an hour on the road."

"I'm coming with you," Lindsay said.

"Don't be silly, you've got Daisy and all. And your dad," she reminded her, nodding toward Dorothy.

"Well, okay. But…."

"No buts. I'll make Trace listen to me and I'll bring him back if I can." She looked at her watch.

"Lexington is about six hours. I'll call when I get there."

———

The end of hunting season signals a shift in the labors of the huntsman and his kennel. The next generation takes center stage now. With any luck, Annie though, there are new puppies being born. They would be a nice distraction from wondering what was going on in Kentucky. Cute as babies are, though, Annie knew it was the yearlings that she could help Gray with. Annie called Gray the day after Sara left and asked if she could help walk the puppies.

"Absolutely," he said cheerfully. "The more hands, the better."

Annie was glad to have something to keep her mind occupied. She went out and rode Warrior most days, but now that Cobie was back at home from the hospital, she was giving him a little space. She told herself she just wanted him to get some rest and recover from the infection that had attacked his lungs. But she was just waiting for Sara to get back before she talked to him again.

Annie went out and helped take the puppies on a long walk. The raucous pack was always accompanied by a handful of adult dogs who were there to set a good example. The youngsters were attached to one another in couples, a comical exercise when the pups learn the art of cooperation. Annie noticed one of the pups with a chain around his neck, but no partner.

"That's Echo," said Gray, chuckling. "Can't for the life of him bear to be chained to another." He paused, considering. "At first I thought he must be the stupidest dog on the planet, but now I'm not so sure. We decided to let him alone. And now he's starting to figure things out."

Gray walked through the neighborhood around the hunt club, with the whipper-in helping to keep the pack in order, off lawns and out of the road. Annie was impressed with the relative order of the group.

"Yeah, once they get a feel for the rules, they get into place pretty quickly. Of course, they see what the older dogs are doing. And you hope at least one of the couple has some sense. The coupling makes it uncomfortable to act independently, so they start learning to think as a unit."

He pointed to Echo, who had run up to the front door of a neighboring house. "There now is the result of independence. Getting into trouble." He issued a sharp whistle. "Here now, here now Echo. Come along. Good puppy." Gray kept his eye trained on the dog, calling and cajoling until he arrived at his feet. He then praised and fussed over him. This scenario repeated itself a number of times as Echo found other ways to get into trouble, and each time Gray was happy and kind and full of praise when the naughty puppy listened to him.

Annie could see why the dogs loved this huntsman. Echo in particular, after being called out repeatedly, soon felt the glow of the attention and trotted happily at Gray's heel. The misfit now felt like the favorite. And his incentive to behave grew before Annie's eyes.

Monty had also come on the walk. He came up behind her, gesturing to the errant puppy. "See that? That Echo may be a loner as far as the pack is concerned, but he knows where his bread is buttered. We'll see in the fall, but he may turn out to be great in the field."

They stood and watched the pack head for home, now clustered around Gray's feet. Monty chuckled. "I know a dozen parents who wish they could send their kids to Gray for just a week." He shook his head. "He's just got a way about him."

Annie dialed Sara's number on her way home from walking the puppies. Once again, it went to voicemail. The women had made Sara promise that she would call from the road, call when she arrived, and call when she found Trace. They had gotten her voicemails, and then a couple of texts to say that she had arrived and that she had found him. And then silence.

It had been over a week now. Rebecca, the college student who was taking care of Sara's barn, called to ask how long Annie thought Sara might be gone. Annie could hear the worry in the girl's voice, and insisted it would be any day now. "Are you okay?" she asked. "I'm sure Lindsay would send Joe or one of the other guys over to help if you need it."

"No, everything's fine here," she assured her. "It's just that I have papers to finish, and finals to prepare for. Just trying to plan my time." She hesitated. "No biggie, if she's back this week."

"Well, don't worry. I'm sure I'll hear from her soon. I'll call you."

But Annie fretted too. It was bad enough that Trace wouldn't answer, but now Sara was MIA too.

CHAPTER 27

———◆———

"YOU ARE EITHER A HOUND person or a horse person," Barrett declared. "Horse people don't tend to have the patience for hound behavior the way real hound people do."

Annie, listening quietly in the corner, nodded in silent agreement. Hounds were a trial sometimes, and you had to have a love for their attitudes. As much as she loved horses, she had to admit that she was a hound person. It seemed to her that they had the biggest stake in the whole thing.

Barrett continued. "When a dog runs riot, that's when you learn a lot about humans."

"What is that, exactly?" Annie asked.

"Anytime he is hunting anything he shouldn't be hunting. In the case of our Meryton hounds, that means anything other than the red fox. They're specifically trained to ignore the scent of deer, coyote, and even grey fox. Gray goes so far as to have a young deer living next to the hounds in the kennel so that they become accustomed to the scent. Nobody wants a pack that chases deer. Some packs are happy to run coyotes, but coyotes are notoriously straight line runners, and they lack the cleverness of the fox. They also can be more aggressive, and to Gray's way of thinking, all together not worth it. Grey fox tend to head straight for heavy cover. Their scent is not as strong either. Gray is a purist; it's red fox or nothing.

"Remember Taper?" said Angus Calhoun. Angus was the huntsman for a club up in Massachusetts, and had come down at Cobie's invitation to give his perspective from another club. Taper, the dog in question, had been drafted from that club into Meryton because of his tendency to riot as a youngster.

"That boy had a bad reputation. I remember when we brought him up; I went out the first day he was entered. They drew that first covert, fanned out and cast themselves. And man, there was something going on. They crash into the undergrowth, up to their eyeballs in briars and tangles, feathering like mad.

"And wouldn't you know it; Taper looks to run riot on a rabbit. Figures, I thought. Going to embarrass me right off. Franklin, he was the whipper-in that day, waves his whip and start shouting "Leave it, leave it." He cracks his whip overhead, just in time to see that bunny hightail it out of there.

"Fortunately, Franklin doesn't rate the dog too bad. He knows that a hound will learn soon enough, and the older hounds will let him know that he is wasting his time. And it turned out; Taper was not on that bunny. He continued to speak, and pretty soon the others have honored his line. Sure enough, they're on a fox that had seen the wisdom of cozying up to the rabbit for a while to give himself some cover. That fox had hoped someone would take the bait, but he quickly saw the jig was up and got out of there.

"So," he said leaning back with satisfaction. "You never know with these hounds. Better to trust first, and not condemn a dog too soon. They do generally grow up and get some sense." He paused a moment and thought. "If Franklin had really lit into that dog over that rabbit, it might have ruined him. Taper had been caught out so many times before. He would have decided that there was no scent that was safe to speak to, and thought twice before trying his luck again. Fortunately, Taper guessed right that day, and he's been an asset to the field ever since."

"It's a rare one who never comes around to understanding, especially when they're given a chance to make mistakes and learn from them."

CHAPTER 28

———

ANNIE WAS IN THE BARN when she heard the distinct low rumble of Sara's truck. Part diesel, part neglected muffler, it was hard to miss. Annie's heart skipped a beat when she recognized the sound. Whether it was the relief or the anticipation that almost took her breath away, she hardly knew.

Sara had finally texted a cryptic message. "On my way home. Not alone." So when Annie peeked around the corner of the barn door, she immediately sought the passenger side of the truck.

And there he was.

She watched the tall man unfold himself from the truck's front seat. His hair was short; the talked-of curls cropped away. Much taller than his dad, she noted. His eyes seemed to drink in the farm, taking in every building. His eyes scanned the paddocks for familiar horses, pausing to check out those that were new. Wanda trotted out to greet Sara, having recognized the sound of the truck. She paused when she saw him, wagging her tail uncertainly, not knowing whether to greet Sara or check out the stranger.

Annie realized with a jolt of surprise that Trace had never met Wanda. It seemed odd that the little matron of the barn had not yet been born when Trace left. That meant that he had never met Lindsay's daughter either. How many years had it been exactly?

She saw Sara come around to his side of the truck, gesturing to the barn, pointing out Lindsay's house, and the field in soybeans. Then she reached out and touched his arm, leaning in to whisper something and nodding toward the house. Trace nodded and headed to the back door.

Sara leaned against the truck and watched as Trace approached the back door. He nervously put on his hat and took it off, finally removing it and smoothing back his hair before reaching for the screen door. She saw Dorothy come to the door just as Trace opened it, and smiled as the older woman throw her arms around him. Trace stiffened at the embrace, but finally relented, reluctantly returning the hug. Dorothy put her hands on his face, studying him closely. He allowed this also. Then she gripped his hand and led him inside the house into the kitchen.

After they had disappeared, Sara turned and walked to the barn. She knew that Annie had seen the reunion, having caught her out of the corner of her eye. She sighed when she saw her, and blew the hair out of her eyes. Then she collapsed onto a bale of hay.

"Quite a week," she offered. Annie nodded.

"Really sorry I didn't stay in touch too well. I lost my battery charger, and by the time I realized it, I was neck-deep in trying to get Trace to talk to me. I just bought a new one on the way out of Lexington."

"I figured it must be something like that."

"I need to call Rebecca. She must be worried sick."

"Don't worry. I called her when I got your text. Everything is fine there. She knows that she'll see you in a day or so."

Sara took a deep breath. "Good. I'm about talked out right now." She looked toward the tack room, nodding in the direction of the refrigerator. "Is there a cold beer in there?"

"Of course, I'll grab you one." Annie grabbed two beers, and they walked out to the bench that sat by the near paddock.

"He's been in rough shape, that boy," started Sara.

"Oh Sara…."

She took a sip from her bottle, and then gestured to it. "He doesn't drink anymore though."

"That's good, I suppose."

Sara shook her head. "He doesn't drive either. Lives in a little place behind the racetrack and walks everywhere. Honestly, he doesn't even ride unless he has to."

"I thought he was working with horses."

"Oh, he is. He said he had no choice; that's all he knows. But the guys around the barn told me he is very matter of fact with the horses. Not hard exactly, but very business-like. He has to get on a horse now and then to show a prospective owner how it moves, but does it reluctantly. No friends either. They're a bit wary of him. Not that he is ever mean. According to his boss, he is unfailingly polite to all." She took another sip of the beer. "They were plenty surprised to see me show up."

Annie chuckled. "I'll bet." She thought for a moment. "So sad though. I guess I had hoped he was just moving on, that you would find him happy and settled, maybe with a wife and kid." She winced. "Oh sorry, I didn't mean anything. Just that I hoped things were better."

Sara shrugged. "Don't worry about it. When it comes right down to it, I haven't moved on either, and god knows people have been telling me to for years."

It turned out that when Trace left, he had just wandered around for a while. He headed in the general direction of Kentucky, not for any specific reason, other than an idea that there would be work there. But when he arrived, he steadfastly avoided anyone who knew his family. That wasn't easy, given his name and his dad's reputation with the Thoroughbreds. He finally sold the truck to get by, and then landed a job as barn help at some third-rate stable. Those guys aren't too picky about whom they hire, and they paid him in cash and a bunk in the tack room.

But over the past couple of years, he had moved into better jobs. His skill as a horseman and his judge of talent was obvious to everyone he worked with. He took to calling himself Joe. He said it just popped into his head one day, and no one but the secretary who cut the checks seemed to pay much attention to his last name.

"He told me that at first he could barely look at the horses he worked with. But eventually, he said he got some relief out of it, particularly if the horse needed him; if it was injured or had been mistreated. It felt like a chance to make amends in some way. But he never let himself get too close. Once a horse was ready, he tried to move him on as quickly as possible. That's probably when owners started noticing him. He couldn't help but tell them what the best job or who the best owner would be for the horse. They quickly saw he knew what he was talking about. If they didn't listen, he just moved on."

"How'd you find him?"

"Pure dumb luck." Sara said. "I pulled into Keeneland and drove around back to the stables. It wasn't busy around there. Hardly anyone around. The two-year-old sale was over, and it was an off day."

"But I ran into a guy spraying down a horse in a wash stall. I asked him if he knew Trace. Of course, he barely spoke English, and my Spanish is terrible. Just as well though. I was describing a guy he would never have known."

"I think he got the idea because he gestured in the direction of a large horse trailer. You know, one of those semi-things? Anyway, I figured I might run into someone who could speak better English, so I thanked him and left." Sara raised her hand over her eyes, scanning the pasture. "I realized later he was probably sending me to the only white guy he knew. It turned out to be Trace."

"How did he react when he saw you?"

"At first, he just stared. Then he looked away, and continued to load the trailer. I stood there and waited. I didn't move a muscle for ten minutes. Just watched him while he ignored me."

She chuckled. "He might have left me that way forever, but a couple of the other guys kept giving me sideways glances and I think it started to make him nervous. He finally walked over."

"And?"

"He just glared at me and said 'what the hell do you want?'" Sara shuddered. "I wanted to slap him."

"I'm surprised you didn't."

She sighed and leaned back into the bench. "Annie, I went through so much with him, and I had no idea what to expect when I saw him. His anger might have helped because anger was the last thing I saw from him seven years ago. So that he picked up the conversation with anger seemed about right. It was like we were right back where we left off." She shook her head. "But this time, I didn't put up with it. Back then, we all thought he was so fragile. We felt like he couldn't take hard truth. We saw how he reacted to Cobie, who was the only one telling him like it was. At the time, we thought he would figure out a way to cope."

"So this time, I told him off. I told him about Cobie, I told him his mom and his sister needed him. I followed him around that trailer, yelling at him and him yelling at me for at least an hour."

She paused, thinking back on that day. "I actually saw him ball up his fist as I laid into him. I didn't stop talking but believe me, in the back of my mind, I was wondering if I still knew him."

"How did you resolve it?"

Sara laughed now. "Well, resolve is not exactly the word I would use. The other horse guys had made themselves scarce, but I saw that the boss had come up and was watching us from a distance. So I walked up to him, told him Trace's dad was ill and that he had to go back home to Virginia."

"What did he say?"

"He said, "Who's Trace?" Sara rolled her eyes at Annie and burst out laughing. Annie joined her, and they laughed until Sara's eyes were filled with tears.

"Okay," said Annie, considering now. "So that was last Wednesday? Where have you been since then?"

"Oh, my quitting his job for him didn't help a bit. He stormed off and said he was planning to quit anyway. I followed him back to his place and watched him as he grabbed his stuff and jammed it into a duffel bag. He swung it over his shoulder and confronted me at the door.

But I just stood there. He would have had to push me over to get by. And I wasn't having that."

"He finally just slammed the door in my face. I stood there for a while, leaning against my truck and trying to decide what to do. I decided to take a chance. I went and got pizza and beer."

"I stayed away about an hour, and was frankly a little surprised that he was still there. Maybe he thought I had given up."

"So I walked in, slapped down the pizza and opened a beer. And I said, *so how have you been?*"

Annie laughed. "How'd he react?"

"He laughed. He took a slice of pizza but passed on the beer. He said, *not bad. And you?*"

Sara's eyes filled with tears again. "I almost saw my old Trace for a moment there. His eyes softened, and his grin crinkled up his face just like Cobie's does."

Annie nodded.

"But then he started to shut it down again. I coaxed him. I fed him, I asked about his work. And he finally started talking."

Sara closed her eyes and held the cold bottle against her face. "You're exhausted," Annie put her hand on her friend's shoulder. "You don't need to tell me right now."

"Annie, we have been talking now for six days straight. Once he got started, it was like he hadn't talked in all those years. That's probably just about the truth. He talked about his work. Then he talked about the farm, his memories of every animal on the place. We moved on to foxhunting, and he asked about everyone, and listened to all the gossip I could muster. I wracked my brain to entertain him with stories about all our goings-on around here. I described every single one of Wanda's puppies individually, and told him about every single junior rider who has gone through my stable. I told him about some of the top students that his dad was still training.

"Finally, we got around to talking about his dad. He had not said a word about Cobie's illness, had not even acknowledged that I had told him about it. But once he mustered the courage, he wanted to know everything. He questioned the diagnosis, Googled it on his phone, railed against the fact that Cobie was refusing chemo. Called him a stubborn bastard."

Annie chuckled. "Apple doesn't fall far from that tree."

"Then he finally talked about Curly. He started with stories of the good times. You could see him embracing the big horse in his mind, reliving every ripple of muscle and graceful motion the horse had ever taken. His eyes would close, and you could see that he saw it all in his head, almost like he was watching a movie.

"He told me a funny story. Seems he had a date with some girl. He called her a fortune teller, but I think maybe she was an astrologist, or that thing with tarot cards. Or a psychic, I don't know. Anyway, she told him that he had an animal once, and that animal wanted him to know that everything was fine. He said to say that he was part of Trace now, that he had entered his heart. She said that the only way the horse could continue to exist is if Trace lived the life he was meant to live."

"Wow."

"Yeah. Of course, Trace thought it was complete bull, and quit seeing her shortly after." Sara took another sip of her beer. "But he admitted to me that he can't sleep. He never gets more than a couple hours at a time. He said the idea of Curly inside his heart weighed on his mind. He knew the girl was right because the horse was always there, in his dreams.

"He finally talked about the night of the accident. He talked about having Curly in his arms, and how he was still alive when he climbed into the trailer. How he tried to stop the bleeding. Curly died in Trace's arms. He wondered for years whether he could have done more. That's what the dream are about—Curly showing up in his dreams, but every time Trace wakes up screaming and drenched in blood."

Annie shook her head and glanced toward the house. "That's a long time to torture yourself."

Sara followed her eyes to the house. "He talked about his dad's reaction. How angry Cobie was at first, and how he had then tried to help him. He said his dad was right about everything. He said over and over what an idiot he had been. That was when I really saw what he had been putting himself through all these years. He spent every night replaying the whole thing in his head. He just couldn't shake it.

"At last, he put down his head and he started crying." Sara shook her head, remembering. "Annie, I don't think he had cried in all this time. He cried for two days straight. And I just stayed right there and let him. I didn't say anything.

"Nothing?"

"No. Sometimes, I made him coffee. Sometimes when he quieted down a bit, I brought him food. He would nibble at it and then the tears would start flowing again. Sometimes when I thought the sobbing would make him sick, I even stroked his head. But I figured this was a long time coming and I wasn't going to get in the way." She considered. "I think it helped that I was somehow bearing witness to the grief, to the truth of the whole thing."

"How did you get him to come home?"

"That's the funny thing. Tuesday afternoon he was just about cried out. He was curled up on the old sofa and he had gone silent. I thought he had gone to sleep, so I leaned my head back and closed my eyes.

"I thought I heard him get up. I opened my eyes, and he was leaning over me, studying my face. His blue eyes looked straight into mine. And he said, *let's go home.* So we did."

"Just like that?"

Sara nodded. "Just like that."

Annie gestured to the house. "What do you think is going on up there?"

Sara shrugged. "I have no idea. It's up to him now. My work is done."

Annie raised her eyebrows.

"Don't give me that. The past is the past. The future is...well...the future. I am not going beyond that right now."

CHAPTER 29

———————

ANNIE GOT SARA INTO HER truck. She protested a little, uncertain whether it was right to leave Trace or more precisely, to leave Trace with Dorothy and Cobie. But there had been no eruptions from the house, and no one had come bursting from the back door. Annie suggested that what Sara really needed to do was go home, check on her place, take a nice hot shower and get some sleep. Sara immediately saw the logic of that, admitting that she hadn't showered in days.

"It'll all be here tomorrow, whatever is going on in there," Annie said, looking over at the house, searching the windows for signs of movement. "If it's going well, we don't want to interfere." She paused. "And if it's not going well, we don't want to be in there."

Sara nodded, rubbing her eyes. The beer had relaxed her, and exhaustion was setting in. "My catching you up has pretty much taken the last of my energy."

"I'm getting out of here too. They know where we are if they need us."

Sara reached out and gave Annie a hug. "Thanks for...everything. Dorothy and Lindsay and I, and Cobie, have been so bottled up for so long, it was high time this happened."

"Well, I'm sorry it took Cobie's illness to do it."

"Me too. But at least it's done now." She gave the house a quick look and moved her lips as if in prayer. Annie thought she heard her say Trace's name.

After Sara had left, Annie wrapped up her work in the tack room quickly, got into her own car and headed home. She was just settling in for a long think, as Elliot liked to call her reveries. But she had barely gotten started when the phone rang. It was Dodie.

"Hey there," Annie said. "Long time no hear."

Dodie chuckled. "Just looking over the new manuscript. Looks good." Annie heard her draw on her cigarette. "I'm sending photographers down to shoot you in the garden."

"Dodie, it's not even May yet. There isn't anything in the garden."

"Nothing?" said Dodie, genuinely surprised. "How does this vegetable thing work anyway?"

Annie wanted to think she was joking, but she knew that was only half true. "I mean, I have some greens and peas. The onions are up. But certainly not photo-ready."

"Okay, when then?"

Annie considered. "Let's wait for the strawberries at least. That's a few more weeks. In the meantime, Elliot can snap a few close shots of asparagus and peas." She thought for a moment, doing a quick calculation in her head. "If I have to be in the shots, I would like a little time to lose weight."

"Oh, good god," said Dodie. "A couple of weeks won't make any difference."

What Annie didn't say, and what she didn't tell Dodie now, was that she had been losing weight. It had been coming off naturally with all the exercise. That and the fact that she was often too busy to worry about food. Riding had made her legs, if not skinny, then at least acceptable. But she would let Dodie just be surprised when she got the proofs back.

"Well, let's just say June 1, how about that?"

"Done. Are you sure I can't just hire Elliot to do them?"

"You know I never let him shoot me."

"You are a weird one."

"Right back at ya."

Dodie took a deep nicotine breath. "Oh, one more thing..."

"Yes?"

"What's your next book?"

"Good lord, I don't know. I haven't even recovered from Garden Fresh yet."

"Still, we should probably select a topic. We want to get another title out on the heels of this one."

"Why? What's the rush? Garden Fresh will be out in September. Isn't that good enough?"

"Practice seems to make perfect. You are getting the hang of this cookbook thing. And of course, Elliot's photos are fabulous."

"Still, why do we need to book another title already?"

"Well, now that Potatoes Galore was picked up by Wal-Mart..."

Annie, as always, cringed for just a split second. God, she hated that title. She had protested it mightily, losing to the wisdom of the publisher's sales and marketing departments. Then she said, "Wait, what did you say?"

She heard Dodie smile. "Oh, didn't I tell you? All fifty states. Sam's Club too." She paused, and Annie imagined her stubbing out her butt. "I was sure I had mentioned it."

Annie tried to ring up the royalties in her head, but she didn't want to get ahead of herself. Wal-Mart, she knew, would buy at a deep discount. No sense in getting her hopes up.

Dodie read her mind. "I mean; it's not going to make you millions. It is potatoes, after all. But thousands seem like a reasonable expectation."

"Thousands is good."

"And now that it's won the Cooking Natural Book Award..."

"Again, what!"

Dodie ignored her. "You really need to stay off that horse and call me once in a while." She paused for effect. "Anyway, as I was saying, Potatoes, followed by Garden Fresh, and then a third title to make a nice trilogy. That square format we used is really appealing. Eventually, a boxed set. Let me think. Kale is hot right now. No, maybe not. Something with more mass appeal...You figure that out."

"Geez," was all Annie could manage.

"Geez, indeed," said Dodie. "Anyway, start thinking."

"Tomatoes?" Annie thought aloud, making a mental run through her file of recipes trying to imagine another vegetable that warranted its own title.

"Tomatoes! Excellent! Red always makes a great cover color."

"Wait, let me think about it."

"Okay, but don't think too long. I'll want a tight turnaround on this. And we will want to book a small tour this summer on the potato thing. Nothing too big. You know how the talk shows are about cookbooks; they always want you to cook them something. They never just talk to you."

Actually, Annie didn't know that. She had never had a book tour.

She rifled through papers on her desk. "Potato Growers Convention is interested. That's June. It might be worth your while. They'll pay you to speak." Annie heard her tap her pen on the desk. "Cooking classes, lectures on cooking with natural ingredients. There might be some more pocket money here."

Annie did not answer. Her head was spinning.

"Your silence speaks volumes. Think about it. I'll talk to you next week."

CHAPTER 30

———

DOROTHY CALLED AND ASKED ANNIE and Elliot to come for dinner. "Nothing fancy," she said. "Just barbecue in the backyard."

"Sounds great." Annie replied, putting down the bowl she was stirring. She almost licked her finger, and then remembered that the batter she was making was for horse cookies. Not that it would be too bad, she thought as she put down the wooden spoon. A little sweet grain and molasses wouldn't kill her. And certainly Warrior would appreciate them.

Now she turned her attention to the call. As normal as it sounded, the invitation struck Annie as quite extraordinary. In spite of the fact that she had been at the farm nearly every day, until that night at the hospital, Dorothy had hardly given her the time of day. She had certainly never suggested that they dine together. With Trace home, Annie had given the family a wide berth. Now Dorothy sounded decidedly upbeat and eager to entertain.

Annie jotted down "Saturday @ seven" on her calendar, and offered to bring something. Dorothy refused politely, her voice a blend of formality and friendliness. It sounded a little false to Annie's ears. After all, Dorothy knew perfectly well that Annie knew all about Trace. Geez, Annie thought, she almost sounds breathless. She had never heard Dorothy like this. Dorothy paused, adding almost as an afterthought, "And we're anxious for you to meet our son."

"Ah," Annie said. Now she understood. The family was circling the wagons. This introduction would be free of awkwardness or explanation.

Dorothy had decided that Annie was no longer inside the secret. The inner circle had shrunk around Cobie, and Dorothy had relegated Annie to revolve in one of its outer orbits. "I heard he was home. It must be wonderful to have him there."

"You have no idea," said Dorothy, sounding almost incandescent with happiness. And Annie suddenly realized that Trace was probably sitting right there in the kitchen, listening to Dorothy's side of the conversation. "He just came and surprised us two weeks ago, and frankly, we have wanted to keep him all to ourselves. Of course, Cobie's buddies have been over. But after so many years, he is anxious to get to know some new people. We just know he will love you and Elliot."

Cobie's buddies had been over? Had they recorded their conversations? Annie shook her head. Their recording sessions had been postponed, or at least she thought they had. But now was not the time to worry about that. "How is Cobie feeling?"

"Marvelous," Dorothy replied. "He's sitting in the sunroom having his coffee right now." Annie heard the clink of a plate and heard Dorothy say, "Trace, could you just take this out to your dad?" Then she turned back to the phone.

"Of course, we told him how wonderful you have been to Cobie, helping him to get his notes and stories together," Dorothy went on. "And he's looking forward to meeting you."

"Of course."

"I thought a big dinner might make Cobie tired, but he insisted on it and Trace likes the idea." Dorothy paused again, and Annie could feel the nervous energy. Then she lowered her voice. "This is best; don't you think?"

"Absolutely," Annie said brightly. "We're looking forward to meeting him!"

But when she hung up, she leaned against the counter for several minutes, lost in thought and cookies forgotten.

———

When Annie and Elliot got to the farm Saturday evening, they brought a bottle of red wine, a six-pack of Guinness and a be-ribboned jar of horse cookies. Dorothy greeted them warmly at the door, and then turned to the tall man who was just then reaching into the refrigerator for a Coke.

"This is Trace," Dorothy beamed. "Trace, why don't you bring one of those to your dad too?" She reached in and grabbed another soda.

Trace extended his hand, first to Elliot and then to herself. He looked over at his mom. "No, I think Dad wants something a bit stronger." He gestured to the Guinness still in Elliot's hand.

Dorothy shook her head. "Oh, don't be silly Trace. The Coke will be fine."

Trace gave her a warning frown that was mixed with gentle good humor. He reached over to pull a bottle from a six-pack, slipping it into the back pocket of his jeans. "My mother here is worried because I don't drink," he said good-naturedly. "I'm not sure there has ever been a non-drinking Grainger in the family and she is not quite sure how to handle it." He turned to kiss her on the top of her head, and then turned to Elliot. "Shall we?" he said, gesturing to the backyard.

Elliot handed the wine to Dorothy and put the beer on the counter. Then he turned to Annie, telegraphing his willingness to wait for her.

"I'll find a place in the refrigerator for that beer," Annie said. "And then I'll be along. Of course, I have to make a detour to the paddock to give Warrior a couple of these." She tapped on the top of the cookie jar.

Dorothy's face clouded a little. "I have been telling Trace to go out and ride him, but so far he's been too busy."

"No way," Trace said, reaching into the cookie jar and taking a bite out of one of the crisp treats.

"Mmm," he said, his mouth filled with sweet grainy crumbles. "Not bad." He made a valiant attempt to swallow, finally taking a swig from his Coke to get it down. "Molasses, carrot, apple, I think?" He saw Annie's eyes widen, and they both laughed. "Believe me, I've eaten worse."

"I'm glad you've pre-tested them," Annie said. "I'll let Warrior know they have been approved."

"Dad says Warrior is your horse these days," Trace said to Annie. "And Sara tells me you're a pretty good rider."

Annie started to answer him, but Dorothy interrupted. "But Warrior is one of the only ones...that you know from before," Dorothy said. She added with a little too much emphasis, "Your dad's horse."

Trace glanced at Annie and then turned to his mother, hasty to brush past Dorothy's rudeness. "Ma, you know there are plenty of horses around here if I want to ride." He said pointedly to Annie, "Dad and I have already talked about this."

Then he slapped Elliot on the back. "We're going to go do the guy round," he said, addressing Annie. "But I'm looking forward to talking to you about Dad's book. Make sure you sit with me at dinner."

Annie smiled and nodded, and then watched as Elliot followed Trace out the back door. It turned out that several people had been invited to the barbecue, so it took the two of them a few minutes to work their way through the back porch and out to the lawn. Annie saw Trace laugh at something Elliot said, and put his hand comfortably on Lindsay's shoulder when making an introduction. He grabbed Daisy from behind and gave her a little toss in the air as she laughed and squealed. Trace stopped by to give his dad the beer, leaning over and smiling as Cobie gestured to another old friend that had just come around into the yard. Trace nodded and immediately headed over to greet the man.

"Trace seems to be settling in nicely," Annie said smoothly, noting that Dorothy's eyes had been following them too.

"Yes, well," said Dorothy, rather brusquely now. "There are still... issues."

"You mean like the lack of drinking?" Annie hadn't meant to say it sarcastically, but she realized that it might have come out that way.

"Well, it's not really natural, is it?"

"Natural?"

"I just think he is still punishing himself for the...the accident."

Annie considered this, trying to put herself in Dorothy's shoes. "Well, I guess I understand you thinking that. After all, you haven't seen him for a long time. But after all this time it must be working for him."

"But he wasn't an alcoholic! He never was…" Dorothy paused to find the right words. "He was just young."

"Still, something like what he went through would make someone re-think their priorities."

"Yes, maybe. But then there's the riding. Sara says he doesn't ride anymore."

"I had the impression he rides for work."

"But only if he has to. He's refused to get on Warrior, and I have asked and asked." She looked at Annie, her eyes narrowed slightly. "He says Warrior's yours."

Annie sighed, a little flustered now. "I'm sure that's just an excuse. He knows perfectly well that he can ride Warrior. And just to be clear, Warrior is Cobie's horse, not mine."

"That's what I told him."

Annie's stomach tightened although she couldn't quite say why. She just knew she wanted this conversation over. Dorothy seemed happy to have her son home, but behind the smile Annie saw a kind of hectic anxiety. She's in protective mode, Annie thought. It's nothing personal.

So she smiled briskly and scooped out a handful of cookies. "I'll just go greet the four-legged critters, and then I'll come back and help with the salad."

"No need." Dorothy turned back to the counter, busying herself with a plate of cheese and crackers. "You just go and mingle."

"Well, if you're sure…" But Dorothy didn't reply, so Annie headed out the door, making a wide sweep around the gathered guests and making her way to the paddock.

She had thought that she wanted nothing more than a few minutes alone to try to puzzle out Dorothy's behavior. But she saw that Sara too had chosen the horses in favor of the human guests, and had beaten her there with treats of her own.

"Hey, if you fill them up on carrots, they won't want my cookies!"

Sara smiled and took a sniff of the treats that Annie held out. "Smells pretty good," she offered. Then she gestured to the two horses that were just finishing their carrots. "When have you ever known these guys to be full?"

"You have a point," laughed Annie as Warrior pushed his head into her chest, angling for her pocket. She reached out and gave each of them a cookie, patting the big necks as they happily munched.

Sara gestured to the backyard, which was still filling with people. "I didn't know there were going to be so many people. Not exactly what I had in mind tonight."

"Were you consulted?"

Sara snorted. "Of course not. I think Cobie just wanted a few people over to see Trace. But Dorothy figures there's safety in numbers."

"Safety?"

"Well, you know. The more people, the shallower the chitchat." Sara scanned the crowd, seeking Dorothy, and found her setting out a bowl of salad. "She is happy to have Trace back, no doubt. But she's about... as comfortable as a canary at a cat convention."

Annie chuckled. That was one of Cobie's lines.

"It's as if she's afraid he'll startle and run off. Or something."

"She does seem a bit wound up."

"To say the least." Sara considered. "I get it, I guess. She and Trace were pretty close—truth be told; he was a bit of a momma's boy. The sun rose and set on him.

"I think Dorothy blamed Cobie for everything that happened." Sara shook her head. "Not the accident, of course." She paused to consider. "No, that's not right. I think she blamed him for that too. She definitely blamed him for the fact that Trace ran off. She never admitted it to anyone, but no question it changed them. Things used to be pretty happy around here." Sara nodded in the direction of the food table. "She's putting on a good show tonight, but I don't think she and Cobie have had a pleasant word for one another in years."

Sara sighed now. "And now she sees him come home and...well, devote seems like a strong word. But Trace has spent almost every waking minute with his dad. They have had some long, long conversations, and I know a lot of tears have been shed. They walk to the barn together, and Cobie has taken Trace out in the Gator to show him all the crops.

"I'm not sure Dorothy has gotten that kind of attention, and I think she may be a bit jealous. Trace, for all his pain, is a grown man now. A pretty good one, from what I can see. But I think maybe she was expecting that hurt boy to come home. This guy is a bit of a mystery to her. I think she thinks Trace is taking sides with his dad."

"Does Trace realize there are sides?"

"No, that's the thing. I don't think he has any idea."

"Sounds like you have been spending some time here."

"No, just like you, I have been steering clear of the place."

"Dorothy implied that I should just introduce myself and not indicate I knew anything at all."

Sara snorted. "Don't be silly. Trace knows everything you've done. I told him myself."

"Then why...."

"Who knows? She thinks she's protecting him. Or maybe she's protecting herself. I don't know. Don't worry about it. She'll get over it."

"So, if you haven't been here, how do you know what's been happening?"

"Oh, Trace calls." She turned her wide blue eyes to Annie. "Late at night, after Cobie's gone to bed. He'll call, and we'll talk for a while."

Annie nodded.

"It's nothing. It's just that I'm the only one he can talk to who knows..."

Annie nodded again, smiling.

Sara colored a little, and then rolled her eyes. "Geez, it's nothing. He just still has a hard time sleeping and needs someone to listen. Stop thinking what you're thinking."

"What am I thinking?"

"I don't know. Just...stop." Sara waved to Archie, who had just noticed them. "Come on; let's go do the social thing."

Elliot met them halfway across the lawn, and gestured them to a round table that had been set up near the apple tree. Lindsay had placed a variety of tables and chairs around the backyard, although many people just chose to eat standing up or balancing a plate on their knees. Trace was already there; his plate overloaded with pork, potato salad and beans. He saw Sara raise an eyebrow at his plate.

"Ma," he said by way of explanation. "She handed me a plate before I got a chance to protest." He dug a fork into the salad. "Figured I had better be a good son and take it."

"Is there any left for us?"

"Oh, she'll probably let you have some." He gestured to where the food was laid out. Annie was glad to see that Dorothy had accepted help from some of her old friends. Lindsay was helping too. She could relax and just be a guest.

They walked over and helped themselves, stopping by the loaded cooler for more drinks. They ran into Gray and Betsy, and invited them to join their table. It was a pleasantly warm evening. Candle lanterns dotted the back yard and tree frogs sang from above.

Trace sat back and observed the crowd. The men were still gathered around his dad, and their wives were in a clutch around Dorothy. Daisy ran around with Gray and Betsy's kids. An older crowd for the most part, he thought. Many of these women had fed him when he was a kid. Their own children were his playmates, but most of them had scattered now.

The men, on the other hand, had been part of the fabric of his life. Archie had advised him on his horses, and Charlie hung around the barn, consulting Cobie on crops and weather forecasts, always having a word for Trace. He had ridden for miles with Barrett and the former huntsman, opening new land and repairing fences. Gray had arrived on the scene a couple of years before Trace had left. He liked the huntsman and was looking forward to getting to know him better.

"So, how long you staying?" Gray asked now.

Trace was surprised by the question. Oddly enough, no one had asked him that. He suspected that the older men just assumed he was home to stay. "Well, we'll see what has to be done."

Gray nodded. "There's a lot to consider. Cobie and I have talked some, but it would be good to have your input on the horses and all." Annie knew that Gray, always practical, saw no need to sidestep what would have to be done in the coming months.

Trace just nodded vaguely. "I guess I was figuring on heading back to Kentucky at some point."

"If that's the case, we can move the horses around a bit. Several of them here are in training or are being boarded. Between Sara and I, we can move them off when need be."

"Don't you think you could talk about this another time?" Sara said.

"I agree. It's a beautiful night." Annie interjected. "You guys can talk business another time."

Trace looked over and saw his dad rising shakily to his feet. "It looks like Dad is calling it a night." He jumped up. "I'll just help him upstairs."

Gray stood up and reached out his hand. "Good to see you home, Trace. Call me, and I'll come over. We'll figure things out."

Trace nodded and shook his hand. "Thanks. I know we will have to deal with things soon enough. Glad to know you're there." And then he hurried off to take his dad by the elbow and steer him into the house.

CHAPTER 31

—————

"GOOD MORNING! WHAT ARE YOU guys up to?" Sara's voice shouted into the phone.

"Where are you? It sounds windy." Annie said, feeling as though she should shout back to be heard.

"Oh, wait. The truck window is down." Annie heard the buzz of the automatic window and then sudden quiet. "There. That's better. Anyway, what are you guys doing?"

"Nothing much. Just did some weeding. Thought I would make some breakfast."

"Well, pack up sandwiches and meet us at Sandhurst. We're taking the bikes out with the puppies."

Sandhurst was a large historic home that was managed by one of the club's members. It sat way off any roads and had no railroad tracks. Even better, there were miles of paved roads snaking around the property. It was the perfect choice for bombing around with the yearling hounds that would be entered in the fall.

Annie smiled. Over the past weeks, she had continued to go out on the puppy walks as often as she could, waiting for the chance to take them out to the farm. But the book and the garden had taken up much of her time, and she had missed their first forays into the field. Now the hounds were starting to get some real exercise.

"I've got Trace with me, and the bikes are in the truck," said Sara. "Come on. Meet us out there!"

Gray and Davis were waiting for them when they arrived. Seventeen couples of hounds milled around, waiting for a word from Gray. Together the six of them were quite a sight. They were decked out for early summer heat in t-shirts and sweat pants, each donning a baseball cap and sunglasses before setting off. Annie chuckled as she helped Elliot pull the old mountain bikes off the rack. If only the walkers, the name given to spectators at the hunt, could see them now. They gave off nothing of the tweedy splendor that the start of the hunting season would require. They wore sneakers or practical boots, but she saw that Davis was riding in Wellies. It seemed an impractical choice.

The bicycles allowed the hunters to get some real exercise, and get the yearlings out into the real country without the worry of horses. Practically speaking, the horses were in their off-season, getting fat and lazy on plentiful meadow grass. So they wouldn't have been much help anyway.

The club's bikes were a little muddier and rusted than Annie would have liked, with balding tires and faulty brakes. She made a mental note to donate the twin's old mountain bikes to the club.

They hit the road, such as it was, and she soon saw that even a new bike would age rapidly in the hands of the huntsman. Annie had expected a somewhat leisurely pace of five or six miles per hour, but Gray often rode hell-bent-for-leather out of sheer exuberance, and to keep up with the young dogs. She wondered what had possessed her to leave her bike helmet behind.

The whips they carried dangled entirely too close to the wheels, and the coupled hounds were constantly threatening to straddle their tires and send them head over heels into a ditch. Nothing about the Virginia countryside is flat, and Annie wasn't sure whether she dreaded the speed of the downhill or the sweat of the uphill more. Sara and Davis whipped in to the left. Trace stayed up front with Gray. She and Elliot stayed right, although Annie found herself often bringing up the rear.

Still, Annie had to admit it was exhilarating finally to be out in the country. The young hounds were enthusiastic, giving a hint of what the autumn's hunt would be like. She watched Trace up with Gray, and saw that the huntsman was filling him in on the quality of the hounds, the condition of the fixture and the likelihood of foxy territory. She wondered, had Trace missed this? Could he be compelled to hunt again? He seemed to be enjoying himself, and Annie saw that he was very fit, keeping up with, and even outdoing the bold riding of the huntsman himself.

After two long hours, they finally returned to the cars, hounds panting heavily and riders dragging. Billy was waiting for them with water for the hounds and lemonade for the riders. Annie pulled out the egg salad sandwiches she had packed into the cooler, and they devoured them along with cold slices of watermelon. She caught sight of Sara looking in the truck's side mirror and trying to make some order out of her hair. Davis pulled off his Wellies, relieved to have his feet out of the rubber prison he had cast them into. Even fit Elliot was rubbing his backside and stretching out a tight muscle. Of the riders, only Gray and Trace looked reasonably fresh.

Annie was muddy from splashed mud and dirty paws. Her sweats had holes in them where they had caught briars and her voluminous red curls were matted to her head. She knew she would need Epsom salts in her bath tonight, and a lot of Advil. But in spite of all that, she found herself laughing. She laughed about the heat. She laughed about the beautiful hounds and the amazing countryside. She laughed because this was her life. And she laughed because she thought she had seen a hint of something between two people who teased each other as they shared a glass of lemonade.

"This is what Cobie was talking about," Annie said as she placed her bike on the Jeep's rack. "This is the perfect venue for teaching kids about the hounds and giving them some off-season fun."

"Oh lord, do we really want to go there?" said Davis.

Sara chimed in. "It's a good idea. We could offer a Junior Hunt on bikes, and charge a regular capping fee. Hunt breakfast after. It could be a good fundraiser." She thought about it a bit more. "You know, we could make it a week, like a day camp. Parents like that sort of thing.

Three days out on bikes, some classroom teaching, and some kennel time getting to know the new litters. I can add in some pool time too. We could even encourage some junior handler training for any kids interested in showing at the Puppy Show in September."

"I like the sound of it," said Trace.

"Okay, but a couple of rules," said Gray, ever the proper huntsman. "Dress code. Rugger shirt, Rohan pants. No Lycra."

They looked around at each other's attire and started laughing.

"Rugger shirts? Really?" Sara said, rolling her eyes. "Gray, your Irish is coming out. They'll be too hot."

"Fine then, collared shirts. Polos. But if you don't require long sleeves, expect some skinned elbows."

"Okay."

"Helmets," Annie said.

"Yes, definitely."

"I'd be willing to organize it," Sara said. She turned to Trace. "Would you help?"

"Uhhh..."

Sara laughed, knowing that she would be able to convince him, especially since this was exactly the kind of event Cobie wanted for the club.

Annie climbed into the passenger side of the Jeep, rolling down the windows to cool off the interior. "I'm in," she said. "I can't be an expert, but I can help wrangle kids, or even be in charge of the breakfasts."

Sara clapped her hands. "It's practically organized! I'll pick a week in July. Okay Gray? We will get it advertised to the members, and I'll put something up at my place. I'm sure we can fill it quickly."

Elliot finished strapping the bikes onto the rack. He knew that now that they had started, this was going to be part of their summer routine. He made a mental note to go shopping for more comfortable bike seats.

He extended his hand to Trace. "Well, looks like you've gotten yourself into something."

Trace shook his hand and nodded toward the girls. "Once they have an idea, there's no stopping them."

CHAPTER 32

SARA WAS INVITED TO TALK with the group. Most of the men there were at least thirty years her senior, but they all had tremendous respect for her. She represented the future.

"You know," she said, "I started foxhunting when I was about eight. And I quickly became obsessed. But to be honest, the adults weren't watching us too close. We were just wild children, left to our own devices. If we fell off, we'd just have to get back on. When we got a little older, we had to watch over the littler kids, and help them if they fell off."

"I agree," said Barrett. "Back in those days, especially when we were kids—well, I'm a bit older than you Sara," He gave her a wink. "The adults didn't want us there. We were a nuisance to them. It took a brave kid to go out, especially if they didn't have a parent there."

Archie agreed. "Hell, even when we did. Sometimes it was even worse when your daddy was there."

"Remember Miz Mosby?" said Barrett. "She about scared me to death. Sent me home one time because there was mud on my girth. I told her I would clean it, right then and there. But she wouldn't have it."

The guys laughed appreciatively.

"That's a good point though," Cobie said. "The Masters set the tone. We're lucky to have Monty, and Deborah before him. They encourage the kids."

"And don't forget Gray," said Sara. "He is very welcoming and patient with them. They adore him."

"It makes all the difference," agreed Charlie. "I've hunted with other places, like up Middleburg way; some of those hunts still don't have much use for the kids. They got the beagle hunts on foot for them, but I don't think they like them in the field."

"Well, I'm lucky then, that I have Meryton," said Sara. "Now that I have the school, those kids don't have much choice, I just bring 'em along."

"I love having the kids there," Monty said. "I love the questions they ask."

"Ha! That's another thing!" Charlie said. "Back in the old days, no kid would dare ask what was happening. They just had to shut up and watch. Pick it up on their own."

Sara smiled at Monty. "I love the questions too, and the stories they tell. And they're usually full of them. I keep a quiet field, but once they're in the truck, all hell breaks loose."

Deborah laughed. "Toby would come home when he was young and tell tales about six-foot fences and monster-size foxes."

"Oh yes," agreed Sara. "Those fences grew taller and taller, the streams forded deeper and deeper."

"Those are the memories that keep them coming back for more," Cobie said.

"No question about it. And we just want them to keep on coming."

CHAPTER 33

———

THE MONTH OF MAY HAD flown by. A wet spring had yielded to mild weather, and there hadn't yet been any of the scorching heat that dried clay to concrete. The garden was thriving, and plans for the new tomato book were well underway. Annie had gone out to Nelson County with Elliot, and they had found a wealth of heirloom varieties of tomatoes. Now that the early season crops were done, there was little else growing in the garden. She counted seventy-three plants in all.

Dodie had sent the photographer down, and had called suitably impressed with Annie's appearance. They took pictures of the spring greens, the peas, the onions and the strawberries. Then they stayed on to photograph Annie with the young tomatoes, anticipating an article when the new book appeared. The publisher's marketing person worked up a small book tour. Annie spoke at the Potato Grower's convention in Minneapolis, where she did a seminar on the versatile potato and its place in a carb-phobic world. It was well received.

Puppy rides had continued in earnest. Between all that biking and her garden, Annie felt that she was almost as fit as Elliot.

Now, the rest of June stretched out lazily before them. Elliot and Annie had long dinners on the back patio, making a ritual of opening a chilled bottle of Virginia Chardonnay after a long day outdoors. Fireflies started the show early in the evening, lighting their dinners with a bit of magic.

Elliot pulled the swordfish off the grill and gestured to the old fireplace where they cooked over the open flame. "You know; this chimney is going to need lining soon." He put down the plate. "Mortar is crumbling."

Annie looked up at the chimney. "It looks okay to me."

Elliot shrugged. "Problem is on the inside. We will probably have to look at the other flues too."

Annie sighed. "How much is that going to cost?"

"About twenty-five hundred dollars?"

Annie gave Elliot a horrified look. "For only one?" He just shrugged in reply and sipped his wine.

"I guess that makes sense. But still…." Annie thought about writing that check, and wondered again where the money would come from. She was so busy with her hobbies, as she called them, that she had avoided her job search. She figured she was just postponing the inevitable, but the reality was that she could hardly imagine herself getting dressed every morning and rushing off to some meaningless job.

More and more, any type of job sounded pretty meaningless. The hounds needed her, she told herself. The garden needed her. Elliot needed her. And Cobie needed her. It was hard to believe that only six months earlier she had been working sixty hours a week, travelling most of the time, and not even living in her own house. She had no idea how life had taken this fast a turn, and she could not imagine fitting any more into her busy schedule. These days, she couldn't even imagine that old life or, as she slipped into her size 10 jeans every morning, her old self.

She sighed again, and agreed that they could probably write the check. Then she turned the conversation back to Cobie, seamlessly shelving the issue of the crumbling house. Cobie's six-month deadline, if one could call it that, had come and gone. Though no one talked about it, she knew that Cobie was pleased with himself. Trace had started taking him to all of his appointments, so now the news flowed a little more freely than it did when Red had driven him to Charlottesville and back. The consensus was that the tumors were growing a little more slowly than anticipated. That was where Cobie liked to stop the discussion, but Trace had told Annie privately that the bone involvement was significant and that there were now shadows in the lungs.

When Trace first came home, he questioned Cobie's desire to avoid chemotherapy and extensive treatments. He argued in favor of extending his life in any way possible. But now he understood that was not his father's way. Better to feel good until you didn't, rather than using poisons to make yourself sicker.

The recordings were pretty much done. Annie and Lindsay had not dared to schedule out this far, and so now get-togethers among the fellows were impromptu. Trace joined them now, which gave them fodder for more stories. He was often the butt of their jokes and he took it with good grace. She could see that the stories worked to heal over some of the wounds he still carried. The men no longer avoided the subject of Curly. In fact, Trace encouraged talk of the big horse.

"I have to go out tomorrow to pick up some photos. I need to start getting serious about the manuscript," Annie said. "Want to come?"

"I promised Lonnie I would do some promotional photos of the vineyard for the new website."

Annie lifted her glass. "I hope you'll be paid in wine."

"I thought you wanted money."

Annie shrugged. Her priorities were clearly slipping. Still wine seemed like the better idea.

———◆———

Annie arrived at the farm with a large cardboard filing box. It was time for her to stay home and start turning the notes and tapes into some hard copy. She would create an outline and have him take a look at it. She was excited that there might still be time for him to get an idea of what the finished product might look like.

"I have good news," she told Cobie as they sat poring over photographs. Trace had come in handy with this task. He had more patience for the pile of memorabilia than his dad did, and he had a great memory for names and dates. Elliot had done most of the work on this part of the project, but Annie liked to put names with faces as she wrote up the stories.

"I got a call from Hounds and Hunting Magazine," Annie said. "They're interested in publishing the book when it's ready."

"That is good news," Cobie said. He smiled blandly. Annie saw Trace out of the corner of her eye. He quickly looked down at the photos on his lap and stifled a small chuckle.

"What am I missing?" Annie looked from one man to the other, and saw them exchange knowing smiles.

"Should you tell her or should I?" Trace said.

"Oh, you tell her."

Trace gave her a big smile. "Fred Willingham, the publisher over there, called the other day. You know Fred?"

"Wasn't he here for the talk about historical stuff?" She looked to Cobie for validation.

"That's the one." Trace picked up the photos and set them aside on the desk.

"Anyway, Fred already told us they wanted to publish the book when it's done. They would also like to archive the tapes themselves." He paused for a moment. "That is, if it's okay with you."

Annie grinned broadly. "Okay with me? This is Cobie's book, not mine."

"Fred wanted to know about your involvement. Dad told him there would be no book without you. Anyway, you have a stake in it," Trace said. "You know, future royalties and all."

"Royalties?"

"Yeah, from the sale of the book. I thought you knew about stuff like this."

"But I don't want any money. I was just doing this for...."

"For dad."

Annie blushed. "For your dad, yes. But also for the chance to hear the stories myself." She turned to Cobie. "You know I can't take any money for this."

Cobie smiled. "I told Fred you'd say that. Good thing too, he'll be here this afternoon."

An hour later, Fred arrived with his editor, and together they discussed the possible format, inclusion of photos, and the deadline. When it came to discussing terms, Annie was adamant. She would not take any money.

"I don't want the money either," said Cobie. "Apparently God don't take hard cash."

Trace rolled his eyes. His dad's macabre jokes were becoming more frequent. His mom and his sister hated it when he talked that way, but Trace was getting used to it. Now he often added his own. "No bribes for Saint Peter?"

"If I knock and he don't answer, I certainly ain't offering it to the devil," Cobie answered drily.

"Okay, okay," Annie said, uncomfortable with this change of subject. "Trace, what about your mom?"

"Nope."

"Well then, I'd like to start a scholarship." She turned to Cobie. "That is, if it's okay with you."

Cobie smiled and nodded. Annie turned to Fred. "We could use it to send a couple of kids to the Junior Hunter's Championship. After that, we can figure out how to spend future earnings."

"Future earnings?" Cobie said.

"The Cobie Grainger scholarship Fund." She looked to Cobie for approval. "We'll have fundraisers, book signings."

Fred joined in. "The magazine would be happy to help."

Trace jumped on the bandwagon. "Maybe veterinary school scholarship?"

"We could help fund a riding program for disabled vets or sick kids," Cobie said, thoughtful now.

Annie grinned. "So, are you in?"

"I'm in," said Cobie, smiling broadly.

"Me too," said Trace.

"So how does this all work? Can we establish a fund now and have earnings placed directly into it?"

"I'm sure Archie could arrange that with Neal." Trace said. In addition to being the club's secretary, Archie had a son in the banking industry.

Fred got up and extended his hand to Annie. "Sounds like a plan."

"I'll walk you out." She stood up and escorted them to the door and out to the driveway.

"You are good to do this for our friend," Fred said.

"The pleasure is all mine," Annie assured him.

"Are you sure you have time for this?"

Annie chuckled. "I've got nothing but time."

Fred gave her a hard look but said nothing. "It's going to be a great book. Lots of good material."

"I think so."

"I'll mail you more details. Maybe you can come up and see us later this summer."

"Sounds good," Annie said. "I'll try to have an organized outline by then."

They shook hands and Annie waved them out of the driveway. Then she went back into the den where Cobie and Trace were still talking.

"I'll be damned," Cobie said to her, beaming broadly. "A scholarship. I don't know why I hadn't thought of that. Come on," he said to her, pointing at the pile of photographs and clippings. "We have work to do."

CHAPTER 34

———

THE MORNING HAD STARTED OUT badly. Annie arrived at the farm right after breakfast. It was her day to take Cobie to the doctor. Trace had promised Gray that he would go out and mend fences with him.

She had her hand on the front door knob when she heard Dorothy's voice. "I think it should go to cancer research," she stated emphatically. "UVA has a wonderful program."

Cobie snapped at her. "Nothing about my whole damned life had anything to do with cancer. I sure as hell ain't going to make it my legacy."

Dorothy didn't answer for a moment. Annie put down her bag and waited on the porch. The argument continued.

Dorothy turned to Cobie. "It's always about the horses, isn't it?"

"For god's sake, I told you before. It's about the kids."

"Kids like Trace? Do you really believe his life is better because of horses?" Annie heard her at the counter, stirring something furiously. "Because I certainly don't."

"I believe it with all my heart," said Cobie.

Annie saw Trace come walking in from the barn, and raised her finger to her lips to keep him quiet. She gestured to the kitchen. He tiptoed up the steps and stopped beside her. Even on the front porch, they could see the confrontation clearly. Annie made a motion to go, but Trace put his hand on her arm and shook his head.

"Trace's life was ruined because of those horses."

They heard a kitchen chair scrape across the floor. Cobie sat down heavily. "Trace ruined his life because he was drinking."

"No, it was ruined because he was so worried about what you'd think, he came home instead of staying overnight the way he should have." Dorothy's voice rose, and Annie heard the catch in her throat.

Annie heard Cobie take a deep breath. "I didn't make him come home."

Dorothy slammed down the wooden spoon. "He was scared to death to disappoint you. He always has been."

Cobie lowered his voice. "He's home now, can't you just leave it at that?"

She turned to him, furious now. "Home now, and to what? To take care of your precious farm when you are gone?"

There was a moment of silence. Trace leaned against the front porch and closed his eyes.

Finally, Cobie spoke, his voice barely a whisper. "You've always hated this place, haven't you?"

"I hated what it did to us," Dorothy answered.

"You knew what you were marrying into. You knew I was taking this place over from my daddy. What did you expect?"

Dorothy was crying now in earnest. "I don't know. I guess I thought that you loved me, and…"

Cobie's voice rose again. "I did love you." Cobie slammed his hand down on the table. "Damn it, I did love you."

"Until that ended, right?" She spit out the words. "Until Trace left, and you took up with that woman next door."

Annie saw Trace's jaw tighten. He started to open the door. This time, it was Annie who stopped him.

Cobie leapt to his feet. "Until Trace left, and you quit talking to me. You never went to the barn again. You never talked to me. You just walk through this house like some kind of ghost." He walked over to her now. "I was here. I was hurting too. Where the hell were you?"

Dorothy knocked over the bowl. They heard it crash to the floor. "I was mourning the loss of my son," she screamed. "That's where I was."

Cobie's voice rose to match hers. "Trace wasn't dead!"

Dorothy knelt to wipe up the mess, her voice low. "He might as well have been. You drove him off." She hesitated. "And then you just went on with your life."

Cobie got up and went to where she was kneeling. He stood over her, his hands slack. "I did my best with him. You would have known that if you had only looked. And I had no choice but to keep this place going." He knelt down beside her. "Here, watch that. Don't cut yourself."

"Hand me that towel."

Cobie reached up to the counter, and then turned to wipe up the mess himself. "I knew the boy was broken. I tried to help him."

Dorothy's voice broke as she started to cry again. "We could have had grandbabies by now. He and Sara…"

Another silence. Trace watched Cobie rise and reach out to take Dorothy's hand to help her up off the floor.

He turned her to him and whispered. "I know."

Dorothy's put her hands on his chest, holding him back. "I hated you for so long…"

"I guess you had the right."

"I don't know if I did or if I didn't." She let her eyes meet his. "I guess we both made mistakes."

"I guess we did."

She dropped her hands and leaned into his chest. "How did we get here?" she whispered.

"I don't know."

Dorothy raised her head to look up at him. "I can't…I have never been able to hate you enough to leave you."

"I don't want to go away, knowing you are mad at me," Cobie choked.

"I just can't forget."

"Trace is working hard to make his peace with it." He reached down and pushed back her hair. "I'd say it's time we do the same."

Dorothy nodded.

"Say you forgive me."

"I...I didn't see how much it was hurting you." Dorothy reached into her pocket for a tissue. "I was just so shattered. I didn't know how to go forward."

"You stayed and took care of us, me and Lindsay. But that's not the same as forgiving."

"I guess it's not." Dorothy admitted. "We've lost a lot of time, you and I. And now I'm losing you." She started to cry again.

"I guess we should have had this fight a long time ago." Cobie drew his arms around her and held her close.

"I just needed to be angry to keep from coming apart," she said.

"I guess it's time that we forgave each other."

Dorothy's voice softened. "I guess it is."

They stood there together for a long time. Finally, Cobie spoke. "And I never did look at that other woman."

She met his eyes now. "Truly?"

"Truly." Cobie paused, searching her face. "You always had the prettiest brown eyes," he said.

"Oh, Cobie."

"Seven years is a long time to be mad."

"I was busy laying all the sins of the world at your feet." She smiled now, through her tears.

"I'm counting on you, you know. To take care of Lindsay, to watch over that little girl of hers."

Dorothy nodded, tears streaming down in her face.

"And Trace will need you too. He's getting stronger now; I can see it. But there's still something of the boy inside him. You need to make sure he keeps growing."

Dorothy turned her head to look out the window. "Do you think he will stay?"

"I'm hoping for it, but I haven't asked. He needs to decide that for himself."

Dorothy leaned in again; Cobie's arm draped over her back. Now they both turned to the window, looking out over the farm together.

Trace looked at Annie. She saw the pain in his eyes and reached out to touch his arm. He shook his head, warning her off. And then he turned and strode back to the barn.

Annie went back to her car and tried to decide what to do. She felt guilty for having witnessed the couple's argument, but it had explained a lot. Dorothy's coldness, the distance she put between herself and those who were close to Cobie. She was relieved that they didn't know there were witnesses to their fight, but she was glad to understand Dorothy a little better.

She would wait for ten minutes, she decided, looking at her watch. Then she had no choice but to go in or they would be late for Cobie's appointment. She reached for the car handle, and drew a deep breath as saw Dorothy coming out the front door. Annie watched as she held it open for Cobie, and helped him navigate the stairs.

"Sorry I'm running late," Annie called, getting out of the car.

"Oh Annie! I'm sorry I didn't call. I've decided to take Cobie to the doctor today." Dorothy smiled and patted Cobie's arm.

"I'm glad," Annie said sincerely. "You guys should stop for lunch at the Horse and Hound Pub afterward."

Cobie smiled at Dorothy. "I think maybe we'll just do that," he said.

"I don't think you are up to fish and chips," Dorothy admonished.

"No," Cobie said, smiling. "But a cup of their potato soup would do." He winked at Annie and added, "Maybe with a sip of beer."

Dorothy started to scold, but she saw the twinkle in Cobie's eye and relented. "The pub it is, then."

Annie looked over at the barn. She should go say something to Trace. But she stopped herself. His parents may have made some progress today, but Annie was afraid that Trace was in a tailspin. He needed time to think.

She pulled out of the driveway, wondering if she should call Sara. She glanced at her rearview mirror and slammed on her brakes. The sight took her breath away. There was Trace, mounted on Warrior, galloping furiously across the back meadow and up the hill toward Lost Legend.

CHAPTER 35

———◆———

TRACE'S HEART POUNDED IN TIME with the gelding's hooves. He didn't know where he was going. He just knew he had to get out of there. His heart had sunk as he listened to his parents argue. This was all his fault. The accident was bad enough. But he hadn't realized how much damage he had done in running away.

He had to admit it felt good to run now. He steered Warrior straight for a coop, and the horse sailed easily over it, cantering furiously on to the next one. The gelding knew every step of this land and could easily take him to the top of the mountain in minutes. But Trace realized the old boy was twenty years old now, and the day was warm. He pulled up the reins and asked Warrior to slow down. The horse, invigorated by the run, danced on his toes, anxious to begin again. But Trace held firm, coaxing him to relax and walk.

Trace looked around him at the hills and valleys of his home. He noted that the stream was running nicely. He saw a fence board that should be repaired. He counted the calves paired together with their mothers down on the lower meadow. He smiled. There was a new fox den along the south-facing hill. He would have to tell Gray.

He got to the top of Lost Legend and drew Warrior to a stop. There it was; the heart-stopping vista that only a few people, mostly members of the foxhunting community, ever got to see. The hills folded and undulated upon themselves, stands of trees and windbreaks dividing them. Trace could see all the way south and west to Charlottesville. The wind blew nearly constant, hot and insistent. He walked over to Lonely Tree, a solitary oak that stood at the center of the meadow. He slid out of the saddle and pulled the reins over Warrior's head, dropping them. He knew the horse would stay put. Warrior sniffed the green grass, and then turned his big eyes to the man, questioning.

"Go ahead," he told the big horse. "Have a snack. Just don't go too far."

Trace walked over to the tree and sat down, leaning his back against the big trunk. He thought he had been doing well. Coming home had felt natural, easier than he had expected. Focusing on his dad's needs had made re-entry easier too. It wasn't all about him, as much as his mother fussed over him.

Of course, he had noticed the friction between his parents, but they had always had a habit of bickering. Now that he thought about it though, it wasn't bickering that he had seen. The tension was thick, and Trace, caught up in his own concerns, hadn't noticed the silence between them.

Now it seemed obvious. He rarely spent time in their company together. Most of his time was spent with his dad, only some in the kitchen with his mom. Mealtime was the only opportunity they had to be together, and he realized that he could count on one hand the number of times they had all sat at the table. He thought his mom had been giving him space to spend with his dad. Now he realized that she was in the habit of avoiding Cobie. They didn't even sleep in the same room anymore, but again Trace had assumed it was because of dad's illness.

Lindsay tried to warn him, he thought now. She said that mom was having a hard time with dad's illness, but he should have seen past that. Sara too, had suggested that he pay more attention to his mom. What an idiot I am, he thought.

Being on top of this hill brought back a flood of memories. Lindsay and he had walked these hills with the beagles. The family had picnicked here in the summer and chased foxes together here every winter. Even mom went out on horseback in those days. In fact, it was she, and not his dad, who had taken him on his first hunt; leading the little pony they called Pumpkin behind the other hill-toppers. Gosh, he thought now. She must have had to walk miles.

He smiled deeply then, remembering prom night. While the other kids had gotten hotel rooms or attended parties, he and Sara had come back to the barn. He was in his tux and she in that long pink gown. They had saddled the horses, Curly and a large mare named Lacy, in the dark, not wanting to attract any attention from the house. She hitched her dress up as he gave her a leg up, and then laughing, she had grabbed a side seam and ripped it straight up to her thigh. Trace thought he would faint on the spot.

Giggling wildly, they walked through the moonlight, sometimes following one another, sometimes side by side and holding hands.

They had ridden right up to this very tree. They slid off the horses and opened the bottle of Boone's Farm strawberry wine that they had swiped from the 7-11. That's not exactly true, he thought. We did sneak it out, knowing they didn't have the credentials to buy it outright. But Trace had left a $5 bill on the counter. He had not wanted Jack, the semi-retired clerk who sometimes worked for his dad, to get in trouble.

He leaned his head back, remembering that night. It was the first time they made love. She remembered it later as prickly, but all he could remember was perfection. She had slipped off the gown and danced in the moonlight in just her bra and panties. She hummed a song... what was the name of it? Something about stars falling from the sky, he thought. He couldn't remember. At the time, all he could do was watch her, mesmerized by her beauty. It was she who made the first move, pulling off his tie and laying it on top of the jacket that he had already discarded. She tried to get him to dance, but he would not, or could not. Instead, he chased her around the field. She screamed and ran, dodging and weaving until he finally caught her and took her to the ground.

Who was he now? He knew he wasn't the same boy who had played here. He wasn't even the same man that Sara had fallen in love with. That man, or rather boy, to be exact, was brash and reckless. Caring, maybe, but selfish too. Nor was he the man who worked in Kentucky for all those years. A non-existence, he thought, pure nullification. He could hardly remember who that man was now, so firmly had he placed walls around him. Trace sighed. It would be good to be happy again, to find a sense of purpose. He just didn't know where to begin.

He looked out over the hills, allowing his mind to wander. Begin at the beginning. That's what his dad always said when Trace brought him a problem with a new colt or a fidgety jumper. Find the parts you want to keep, and then work on discarding the ones you don't.

Trace nodded. Still good advice, he thought. The list would be long, but he would get started right away. The first step was to talk to his mom and apologize for what he had done to her. His dad, he thought, already understood. He stood up and dusted off the back of his jeans, and then whistled for Warrior. He swung easily onto the horse's back and headed for home.

He needed to talk to Lindsay too, he thought. He had assumed she was unscathed by it all, having gotten wrapped up in her marriage and child while he was away. But he saw now that he had left behind a huge burden -- to be a bridge between angry, silent parents. He would get his house in order. Then he would get started on the farm, starting with that broken fence over there.

After that, he would see about Sara.

CHAPTER 36

———————

"DAD WANTS TO TAKE A tour on the Gator. Anyone want to come?" Trace addressed the women who had congregated in the kitchen.

Dorothy brightened, pleased to be included in the invitation. She demurred, however, pointing out that the ride would be hot and bumpy. "Doesn't seem like a good idea for your dad either," she declared.

Sara and Lindsay shook their heads in unison. They were getting Daisy's riding lessons started, and had already promised her the afternoon.

"I'm up to my ears in papers here," Annie said. "And I have to head up to Leesburg later today. I guess I'll pass too."

Cobie hobbled out of the den. There was a distinct hitch in his gait, and he steadied himself at the kitchen counter. He had weakened recently, and though both he and Dorothy had said the doctor told them there were no changes, the rest of them watched his ragged breathing and unsteady gait with alarm.

"Dad, where's your cane?" Lindsay jumped up to retrieve it for him.

"I don't want that fool thing. I'll be sure to fall if I use that thing."

"It's okay," Trace told her. "Joe's brought the Gator to the back door." He took Cobie by the elbow to steady him. "We'll manage just fine." Annie saw Cobie start to protest. He hated it when they made a fuss over him. But this time he took Trace's arm and held it tightly.

"Are you sure he can handle that drive?" Sara whispered to Trace when he came back in from getting Cobie settled.

Trace opened the refrigerator and grabbed two bottles of water and an apple. "I'll take it slow. I don't know if it's a good idea, but he insisted."

Dorothy placed some cookies and a protein drink into a paper bag. "Here, take these too."

Trace kissed her on the cheek. "Thanks Ma."

"We're off," Trace called. The two men waved as they headed out toward the soybean field.

Cobie directed the trip, pointing first to a field near the edge of the road. He had told Trace that he wanted to see it all one more time. Trace hadn't told the girls what he said. But he understood.

"Let's ride the edge of that field and check the corn."

"Okay," Trace agreed, following the hard track around the perimeter.

"Did I ever tell you about the time your mother and I saw the bear in this field?"

"I'm not sure I remember that. I think I remember you warning me about seeing one sometime."

"You weren't very old, I guess. Maybe twelve or thirteen." Cobie remembered. "You ma liked to ride that old Quarter Horse, what was her name?"

"Misty?"

Cobie slapped his knee. "That's right. Misty. She never cared for the big Thoroughbreds. Could have had her pick but always preferred the smaller ones."

Trace smiled. "I remember. She'd have to trot like crazy to keep up with us."

"Anyway, we were riding right along this edge here. Just heading over to see Gladys, I think." Cobie gestured to the middle of the field. "And suddenly this big sow rises up from the corn, standing up to see who was passing by."

Trace chuckled. Cobie pointed left, and they followed the edge of the river, checking out the crops planted in the river bottom.

"Of course, the horses smelled her before they saw her, so they were getting skittish before we even knew why. I managed to stay in the tack, but Misty reared up and off your mother went." Cobie rubbed his jaw. "Pride more hurt than anything. But now we had a loose Quarter Horse and a nearby bear."

"What happened?"

"I went to reach down for her, thinking to pull her up with me. But my horse reared suddenly, and off I come too."

Trace laughed. "You came off?"

"Hmmm…" Cobie considered. "Maybe that's why I never told you the story. Didn't want to admit I came off."

"Ha!" Trace laughed. "You came off plenty of times."

"Not standing still, I didn't." Cobie said, smiling. "Anyway, both horses took off, and we limped back towards Gladys' house. A farm worker saw us and picked us up in his truck. Here," he pointed. "Let's head up to that high pasture up there."

Trace did as directed. "So what about the bear?"

"No one wanted to shoot her, so we just avoided the field until it got cut down." He thought back. "I think everyone just hoped she would move on. I guess she did." He put his hand on Trace's arm, indicating that he wanted to stop and inspect the cattle.

Cobie got out slowly, reaching for the handrail on the Gator to steady himself. He stood there for a number of minutes looking out over the field. Trace didn't rush him, and he didn't say anything. He knew his dad was saying goodbye.

When Cobie climbed back in, Trace got out the water and handed him a bottle. He broke open the bag of cookies and offered Cobie one, but he waved it off. "Protein drink?" Trace offered, chuckling.

"I hate them things. Taste like chalk." Cobie lifted the bottle and tapped it against Trace's. "Water'll do."

Cobie pointed straight ahead, and Trace drove further up the hill. Cobie picked up his story right back where he left off. "Your mom didn't ride too much after that. I think it spooked her good. She was always a pretty good rider, but on the timid side. You know that."

"Yes, she was always worried about us. She was proud of me, but I always knew she hated to come and watch me jump."

"Scared her right out of her mind. She'd put her hand over her eyes on every approach and only put them down when the crowd noise assured her you had gotten over." Cobie chuckled. "Course, that didn't keep her from filling every damn room with pictures of you jumping fences."

"I notice Lindsay doesn't ride much anymore."

"Well, Lindsay's a little more like your mom. Conservative. And more interested in being a mom than riding horses." Cobie considered. "I wish she would give Daisy her head a bit more. That little one has potential. But I guess that's not up to me now."

"Don't worry," Trace said. "Uncle Trace will see what he can do."

"I suppose your mom had a little more influence over Lindsay than she did over you."

Trace laughed out loud. "That's about right. I didn't give that poor woman a restful night's sleep since I started riding."

"Probably not before that either. You didn't sleep through the night until you were about three. At that point, you were running the farm from dusk to dawn, and you collapsed every night right there at the dinner table."

Trace smiled. "I remember getting carried off to bed. Sometimes mom would wake me up and toss me in the tub because she couldn't bear to put me to bed so dirty."

Cobie smiled and nodded.

"I remember you arguing about me," Trace said, his voice softening. "It seemed to be a running theme. She wanted to keep me under control. And you encouraged me to go out and seize the day. Hell, Lindsay and I were like wild Indians, going out and catching the horses, swinging right up on them in the field and tearing off bareback to go swim with them in the pond."

Cobie shook his head and laughed. "I don't know if your ma was more scared of you getting thrown or drowning."

Trace grew serious now. "I'm sorry I put you through so much. Mom too."

Cobie waved off his comment. "Life gives us lessons and we got to learn 'em. Why else are we here?"

"Still..."

Cobie interrupted him. "She's as fierce as a lion about you kids. Daisy too. Once she decides something, it's hard to get her to change her mind."

Trace raised his eyebrows. Cobie saw his expression but ignored it. "Anyway, you know you can trust her. She might be a bit cautious, but she always did right by me. And she'll do right by you too."

"I know, dad. And I'll take care of her. I'll help her with the farm as long as she needs me."

"Son..." Cobie put his hand on Trace's arm and motioned him to pull over. They had arrived at the high meadow just below Lost Legend. Trace stopped the Gator.

"All this here," Cobie said, sweeping his arm across the wide expanse of land. "All this here," he repeated. "It belongs to you."

"To me? But it should go to mom."

"What is your mom going to do with a big farm like this?"

"I just assumed...."

"Your mom wants her kitchen, her girlfriends. I wouldn't be surprised if she doesn't want to travel some, now that she gets to shed this old country boy."

"Dad..."

"Lindsay's got her place. We gave it to her as a wedding present, house and all. Don't you worry, she knows about this. This farm passed to my daddy from his daddy. And then to me from my daddy. And now I'm passing it to you."

Trace hung his head.

Cobie avoided looking at his son, instead gazing out over the land that had been in the Grainger family since time long gone. "Do with it what you will. But it's your responsibility now."

CHAPTER 37

Since overhearing the argument, Annie had felt conscious of intruding. She knew things were better between Cobie and Dorothy. They almost seemed light-hearted around each other now. Annie had promised herself to do more work on the book from home. There were tomatoes to tend and the other books to work on. The problem was that Cobie liked having her there so he could look over her shoulder as she worked. It made slow going, particularly if she was typing. But she shook off those thoughts. Elliot was taking care of the tomatoes, and she had a feeling she wouldn't have to be here much longer.

She would have understood if Dorothy preferred that she not be there. But the older woman had become markedly more tolerant of her presence, even taking an interest in the book. Trace had changed too, she noticed. Annie had been afraid for him, but since disappearing that day, he had taken on a more active role on the farm. Sara told her that he had a long heart-to-heart talk with Dorothy and that he had been spending more time over at Lindsay's house and with Daisy.

It was clear now that Cobie was slipping. He had allowed a recliner to be installed in the den so that he could rest comfortably without having to lie down. Cobie hated, above all things, to lie down. "Reminds me of dying," he had said. Now he sat for long hours in his recliner with a blanket wrapped around his legs. He slept there too.

The doctor had recommended that they talk to Hospice. Now that the stairs were no longer possible for him to navigate, he suggested that they put a hospital bed in the den. Cobie wouldn't hear of it, but Dorothy arranged that it be brought in anyway. It sat unused in the corner.

The friends who had beat a steady path to the door trickled to a stop now. Cobie didn't have the energy for much more than a short conversation before dozing off again. Annie and Elliot tried to stay in the background, fielding phone calls, carrying food and making coffee. Sara came too, sometimes sitting alone with Cobie for long periods, murmuring gossip about horses and riders as he held her hand and nodded. Dorothy declared that Cobie was never to be alone, so one of them sat with him twenty-four hours a day.

On a warm Sunday night, they were all in the den together. A steady wind was blowing, rattling the windows and carrying with it the threat of rain. Cobie looked around the room at the assembled faces. Dorothy sat nearest to him, holding his hand.

Elliot had gone to pick up a casserole that Red's wife had made. Annie slipped out of the room, thinking to check on him and give the family a little private time together. Cobie looked around. "Where's Annie?"

"I think she stepped into the kitchen," Lindsay said.

"Well, get her back in here. I'd like to talk to her."

Trace nodded, and went into the kitchen just as Elliot came in, laden with a hot dish, a bowl of salad and a foil wrapper containing fresh bread.

"Food's here," Trace called.

"Go eat," Cobie said gently. He reached out and touched Dorothy's face. "Annie will sit here with me for a while."

When everyone was gone, Cobie slumped back into his recliner. The strain of staying alive wore on him now. Annie could see the effort it was taking. She sat next to him in silence.

Cobie closed his eyes, and she thought he had gone to sleep. She reached out to hold his hand. He opened his eyes and looked at her. His blue eyes were shining.

"You know," he began. "When the fox sees us all comin', he knows he's the prey. He's no fool." Cobie's voice cracked, and Annie reached for his water glass, but he shook his head. "Scent is everything," he continued. "Of course, we humans can hardly smell a damned thing. We have no idea what's going on.

"Folks fret about the weather on the day of the hunt," his voice now thick and hoarse. "Mostly, they just want to pick out what clothes to wear." Annie smiled and squeezed his hand.

"Cold, wet, sunny, snow—everyone thinks they gotta be ready for what's coming. Doesn't really matter; we're going out anyway. But the huntsman, he's looking for clouds. He knows if you got clouds; there's a good chance of foxes."

Annie nodded.

"You recording this?"

She shook her head, smiling weakly. The wind gusted outside, shaking the windows again. Cobie turned his head to the window.

"That wind there is like an invisible river. It bounces, and it splits and it rises. That wind makes folks nervous; we can't make heads or tails out of what's going on around us." He turned his head back and met Annie's eyes. "The clouds are there to keep the wind down closer to the earth; it helps to move the scent along where the hounds can find it." Cobie breathed deeply, his throat catching for just a moment, making his breath ragged.

"That old fox understands the stake he has in the wind. He knows the hounds can follow his scent as long as he's running with the wind."

His voice grew softer. "Sometimes the only thing he can do is stop. If he ain't laying down any more tracks, the horses and the hounds and the people might just gallop right past him. Like he weren't there at all."

Cobie sighed deeply. "Us fool humans have no idea. Sun or clouds, we're always guessing our place in the world. We pick up ideas and then run off in the wrong direction. For us, the wind might as well always be blowing. We have no idea where we are."

"But the wind talks to that fox. And he knows what to do."

CHAPTER 38

———————

ELLIOT HELPED DOROTHY CLEAN THE kitchen and put away leftovers while Annie talked to Cobie. Trace walked Lindsay home.

When Elliot and Annie were leaving for home, Trace came in the back door. "Crazy weather out there." He looked back over his shoulder. "Threatening to storm. I see it up there over the mountains, but it may pass us by." He took off his hat. "Where's mom?"

"She's in with your dad."

Trace nodded. "I think I'll take the late shift. Let mom get some rest."

"Good idea," Elliot said. "She's looking pretty tired."

"I think she's trying to make the most of her time with him."

"Glad for it," Trace nodded. "But still, we have long days ahead."

Annie nodded, wondering if that was true.

Trace tiptoed into the room and placed his hand on Dorothy's shoulder. "Mom, I'll sit with Daddy."

"No," she said. "I thought I'd stay a while."

Cobie shook his head. "You already had a long day. Go take a little nap. I'm fine."

Dorothy reached out and stroked his rough face. "Are you sure?"

Cobie nodded. "Me and Trace will watch the storm come in."

Dorothy leaned over and kissed his forehead and smoothed his blanket. Then she straightened up and leaned against Trace for a moment. "Call if you need me."

"I will, I promise."

Dorothy slipped out of the room and shut the door gently. For a few moments, the men sat quietly.

"I'm glad they're gone," Cobie finally said.

"Who?"

"The girls," Cobie swallowed hard. "Hard to leave with them here."

Trace pressed his hand into his father's. "You leaving, daddy?"

"Soon, boy. Soon."

"I want you to ride Curly for me, once you are up there."

"Curly's not there, son. He's right here." Cobie took his hand and pressed it to his son's chest.

Trace bowed his head, tears filling his eyes and running down his face. He knew it was true. His dreams had told him that, but he had not been able to accept the horse's messages to him. He had continued to fight the dreams. He saw now that he had been fighting Curly all along. Recently the dreams had mellowed. Curly had come to him, healthy and whole, galloping, jumping, following him through the fields. Trace knew now that the horse was at peace, that Curly would stay there safe in his heart, if he could only accept him. Well, maybe he could.

He looked down at his dad to tell him he still wished Curly was in heaven, waiting for his dad to jump high fences again. He saw that Cobie had closed his eyes. Trace looked up as heat lightning flashed in the distance. He gently released his dad's hand and walked over to the window. He watched the trees swaying against the breeze and saw small droplets of water spattering the front porch.

Trace thought of the stories he had heard as a child, particularly the ghost stories Cobie had told around the campfire up at Lost Legend. Cobie had put up a real Native American tipi, complete with hand painting and long wooden poles for support, on top of the hill back then. It was huge; big enough for all of them to sleep comfortably. He had called it their summer vacation home.

Cobie told him that when someone died, their spirit would escape through the opening at the top of the tipi. It occurred to Trace now that a window might do just as well. He reached for the sash and threw open the window, inviting the storm into the room. The air was warm; the breeze scattered and disorganized. The rain would not amount to much, he thought. The storm was just a lot of bluster.

He sat back down next to Cobie. "Go ahead, daddy. Now's your chance." He felt his dad's hand go limp. Trace watched him closely. He saw Cobie's jaw go slack, and his breathing become shallow. Soon he realized that Cobie had drifted off to sleep. He put his head down on the arm of the chair and stayed there with him all night long.

When Dorothy tiptoed into the den before 5, she went straight to the open window, thinking to close it. The clouds were passing quickly now. Dorothy watched the wind push them across the sky, revealing pockets of brilliant blue in their place. A breeze still blustered among the branches, bouncing across the grass and rustling the rosebushes. It occurred to her that the birds singing in the boxwoods might be a welcome sound to Cobie. She left the window open, and walked over to touch his sleeping head. She found him peaceful and still, one hand still holding Trace's, the other hand resting on the young man's head. She put her hand on Trace's back. He woke and lifted his head.

Dorothy quietly reached for the blanket to tuck it closer around Cobie. His eyes flickered open, taking in her face and then Trace's. His brilliant blue eyes shimmered now, bright with expectation.

"Gone home," he whispered. And then he slipped out with the clouds on that river of wind.

CHAPTER 39

———

THE THREE DAYS LEADING UP to Cobie's funeral were a blur of faces. Old friends flooded through the house to pay their condolences. The older men formed the nucleus of the group, positioning themselves on the back porch, their wives busying themselves in the kitchen. The men tried to keep Trace close by, as if to shield him from the onslaught of neighbors, students and friends that streamed through the door. But Trace refused to let Dorothy and Lindsay bear the burden alone, manfully standing in attendance for everyone that came through the door.

The people who came now presumed a strong enough acquaintance to stop by the house at all hours. Annie knew that the night of the wake would be even worse. And Grace Leighton, Trinity Episcopal Church's pastor, had been warned to expect attendance for the funeral to be in the hundreds.

Barrett came in carrying a scarlet hunt coat. He handed it to Dorothy. "For Cobie to be buried in," he said.

"Oh, but he has his own scarlet coat," Dorothy replied. "I was going to bring it to the funeral home later today."

Barrett rolled his eyes. "When's the last time you took a look at that coat, Dorothy? The man nearly ran it to bare threads. He can't be buried in that."

"Don't you think that's just what he'd want? Cobie was never one for new things." In spite of all his connections in the equine world, even the saddle he used was almost forty years old. Dorothy peered up at Trace, who had seen Barrett arrive.

Trace took the hanger from Barrett's hand and held it up. "It's a beauty," he said, fingering the gold buttons that he knew cost at least $50 each, all by themselves. "It's a shame to bury it." He handed the coat back to Barrett. "I think Ma's right. I think daddy would want the old one."

"I thought you might want to keep that one for yourself, Trace," Barrett replied. "That jacket has seen a lot. I know it won't fit, but it's a nice keepsake." He winked at Dorothy. "Seems like Cobie might want to meet his Maker in a decent coat."

Annie came around with a tray of brownies. Trace caught her eye and waved her over. He held up the coat. "What do you think? Should daddy wear his old coat or this new one?"

"Oh no, I'm not getting involved with that." Annie offered up the tray. Barrett accepted a brownie.

"You decide, Trace," Dorothy said. "Either way is fine with me."

Trace sighed. "Tell you what. I'll take this one upstairs for now. I'll decide later this afternoon, I promise."

That much decided; Trace went off with the coat and then back to his duties at the door. Annie and Elliot made coffee, served food and gently moved people on when they saw that Dorothy was wearing out.

"I have an idea," Annie said to Sara as she walked around picking up coffee cups and discarded napkins. "What if we have the wake in the barn? We could set up a food table and a bar, and people could wander in and out. We could string up lights if you think it's too dark."

"That's a great idea," Sara agreed.

"I'll get Elliot on it. I think he would like a project. Maybe Joe can help him."

Sara nodded. "I'll just make sure it's okay with Lindsay and Trace, but I think they'll agree." She looked around at the scattered clusters of people. "Is it supposed to be like this?"

Annie shook her head, smiling. "Cobie had a lot of best friends." She paused, considering. "What is a wake, anyway?"

"I think the point is to get drunk and tell stories."

Annie took in the faces of the assembled group. People milled around the living room, the kitchen and the back yard. Only the den had been closed and declared off-limits. Her eyes went to the men on the back porch. "They've been doing that for months."

Sara laughed. "Yeah, well the wake will be a more concentrated version." She wiggled her eyebrows. "Get your tapes ready."

"Sara! I'm not taping Cobie's wake!"

"Well, maybe not. But keep your ears open. I guarantee you the stories are going to fly."

"Honestly, I'm not really sure how funerals are supposed to work," Annie said, considering. The only funerals she had ever attended were small services, and her parents' deaths had been quiet affairs. "Especially one like this."

Sara chuckled, handing her another tray of brownies. "I guess we'll find out."

Annie looked at her watch. "It's after four o'clock. I'll try to sell these brownies, but I would say some of them are thinking about drinks right now."

Sara shook her head and turned to Elliot. "Go see about them, would you?"

———◆———

Wednesday morning dawned bright and clear. The weekend storm had chased away the heat, tamping down the humidity that plagued central Virginia this time of year. It was shaping up to be a blue bird day, as Cobie had always referred to perfect weather days. Trace and Lindsay had done their best to spread the word that Wednesday was not a day for calling at the house, telling everyone that they would see them in the evening for the wake.

Annie and Elliot worked out in the barn all day, stringing lights and setting up tables. Joe swept the barn clean. Every stall had been emptied and washed down. Dorothy had called the caterer in Orange to bring a spread of barbecue, and she and Trace stopped by the funeral home and church for last-minute arrangements. Lindsay and Sara went off to Charlottesville to buy beer and wine.

"Use these checkered tablecloths on the round tables," Annie directed as she hauled things out of the Jeep. "We can use these other cloths on the picnic tables."

"Where'd you get all this stuff?" Joe asked.

"Years of entertaining," she replied.

She handed him a couple of folding chairs, gesturing to the lawn on the western side of the barn. "We don't have enough seats for everyone, but most people will just mill around. As long as we have chairs for the older folks."

"I'm setting up a bonfire back there," Elliot pointed behind the barn. "Joe just went down with the Gator to get a pile of firewood. And I'll drag over the Adirondack chairs and porch rockers."

"Perfect."

Everything was set up by three o'clock, and they made their way back to the house for showers. Annie and Elliot went to Lindsay's house to clean up. They all agreed to meet by 5 to have a quiet drink before the onslaught began.

When Annie got to the big farmhouse, clean and refreshed, Dorothy was waiting on the back porch. She gestured to the chair next to hers, inviting Annie to take a seat.

"Where are the others?" Dorothy said.

"Trace is pushing Daisy on the swing while Lindsay gets ready. I think Elliot went down to the barn to meet the caterers. So it looks like it's just you and me for a few minutes."

"I'm glad. I had hoped we could talk." She shook her head. "These last few days…"

"I know. How are you doing?"

Dorothy smiled. "I'm okay. I'm better than I expected to be. It may sound odd, but in a way it's a luxury to know you have several months to say goodbye. The end comes a little easier."

She gestured to the pitcher on the table. "Lemonade? Or something stronger?" she offered.

Annie reached for the pitcher to help herself. "Definitely lemonade," she said. "I think I need to keep my wits about me tonight."

"Me too." Dorothy sipped her lemonade. "I'm beginning to think Trace has a point about drinking."

"Oh, I'm not sure he's trying to make a point."

"Maybe not," Dorothy said. "But there is something to be said for facing everything straight on, and not relying on 'liquid courage' to get through the day." She shrugged. "I don't imagine I'll be giving up my nightly bourbon, but I think I understand."

Annie looked at Dorothy thoughtfully. "How are you feeling about Trace these days? I know you were worried when he got home. What do you think now?"

Dorothy smiled. "I see a young man who came through a tough situation. Not unscathed, of course. But wiser. Stronger. Kinder, if that is possible." She shook her head. "He took care of Cobie like no nurse would ever have been able to. You didn't see the things he did. He wanted his dad's dignity intact, and he saw to it until the very end."

Annie nodded thoughtfully. "He seems a remarkable young man."

"So like his daddy." She paused and chuckled. "Taller of course. Took after my side of the family for size."

"I see he's riding again." Annie had noticed Trace patrolling the fields, on Warrior or one of the other horses.

"Yes, he said it was a stupid notion, refusing to get close to another horse. It was just part of shutting down anything that could hurt."

Annie nodded.

"He said it wasn't practical anyway. He's got to ride those fences and check on things. He could drive the old truck or the Gator, but he'd much rather be on a horse."

"I'm so glad," Annie said.

"It does my heart good to see him on his Daddy's horse."

"I'm sure it does," Annie responded quietly. "Do you know what Trace is going to do, I mean, now that Cobie is gone?"

Dorothy sighed. "I was going to ask you the same thing."

Annie chuckled. "How would I know?"

"Oh, don't think I can't see the influence you have around here these days. Cobie...well, Cobie couldn't do without you these last months."

"Dorothy..."

She waved her hand. "No, it's okay. It's good. I have to admit; I was a little jealous at first." She sighed. "I wasted a lot of years being jealous of just about every pair of skinny breeches that came around." She looked thoughtfully at Annie. "But you were different. You hadn't been hanging around. Cobie didn't even know you that well." She put her hand to her mouth. "That's not what I meant. I know Cobie knew you from the hunts."

"It's okay." Annie said. "You're right. I wasn't around much. Cobie knew Elliot, of course. But I have been pretty scarce over the years."

"Well, anyway," Dorothy went on. "I just want you to know how grateful I am. Cobie and I, well, let's just say we had our problems. But in the end, we made our peace with each other, our son is home and the world was set right before he left us." She looked into Annie's eyes. "And I think you had a big hand in that."

"Me!" Annie shook her head. "I didn't do anything."

"Oh, you did more than you know." She gestured to the den. "Those tapes of yours. They gave Cobie the chance to talk, to work things out for himself." Dorothy stood up and looked out the window. "I mean, who did he have to talk to? Not me. Not Lindsay. And he wasn't going to open his heart to his cronies."

Annie hung her head, blinking back her tears.

"I was happy to..."

"I know. The book," Dorothy said. "And if a book comes of it, well, that would be fine. The scholarship too. But the real value," she choked back tears. "The real value..."

Annie stood up and crossed to Dorothy and put her arms around her. "I know."

"He wanted to leave something behind. He said it was for the kids, I know. For the future of foxhunting." Dorothy's voice softened. "But he was making those tapes for Trace. He didn't think he was going to see him again." She shook her head. "I don't know why he wouldn't just reach out to Trace. Lindsay and I, Sara too, tried and tried, but I think it was his daddy he wanted to hear from."

"But Cobie did call him," Annie said gently.

Dorothy searched Annie's face. "But, I thought…he always said it was up to Trace to come back if he wanted. He said he wasn't doing it for him…" She shook her head. "No, I think you're mistaken."

"I heard the call myself. It's on one of the early tapes."

Dorothy sat down heavily. "Well, I'll be. "She sighed and looked up at the sky. "Well, Cobie, check off another sin that I laid at your feet." Dorothy broke down crying again. "I was so foolish."

"You went through a lot."

She looked at Annie and smiled. "He was smart enough to ask for help. And it came in the form of you."

Annie hugged her, tears flowing now.

"And I stupidly went through it alone. I didn't want help. It felt good to hurt, I think. I couldn't accept…" She stopped in mid-sentence, and her voice caught. "Oh my," she said as the realization lit up her face. "Just like Trace."

Annie squeezed her shoulder. "I guess he got more than his height from you."

Dorothy smiled, blinking back her tears. "I guess he did."

Dorothy and Annie sat back. They did not speak for several minutes. Then Dorothy said, "So what are we going to do about him and Sara?"

Annie laughed softly. "I'm afraid we're going to have to leave that in his hands."

Dorothy thought for a moment. "I guess so," she said reluctantly. "But it may be safer in Sara's hands."

CHAPTER 40

———

THE EVENING BEGAN QUIETLY. THE elderly members of the church led the
way. Old people seem to arrive promptly to these things, Annie thought.
Maybe it's just the hours they keep. Or maybe they want it known that
they had done their duty to the deceased, to ensure good attendance
when their own time came. Since there was no funeral home to go to,
their instincts told them to go to the front door of the house. Annie
stationed herself on the front porch and steered them, somewhat confused, toward the barn.

Dorothy met each person and accepted their quiet condolences and
kind thoughts before directing them to the food and the tables. Cobie
had been a deacon at the church, so a number of the old men claimed a
special acquaintance with him. Elliot positioned himself near the drinks
table so he could tend to the bar. For the first hour, he only poured lemonade and ladled punch. With their obligation to the family fulfilled,
the old folks sat together somewhat stiffly at the outdoor tables, nibbling
sandwiches and peering around at the horses. Most of them had not
been to the farm before, and it occurred to Annie that this was not quite
what they were expecting when they came to make their call.

Next came the students, some alone and some with their parents.
Elliot pointed out Andrew and Leigh Landers and their daughter Fiona.
Annie didn't recognize the parents, but she was pretty sure she had seen
the exuberant teenager out in the field. Cobie had coached advanced
jumpers for many years, always at Sara's request. He had trusted her to

only pass on the truly talented ones. Fiona Landers was one of them. Annie saw Fiona's eyes shimmer with tears as she greeted Sara and Dorothy.

"I'll miss him so much," Fiona said to Sara. "Nobody got so much out of me and Plato, ever. I'll never forget when I won the Children's North American Field Hunter Championships with him." She looked over at the tall man chatting with a group of young people. "Is that him?" she whispered.

"Yes, that's Trace. You should remember him from the hunt. You were little, I know, but he was there then."

"I'm not sure I would have recognized him, and he sure wouldn't recognize me without braces and pigtails." She nudged her. "Introduce me. Is he taking any students?"

Sara rolled her eyes. "Fiona, introduce yourself, or have your mom do it." She turned to walk away. "And for goodness sake, don't mention training. He's here to be with his family."

Sara walked away, taking a look back over her shoulder at the group surrounding Trace. She noticed that some of the other former students remembered Trace too, and seemed surprised to see him, trying in vain to bridge the intervening years with awkward chat. Sara wondered how many were hoping to learn whether he would be taking his father's place as a trainer.

Trace's strategy, Annie noticed, was to act as though those years had never happened, taking up with people he knew right where they had left off, brushing away any reference to the accident or his years in Kentucky. He fared better with the people he had not met. They merely registered surprise at not knowing about Cobie's son, and he smoothly maneuvered them into talking about their relationship with his dad.

By seven o'clock, the place was crowded with people from every walk of life, young and old, farmhand and CEO. Each one of them had a story about Cobie and how he had touched them. It seemed that to meet him was to become his friend. Annie thought at this point she knew much of what there was to know about him, but she found herself surprised at every turn.

She met a sincere young woman who worked with Cobie to raise funds for retired racehorses. Another woman, the widow of a jockey who Cobie had ridden with, told her how Cobie sent them money every month while her husband was recovering from a back injury that kept him off the track. Still another person, a farm worker from Gladys' place, told of Cobie coming to bail him out of jail after he went on a bender. Cobie then went over and asked Gladys if he could borrow him for a while, so he could complete detox without her being the wiser. Now he was ten years sober, and he still had his job because of Cobie.

Everyone from the Meryton Hunt Club was there. Annie realized she didn't recognize many of them without their tweeds and boots. Cobie's standard bearers came in force but were surprisingly subdued. The mass of people seemed to diminish the force of their presence. She found it hard to believe that they had talked themselves out, but maybe they were glad for others to take over the storytelling now. They looked comfortable sipping their beers and chatting with their many friends and acquaintances.

The early guests came and went quickly, and now the crowd was down to a hundred or so of their closest friends. Annie said hi to Kiernan and Alexis Lynch, the red-headed twins from Ireland who had come to study at UVA. They were on the school's polo team, and rode with the hunt as often as they could. "Have you seen Trace?" Kiernan asked.

Annie looked around. "Over there," she pointed to where a clutch of men stood near the front paddock.

Kiernan nodded. "Thanks." Annie saw her go and whisper something to Trace, and then nodded and walked over to her car. Annie saw her take out two cases. One was fiddle-shaped, the other she wasn't sure. Alexis opened her case, and Annie saw that it was a flute. Kiernan and her sister leaned together, quietly tuning the instruments. Then they began to play a soft Irish ballad, strings blending seamlessly with the haunting sound of the flute. People heard the girls and turned to listen.

They played another ballad, this one a sad love song called "Donegal Rain."

When they finished the tune, Alexis nodded to Trace. They had only struck the first chords when Annie started to smile. She knew this one. It was "The Ballad of the Foxhunter." She remembered hearing the Celtic band 'Cherish the Ladies' sing it at Wolf Trap. She still had the CD that she had gotten at the concert. She leaned against the barn to listen. The girls played it slowly, not at the brisk pace that Annie thought she had remembered. Kiernan's plaintive voice opened over the strings.

"Lay me in a cushioned chair. Carry me, ye four…"

She saw Barrett walk up to Dorothy and tap her on the shoulder. He bowed slightly, clearly asking her to dance. Dorothy looked around awkwardly at first but then accepted his hand.

"To stable and to kennel go, bring what there is to bring…."

The moon illuminated a wide swath in the middle of the yard, and white lights twinkled from the big oak that hung over it. Barrett was a good dancer, and the couple looked beautiful in each other's arms. Annie wondered what to make of the gesture.

"Put the chair upon the grass, bring Roddy and his hounds…."

Just then Archie came over and cut in, taking Dorothy smoothly in the next beat as Barrett stepped away.

"Huntsman, come blow the horn. Make the hills reply…"

Elliot slipped beside Annie and squeezed her hand. It was pure magic, this impromptu ritual. The men in Dorothy's life could not have put it into words. It was their way of letting her know that they would always be there for her.

Gray took his turn, as well as Monty and Charlie. Even Red came forward, red-faced and awkward. Then Trace came forward to release him and claim his mother for himself.

"I cannot blow my horn, but only weep and sigh."

The girls lingered now over the final refrain, Alexis stretching the final flute notes and releasing them mournfully into the air. Trace turned his mother in a wide circle. Then he leaned down and kissed her hand.

The final chord hung in the air, mixing with the singing of crickets in the trees above, before evaporating into the soft night. Dorothy looked around, slightly embarrassed by the applause. She made a small curtsy which was met with more approving applause. She accepted kisses from each man and spoke her thanks in low whispers to each one. Then she excused herself and said good night. Lindsay walked her to the house, knowing that she must be overwhelmed with this outpouring of affection. Annie knew that Dorothy often felt that she spun in the outer orbit of Cobie's world. It must have been gratifying to her to know that she had a piece of their hearts too.

Some people gravitated to the bonfire while others started to say their goodbyes. Annie thought it was safe to start picking up plates and bottles, but she found that Joe and his family had been quietly keeping up with that task throughout the evening. There wasn't a lot to do. She surveyed the food table, happy to see that almost everything had been eaten. Foil trays could go straight into the trash. She sighed with relief. She and Elliot could be home before midnight, she thought. That was good. Tomorrow was going to be another big day.

Annie went down to the bonfire to find Elliot and make their departure. Kiernan had brought her fiddle to the fire, and the songs now took on a rowdier tone as people started to sing along. Annie noticed that Fiona Landers was flirting with Davis, who had clearly had a few more beers than were good for him. She nodded to Gray. "Looks like your boy may need a ride home."

Gray cast his eye over to the youngster, his jaw set in a disapproving frown. "I'll take care of it."

Elliot came over and put his arm around her waist. "I think we'd better get out of here before they start singing 'Danny Boy'."

"Wise choice," Gray stood and held out his hand to help Betsy up from her chair. "I think it may be just around the corner."

"Have you seen Trace and Sara? We wanted to say goodbye."

"Sara may have gone up to the house," Betsy said. "I saw her carrying Daisy up there earlier."

"I'll just go see if I can find her," Annie said to Elliot. "Keep an eye out for Trace."

Annie decided to walk through the deserted barn and snap off a few lights. As she exited the other side, she caught sight of Trace. He was standing under the big branch of the big oak tree; his shadow just illuminated by the twinkling lights. She started to call out to him but caught herself. She realized he was not alone.

Annie backed quietly into the shadow of the barn. But she couldn't resist just one more peek. There was Trace; his arm wrapped around Sara's tiny waist, leaning in for a kiss.

CHAPTER 41

"LET'S STOP AT THE BARN before the funeral," Annie said to Elliot as they dressed. "Gray and Betsy are getting Warrior ready and I want to be there."

"Are horses generally invited to funerals?" Elliot teased, pulling apart the knot on his tie and starting again.

"They are when it's Cobie Grainger's funeral. I expect there will be hounds too."

"Seriously?" Elliot turned to her for inspection. Annie reached up to straighten the tie and smooth down his collar.

"This is a huntsman's funeral we're talking about."

Annie and Elliot got to the barn just past 10:15. The family had already left to meet with the pastor and say their goodbyes in private. They found Gray and Betsy in the barn with Warrior. He had already had a bath. His white coat gleamed. Betsy was on a footstool braiding his mane, and Gray was putting the finishing touches on the tack.

"How did you do that?" Annie said, looking approvingly at the horse.

"Do what?"

"How did you get him so white? I have tried, but he always seems to be the color they call "Virginia chestnut."

"What's that?" Betsy asked, climbing down from the footstool and standing back to admire her work.

"The color that a white horse gets by rolling in good Virginia clay."

Gray laughed. "I'll give you my secret formula sometime." He went back to his work. "Annie, would you go get me the neat's-foot oil underneath the sink in the tack room?" He put down the sponge he was holding and reached for a cloth. "I had thought to knock a bit of mud off this saddle, but it's fairly clean. Still," he said, pointing to the knee roll of the saddle he was working on, "I swear Cobie nearly wore this leather through. I'm having a devil of a time making it look good."

Annie chuckled. "He hated to hunt in anything else."

Gray shook his head. "Cobie didn't like to waste anything."

"That's a fact. Here, let me do that." Annie reached for the cloth.

"Okay, I'll just put the finishing touches on the old man." Gray looked on the grooming shelf. "I don't see the hoof oil."

"Right there," Annie said. "In the butter tub."

"This?" Gray held up an ancient little bucket. He opened it and sniffed. "Where did he get this?"

"Cobie told me he always makes his own hoof oil. Pine tar and shortening."

"Good lord." Gray reached into the tub and fished out a small brush. He swabbed Warrior's hooves. "Goes on nicely." He stood up and admired the horse. "Nice looking fella, you are."

Annie patted Warrior on the neck, slipping a peppermint from her pocket. "You need fresh breath today," she whispered to him.

"Let's get him on the trailer," Betsy said, slipping the halter over his head. She looked at her watch. "We need to get to the church. It's almost 10:30."

Annie helped load Warrior, stopping to reach in and pat the three hounds that would also be in attendance. "Let's see," she said. "Dandy. Winston. Lotus." She turned to Gray for confirmation.

He smiled and nodded. "Not bad."

"Why these three?"

"Dandy because he was always Cobie's favorite. He stayed with the bitch all night when that litter was born. She got sick, and he hand-fed that puppy himself. Always had a watchful eye for him from the day the dog was entered." Gray reach in and fondled Winston's head. "Winston is the old warrior. He's retired, but would go out to the field to this day if we let him. Seemed right that he should be here." He nodded to Lotus. "And Lotus there. I chose her because she'll be sociable to the guests." Gray winked. "Our goodwill ambassador."

He closed the trailer and patted it for good measure. "Okay, let's get on with it."

The church parking lot was filling with people when they pulled in. Gray pulled the trailer behind the church. Annie and Elliot swung around, taking a distant spot. "I'll just leave the last closer spots for the late arrivals," Elliot said. "They'll be in a hurry."

They walked to the door of the church and saw that it was nearly full. "I don't see a place to sit," she whispered. She knew that Gray and Betsy had a spot reserved for them.

"Sorry," said Gray as they walked by.

"No problem," said Elliot. "Look, they put chairs outside for the overflow."

"Speakers too, at each window. That was thoughtful of Grace," Annie observed. "This will be fine. We can hear everything and stay out of the way."

As she was sitting down, she saw Betsy wave them in. "Dorothy wants you to come in."

"But there aren't any seats."

Betsy looked around. "I think you're right. But at least come and see Cobie before the service starts."

"Isn't it supposed to be closed by now?"

Betsy shrugged. "No visitation at the funeral home, so I guess this is what they decided."

Annie swallowed hard and nodded. She had always dreaded open caskets. She just couldn't see the point of remembering someone this way when she could hold the memory of them alive and vibrant. But she walked to the casket as she was told. When she saw Cobie, she had to smile. Trace had chosen Cobie's old coat. One lapel was torn, and the collar was frayed and worn. The vibrant scarlet was a soft shade of red. Not pink exactly, as the jackets were sometimes called, but worn and buffed to a soft patina. Trace had opted for a new white shirt, however, and the white stock tie was meticulously tied, a long stick pin holding it in place. Someone had pinned a snippet of blue cardinal flower onto the lapel. Annie wondered what Cobie would have thought of that, a decidedly out-of-regulation adornment for a huntsman.

In spite of herself, she reached for his hand. His face, artificially smoothed now by the skill of the mortician, seemed serious and statesman-like, so unlike the real Cobie. She was especially glad now for the ragged coat. It put an authentic stamp on him, and she was sure that it would make him happy to appear at the gates of heaven thus outfitted. Her throat caught, but found that she couldn't cry. In fact, she hadn't cried at all, through the final days or even when news reached them that Cobie was gone.

Annie stepped back as an attendant approached to close the casket. The air seemed to go out of the room for a moment, and Annie reached blindly for Elliot's hand to steady herself. Elliot guided her away from the casket, but Annie paused to squeeze Dorothy's shoulder as they passed. "We will see you later," she whispered. Dorothy nodded.

"It's better this way," Annie said to Elliot as they reached the back of the church. "We'll be outside to tend the horse and hounds when the service is over." Before they turned to leave, she looked around at the church. Every possible space was taken. People were standing three to an aisle. The choir loft was full too. In the July heat, the temperature was already stifling. Annie looked at the altar, where large pictures of Cobie dominated the sea of flower arrangements. There was a photo of Cobie jumping a fence, and another of him leaning against a rail, watching a Thoroughbred gallop past.

"Look," Annie whispered, nudging Elliot. She gestured to a shot of Cobie and Gray, both on horseback. They were each pointing in opposite directions. It was a comical sight for those who understood the vagaries of foxhunting. "I remember that day," she said. "They were arguing about where to start the field." Elliot nodded.

"Isn't that your shot?"

"Yes," Elliot whispered. "Trace asked me for it a week or two ago. I think he and Cobie chose these pictures together."

Annie and Elliot made their way outside; this time skipping the chairs and opting to stand under the enormous tulip poplar that overshadowed the churchyard. They could hear the speakers clearly there. A little breeze rippled through the leaves. It was far more comfortable out here too, she thought, than in the stifling church.

The service was a traditional one, with readings from the Book of Common Prayer, the singing of "Amazing Grace," and the requisite eulogy. This was delivered by Barrett, and in typical grand style, he had the crowd laughing and weeping. Just as he finished, everyone's heads turned to the windows. As if on cue, the hounds had begun a mournful howl. A chill rippled over Annie's skin, and she unconsciously rubbed her arms to tame the goose bumps. In the still summer heat, the hounds' cry was haunting.

Grace Leighton paused at the lectern, allowing the hounds to say their final goodbye. The young pastor, who had come to the church only a few years before, had quickly adjusted to her duties with the hunters. She had learned to appreciate the annual Blessing of the Hounds and the prayers for safe sport.

"When the field is called in," she said now. "The huntsman goes reluctantly, never one to leave before his time. Our brother Jacob heard the call home, and he followed it." She paused and nodded to Barrett. "I won't try to follow Barrett's illustrious oratory," she smiled, "nor the eloquence of the hounds. So please allow me to read a poem written by William Ogilvie in the 1930s."

She began.

"The hoofs of the horses! Oh witching and sweet
Is the music earth steals from the iron-shod feet;
No whisper of lover, no trilling of bird
Can stir me as hoofs of the horses have stirred.

They spurn disappointment and trample despair,
And drown with their drum-beats the challenge of care;
With scarlet and silk for their banners above,
They are swifter than Fortune and sweeter than Love.

On the wings of the morning they gather and fly,
In the hush of the night-time I hear them go by-
The horses of memory all thundering through
With flashing white fetlocks all wet with the dew.

When you lay me to slumber no spot you can choose
But will ring to the rhythm of galloping shoes,
And under the daisies no grave be so deep
But the hoofs of the horses shall sound in my sleep."

Annie felt her throat tighten. She turned to whisper to Elliot, but he had already turned at the sound of the horses. Rounding the corner of the church was a black caisson pulled by two black horses. The driver, wearing a black frock coat, turned the pair and stopped at the door of the church. Soon, the pallbearers, each of them wearing the traditional scarlet coat, carried out the closed casket. They slipped it onto the caisson. The driver made a wide turn around the churchyard and then waited for the church to empty. Gray appeared leading Warrior, Cobie's worn boots reversed in the stirrups. The three hounds walked at Warrior's heels. Gray fell in behind the caisson as it proceeded to the cemetery.

A car had been waiting for the family, but Trace waved the driver off. He took Dorothy's hand and followed Gray and Warrior on foot. The crowd followed; a long, winding procession down the hill and across the park. The cemetery sat atop a small rise beside the church, the soft, rounded mountains of the Blue Ridge etching the horizon. It was a good place for Cobie, Annie thought.

Gray paused with the horse at the entrance to the cemetery. The caisson went on, followed now by the three hounds. It followed the trail leading through the gravestones and then across the field to the top of the hill. There it paused, a sober silhouette of horses, carriage and hounds carved into the lush vista of the Virginia landscape. The crowd fell into a moment of silence as the land said its last goodbye to its fallen brother.

Blood pulsed in Annie's head; it felt to her that everyone's hearts were beating together. She looked around at the crowd of people. These hearts, she thought. The hearts of friends and animals past. The heart of the earth. The heart of Cobie himself. She felt the sun as she had never felt it before, embracing her flesh with its warmth. She felt the wind, feathering gently across her skin. The mountains in clear relief on the edge of her vision seemed to spread and blend with the unknown vistas that spread behind them, on and on without end. Annie trembled, a long unknown presence suddenly filling her from head to toe. She felt filled with light.

When the caisson moved to complete its circuit to the gravesite, Annie gasped. She hadn't realized she was holding her breath until that very moment. Elliot reached toward her, and she fumbled to take his arm. She shook her head to warn off his questioning look, and took a deep breath to regain her equilibrium.

At graveside, the prayers were said. One by one, Cobie's friends stepped forward and shoveled a little dirt into the hole. The air was thick and silent, the only sound the rasp of the shovel as it struck the sand. Annie tried to tame her wandering mind. But she wasn't sure which world she was in, so blurred was the distinction between this one and the next.

Her reverie was broken by the sound of Archie's voice. His deep voice resonated with the part of her mind that belonged to the here and now. She turned to listen. He spoke the words of the chorus from "The Ballad of the Foxhunter."

"Huntsman blow the horn
Come make the hills reply
Loosen on the morn
A gay and wandering cry
Roddy blow the horn
Come make the hills reply
I cannot blow my horn
But only weep and sigh"

Then the haunting sound of the huntsman's silver horn filled the air. Gray blew the call for the end of the day. The long extravagant notes floated across the Virginia hillside, sweeping up on a breeze of their own making. So mournful and deep was the sound, Annie felt the hairs on her arm stand on end. Elliot put his arm around her as Gray continued to blow the final call for home for his fallen friend.

The mourners streamed back down the hill to the church hall where they would be met with a reception organized by the church's women's group. Annie and Elliot lingered behind, waiting for the crowd to clear. Truth be told; Annie wasn't sure she could stand. They said good-bye to Lindsay and John as they passed, Daisy clinging tightly on her father's shoulder.

Annie and Elliot had already decided not to stay for the reception. It had been a long few weeks. She knew that it would be another long day for Dorothy, Trace and Lindsay, with a number of out-of-town relatives to entertain tonight. But she thought that a family evening was long overdue for them.

"Annie." She turned at the sound of her name. Trace was walking toward her with Warrior.

"Would you like us to take him back to the trailer?" Annie asked.

"If you would," he said. "I want to walk back with Mom."

Annie stood up on trembling legs and accepted the reins from him. "Glad to," Annie said.

Trace turned to Dorothy. "Mom? You ready?"

Dorothy turned from the grave and nodded. Then she walked up to join them. She smiled at Annie.

"You must be tired," Annie said.

"I'll have plenty of time to be tired tomorrow." She paused and looked at Trace. "Did you tell her?"

"I wasn't sure this was the time."

"Oh, I think it's the perfect time," said Dorothy.

Annie looked from Dorothy to Trace and back again.

"You see, Warrior here has just done his last job for my dad," Trace began. "Daddy wanted to make sure he was passed on to the right person, so maybe it's best to tell you right here where he can see."

"I don't understand." Annie felt Elliot's hand close around her waist.

Trace stepped forward and rested his hand on Warrior's neck. "Daddy said he belongs to you now."

Annie pressed the reins back toward Trace. "No, I couldn't. He's Cobie's horse. He's...your horse, Trace."

"I've got a farm full of horses, and Daddy said the only good job for Warrior now is to take you out foxhunting."

"Hunting," whispered Annie, her voice cracking.

"Daddy expects you in the hunt field come fall, and he wanted to make sure Warrior is there to take care of you."

Dorothy reached out her hand, smiling. "Please take him, Annie. It was Cobie's last request. He said he belongs to you." She saw the horse lean his big head into Annie's, nuzzling her pocket in search of a peppermint. "I can see that it's true."

Annie took the reins back from Trace. She was so full of emotion; she thought her heart might burst. How had she gotten here? It was all just too much. She looked from Trace to Dorothy, and then to Elliot. He smiled and nodded. Then she threw her arms around Warrior's big neck and at last she wept.

———

CHAPTER 42

ANNIE POURED HER COFFEE AND then reached over to top off Elliot's cup. "Did you see Sara at the funeral?"

Elliot nodded, peering over his newspaper. "She was with Rebecca and some of the students." He folded the paper and put it down. "Why?"

Annie shrugged. "Just wondering. I never saw her with Trace or the family."

It had been a little over a week since the funeral, and she hadn't talked to anyone. It felt odd, like she was out of the loop. But she felt the need for some space and she imagined everyone else did too. And she really needed to get her head back into her own life. The tomatoes were ripening. She picked them as they were ready, and her counter was almost completely covered with them.

Elliot shrugged. "Well, there were a lot of people there. She probably felt like we do. Time to back off and give them a little space."

"Do you think Sara falls into the same category we do?"

Elliot frowned as he stirred sugar into his coffee. "What do you mean?"

"Well, with Trace and all. She was almost family."

"That's old news," Elliot said. "That ended a long time ago."

"Well, actually...."

"What?" Elliot raised his eyebrows. He was accustomed to Annie's conspiracy theories, especially when matchmaking was involved.

"I didn't tell you when it happened, things have been so busy." Annie paused to think about what she had seen. "But I saw Trace and Sara kissing under the big tree out by the barn the night of the wake."

"No kidding," he mused. "I hadn't seen any sign of that. But then..." He tilted his head at her. "I don't watch as closely as you do."

"Or talk to anyone either," Annie said. "Sara tells me that Trace calls her a lot. And Dorothy has been hoping they would get back together."

"Well, none of our business." Elliot picked up his paper again.

"Don't you think it was odd that we didn't see them together at the funeral, given the...kiss?"

Elliot sighed and put the paper down again. "Look, maybe it was just a beer-driven moment. Maybe it was awkward after. Maybe...I don't know. Maybe it was any number of things." He looked at her sternly. "Stay out of it."

"Oh, definitely," Annie said lightly. "Not my place. Still...I wonder if they're okay." She smiled at the warning look Elliot gave her and then looked at her watch. "Well, I had better go and see my new horse."

Elliot smiled. "I still can't get over it. That was quite a gesture on Cobie's part."

"I know; I keep pinching myself. Do you think we should bring him here? I can get the paddock back together pretty easily. Of course, we don't have the barn he is accustomed to."

"I was thinking about that when Trace told me..."

"You knew about this?" Annie was incredulous.

Elliot smiled. "I think he thought it was an awful big thing to do without some kind of permission. He knew you'd say yes but I think he just wanted a sensible view of it before he made the offer."

Annie shook her head. "Well, what did you in your infinite wisdom decide?"

"I don't know. Really, it's up to you. But that's the only home Warrior has ever known."

Annie nodded. "That's what I was thinking. He'd be alone here, unless we brought Mink with us." She chuckled at the thought of the miniature donkey whose only job was to roam the farm and provide companionship to the thoroughbreds.

Elliot chuckled too. "I don't think anyone would agree to that."

"No chance," Annie agreed. "The only one around there more popular than Cobie is Mink. I'd be hung if I tried to take him."

Annie stood up and stretched her back. "Okay, I'll talk to Trace about boarding him there then."

"I'll bet he refuses your money."

"I thought of that too. But I have to contribute somehow. Warrior won't feel like mine unless I do."

Elliot nodded. "You're right, of course. Just be prepared for an argument."

Annie nodded. She stood up and grabbed her bag, sending a half dozen tomatoes skittering to the floor. She bent to pick them up. "Geez, I have to do something about these tomatoes."

Elliot reached over and pinched her bottom. "God, I love riding pants."

Annie straightened up and swatted at his hand. "That's practically all I own these days that fit. That, blue jeans and some t-shirts. I don't seem to wear anything else." She shrugged. "I guess my transition to country girl is complete. I don't even know who that other person was."

Elliot smiled. "I wouldn't have it any other way."

Annie had intended to leave earlier, but lingering over coffee with Elliot had become a favorite pastime. Lately, it was the only time of day they had all to themselves. They liked to carry their coffee to the garden and wander there early in the morning, pausing to pick a weed here and there, or harvest a few ripening vegetables.

Now it was almost eleven, and the heat of early August was bearing down on her. Annie figured she wasn't going to ride at this point, so she decided to stop by Sara's on the way over to the farm. She wanted advice on a new saddle, and she thought, maybe she could get some news on Trace.

She pulled into Sara's tidy stable, slowing her car to admire the front paddock where several of the school horses grazed. Annie was always amazed at how well turned out they all were, but then, she reminded herself, Sara had a wealth of slave labor in the students that came and went all week.

The mini-camp on bikes had gone well, and a number of kids had been identified to take part in the showing of the puppies. Annie had agreed to help with some of the basic handling classes, knowing that Gray would have no time for such things in the month of August. She thought that she and Sara could take a look at the calendar and make some plans.

She pulled the car into a space near the barn and got out. She heard laughter coming from one of the nearby rings and saw a class in progress. She identified Rebecca as the instructor, so she wandered into the barn to see if Sara was in the office. She found her there on the phone. Sara held up a finger, indicating that Annie should wait. Annie sat down.

Sara spoke into the phone. "When did it happen?" Annie raised an eyebrow, and Sara shook her head in response.

"Figures it would be something stupid," she said. "Okay, Betsy. I assume you've talked to Monty." She paused to listen, nodding. "I'll certainly do what I can to help. Davis isn't up to doing it by himself, but the hounds aren't my specialty either."

She paused again to listen. "I agree with that. Has Monty called him yet?" She listened to the answer and then sighed. "No, you wouldn't have gotten an answer on the house phone. Dorothy went to stay with her sister for a few weeks."

She nodded. "Okay, I think that's the only answer. Let me know what you hear."

Sara hung up the phone and leaned back in her chair. "Gray broke his arm."

"What! When did that happen?"

"Last night. Apparently one of the horses was colicky, and Gray was walking him in the dark. Tripped and hit a rock as he went down. Compound fracture. He went straight into surgery last night."

"Damn. What stupid luck."

Sara shook her head. "Bad timing. August is so hectic for him. He hunts every single morning on horseback in order to get the new hounds trained and to give the veterans a chance to get into shape before the season begins. It is a grueling schedule."

"I had no idea August was like that. I guess it never occurred to me."

"Six days a week. He takes half the pack out one day, the other half the next. They get up before dawn so they can hunt as the sun comes up. Otherwise, the heat would just be too much for everyone."

"So, what can be done?"

"Well, Betsy says Gray is determined to get back out there and soon as he can, cast and all. But the doctor is saying no way, not as long as the cast is on."

"How long is that?" Annie asked.

"He said several weeks."

Annie blew out her breath. "Wow, that bumps right up to cubbing."

"Yes. I'm sure after a few weeks, he won't be able to help himself. But he can't do anything now, and a fall would be disastrous in the first month."

"I'll say."

"Betsy is worried that he won't stand for it unless he feels like the hounds are on schedule. But Monty can't go fulltime, and Davis is pretty green. Everyone has commitments. Archie is in the Outer Banks with his family. We can cobble some kind of schedule together, but that's not enough."

"Another huntsman maybe?"

"They're all facing the same schedule. There might be a young man around to help, but that's not the answer."

"Then what are they thinking?"

Sara hesitated. "Trace."

"Trace?" Annie said, surprised. "He hasn't hunted in years."

"No, but he has been out with the puppies a lot this summer. He and Gray have become close friends and Gray could work well with him. Of course, he knows the hunt field as well as anyone, and he's an expert on horseback."

"Has Gray talked to him?"

"No," said Sara. "Betsy says he's on pretty heavy pain meds at the moment. He won't want to ask for help anyway. Monty is going over to find Trace. They're hoping if Trace approaches Gray, he might be able to accept the plan."

"What's the plan until then?"

Sara rolled her eyes. "More bicycling."

CHAPTER 43

———◆———

THE HUNT CLUB BOARD HELD an emergency meeting to work out what to do.
Monty asked Trace to attend the meeting too, but he was reluctant to do
so. He agreed to come along and have a talk with Gray.

"Davis doesn't have the experience to lead the field," Archie began
hotly.

Monty raised his hand to stop him. "Relax. We know that. We're going to have to work out some kind of schedule…"

Archie threw up his hands. "The dogs need consistency. We can't
just have every Tom, Dick and Harry out there with them."

"I agree," said Monty smoothly. "They need a leader. But we can take
turns as whippers-in."

"Maybe," said Barrett. "But with who at the head?"

"Well, one of the current whippers-in would make sense. But Barrett,
you work in DC much of the week, and Archie, I can't see you going out
every day."

Archie rubbed his face, considering. "True. I'm not as young as I
used to be."

Monty glanced over at Gray, who nodded his assent. "We were thinking Trace."

The men all turned to look at the huntsman. Barrett raised an eyebrow. "Gray?"

Gray nodded, looking down at the table. "I think it's the only way.
Trace knows the youngsters, and they respect him. He can take my place."

"But is he willing to do it?"

Gray nodded. "I have already talked to him. He was reluctant, but I think he sees it's the only answer."

Archie leaned back and sighed, raking his hand through his sparse hair. "Well, I guess that's as good an answer as any." He looked around for agreement and got nods from the faces around the table. "I guess we should talk to him."

"I'll text him," said Gray. "He's up at the house."

"Why didn't you just bring him down in the first place?" Barrett said.

"We thought it would be best to discuss it first," Monty said diplomatically.

Gray looked around the table at the men, raising his own good hand. "Wanted to spoon feed it to you, more like. Wanted to know there wasn't a serious objection before we subjected him to the likes of you all."

The men laughed, in spite of themselves.

"Actually, I think it will be good for the boy. Get him into the thick of things where he belongs," Archie said.

"You might want to lay off calling him 'the boy,'" said Sara.

Archie started to reply, but he heard the door open and turned to see Trace walk in.

Gray smiled up at him, gesturing for him to sit in the seat beside him. "Anyway," he smiled. "I can't imagine partnering with any of you boneheads. You'd want it all your way." He smiled apologetically at Sara and Deborah.

"Don't treat us any different," Deb said. "We agree completely."

He looked at Trace and gave him a grateful nod. "I know it's a huge task, especially with you just taking on the farm."

Trace shrugged. "Not so bad a time, really. Joe has been doing most everything all summer, and they can just keep on with it. Harvesting and all was settled a while ago. I guess I can find the time."

Gray nodded. "And I can come out in the truck at least. Watch and do some walking." He moved his arm and winced a bit. "At least, in a week or so."

Monty pulled out his notebook. "Well, let's see if we can get a schedule together and do this." He considered. "Davis will go out every day, of course." He jotted down his name and then looked around the table. "And we should have one or two more every day."

"I'll take Tuesday and Thursday," said Archie.

"Monday too?" Monty asked.

"My wife'll kill me. But sure, Monday too."

Barrett volunteered Friday and Saturday. Sara offered three days. Deborah volunteered four and so did Monty. Monty wrote down everyone's names and days, and promised to email them. He sat back to look over the sheet. "More than enough," he said. "Gives us a little wiggle room."

"Now then," said Gray. "Trace and I have already talked about this. We will use Belle Deane farm most mornings, as least at first. He'll be at the kennels by 4…"

"Four what?" said Archie.

"Four a.m." Gray replied, ignoring Archie's groan. "Don't worry, Trace and Davis will have Billy to get the hounds loaded." Gray turned to Trace. "Did you have a hunter?"

"Not really," said Trace. "Daddy gave Warrior to Annie and…"

Barrett raised an eyebrow. "He did what?"

Trace waved him off. "He wanted to re-pay her for all she's done. Warrior is too old for that kind of pace anyway."

The men exchanged glances. This seemed like big news, but they would need some whiskey and some time to process it.

Trace continued on. "There are plenty to choose from, I suppose. But I don't know them all that well yet. I think I can count on Bedrock. He's young but sensible."

Gray said, "Plan on taking my Titan. Rogue too. You'll need more than one horse to choose from. And they need to get into shape too."

Trace nodded. "Sounds like a plan."

Gray said, "Anyway, if it's your day, try to be at the farm by 6, tacked up and unloaded. I like to leave with first light. Get it over with before the heat strikes."

Everyone nodded. Those who groaned inwardly had the good grace to remain silent.

"Okay then," said Monty. "We'll see you on Monday. Meeting adjourned."

Trace walked out with Gray. "Come for a drink," Gray said.

Trace gave him a wry smile. "I don't drink, remember?"

Gray shrugged and held up his cast. "I don't either, I guess, at least until I'm off these pain pills. Still, I think Betsy can rustle up some Coke or lemonade."

Trace considered, glancing back to see if Sara had come out of the clubhouse.

Gray followed the track of his eyes and said casually, "You know, why don't you grab Sara and see if she'll come in too. I'll bet that Betsy would be happy to throw something on the grill."

Trace looked at him gratefully. "Okay, let me just see if…"

Gray interrupted. "Sara, come over here, would you?"

Sara walked over reluctantly. She avoided Trace's gaze, concentrating on Gray. "What's up?" she said lightly.

"Come on in for a bite to eat. Betsy has been wanting to see you."

"Oh, I don't think so." Sara protested. "I have a lot to do, especially with this new schedule."

"It's after 7. There's nothing more you can do tonight."

"Really? Invoices, schedules, feed orders, mothers to call…" Sara protested.

Gray laughed. "Okay, okay. But you have to eat. Come on in."

Sara was trapped. She sighed. "Fine, but only for an hour or so."

Gray smiled. "Plenty of time."

"Shouldn't you rest?" She asked.

"Good lord woman, this is rest. I haven't done so little in the past few days since 1998. I already don't know what to do with myself." He smiled. "Help me out. Entertain me for a bit." He glanced to the kitchen. "And save my wife. She already can't bear to live with me."

Sara rolled her eyes. "Fine."

Gray walked ahead to tell Betsy about their dinner guests. Trace slowed and placed a hand on Sara's arm. Sara flinched and pulled away.

"What's wrong?" said Trace, taking her arm and turning her to him.

"Nothing's wrong."

"Then why are you acting like this?"

"Like what?" Sara pulled her arm away and turned to the door.

"Like this!" he said, taking her arm again.

This time when she turned to him, she was in a fury. "What do you want from me?"

Trace backed up and held up his hands. "Sorry. I thought that we…"

"You thought that we… what?" She looked toward the house and lowered her voice. "What did you think, Trace? That I was your girlfriend again?"

"Well, after the other night, I thought…."

"Thought what? That we could take up where we left off seven years ago? That I was over what happened? That I didn't stew and fret and cry for much of that time and that I could just let bygones be bygones?" She pushed him, her hands hitting his chest and forcing him back. "Is that what you thought?"

Trace retreated, silent now.

"I've been your nursemaid, your shoulder to cry on, your confidante. Isn't that enough? Now you want more?"

Trace looked down at the ground. "I had no idea you felt this way," he whispered.

"That's because you never asked!" She was yelling now, forgetting to care who heard. "It's all about you. It's always been about you. How do you think I felt? Do you know…" she said, coming close and looking him directly in the eye. "Do you know how it feels to see someone you love, someone as talented and bright as you, fall apart before your very eyes? To pack up and throw away every plan I had ever made for the future?"

He didn't answer.

"Do you really think you are the only one who suffered? My god..." Sara ran her fingers through her hair. "But I carried on, Trace. I sucked it up and kept going. What the hell did you do?"

"I killed my best friend."

She shook her head, her eyes now slits of anger. "Yes, you killed Curly. But..." she waited for him to look at her. "You killed me too."

Tears sprang to his eyes, but he blinked them away. "Sara, I never meant to..."

Sara turned away. "I know. You never meant to do anything. Things just happened to you." She faced him again. "And I wanted you back so badly, I wanted you here at home, I thought I would do anything to make that happen. I wanted you to be all right. I wanted you to be happy. I wanted you to be with your dad. But after the other night..."

"Yes?"

"After you kissed me, I realized it's not enough. You can't just come back and pick up where we left off. Good old Sara. You have your farm. You're the golden boy again. It's too easy. It can't...I mean, I can't...." She looked to the house. "Tell Betsy I'm sorry, I can't stay." She turned toward her truck.

"Sara, don't leave like this." Trace pleaded. "I thought we were..."

"A couple? Well, think again, buddy. I have a life too, and it is high time I live it." She turned on her heel, got into her truck and pulled out, sending pebbles flying in the spin of her tires.

Trace watched her go, hands jammed into the pockets of his jeans. "I was going to say, I thought we were friends."

He started to the house to make his apologies. Then he looked down the road as the brake lights of her truck disappeared into the dusk. "Screw it," he said to himself. He turned on his heel, got into his own truck and sped off too.

Betsy and Gray were on the front porch as one, and then another, truck spun out of the driveway. Betsy raised her eyebrows at him.

"Well then," he said. "That went well." Betsy rolled her eyes.

Gray pulled out his bottle of painkillers. "I guess it's time for one of these," he said. "I hate these blasted things." He held out the bottle. "I don't suppose you would trade me these for a cold Guinness and a couple of Advil?"

Betsy groaned and reached for the pills. "If a Guinness will do it, then a Guinness it is. Stay out here," she said, gesturing to the porch swing. "I'll go get you one." She turned to go in the house, stepping over a sleeping hound. "It's going to be a long month," she said to the dog.

CHAPTER 44

———————

ANNIE TRIED TO SEE TRACE at the farm, but she always seemed just to miss him. Lindsay explained his schedule, telling her he left before daylight every day and took a nap when he got home. She said it seemed to be going well with the hounds and Gray was mending nicely.

"The only thing is Trace always seems like he's on a low boil," she said. "I know Gray always gets testy in August too, so I've tried to cut him some slack. The schedule's just really tough." She laughed. "I leave dinner in the refrigerator for him. That way I don't have to deal with him."

"How's your mom?"

"Good. She decided to stay with Aunt Ginny a little longer. Massachusetts is pretty nice right now, and they're going to the Cape for a week or so." She sighed, wiping the sweat from her brow. "Sounds good to me."

"Me too," Annie said. "This heat is just too much." She looked toward the barn. "I wanted to ask about a couple of things for Warrior. His supplements and all. And the farrier's schedule."

"Joe will know all that."

"Okay," Annie paused. "Have you seen Sara?"

Lindsay thought about it. "Gosh, not for ages. Now that you mention it, I don't think I've seen her since the funeral. I know she's a whipper-in a couple of days a week. I saw it on the schedule Trace has hanging on the refrigerator."

"Yeah, I suppose adding that into her week is keeping her pretty busy."

"The weeks are flying by. I have to take Daisy school shopping soon. First grade, you know."

"Wow, already?"

"Yeah." Lindsay sighed. "It was nice to have John home for the funeral, even though it was only a couple of days. It sure feels good to know that he's back in the States. He will be off deployment by November, so maybe things can start feeling a little more normal around here."

Annie nodded. "That would be great. I'm sure you've miss him."

"Like nobody's business. Daisy too, especially now that her grandpa is gone."

Annie put her hand on Lindsay's shoulder. Lindsay looked up and smiled. "It's okay," she said. "We're strong."

Annie gave her a quick squeeze. "OK then, I'm going to go find Joe and then head home. I'm up to my eyeballs in tomatoes. Want some tomato ginger chutney?

Lindsay wrinkled her nose. "Uh, I'm sure it's great Annie, but…"

"Don't worry about it. I don't like it either." She chuckled. "But I'm running out of things to do with tomatoes."

"Well, good luck. Remember, I'm always up for a jar of your pasta sauce."

"Oh, I have several variations now."

"Well, go easy on us," Lindsay said. "Daisy has simple taste."

"I'll bring some out next time I come."

She left Lindsay hanging her laundry and wandered down to see Joe and visit Warrior. She was tempted to bring the horse a treat, but a month of relaxation and grazing was making him round enough.

Annie got into the car. She rolled down the windows, but the air that blew in was almost as bad as the heat itself. She closed up the car and cranked up the air conditioning. Her thoughts went from the pleasantries of the farm back to her own life. The tomato book was almost done. The last bit was always the hardest, she thought. She needed to make sure she tied up all the loose ends, edit it for consistency and look for holes in the logic of the content. A week or two should do it.

Annie ran their expenses up in her head again. It would probably work itself out, she thought, trying to shake off the insistent nagging that lodged itself in the back of her head. She'd get that small second half of the advance when she sent in the manuscript. And more royalties would come in eventually, but given the vagaries of order and delivery times, terms and returns withholding, Annie never felt she knew what she could count on. The amount of a royalty check was always a surprise, sometimes pleasant, sometimes not.

It was probably time to look for a job again. She had not sent out a resume since spring. Elliot told her that her writing was enough, but as much as she wanted that to be true, she still felt the need for some security. In spite of the Grainger's generosity, Warrior would create expenses. And the next book she had to work on was Cobie's, and that was all for charity. No money there. The boys were entering graduate school, and although they said they were prepared to pay for it themselves, Annie wanted to provide some back up. She shook her head again. The same old story. When would she shake herself free of it?

Annie wondered why she still felt the need for a job so keenly. It's my age, she decided. I don't have many more chances to hold down a real job. Life is passing me by. At least my work life is.

Annie sighed again. She was anxious for autumn and cooler weather. She wanted wool coats and riding boots. She wanted the money to buy them. And most of all, she wanted to be done with tomatoes.

CHAPTER 45

———

AUGUST DRAGGED OUT, HOT AND sticky. Annie was grateful to be inside, and buckled down to the work of finishing the tomato manuscript. Testing new recipes every day was a grind, but she cranked up the AC and made the most of evening and early morning hours when the oven needed to be on.

She sent the final manuscript off by email early one weekday morning and sat back in her chair with a sigh of relief. She glanced at her watch. It was only 6am. She stood up and walked into the kitchen to check the thermometer mounted on the outside of the window.

"That's what phones are for," Elliot commented, pouring coffee and watching her squint at the large dial.

"What?"

"I said your phone will give you the temperature."

"Yeah, I forgot. What happened to simply going outside and seeing how things feel anyway?"

"Over-rated," he said. Elliot held up the coffee pot. "Hot? Or would you like me to pour some on ice."

"Ice, I think." Annie walked to the counter and reached into the cupboard for a tall tumbler. "The book is gone. I thought we might go out and celebrate by watching the progress with the hounds."

"Is that okay? I thought this training was strictly for the hounds and the horses."

Annie shrugged. "They've been out there for three weeks now. We'll just go and see if we can spot them. I still haven't been able to see Trace. I thought maybe I could catch them when they're packing up." She thought for a moment. "Anyway, it's Wednesday. Sara should be riding too. I haven't seen her either. I wanted to catch her up on those Saturday morning handling classes I have been doing at the club for the kids."

"Gray has been coming to those, right?"

"Yes, he might have been able to do them himself, now that he has extra time on his hands. It's been great to have him there. He has so much knowledge." She smiled. "And it's a small distraction for him. Betsy says he's bored out of his mind."

Elliot chuckled. "I'll bet. Will he be out there? I thought he was following in the truck."

"Yes, he and Billy should be there." Annie swished the coffee in the ice, waiting as it crackled and melted. Then she poured it over a second glass of ice. "What do you say? Up for it?"

Elliot was already transferring his coffee to a travel mug. He nodded. "Better take off now. They'll be gone before you know it."

On the way to Belle Deane, Annie talked over the outline of the new book. "Cobie's book needs to cover a lot of topics."

"You know, someone's name will need to be on it," Elliot remarked. "He can't be listed as the author."

"I know, I've been thinking about that," Annie nodded. "Maybe "from the stories of Cobie Grainger and the members of the Meryton Hunt Club, compiled and edited by Annie Gentry."

"That's a mouthful."

"I know," Annie shrugged and sipped her coffee. "I'm not going to worry about it. Fred will have an idea."

"It seems like the title outlines the book pretty well. "The Foxhunter's Year" says it all."

Annie nodded. "I agree. I just want to sit down with Gray and make sure I can line up the subjects in the right places."

Annie scanned the open field that led to Belle Deane's barn. She pointed to the hillside directly east of the barn. "There they are."

"Looks like they're already on a scent."

Annie nodded, opening the door and putting her feet on the ground before the Jeep had come to a stop.

"Hang on; I want to grab my camera."

"Catch up with me," she called over her shoulder. "I want to see the yearlings at work. I see Echo already. He's up front." Annie ran to the top of the ridge, her eyes following the three horses and the pack of hounds. She counted sixteen couples, thirty-two hounds in all, making their way along the ridgeline.

There was a yellow truck heading overland. She didn't recognize it, but she assumed it was Gray and Billy. The pack quickly moved over the hill and out of sight, but Annie heard the telltale singing that indicated that they had found a line. She saw a herd of deer burst from the woods, and was relieved that no hounds followed at their heels. "Good puppies," she murmured to herself.

Elliot caught up with her. "Where are they?"

Annie pointed toward the last place she had seen them on. "Up and over," she said. "Too far to catch them on foot."

Elliot nodded. "If I'm not mistaken, they'll cross north and back up over that ridge." He pointed to the left. "If we stay here, I won't be surprised if they double back to where we're standing."

"As good a plan as any," Annie said, finding a smooth spot on the ground and sitting down. "Darn, I forgot my coffee in the Jeep."

"I'll go get it."

"No, never mind," she said, reconsidering. "I don't think I want it." She stretched back. "It's going to be a scorcher today." She smiled and reached for her phone to consult it. "It's already 80. They're expecting 100 degrees."

"August in Virginia."

Elliot sat down beside her. "Well, I think I'll join you. No sense in expending more energy than I need to."

Elliot fussed with his camera as they waited. He was never at a loss for things to photograph, thought Annie. A hawk circled overhead, a butterfly landed lightly on a stem of grass, small wildflowers grew on the floor of the field. It was so easy to keep him occupied. Without a distraction of her own, Annie laid back and let her mind wander. Light clouds floated overhead, and she could just detect the smallest of breezes tickling the grass. How long had it been since she lay in an open field and watched the clouds?

She must have been just a child. Now the experience filled her with the same kind of wonder she thought she remembered when she was young. How is it that we forget these things, she thought? Why can't adults keep their senses of wonder? She vowed silently to try to make time for these moments.

The rumble of an engine and the crunch of wheels woke her from her reverie. Annie sat up and saw the yellow truck approaching. It was in fact Gray, but she didn't recognize the driver.

Gray swung easily out of the truck, raising his cast in greeting. "Good morning! Glad to see you out."

Annie smiled. "I just finished the tomato book. It's time to turn my attention to foxes."

"Glad to hear it." Gray said.

"Tomato book?" said the man, extending his hand to greet her.

"Long story," she smiled. "For another time. Nice to meet you."

"You as well," he said. "I'm Angus." He walked over to shake Elliot's hand before turning back to her. "Although, I think maybe we have met before. Weren't you at one of Cobie's fireside chats?"

"Angus here is the huntsman at a hunt up in Massachusetts." Gray said by way of explanation. "He's here to talk about drafting a couple of our hounds."

"Ah, now I remember. The dog that ran riot," Annie smiled. "Well, welcome back." Angus nodded and tipped his hat.

Annie turned to Gray. "Speaking of the book, I want to take a bit of time with you on the outline, if you can make time."

"Absolutely," Gray said. "We could meet after the handling class on Saturday." He raised his cast. "That is, as long as I don't have to write anything."

Annie smiled. "No, talking only."

"Never had a problem with that."

Elliot chuckled. "How's the arm doing anyway?"

Gray shrugged. "I think the cast will be off by mid-September. I can't wait. With this damned heat, it itches like the devil." He looked over his shoulder toward the hills. "Something doesn't seem quite right."

Annie looked toward the hills. She didn't see anything. "What makes you say that?"

"The horn. Trace is blowing out."

"That just means he's calling the hounds to him, right?" Annie said.

Gray nodded. "But he's doing it again and again." He paused to consider. "Too much. I wonder if they have lost count."

"Who's out there?" Elliot asked.

"Davis and Sara." He pointed toward a stand of trees in the distance behind the barn. "Look, I think I see them."

Annie watched Trace trotting toward the farm. He was riding Bedrock today, the brilliant black Thoroughbred from Trace's barn. Annie couldn't help thinking the black horse must be hot already, with the sun beating down on his shiny coat.

"I count thirteen couples," said Angus, his eyes scanning the field.

"Yes, me too," said Gray, shielding his eyes from the glare with his good hand. "There's Davis there to the left. Looks like he has a couple with him."

"That's four hounds missing. Sara must be after them."

Gray nodded thoughtfully. "Trace would have wanted to turn back before they hit the train tracks. She was probably patrolling there."

They watched together as the hounds came in. Annie hadn't noticed the hound truck when they arrived, but she now saw Billy exit the cab and go around to the back to open the trailer.

Trace approached the group, still on his horse. "We lost part of the field past the river over there," he told Gray, gesturing toward the eastern slope. "They ran riot on a coyote. Sara went after them."

Gray gestured for Trace to hand him the horn. "Angus and I will drive up that way as far as we can." He gestured toward Bedrock. "Get him some water before you go back out. Get yourself some water too."

Trace nodded. "Not the ideal horse for today, I have to admit. He doesn't like the heat." Billy had already handed him a bottle of water, which he quickly downed. He slid off the horse and handed the reins to Billy. "I'll just take a few minutes to freshen him up, and then I'll head back toward the train trestle where I last saw them."

"Keep your phone nearby," said Gray. "I'll call you if I get a location."

Annie looked at her phone. "Service out here is pretty bad. Does Sara have her radio?"

"No. We realized after we got here that the batteries were dead." Trace scuffed the ground with his boot. "Bad luck. She does have her phone, but you're right. We may not be able to reach her."

"Texting might go through, even if signals are weak," Elliot offered.

"I'll remember that."

"If you are going cross-country," Elliot said to Gray. "We will get in the Jeep and follow around the nearest roads and see if we can come across them."

"Okay. We can make it by truck as far as the river." Gray shoved his phone in his pocket and turned to get back into the truck. "Billy, is that other horn in the truck?"

"I think so."

"Good, Trace can take that." Gray looked around at the group. "Looks like we need all forms of communication at our disposal today."

Angus and Gray took off up the hill while Billy poured water for the horse and tended to the returned hounds. Annie could hear Gray already blowing for the hounds.

Billy turned to Trace. "Do you want me to take these guys home?" he said, nodded to the trailer.

"I think so. It's going to be blasted hot and it's only a couple of miles," Trace said.

"I'll bring back more water."

"Okay, leave me what you have." He looked at Bedrock. "I wish I had Rogue with me today."

"I can bring him back if you want."

Trace thought for a moment, looking out over the hills. The super-heated air was already rippling over the fields. "I might be over-reacting. Sara could turn up any minute now. But go ahead and tack him up and come back with him."

Billy nodded. "It won't take me more than thirty minutes. Levi can put the hounds up when I get there, and I'll turn right back."

"Okay." Trace looked at Bedrock. The sleek gelding's breathing had gone back to normal, and he stood comfortably in the shade of the trailer. "I think we're ready to head back out." He nodded to Davis, who had been tending to his own horse. "Ready?" Davis nodded.

"You take the north ridge," Trace told him, pulling off the long sleeve shirt he wore. He tugged at the t-shirt underneath, tucking it into his riding pants. "I'll follow the train tracks to the trestle." He tossed Davis two bottles of water. "Here, take these with you."

Davis nodded and leaned over to squeeze the bottles into his saddle bag.

Annie and Elliot got into the Jeep. "Good luck. We'll try to let you know if we see anything."

Elliot drove out of the farm's long driveway and made a left onto Fairgrounds Road. "I'm going to take this down to Bayar's Ford road and see how far we can get. If they crossed that, we might be able to go off-road on the old Mill place."

Annie nodded. "What a day to lose hounds," she said, shivering as the air conditioning made contact with her damp skin.

CHAPTER 46

———◆———

MORNING WORE ON WITHOUT A sign of Sara and the missing hounds. With poor cell service, Elliot and Annie found themselves circling back to the farm, hoping for word. They found Billy waiting with Rogue.

"Gray called when I was at the kennel," he said. "They saw tracks headed past the river. He and Angus were following on foot."

"It's almost noon. Have you heard from Trace?"

Billy shook his head. "Not a word. Davis neither."

They all turned at the sound of a truck off in the distance. For a moment, Annie thought it must be coming from the road. But then she caught sight of the bright yellow truck. It approached quickly, and she saw Gray swing out of it before it had come to a full stop. He went straight to the truck bed and put down the gate. "Billy, come here. Now." Annie saw Gray scoop the hound into his arms, balancing the bleeding dog over his cast.

Billy ran to relieve him of his burden. "Let me have him. I'll tend to him in the trailer."

"Water first, and put him in the cab with a bit of AC. The poor boy is ragged."

Annie's heart stopped. It hadn't even occurred to her before to question exactly which hounds were missing. Now she saw the telltale markings on the dog's back. "Echo," she whispered. She had formed a special bond with the crazy, boisterous youngster. Her heart sank.

Angus got out of the truck and followed Billy. "I'll help your kennel man," he told Gray. "The dog needs stitches. And I want to check that front leg for a break." Gray started to follow, but Angus waved him off. "Find out if they've seen anything."

Elliot was already shaking his head when Gray turned to him. "Nothing," he reported. "We drove all the way down to the ford and crossed around the Mill's soybean field. No tracks. I don't think they came out that way."

Gray nodded. "I'm afraid how far they might travel if Trace is right about the coyote. Those beasts tend to run straight and far."

"Where did you find Echo?" Annie asked, her voice shaking.

"We walked past the river to that coop that divides Belle Deane from the next place over. He was caught in some barbed wire."

"How bad is he?" Annie asked. She felt a chill in spite of the heat.

"Pretty torn up. Lost a lot of blood. Angus is right. He couldn't put weight on that front leg. But I doubt it's broken. I think he was just fighting like crazy to get himself out of the wire."

"I'll just go see if I can help," she said.

"You might not want to do that," Gray said. "Billy will be sewing him up."

Annie nodded resolutely. "I can handle it." She saw Gray's doubtful look. "Don't worry. He'll be glad to see me."

Gray chuckled. "You're right. If may be a comfort to him. Go ahead."

Annie made her way to the cab of the club's truck and opened the passenger door. Echo winced with pain as Angus held the leg for Billy to stitch. "I'll take over," she told Angus.

"You sure?" he asked.

Annie nodded. "I'm sponsoring this dog, he's my pal." She saw him hesitate and look at Billy. Billy nodded his assent. "Anyway, I think Gray could use you."

"Okay then." Angus gently moved the dog's head off his lap and got out of the truck, waiting as Annie took his place and braced the dog's leg in her hand. When Billy started stitching again, he closed the door and went back to Elliot and Gray.

"Good puppy, good puppy," Annie crooned to the dog, stroking his head. She reached for a water bottle and poured a bit of it onto his head, smoothing the crusted blood off his ears and muzzle with her shirt. Echo closed his eyes and relaxed.

"Tough boy," Billy said. "I put some painkiller in there, but he's such a lunatic, I didn't think he'd cooperate."

"Will he be okay?"

Billy nodded, beads of perspiration building over his eyebrows as he worked. "Lost a lot of blood. Going to have some real battle scars." He sat up for a moment, stretching his back. He patted the dog's head.

"Aren't you, fella?" He looked up at Annie's worried face. "We'll just keep pumping him with electrolytes. Don't worry, he's young and strong." He bent back to the dog's leg. "Here, were almost done. Just stretch his leg out here and let me get at the back."

Annie did as she was told. Billy worked methodically, finally laying down the needle and checking over his handiwork. "That should do it. I'll cover it with gauze for now." He looked around the cab. "It's in the back. You okay to stay with him? He might jump up when I open the door."

Annie nodded, reaching to take a firm grasp of the dog's collar. But Echo did not jump up. He turned his head slightly at the sound of the opening door, and then laid it back down on Annie's lap. "Well, he's comfortable anyway," Billy said. "I'll be right back."

Annie waited for several minutes, petting the dog's head and looking over the stitches. The wound was the type of ragged cuts that only barbed wire can inflict, but she thought that Billy had done a good job. Echo would have an interesting scar, she thought. Something to brag to his pals about one day.

She heard a thumping sound behind the truck and looked into the rearview mirror to see Billy off-loading Rogue. She wondered if Trace had come back. She looked for a sign of him, but didn't see him or Bedrock. She knew she couldn't leave the truck without upsetting Echo. Who was going to ride Rogue? Surely Gray wasn't riding out, she thought. He couldn't be that daft, no matter how worried he might be. And for all his skill with the hounds, Billy was no horseman.

Annie got her answer when she saw Angus trot across the field on Rogue. Elliot came around to the passenger door, and Annie rolled down the window and nodded to the field. "What's going on?"

"Angus thought the best line on them was from the fence they found Echo. He's going out to look."

"But he doesn't know the area."

Elliot shrugged. "He's a huntsman. He's hunted here before, and he knows what he's looking for. With no sign of Trace and Davis, much less Sara, it seemed the only answer."

Annie felt a rush of heat into the cab. "My god, it's hot."

Elliot nodded. "Gray is beside himself. The hounds can find their way back or be picked up by others, but now he has four people out in this heat."

Annie looked out the front windshield of the truck. Heat vibrated off the truck's engine. She had forgotten that the truck was still running. "Why don't we move Echo into our Jeep," she said to Elliot. "Maybe we can take him home."

"Okay," Elliot said. "Let me ask Gray."

"Wait!" Annie put her hand on Elliot's arm. She pointed straight ahead. "Someone's there. No, it's two horses. Who is it?"

Elliot stepped to the front of the truck, shielding his eyes from the sun. "It's Davis," he called back.

"Who's the other rider?"

Elliot watched for several moments, and then turned back to the truck. Annie looked at him expectantly.

"Who was Sara riding today?"

Annie shook her head. "Not sure. She likes that young chestnut with the white back leg. Tater."

Elliot looked again at the pair of horses. "Yeah, that might be right."

"Oh gosh! Davis found her!" Annie looked back to see if Gray had seen them, but he was walking the edges of the far field.

"Annie, no."

"What?" she said, turning her head back to Elliot. He frowned at her. "No, it's not Sara. Davis is leading a riderless horse."

———

Davis slid off his horse and handed Tater's reins to Billy. He leaned heavily against his own horse for a moment and then reached to loosen the horse's girth. Billy led Tater back to the trailer to remove his tack.

"Where did you find him?" Gray asked; his forehead furrowed with worry.

"About a half mile past the trestle. I saw no signs headed north, so I figured I would run into Trace if I followed the train tracks." He nodded toward the retreating chestnut. "Tater there was standing in the river, cooling himself off." He spat on the ground and took a drink of water. "No sign of Trace or Sara."

Gray nodded, going over the terrain in his mind. "Well, you've covered the better part of several square miles. The horse couldn't have gone too far after losing Sara."

Davis nodded. "I saw Angus on the way back. He told me about Echo. He was headed back to that fence. I'll go back out in a few minutes."

Gray shook his head. "I don't think so. It's nearly a hundred degrees. I can't put anyone else in jeopardy."

"You can't just leave them out there!" The words burst out of Annie's mouth before she could stop them. She knew better than to question the huntsman's judgment. "Sorry," she said sheepishly.

Gray put his hand on her shoulder. "I understand how you feel. But I just can't jeopardize anyone else. Angus will be back soon. I made him promise he wouldn't go too far. If he doesn't find any signs past that fence, he'll turn back."

"But that leaves Trace to find her alone."

Gray nodded, distracted by his thoughts. "Has anyone tried their phones lately?"

"I have," said Elliot. "Nothing."

"Okay, then we wait." He pointed to the near rise of the field. "There's Angus now."

When Angus returned to them, he reported nothing new. After he met Davis, it occurred to him that Sara might find the river and stay near there to keep cool, but he hadn't seen any sign of her.

"Good point, though," said Gray. "Sara would do something like that, unless she got turned around. She knows what she's doing."

Their silence was broken by the sound of Billy's cell phone. They all looked at him eagerly as he pulled it out of his pocket and looked at the caller ID. He shook his head as he answered it. It wasn't Trace or Sara.

"Hello," he said. He listened and nodded, repeating the caller's words for the benefit of the others. "You found two hounds?"

Gray slapped his forehead.

"Really? Way over there? Can you hold onto them for me?" He paused to listen. "Okay, thanks very much for calling."

Billy slipped the phone back into his pocket. "Lisle and Maybe are at Ainslie. The farm manager has them in a stall."

"Ainslie! That's got to be ten miles from here," Annie said.

"By road," said Elliot. "Probably less across country."

"Still…" Annie thought for a moment. "Who does that leave missing?"

"Opal," Billy said.

Annie nodded. The pretty bitch with the star on her back was a mild-mannered youngster. Annie was a little surprised. Opal didn't seem to her as one who would out on an adventure. Her heart tugged at the thought. The little thing was probably scared to death, especially now that she was alone.

"Billy, you drive over to Ainslie and get them. Take a look around the roads near there. You can take Echo with you."

"Actually, I hoped you'd let me take care of him," Annie said. "Echo doesn't need to bounce around a bunch of country roads right now."

Elliot nodded. "I agree. Let me run Annie home with him and I'll come back out and help you search."

Annie protested. "Wait a minute!"

But Gray nodded at Elliot. "Good plan. We need to take care of Echo and there's only so much everyone can do here. You go." He smiled at Annie. "I appreciate your help. Billy will take care of the other animals. Angus and I'll see what we can do by truck. Elliot, call me on your way back. I'll tell you what roads to cover."

Elliot nodded. He and Billy moved Echo to the back of the Jeep. Annie insisted on climbing in next to the dog. "I don't want him trying to jump over the seat or something."

"Fine," said Elliot. "You can explain it to the cop if we're pulled over."

"I'll just do that," Annie said fiercely. She was hot, and she was annoyed at being sent home. She certainly wasn't going to let anyone tell her how to take care of Echo. Elliot slammed the hatch and climbed into the driver's seat.

"I get it," he said mildly as they drove. "I really do. We're all worried. But you are doing more good taking care of Echo than you can do riding around with me."

"I know. I'm just frustrated," Annie admitted. "My heart nearly fell out of my chest when I saw Tater come in without her. What if she's hurt?"

"They'll find her," Elliot said. "She's sensible. She knows her way around. I'm sure she's fine."

"Humph," Annie answered, stroking Echo's head. The dog raised his eyes to her and responded with a couple of thumps of his tail. She ruffled his ears. "At least you are okay, buddy. Let's get you back to the house and…." She looked up and caught Elliot's eyes in the rearview mirror as they pulled into the driveway. "Our dogs. They'll go nuts."

"Yeah, I thought of that. I'll go in and set up the big crate in the breezeway. Then I'll put up a gate to keep them out of there."

"Okay," Annie said. "I'll just stay here with Echo."

"I'll be right back."

Annie leaned back against the seat and waited, stroking Echo's head. She could hear her own dogs yipping to receive Elliot and wondered how they would receive the arrival of this big dog. She sighed. At least they were all hounds. They should find common ground. Right now, though, it didn't matter. Echo would be in confinement for a while.

Annie's phone buzzed in her pocket. She scrambled to retrieve it from her pocket, moving the weight of Echo's body off her leg. "Hello?"

"It's Gray. I just got a short text from Trace. It just says, "I've got her.""

"What? Where are they? Is she okay? Can we go get them?"

"Don't know the answers to any of those questions. I texted back but can't get it to go through."

"But it's so hot! Surely we can do something."

"I think for now we just have to wait. The two of them are together, and I'm sure we'll hear again soon."

"What about Opal?"

"I'm afraid she is on her own for now." He heard the catch in Annie's voice. "I'm sure she'll be okay. Annie..." he said. "If you are going to hunt, you have to toughen up a little."

Annie choked down a laugh. "I've heard that before. Why do you think I quit breeding my own dogs? I can't bear to give them away."

"We'll find her. My dogs sometimes go astray, but I haven't actually lost one in years."

"Okay. Thanks for calling, Gray. Let us know as soon as you know any more. Do you want Elliot to do anything?"

"No, we will stay nearby. I'll let him know if we need him. Thanks for your help this morning."

Annie glanced at her watch. "It's almost 3 o'clock."

"Is it really? I hope they found someplace to rest out of the heat."

Annie hoped so too.

CHAPTER 47

———————

TRACE WAS FRANTIC WITH WORRY. He and the horse were both drenched in sweat. Flies and mosquitoes buzzed around them, and he had just drunk the last of his water. He had covered the forested area along the bottom of the ridge, now he decided to head back toward the river. Both he and the horse needed a bit of relief from the scorching heat.

He caught sight of Sara before she saw him. Relief flooded him from head to toe, and he immediately called out to her. But when she didn't hear him above the babble of the stream, he couldn't help but sit back and watch her for a moment.

She sat on a rock just below the ripple of a small cascade in the river. She had pulled off her boots and was soaking her feet in the cool water. She cupped some of it into her hands and splashed it over her head, and then pulled off her shirt and dipped it in the water. She let it swirl there for a minute, and then wrung it out and put it around her neck. She leaned back against a rock and closed her eyes, humming quietly to herself.

Trace slipped off the horse's back and looped the reins around a tree. Then he walked to where she was laying. "So you're okay," he said grimly.

Sara opened one eye, and then closed it again, feigning to resume her nap. "It took you long enough."

"What the hell? We were worried sick. I...." he hesitated. "I was scared out of my mind."

She opened her eyes and looked at him. "Why?"

"Why? Are you kidding? I'm responsible for three people, three horses and thirty-two dogs. It's a hundred degrees, and I lose six hounds and…. you. Why wouldn't I be frantic?"

She closed her eyes again. "That's what I figured. It's all about you."

Trace started to respond, but a thought occurred to him. He turned around in a complete circle. "Where's your horse?"

"I have no idea."

"You lost your horse?"

"Yes, he bolted at some damn thing when I got off to open a fence. It was too hot to keep jumping, and I was trying to give him a break." She gestured to the river. "I thought he might be smart enough to come back to the river. Given the tracks over there," she gestured to the other bank, "he did just that. But there are more tracks too, so I suspect someone found him and took him back. I was going to walk back. I think the road is only a mile or so away, although Belle Deane would be a long walk. I thought I had better stop to cool off."

Trace nodded, his eyes travelling along the opposite bank to see the evidence she described. "What about the dogs?"

"Well, I have Opal here…"

Trace had not noticed the petite hound that had lifted her head to regard him. "She never goes far from me. The others were high-tailing it after a coyote, heading east. No telling where they are. I was about to stop and turn for home when I lost my mount." She looked over at Bedrock, standing patiently under a tree. "Don't you think your horse would like some of that water?"

"Oh hell," he swore. "I'll be right back." Trace loosened the horse's girth and led him to the stream, where he drank thirstily. Soon, he started pawing the water with his large front hoof.

"Watch it," Sara said. "He's going to lie down."

Trace grabbed the reins just as the horse went down into the cool stream. "Damn," he said. "My saddle."

Sara chuckled. "Well, I'm sure it feels great after the day he's had."

Trace lifted the horse's head to raise him. The horse obliged and stood up, then gave a great shake, spraying Trace with sweaty water. "Okay, you've had your fun," he said to the horse. He led him out, removed the tack and laid it out to dry.

Trace sat down beside the stream, peeling off his own boots and dipping his feet into the water. He splashed his face too, and then leaned back. For a few minutes, they were both silent. When Trace finally spoke, his voice was quiet.

"It's not all about me."

"What?" Sara said, turning to face him.

He sat up and looked at her. "It's not all about me, damn it."

"You could have fooled me."

"Sara, I…I was so ashamed. I had disappointed everyone. I had ruined my life."

"You. You. You." Sara summarized.

"My world was pulled out from under me. How could it not be about me?"

Sara paused to consider. "Trace, did you ever think about me when you were gone?"

"How could you ask that question?" he said. "Of course I did. All the time."

"And what was the content of those thoughts?"

"Am I on trial?"

Sara sat up now to face him. "I don't know, are you? Has anyone ever called you on your behavior?" She stared him down. "Because it looks to me like all you got was a hero's welcome."

Trace looked down sheepishly.

"Can you answer me?"

Trace sighed, and swatted at the mosquito that buzzed around his neck. He was silent.

"That's what I thought," Sara said finally, lying back against the rock again.

"No, damn it," Trace yelled. He jumped to his feet and turned to her. "You're wrong. I was thinking about you. I thought you were better off without me. I thought I had... I mean..." he stopped, trying to re-phrase his statement. "Your future, your stable might be ruined with me around. Our kids, the stories about their old man..."

"Are you kidding me? You were worried about all that?" Now Sara was on her feet. She pushed him.

"Did it occur to you the gossip I endured after being left at the altar? How I had to make a go of the stable and the riding school alone, when I had started it with the belief that we would do it together. My god, your dad could barely be around me; it hurt him so bad to be reminded." She pulled at her hair. "And your mother. Her mind had been on grandchil-dren. It almost killed her."

Sara paced back and forth now, her socks squishing in the mud. "Poor Sara, poor Sara. People could barely talk to me. Oh my god, it's only let up in the past couple of years, now that I have the school go-ing and a new crop of parents and kids who don't know about it." She shook her fist at him. "Do you have any idea what you did to me, you idiot?"

Trace's mouth hung open. He couldn't bring himself to say what he was thinking. He had only thought of Sara in the abstract. How he had left for her sake. The day-to-day realities had not hit him. "I thought you'd move on, find someone better." He shook his head. "It never oc-curred to me that you would still be alone."

Sara dropped to her knees in front of him. "You are dumber than I gave you credit for," she said. "Don't you remember I said you were the only one I would ever love?"

Trace shook his head again, this time hoping to hide the tears that stung his eyes. He sat down next to her. "Everyone says stuff like that," he muttered.

Sara touched his face and looked into his blue eyes. "I am not every-one," she reminded him. "We are not everyone." She smiled now. "Don't you remember that? We are...unique."

Trace smiled too. That had been their inside joke for everything. They would not make any decisions based on other people's ideas. They would invent their world together. He touched her face now, smudging it with his dirty hand. "You were so good for me. You made me believe."

"And you made me believe," she said softly. Then she sat back. "That is, until you didn't."

Trace's heart sank. He thought they were getting somewhere. Now he saw her face shut down again. "But you did it," he said. "You did it all. The stable, the school, it's so successful. Your student list has some of the top riders…"

Sara nodded her agreement. "Yeah, I did it. But I didn't do it because I believed. I did it because I had to. I did it because the ink was barely dry on the mortgage, and because I had no other way to support myself." She looked him square in the eye now; her arms folded over her chest. "I did it because I had to, Trace," she repeated. "I didn't have the luxury of running away."

He couldn't respond to that. He was guilty as charged. Finally, he whispered. "Mistake after mistake after mistake." He looked up and caught the look in her eyes softening. He jumped at the opening. "How can I make it up to you?"

Sara dropped her arms at her sides and sighed deeply. "I don't know Trace. How can you make it up to me? God, do I have to do everything in this relationship?"

"We have a relationship?" he asked, hopeful now.

Sara sighed. "That's up to you, I guess. I seem hopelessly stuck with you." She held up a warning hand as he jumped up to hug her. "Not so fast," she said. "I didn't say we had a good one, or that I am sure we ever will. I'm just saying that maybe we can start over."

Trace nodded. "We can do that," he agreed. "But not from the beginning. We start from right here today, right where we are. We take everything that happened and everything we learned, and we forge ahead. No more sweeping it under the carpet." He paused to watch for her reaction. "We can do it," he smiled. "We are unique." He saw her smile now, in spite of herself. "And I can make you believe again, I promise." When she did not move away, he held out his hand. Deal?"

Sara smiled weakly and took his hand in hers. "Deal."

He reached out and this time she accepted his hug. Trace closed his eyes and held her tight. He ran his hand on her bare back, flicking a mosquito away. "So," he whispered into her hair, "Did you forget about your shirt?"

Sara's hands hit his chest hard, knocking him off his feet and into the water. He scrambled to his knees and then reached for her, tumbling her into the stream with him. They sat in the water, laughing and wiping water off each other's dirty faces. Opal jumped in with them, barking her joy at the unexpected play time.

"Get down, you fool dog," Trace said as he pushed her away.

Sara laughed and tousled the hound's head. "I guess we should get back," she said.

"Everyone is worried sick," he agreed.

Sara nodded. "They should know me well enough to know I'll always be okay."

"No one would ever doubt it," Trace said. He pulled her to her feet. "And whatever happens, I'll never forget it either." He bent down to kiss her.

"Okay, okay," she said, holding him at arm's length. "Where's my shirt? I'm getting eaten alive."

"I'll eat you alive," he continued, wrapping his arm tightly around her waist.

"Not so fast, stud," she warned. "We have a long way to go." She pulled away and turned to grab her boots.

Trace dropped his hands. *Slow down, you idiot,* he thought. She just looked so damned cute in her wet bra and breeches. "Yes, ma'am."

"Ugh," she said. "Boots over bare feet or boots over wet socks. Not sure which is worse."

"You can ride Bedrock."

"No, I think we'll all walk out of here together."

Trace nodded and reached for her hand. "Together it is."

"Come on, Opal," she called to the waiting dog. She stood up and pulled her damp shirt over her head.

"I think we can get a signal once we're over the embankment." She picked up her phone. "At least I hope so. Anyway, we should be able to get one once we're on the road. Someone will come get us."

Trace put the tack back on the damp horse, tightening it only enough to keep it on. He nodded. "Let's get out of here."

CHAPTER 48

AFTER MONTHS OF HEAT, THE October sky broke clear and cool. Fall had finally arrived. To Annie's mind, the weather brought nothing but pure possibilities—and all of those possibilities centered around foxhunting. The opening meet was scheduled for the end of October. This was it; her chance to immerse herself in the adventures that she had only tasted in the past.

Warrior was ready. In spite of the long summer of grazing, Annie had made sure to get him out as often as she could so he wouldn't have to start the season with flabby muscles and a giant belly. Annie was ready too. Months of riding and gardening had turned her flabby office-bound body into a solid machine. She was still not exactly thin, she thought, looking herself over in the mirror. But she was fully functioning, and that was all she really wanted.

Annie dug into her savings account for the event she had waited for all summer—shopping at Horse Country for her hunting clothes. She had braced herself for the big outlay of cash this purchase would entail, justifying the cost as an essential, and deserved, treat after the summer of cookbook writing.

Dodie came for a visit, ostensibly to go over the galleys of the tomato book. But Annie knew this was her yearly fall pilgrimage out of the city so she had made sure to give her the tourist's tour of the vineyards and Monticello. She had planned to shop that Thursday but decided to put it off until Dodie's visit was done. When Dodie heard about the shopping trip, she wouldn't allow her to put it off.

"Shopping! Thank goodness!" she exclaimed. "Something I know how to do." She raised her eyebrows at Elliot. "Other than drinking wine of course, I am pretty good at that."

Annie wasn't entirely sure this was a good idea. She had thought to bring Sara or Lindsay; someone who could give her good advice. But she had to admit that watching Dodie's eyes goggle over wool coats that ran in to the thousands of dollars might be fun. On the other hand, Dodie's normal shopping life was in New York City. Maybe she wouldn't be shocked at all.

"So tell me again what we're doing," Dodie said as she climbed into Annie's Jeep. She reached down to wipe dog hair from her pants. "God, don't you ever vacuum?"

"It wouldn't help," Annie smiled. "They just keep putting the hair back." She looked down at Dodie's outfit. "I told you not to wear black."

"Black is the only color I own, as you well know," Dodie sniffed. "Oh well, the dry cleaner can deal with it when I get home." She brushed her hair from her eyes and picked up a copy of the catalog that Annie had brought along. "Okay, do we need a list?"

Annie thought for a moment. "That probably wouldn't hurt," she said. "There's paper in the glove compartment."

"Well, you'll need everything," Dodie said, reaching into her purse for a pen. "You're practically a rail."

Annie laughed. "Hardly a rail, but you're right. Aside from a few breeches and my paddock boots, I don't have much that's right for the hunt field."

"Okay," Dodie nodded. "So you need one of these jackets..." She tapped her finger on the picture of a pretty tweed coat.

Annie glanced over as she turned the car onto Route 29. "Yes, that's beautiful. And I'll need a black one too."

"Why is that?"

"Ratcatcher attire is tweeds. Brown accessories, colored ties. More casual, you know."

Dodie's eyebrow shot up as she perused the catalog. "Casual? At $1,400?"

Annie chuckled. "You chose the most expensive one in there. But you're right; hunt clothing is expensive. Forget evening gowns, these will absolutely be the most expensive clothes I will ever own."

Dodie nodded. "Okay, then if these are casual, what else do you need?"

"Formal days call for a black coat, black accessories, white stock tie…."

"What's a stock tie?"

"A white tie you wear around your neck." Annie stopped at a stop light and reached over to flip a page of the catalog. "Like this," she pointed.

Dodie laughed. "This traditional garb is something else. What on earth is that for? Won't a regular scarf do?"

"Oh, you would be surprised by how sensible this clothing is. Yes, it was born out of the British tradition. But everything actually has a good reason." The light turned green, and Annie proceeded up the road toward Warrenton. "That stock tie started out as a safety thing. It is quite long and wraps around your neck a couple of times. If there is an injury, it can be used as a bandage or sling. Heck, it can even become a leash for a stray dog."

"Ok," said Dodie, lifting her pen. "Two jackets." She circled some photos and then bent down to reach for her cigarettes.

"Not in the car," Annie said.

"I'll keep the window open."

"Not in the car. You can wait until we get to the store. I'll give you time before we go in."

"God, it's enough to make me quit. It's bad enough being banished to your back porch…."

"You should quit," Annie said firmly.

Dodie reached down and picked up a packet from her purse. "I'll compromise," she said. "Nicotine gum. I only got it to use on the plane but I'll make an exception."

"Thank you." Annie nodded her approval. The drove silently for a few minutes, Annie lost in thought while Dodie pouting over her gum.

"You know," said Annie. "I could make do with less, but I want to do this right." She sighed. "And I haven't shopped in months, except to run to Old Navy for a couple of cheap t-shirts now and then. And of course, jeans. So I have a lot of pent-up shopping need."

Dodie nodded, brightening. "Well, you have the right partner in crime for this escapade. I'm all for shopping. Let's do this."

Annie always felt like she had gone back in time when she entered the Horse Country store. The smell of leather and books pervaded the place. Decorative items and china were the first things that caught her eye, but there would be plenty of time at Christmas for such things. Right now, she wanted clothes and boots.

Annie made a beeline for the tweed coats, immediately landing upon a luxurious hacking jacket in a warm tan and green hounds tooth. "Oh, this one," she said, rifling through the rack for one to try on. She frowned. "I don't think any of these are big enough."

Dodie looked around for signs of sales help. "If we're going to spend some serious money, I think we could use some assistance."

"No, that's okay," Annie said quickly, remembering her last embarrassing trip to the store. "I'll just poke around a bit." But Dodie had already left in search of someone. Annie located the biggest jacket on the rack and slipped it off the hanger. She swung her arm into it as she walked toward the mirror. She stopped in front of the mirror and stifled a giggle.

Another chuckle echoed her own and she turned at the sound. "I think you need something a bit smaller," the woman said. Annie turned to see Aideen, the woman who had waited on her before. But if Aideen remembered her, she didn't react. "What size is that?"

Annie looked down at the tag. "Thirty-eight."

Aideen shook her head. "Well, no wonder. I'd say a thirty-six might do." She expertly lifted a jacket from the rack. "Try this one."

To Annie's surprise, it fit beautifully. She buttoned if up and stood back to admire herself. She couldn't believe it. Last time she was here, not a single coat would have fit.

Dodie clucked her approval and turned to Aideen. "We have some money to burn here. Ratcatcher attire," she looked to Annie. "Is that the right word?" Annie and Aideen nodded. "Fine, and then something dressier."

Annie rolled her eyes. "I'd like a nice hacking jacket. I'll need a black frock coat. And probably some boots."

"And that tie thingy," added Dodie.

Annie glanced sidelong at Aideen, who watched the slick urbanite with a trace of a smirk on her face. "Don't mind her, she's from New York. She has no idea what I need, but I promise, she does know how to spend money."

Aideen's eyes brightened, and she clapped her hands. "As good a qualification as any, I would say. Let's get started."

Annie purchased the hounds tooth hacking jacket, as well as a black frock coat. She got two white stock ties, and because Dodie was so taken with them, a couple of colored ties for rat catcher days. In addition to white shirts and stock pins, she also bought a couple of new breeches and a pair of gorgeous black boots.

"Don't you need brown boots?" Dodie asked, admiring the display of sleek leather hunting boots. She sighed as she fingered a fine pair of Italian boots. "I wish I could justify these for myself. They're spectacular."

"Yes, they are," said Annie, looking over from the bench where she tried on her black boots. "And over $750."

"Still…"

Annie shook her head. "I have brown paddock boots and half chaps. They will have to do. I have already bought more than I intended." She felt a touch of dread at the growing pile on the bench beside her.

Aideen gave Dodie a smile. "Let me just take these to the register. You can keep shopping."

Annie gave Dodie the eye. "You are a bad influence."

"God, I love this place," Dodie said, having turned her attention to a rack of gloves. "Don't you need these?"

Annie shook her head in resignation. "Yes, pick out the yellow chamois, and maybe..." She looked over the rack. "I like those tan ones of the end."

Dodie nodded and added them to the pile in Aideen's arms. As the woman walked away, Dodie turned to Annie and raised her hands. "Anything else?"

"I can't imagine another thing...oh, look at that canary waistcoat!"

Dodie picked it off the rack. "Do you need such a thing?"

Annie screwed up her face. "Well, not essential, but very much the thing."

Dodie checked the size. "Medium. Perfect."

"No! Wait! It must be $200!"

Dodie looked at the tag. "$300."

"Put it back."

"I won't. When in anyone's whole life can they say they *need* a canary-colored vest? You are getting it." She paused for a moment. "A gift from your editor."

"Well, if you put it that way...."

It took two trips to the Jeep to carry all their purchases. Annie climbed in and looked at the back seat in dismay. "I can't believe I just did that."

"Oh, don't be silly," said Dodie. "It's one royalty check."

"One royalty check I should be living on."

"Well, as you say, you only need to buy most of this stuff once in your life." She sniffed. "A shame really, I'd like to do this more often." She turned around and fingered the herringbone. "And it's a good incentive to keep the weight off."

"That's for sure," Annie said. "I wouldn't dare grow out of a $1,200 frock coat." She looked in the rearview mirror and pulled out of the tight parking spot and onto the busy street. "Speaking of that, I'm starved. Let's go to lunch."

CHAPTER 49

Opening day dawned crisp and cool. Annie stepped on the back porch and looked up at the sky. There was a high layer of thin clouds. Perfect, Annie thought. Cobie would approve. She dressed carefully, fussing with her stock tie, smoothing it until it was perfect.

"Well," she said as she presented herself to Elliot, who was finishing his coffee. "What do you think?"

"Turn around," he said, gesturing for her to spin. She did as she was told. "Nice," he observed, smiling. "You look like the real thing."

Annie nodded. "I feel a little too squeaky new," she said. "I feel like I should rub a little dirt on myself."

"What would Gray say?" Elliot smiled. "He likes a perfect turnout."

"Well, I am that," she said, looking down at the gleam of her black boots.

"Let's go," Elliot said, reaching for his camera bag. "Trace said the trailer leaves promptly at 8:30."

They got to the farm at 7:45, just enough time for Annie to brush Warrior and braid his mane. She had bathed him the night before and kept him in the stall, nervous that he would make a mess of himself back in the paddock. Trace had Bedrock on the crossties. He waved to them as they entered the barn.

"Ready for this?" he smiled, nodding approvingly at Annie's clothing.

Annie removed the jacket and pulled a hoodie over her pristine white shirt. "I can't wait," she admitted, opening the stall to retrieve

Warrior. The horse seemed to know what day it was too. His flank quivered in anticipation. "I just hope I don't disappoint this one," she said, smoothing her hand over his flank. He's used to first flight."

Trace raised his eyebrows. "He'll be fine, wherever you ride."

"That's why we are well-suited." She brushed out Warrior's long tail and got a small step stool so that she could work on his mane. "We trust each other; don't we buddy?" She put her arm around the horse's neck and slipped him a peppermint.

She heard a series of sharp clicks, and turned to see Elliot busy snapping pictures to commemorate her first Opening Day. "Go get me some elastics, would you? They're in that little drawer in the tack room." Elliot nodded.

When he was gone, Trace turned to her. "I'm nervous too," he admitted.

"You? That's crazy. You've been out hunting every day."

Trace nodded, pulling his saddle from the rack. "Yes, but thank goodness Gray's got his cast off. I couldn't have led the field myself to save my life."

"Of course you could…" Annie paused when she saw the look in his eye. "Oh," she said.

"Here I am, in the field after being absent all this time, and my dad gone." He shook his head. "All those people. I want to just blend into the woodwork."

"You'll ride First Flight, right?"

"Of course, but I wouldn't mind being back with Sara and the hill toppers."

Annie snorted. "Don't be silly." But Sara's name made her wonder again what was going on with those two. It seemed like the tension had lessened there, but she hadn't seen much of them together lately. They had sat together at dinner after the puppy show, and they seemed friendly enough. Still, if he would rather be back with the slowpokes, Sara could be the only incentive.

Elliot came back with the elastics and they watched as she finished the mane. Trace nodded his approval. "I hate braiding."

"I can do yours in the future," she said. "I don't mind." She gave Warrior a quick once over with a damp cloth and then tacked him up. "Ready?"

"Stop," Elliot said. "Let me get one shot with you standing there with Warrior." Annie rolled her eyes again, but Elliot wouldn't take no for an answer. "You too, Trace." Trace edged into the frame, leaning his hand on Warrior's neck. Elliot focused and shot. "Nice," he said. "Of course, I'll need another one in the field once you have your coats on."

"Do you always travel with the paparazzi?" Trace teased.

"Oh, you have no idea," said Annie. "I use to forbid it, but I guess I'm starting to get used to him." She winked at Elliot. The real reason for her patience with his camera was obvious, to her at least. She was looking a whole lot better in pictures these days. She rolled her eyes for Trace's benefit. "I just hope we get a good view, and then we will be forgotten. He'll be after the fox."

———

Trailers were already lining up when they arrived at Fox Haven Farm. The autumn colors were on full display, and there was just enough nip in the air to make for comfortable riding in the warm wool jackets.

Trace and Annie unloaded the horses as other members of the club stopped by to say hello. It seemed impossible to Annie that there were people who had not seen Trace all summer, with the funeral and all. But as he expected, he had to endure rounds of greetings and explanations to a host of club members who knew nothing of his arrival. Fiona Landers brought over a couple of younger women who Annie knew to be students at UVA to meet the "new talent" in the field. Annie shook her head. With any luck, this would be the last major coming out he would have to endure.

Sara rode up on Sparkle, her young Thoroughbred draft cross. Trace whistled appreciatively. "Nice looking...horse," he said with a smile. Annie looked at Sara, who was smiling back with apparent pleasure.

Annie raised her eyebrows and gave Sara a look, which she studiously ignored.

"I know, huh?" Sara said, patting the big chestnut's neck. "She's really filling out. Going to be a beauty. Smart as a whip too, she's taking to the field like crazy."

Sara noted the folks still lingering around Trace, letting her eyes linger on Fiona and the other girls who were in full flirt mode. She said mildly, to no one in particular. "Riders up soon. You know how Monty hates to wait." This was enough to remind those who had still not entirely satisfied their curiosity about Trace what they were actually doing in the field today. Fiona giggled and said her goodbyes, and the girls dispersed quickly to mount their horses.

"Thanks," he said. "There are a lot of people I don't know." He raised his eyebrows. "But apparently they know me."

"Hmm…or would like to," Sara said, eyeing the departing backsides of the girls. Trace followed her eyes.

"Not for me," he said casually. Annie looked at Sara again, whose smug look seemed to hint at something more. Annie was sure now. There was more going on with these two. But why hadn't she heard? Were they keeping it a secret?

Annie didn't have any time to dwell on this latest revelation. The hounds were released from the trailer and there was no time to waste. Her heart pounded in her chest as she mounted. She did not have to endure the attention that Trace had, but she was very aware that she was riding her first hunt on Cobie's horse. Warrior was a distinctive fellow and everyone knew him. There were sure to be whispers about her, and she only hoped for two things from today's hunt. First, that they would keep their comments to themselves, and second, that she would do both Warrior and Cobie credit. Well, third, she thought to herself. Don't come off the horse.

Elliot had already gone to listen in as Gray and Monty decided on the first draw. Annie saw them pointing west, and she knew that they planned to make for Layton's Ford. Good, she thought. An easy start while she got her bearings, and her nerves, under control.

Trace saw them gesturing too. "Good," he said. "There's a big red living over there. I've run into him several times this summer. I call him Dallas."

"Why Dallas?" Annie said.

Trace shrugged. "I don't know, there is something bold and rugged about him. Seemed about right." He smiled. "Ready?"

"As I'll ever be," Annie replied with a smile. She turned her horse to walk with Sara, but Trace stopped her.

"Aren't you riding First Flight?"

Annie blanched at the thought. "Oh, I wouldn't dare. We aren't ready."

Trace shook his head and smiled. "Annie, you don't think I have seen you out on that horse? I know perfectly well you have been preparing all summer. You take those jumps like a pro."

Sara nodded. "I coached her some. You're right. She's fine, and Warrior will take good care of her."

"Warrior's getting older, I thought that was the whole reason Cobie gave him to me…"

"If you believe that, you are dumber than I thought," smiled Trace. "That horse has a few years of jumping in him." He nodded to the big fellow. "As a matter of fact, I imagine he will be pretty offended if you don't come out in front."

Annie's heart thudded harder than before. There would really be something for the field to talk about now. First time in the field, riding a legend's horse, and in the front of the field. She swallowed hard, tears stinging her eyes. No, it was too much.

Trace saw Annie's panic and relented. "It's okay if you don't want to," he soothed. "Dad would understand."

At the reminder of Cobie, Annie looked up. She saw Warrior's ears pricked forward, already aware of the field shifting into place. She steeled herself and nodded. "Warrior's place is in front, and that's where we're going to be."

Trace smiled. "Just remember, heels down and stay on."

Annie set her jaw and nodded. "Got it."

Elliot saw Annie ride up to take her place with the first flight. He started to walk up and ask her what she was doing, but Sara caught his eye and shook her head.

Monty made his announcements. "Hunt Breakfast after, of course. Don't forget to get your reservations in for next week's dinner." He paused and cleared his throat. "I don't think we could start the season without a mention of our brother Cobie's departure." The hunters bowed their heads, some of them taking off their caps.

Monty looked around at the somber faces. "Not going to make a speech here, just wanted to acknowledge that this will be the first season without him in forty years, and we will miss him." People nodded. "We're pleased to have his son Trace with us. Many of you might not know this, but he did the club a tremendous service this summer when Gray broke his arm."

Congratulations and thanks were called out, and Trace nodded his appreciation.

After the field had moved on, Annie noticed some casting sidelong glances at Trace, and she was aware of pointed looks at her and Warrior riding alongside him in First Flight. She blushed, in spite of herself.

Annie finally caught sight of Elliot among the people on foot and shrugged her shoulders. She shook her head and gave him a resigned look that said "what am I doing here?" Elliot smiled and gave her a thumbs-up. And then hurried with his camera for the first coop the field would be jumping.

Annie took the first jump smoothly. But her mind was racing. Of course, that one was easy. I saw it coming, she thought to herself. There was an easy approach, a smooth landing area. But how many others would there be? She was so pre-occupied with her worries that she hardly noticed the call for the fox. Dallas was sitting at the top of the hill waiting for them. Annie saw him watch their approach, only turning to run when he was sure the hounds had caught his scent. Then they were off and running.

Jump after jump came now, as the big fox took them on a merry chase. Together, horse and rider took each one smoothly. She felt a kind of divine inspiration take hold of her as they followed the huntsman, heard the cry of the hounds and caught sight of the wily fox. Cobie was with her today, she knew. There was no way he would miss this opening day.

In the heat of the chase, Annie's mind cleared. Worry was replaced with exhilaration, a pure rush of adrenaline like she had never felt before. Aboard Warrior, she was free. She belonged here, she knew. She belonged to the field, to the hounds. Her heart now beat in time with the horse. The fear was gone. If she died in the field, so be it. She was home.

When they trotted in almost three hours later, hot and perspiring, every molecule in Annie's body tingled. She didn't even realize that she was grinning from ear to ear until Monty caught sight of her and smiled.

"Good sport today," Monty said.

"Yes, amazing," Annie nodded. "Three great views. Dallas was all in, wasn't he?"

Monty smiled. He had heard Trace's name for the big red too. "Got the bug, eh?" Monty said.

"More like the fever," Annie replied. "How have I gone all these years without hunting?"

"Well, we got you now," he answered smoothly. He nodded at the horse. "Good job out there."

Annie tucked her chin, embarrassed. She knew that she had done okay. That is, she was still in her tack at the end of the meet. But she had forgotten that others were watching. She nodded uncertainly and dismounted. She ducked behind Warrior and fussed with loosening his girth until she was sure Monty was gone.

Trace came up beside her to take Warrior's reins. "He's right, you know. Dad would have been proud."

Annie nodded, tears springing up once again. "I felt him with me."

Trace rolled his eyes. "If you are going to cry every time we hunt, I'm going to have to find someone else to ride with."

Annie laughed, wiping her eyes. "Okay, okay, I'll get it together for next time."

"See that you do." Trace took Warrior and loaded him on the trailer as Elliot came to find them. "Hunt breakfast is starting. Ready to go?"

Annie nodded. "Let me just get the food I brought out of the cooler."

She heard Trace slam the trailer door. He came around the corner and peered into the cooler.

"Tomatoes?" he said.

"Absolutely not," Annie laughed, lifting the big tray. "Deviled eggs. I'm off tomatoes indefinitely."

CHAPTER 50

EARLY NOVEMBER BROUGHT CRISP, CLEAR weather. Annie lived for the Monday, Wednesday and Saturday meets when she could take to the hunt field. She couldn't bear to miss a single day. Three days a week was a bit more than Warrior needed, especially riding First Flight. But Sara always had a horse for her to use on odd days. Annie resisted at first, not wanting to take advantage of her generosity, but Sara made a point of telling her it was a favor to her to give some younger horses the experience.

"I can't put the kids out on horses that haven't got some credentials in the field," Sara told her. "You are a good rider, better than you give yourself credit for. You have a way with the young horses."

Annie nodded shyly. "I'm just an old cowgirl," she said. "No technique to speak of."

Sara brushed away her protests. "Well, you make up for it in confidence. And you impart that to the horses. That's all they need."

"Okay, I'm happy to help, if that's what I'm doing. And I can learn along the way."

She had gotten up early this morning to help Sara with a new colt. Dumphrey had just arrived from Massachusetts, the planned mount for a young student just started in her hunter jumper program.

"I want to get the kinks out of him," Sara told her. "Little Petra is pretty strong in the saddle, but she doesn't have much sense. I want to see what we're working with before I put her on him."

Annie nodded and clipped the lunge line onto the horse's halter, gently placing the chain over his nose. "No bridle?"

Sara shook her head. "Let's see what happens with this first. He seems like a compliant fellow."

They lunged the horse for twenty minutes. He was calm and responsive, and seemed to be everything that Sara had hoped for. "Would you ride him in the field on Monday? Petra will be home from boarding school and will want to try him on Saturday."

"Sure," said Annie. She had hoped to take Warrior out on Monday but helping Sara came first. "Maybe Trace will take Warrior."

Sara shook her head. "I have him on that new black horse, Manfred. What a handful he is."

"Do you see much of Trace?" Annie asked mildly.

Sara shrugged. "Some." She looked up and caught Annie's eye. "It's a process."

Annie nodded. As much as she wanted to know more, she knew she should let it go. Sara seemed happy, and that was enough for her. "I'll help you do grain," she said as she turned the colt into a stall. "There you go, Dummy," she said. She turned to Sara. "Oh dear, that's an unfortunate nickname."

Sara chuckled. "I called him that too. Better be careful, we don't want to give him a complex."

She worked in the barn with Sara for the morning, trying to absorb everything the young woman showed her about supplements and medications. By noon, she was anxious to get home and sit down for lunch with Elliot.

Annie drove into town, her head full of horses and hunting. Almost a year after quitting her job, she thought. Had it really been that long? And she still found her new life remarkable. At fifty-five, she had been re-born. She had taken up with horses like she had never been away. It still seemed surreal.

If only she could shake the feeling that she was living in fantasy land. There was no way she could keep this up. In spite of the royalties trickling in from the books, she still had to face the fact that she needed a job. Health insurance alone was costing them over $1,500 a month, which was ironic, since neither of them was ever sick. Still, a good fall off her horse could cost a lot of money…

She still looked half-heartedly at the job boards, but could not imagine a company that would accommodate her hunt schedule. Who had time to work when there were foxes to chase? She chuckled at the thought of an old illustration she had seen hanging on the barn of one of the more well-to-do members. It was a pen-and-ink drawing of a group of foxhunters. The caption read "The Society of Unemployed Gentlemen." That's about right, Annie thought. She shuddered. The thought of going back to an office made her physically ill.

Annie walked in the back door and peeked into the kitchen. She was pleased to see the makings of sandwiches already laid out on the kitchen counter.

"There's a letter for you," Elliot said when Annie walked in the door.

"You mean actual mail? Not just the electric bill?"

"The electric bill comes by email."

Annie rolled her eyes. "You know what I mean. Nothing interesting comes by mail anymore."

Elliot raised his eyebrows. "Well, since you are that excited about it, there are actually two letters."

"Even better!" Annie dropped her bag and kicked off her boots. She was tempted to peel her sticky shirt off at the door too, but the thought of Elliot's arms around her sticky flesh seemed unappealing. It was warm for November, and she had worked up quite a sweat lunging the young horse. She walked through the kitchen and to the front door where the mail usually accumulated.

"Hmm," she said to herself as she scanned the contents of the first envelope. "The contract for the foxhunting memoirs. Fred was as good as his word. The royalties will go to the scholarship fund, and there's an advance of $10,000."

"Nice start," Elliot said. "And with the proceeds of the puppy show going to the fund also, you already have about $15,000."

"Yes," she said, still reading. "They want a pub date of March 1. That should be okay, but I'll need to concentrate on the tapes soon." She handed Elliot the contract to peruse and picked up the next letter. 'Glad the tomato book is gone. I have to go at this new one full time." She looked at him guiltily. "That means no time to look for a real job."

He looked at her over the contract he was reading. "I didn't have the impression job searches were a top priority right now. We're getting by."

"I know, but a little steady income would be a good thing." She looked over at him. "We have to retire at some point."

"Isn't that what this is?" Elliot grinned. "Doing whatever we want? Seems like retirement to me." This was an old joke. They both knew they would never retire. Projects piled up around both of them unbidden. The money wasn't always great, or consistent, but there was always something to do.

Annie's heart sunk at the thought that he considered them retired. Just the other day one of the boys had asked for a small handout to cover school books and there had been an expensive repair on the house's heat pump. "It's too soon. We need fewer expenses before we're free to do whatever we want." She popped an olive into her mouth. "And downsizing is not going very well. We have that extra mouth to feed."

"Oh, Warrior isn't adding much to the bottom line."

"I know," she agreed, tearing open the second envelope. "I still haven't been able to get Trace to set up boarding fees, but the expenses will be coming along soon enough." Annie sighed. "If only Dennis' house would sell."

"The books should cover those expenses." Elliot said, putting the contract back into the envelope. "You worry too much."

Annie nodded absently, her eyes scanning the next letter. "Well, look at this," she said to herself, holding up the letter and reading it to Elliot. "We know you have out of pocket expenses related to the book." She hesitated for a moment, digesting the next sentences. Then she began again. "We don't really have the staff to do the archiving and sorting."

"You could help them," Elliot said.

"Hang on. This is interesting," she said, continuing to read. "In addition to Cobie's files, they have more materials than they know what to do with. Harry Stapleton offered to foot the bill to get this project published, as well as to organize some long neglected assets that his family had bequeathed. Of course, the salary isn't huge but the hours are flexible and I can work from home as needed."

"Salary?" Elliot raised his eyebrows.

Annie nodded and continued to read. "I understand how you feel about Cobie and this project. We're all glad that we can get it underway. But Harry needs to know that someone will actually be devoting their time and energy to these historical materials." Annie nodded thoughtfully. "If we can put you on the payroll," she read, "we know it will get finished."

Annie smiled and handed Elliot the letter. "From Fred. He's going out of town but wanted to dash off a note before he left. It just ends with let's talk, give me a call next week, etcetera."

Elliot took the letter and scanned its contents. "Looks like you have a job," he said.

"Well, I'll be damned," she said, reaching back for the letter and holding it up to confirm the words. "I'm not retired after all. It looks like I'm the new archivist for the Hounds and Hunting Magazine."

CHAPTER 51

———

"CAN YOU GET ME A coat?" Elliot asked one night after dinner. They had just poured their nightly bourbons and lit a fire. They had settled into the leather chairs in the great room, the twinkling of the Christmas tree the only other light in the room.

"A coat?" Annie asked absently, her mind on the file of hunt club clippings in her lap. If she were going to look at them, she would need to turn on the lamp, she thought. But she didn't feel like breaking the mood of the room.

"A hunt coat," Elliot repeated. "I thought I would like to go out on horseback. Now that you are in the field, I'd like the option."

"Oh course," Annie said, placing the file on the side table and sitting forward. "When did you decide this?"

Elliot shrugged. "I don't know. Everyone expects me to take pictures at the hunt. But I have enjoyed the trail rides you and I take, and I thought it would be fun to join in."

"I think that's fantastic," Annie said. "We can go to Horse Country on Saturday."

"No, no," Elliot protested. "Find me something on EBay. I'm a straightforward 42. I have a helmet, breeches and paddock boots. You can pull the rest together for me easily enough." He raised his hand to warn her. "Don't get carried away, I mean it. I only want to go on horseback now and then. Don't spend a lot of money."

Annie nodded. She was already racing through a list of needs. He was right. His boots were fine, and she could lend him a pair of half chaps. Of course, he would need a long stock pin. But everything else could be cobbled together. Except....

"What about a horse?" She asked. "I can ask Sara..."

"Taken care of," Elliot said. Annie raised her eyebrows. "Trace is lending me Palmer."

Annie raised her eyebrows. "You've already talked to Trace?"

Elliot shrugged. "It came up the other day at the hunt breakfast."

"I'm impressed," Annie said. "I had no idea you wanted to ride. When do you want to go? We're at Faraway Farm on Saturday."

Elliot sipped his bourbon. "I thought I would go out on Boxing Day."

"You seem to have thought this out. Why Boxing Day?"

"Well, it's one of the High Holy Days. And I thought with Emily and Bella home for Christmas, we might all go out."

"I love the idea," Annie agreed. "Especially with the boys gone for the holidays." Jack and Galen had both made other plans, making this the first year they would not all be together. Jack was going skiing in Vermont and Galen had taken the enormous step of accepting an invitation to spend Christmas with his girlfriend's family in Alexandria.

"Do you think Bella will want to go? I mean, Emily can bring clothes for both of them. She hunts in Colorado with her club. But Bella hardly ever rides. Are you sure she will be comfortable with this?" Annie thought about the other obstacles in the way of the idea. "Sara needs a head's up too. She'll need to give them horses. But she'll be pleased to see them."

"Don't worry. I mentioned it to them the other day," Elliot said casually.

"You already talked to the girls?"

Elliot nodded. "Don't look so surprised. They are my daughters too." He saw Annie's skeptical look. She was the planner in the family, after all. "Emily called the other day when you were at the magazine. I told her I thought I would ride and she hatched this scheme. She's already called Bella. It's settled.

Bella and I will ride with the hill toppers. Emily will go First Flight with you." He took another sip of his bourbon and then got up to refresh it. He held out his hand to take her glass. "Ready for more?"

Annie nodded and handed him the tumbler. She picked up her IPad, anxious to pull up her eBay app and look for coats. "I have to find something for sale; we don't have time for auctions. She thought for a moment. "Three weeks until Boxing Day. I should be able to get something here by then." She felt a ripple of pleasure. "Oh, Christmas will be so great this year!" She thought of last year's frantic attempt at cheerfulness. This year she was so busy, she had only managed to get the one tree up. With her work for the magazine and three days of hunting every week, there was simply no time for more. But somehow one tree seemed like plenty.

She clapped her hands like a child, causing the eight PBGVs asleep around the room to wake up. Most of them just lifted sleepy heads, but Chanel leapt from her sound sleep straight into barking, and Freddie walked over to the window to check on security. Annie watched them happily.

"Lay down, you fools," she said to them, accepting the refreshed tumbler from Elliot. "Haven't you ever seen happiness before?"

Elliot smiled down at her. "They're getting used to seeing you happy." He leaned down to kiss her. "Me too."

Annie smiled up at him. "I spent so much time inside my head all those years, so busy with kids and business, I'm not sure I knew what true happiness was. "She hesitated. "No, that's not true. You've always made me happy."

Elliot smiled again and returned to his chair. "I did what I could, but I have known for a long time you weren't entirely happy. I mean, you always throw yourself into your work and I know you get a lot of satisfaction from it. But I have always had my camera, and I couldn't help feeling like something's been missing for you."

Annie nodded, thoughtful now. "I told myself being outdoors was something I did outside of the office. It seemed enough to think of myself that way, even in the abstract. I think I denied how fundamental it was to my well-being." She took a sip of her drink. "It was so easy wrapping myself in other things all these years. I was glad to get the girls into riding lessons, of course, and attend the hunts, but it seemed like living on the periphery of a horsey life was all I was ever going to have."

"It turns out you are still the young cowgirl I married."

Annie chuckled. "Hardly. But this new life suits me. I feel authentic. I feel whole. I don't understand exactly what's come over me, but for the first time in my life, or at least in a very long time, I feel real."

Elliot shook his head. "I'm sorry it took so long."

"I'm sorry too. You didn't deserve a fat wife who spent years in the rat race."

"I never, ever saw you that way."

"It had its upside. Money, of course," she mused. "But the rest of it? I honestly can't think of a single thing I miss." She took another drink. "Or a single thing about it that was real."

"You should have been doing this a long time ago."

"I don't look at it that way," Annie said. "No, that's not true. I do sometimes wonder what it would have been like to be one of those people who hunted for decades. But I needed to do what I did to get where I'm today. I'm here now, and that's all that matters."

"You have the perfect job. Your marketing background is a huge asset to them. And of course, they would never want to interfere with your hunt schedule."

Annie nodded, smiling. "Fred and everyone are so great. Of course, everyone is as hunt-crazy as me." Annie's mind drifted away for a moment.

"Annie?"

"Sorry," she said, shaking her head. "I was just thinking about Cobie. None of this would have happened without him."

Elliot nodded. "He was a special guy."

"He was more than that," she mused. "It's like he was an angel sent to shake me out of myself. He sent me Warrior in a dream…."

Elliot nodded uncertainly. He wasn't used to Annie talking of angels and dreams.

She shook her head, dismissing the thought. She didn't want to talk about it. "However it happened, I realize now that everything that happened was exactly the way it was supposed to be."

Elliot raised his eyebrows. "That's a big statement, coming from you."

"I know. Control freak that I am, I always thought I was in charge. Now I realize that not only am I most decidedly not in charge, I'm better off not being. Somehow there is a plan for me, and I'm going to get to it a lot faster if I stay the hell out of the way."

Elliot eyed her suspiciously. "Who are you and what have you done with my wife?"

Annie chuckled softly. "I know, I know. It's still me." She lifted her glass. "Maybe just a better me."

"Here's to better of everything," Elliot said, lifting his glass too.

Annie smiled and took a sip of her drink. Then she looked down at the floor. "You know; these floors need waxing again. I can't believe it's been a year. Maybe I'll do them after the holidays."

Elliot looked at the floor. It looked the same as it always did. "Maybe you should work on that multi-tasking problem of yours."

She thought for a moment. "Or maybe I can do them after hunt season."

Elliot nodded. "I agree. But remember you plan to take the dogs out this spring to get their hunting certifications."

She chuckled. "Right, we'll start right after foxhunting is over." She was excited by the thoughts of honoring her dogs' natural instincts and had already booked the pack for the hunting instinct tests. She wasn't sure about dog shows anymore. They might come again in time—but right now she wanted the thrill of seeing her dogs do what they were supposed to do. Their job, as Cobie had reminded her.

"Anyway, there's still a lot of riding to do this winter." Elliot gave her a wink. "You need to get as much in as you can while you are still young."

"Oh, I think I still have several years to ride. I'll end up being one of those eighty-year-olds out in the field that everyone worries about."

"And I'll still be taking pictures of you," Elliot promised. He nodded at the tablet on her lap. "Now show me what you found. I need to look good when I'm riding next to you."

———

CHAPTER 52

THE GIRLS ARRIVED, FLUSH WITH excitement for the holidays. Annie had always attempted to make Christmas a special time, but they felt that this year would be different the minute she picked them up at the Charlottesville airport.

"Mom, you look fabulous!" Emily exclaimed. "Why didn't you tell us how much weight you lost?"

Annie chuckled. "I thought I mentioned it. And I know there have been some hunt pictures on Facebook."

"It's hard to tell with a big jacket on."

"Well, I feel great."

"Tell us everything. What's the plan?" said Bella from the back seat.

"Oh, you know, just some shopping. I planned a dinner or two. But kind of low key." Annie looked in the rear view mirror at her younger daughter. "I hope that's okay."

Bella smiled. "It's kind of a relief, honestly. Work has been so hectic; I'd like to kick back. I was afraid you had lined up a string of parties like last year."

"No, I thought we would do Chinese take-out Christmas Eve."

"Really?" Emily said. "We haven't done that since we were kids."

"Is it okay?" Annie said. "I can cook if you'd prefer. But the two of you eat like birds and without the boys here…"

"It's perfect!" they cried in unison.

"Of course, we will still have a big Christmas breakfast. Dad wouldn't stand for missing that. Anyway, he does a lot of that cooking. Oh, and of course, there's the Boxing Day Hunt."

Emily nodded, smiling. "I'm really looking forward to that. I talked to Sara the other day and…"

"Sara called?"

"Yeah," Emily said, digging lip balm out of her bag. She applied some and handed it back to her sister.

"She wanted to make sure we were riding."

"Did she say anything else?"

Emily shrugged. "Not really. Just that things were going well, new horses, new students. All the regular stuff. Oh, and she was gushing about you."

"Me?"

"Yes, what a good rider you are, how much you've helped the club and her. She went on and on."

"Really? I thought she was the one helping me."

Emily rolled her eyes. "Mom, have you forgotten? You are…Mom."

Annie glanced over at her. "What does that mean?"

Emily looked back at her, incredulous. "You're just mom. You know, you have always been everyone's mom. Sara really appreciates that. She said she has missed her mom so much since she died. It's just really nice to have you around."

Annie had to think twice about that. Emily was right. She had been everyone's mom when the kids were younger, and she regretted that most of those young people had drifted out of her life. But she honestly had not thought of herself that way around the hunt crowd. Age seemed irrelevant around them. And because she was usually the one learning, it never occurred to her that she was mentoring anyone back. She knew she would have to come back and think about this some more. Another part of her true self.

But what the heck, she thought. Since she's in the mom role, she might as well play it out. "Did she mention Trace?"

"No, she didn't mention him. Why?"

"Oh, no reason."

Emily eyed her mother suspiciously but said nothing. "Anyway, I'm looking forward to seeing her. Don't worry," she told her mother, "If there's gossip to be had, I'll get her to spill it."

Christmas Day was quiet and happy, as promised. Elliot made omelets to go along with the fruit salad, sausages and hash browns that Annie produced. The four of them drank mimosas and opened presents, staying in their pajamas until afternoon. They put the boys on Skype on the large TV in the great room, and it was almost like being together.

Elliot gave Annie a beautiful St. Hubert's medal on a silver chain. Annie knew that St. Hubert was the patron saint of hunting. She admired the relief image of the stag and hound on the surface of the medal.

"I love it," she said. She placed it around her neck. "I'm not going to take it off until after hunting season is over."

Emily gave her a hand-crafted stock tie in a beautiful paisley that went perfectly with her hounds tooth coat. Bella gave her a thin silver flask.

"I wasn't sure you would actually carry it in the field," Bella said. "But I wanted something that said "foxhunting.""

Annie held it up and admired it. "I'm not sure I would normally bring a drink to the field, but I don't see how I can resist now. It's beautiful." Annie examined the flask closely. It was engraved. It said "Annie and Warrior. Meryton Hunt Club. 2015." Tears spring to her eyes. "Oh, Bella! It's beautiful."

"I wanted you to remember this year forever," she said shyly. "The year that mom grew up."

Annie's tears fell for real now. In all her years of creating perfect Christmases, she never remembered receiving presents so meaningful or so perfect.

When the girls went to the kitchen to make more drinks, Annie turned to Elliot. "The year that mom grew up?" she asked. "What is that supposed to mean?"

"Give your kids a little credit," he said. "They can see for themselves what you already know. You are a brand new person." He paused. "But maybe you're right. Maybe Bella should have said "the year that mom became a kid again.""

CHAPTER 53

———

EVERYONE TURNED OUT FOR THE Boxing Day hunt. It was a given that no one in the hunt club traveled at Christmastime—it would put too big a crimp in their hunting schedule. Even those who missed much of the rest of the season turned out for this one.

This year, it was expected to be extra-special. Dorothy had decided to host it at Pegasus Farm. When she called Monty to suggest it, he made a quick change to the fixture card to accommodate her wishes. Marjorie Adkins, who usually had the honor of this breakfast, readily agreed. She knew, as well as the other board members did, what a big statement this was for Dorothy. Dorothy had avoided the club and all its members to the best of her ability over the years, and this gesture was meant to thank the club and, he suspected, to welcome her son back into the fold.

Trace already had Warrior and Palmer on the crossties when Annie and Elliot arrived. They had planned to be dropped off so the girls could go on to Sara's. Annie was surprised to see the mounts that Sara had promised the girls there too.

"Why are Ladysmith and Blaze here?" Annie asked Trace.

"Lots of juniors today," he said casually. "I think it was easier to get those two over here since you were coming early anyway."

Annie nodded and looked him over. "You look nice today," she said.

Trace grinned. "All I did was polish my boots," he said.

"Hmmm…maybe it's the scarlet coat. I haven't seen it on you yet." Trace had officially been awarded the colors at Thanksgiving and had immediately ordered his coat. In truth, he had received it earlier but had saved it for today.

"How's Dorothy doing?" Annie asked, looking over to the farmhouse.

"Woo! I got out of there as quick as I could. The place is a whirlwind."

"Maybe I'll just stop in…"

"Do so at your own peril. She has the folks from Peachtree Catering helping her and she's got the place turned upside down."

Annie hesitated. "Well, maybe I'll just let her be."

Trace nodded. "Good idea. Lindsay might want some help though. Daisy's going out on lead and she's getting her dressed."

"Oh, here they come!" Annie exclaimed, nudging Elliot and pointing at the pintsize girl in her jacket and riding boots. "Look how cute she looks."

Elliot tugged at the gloves he was trying on. "See? This is why I keep my camera around. Let me get it out of the car…" He dashed off and quickly had Daisy posing under the big oak tree with Blondie.

Annie sighed. "Well, I guess I'm saddling his horse."

"I'll do it, mom," Emily said. "It looks like Sara has our horses all groomed. I'll just tack Palmer up, and then we'll get ours ready." She looked around the farm. "I haven't been here in years," she said to Trace. "Ever since…" She looked up at him sheepishly. "Sorry," she said.

"Nothing to be sorry for," he said brightly. "My own fault. Anyway, glad you could be back here today."

The farm yard soon filled with trailers. Annie counted at least seventy-five, meaning there were well over 150 horses present. She wondered how orderly the hunt field would be on a day like today.

Annie saw Sara's big truck come in, pulling her multi-horse trailer. She went over to meet it. Rebecca was at the wheel. "Where's Sara?" Annie asked.

Rebecca shrugged. "Said she wasn't hunting today. Sent me a text and asked me to lead the hill toppers." She looked at Annie's skeptical face and shrugged again. "Don't look at me. I'm as surprised as you are."

Annie went to find Elliot. He was fussing with Palmer's girth. She told him about Sara. "Where's Trace? Maybe he knows," she said.

"Trace has his hands full parking the trailers," Elliot said. "Anyway, what difference does it make? Rebecca can handle the field just fine."

"Very odd," Annie said. "You'd think she would have told the girls. They're expecting her."

"Maybe she'll turn up for the breakfast."

"Maybe, still I just don't understand…."

Elliot turned to her. "I just can't get this thing tight. I forgot to put on the martingale, and I'm having trouble putting it all back together."

"Okay, move over," she said. Annie took off the girth and threaded it through the martingale and then tightened it. Then she put on the horse's headset and threaded the reins into it. "There you go," she said, handing Elliot the reins.

"Thanks. You'd better get Warrior going. Riders' up will be any time now."

"Damn," she said. "Time got away from me. She finished tacking Warrior and mounted him just in time for Monty's announcements. She looked around one more time for Sara, not really believing she wouldn't be there. Then the call came for the hunt to begin, and soon Annie's head was full of nothing but foxes.

It was a successful hunt, mostly for its picturesque beauty than for the success of the field. Big fat snowflakes fell and layered the bare ground with a blanket of white. The ground was soft, so the footing did not get slick the way it might have if it had been frozen. With a lack of viewings, the field chatted and laughed more than was normally accepted, and more than one flask was produced. There were plenty in the field who had already arrived with hangovers, and were happy for a sedate ride in the countryside. They crested Lost Legend, and Annie caught sight of a tipi.

"Where did that come from?" she exclaimed as she rode up along-side Trace. "It's gorgeous!"

"I found it in the barn," Trace said. "Dad put it up when we were kids. When it came down, I assumed it was gone. But I found it in the rafters and rolled it out. Still in good shape."

"It's amazing," she agreed. "Can we go look at it?"

Trace chuckled. "I think the master might disagree with a move like that in the middle of the hunt."

"You're right, of course," Annie said. "But I'd love to see it sometime."

Trace nodded. "Absolutely. I'd like Elliot to take some pictures of it anyway."

Annie looked back to where the hill toppers were riding. "He'll have a fit when he sees it. He wanted to bring his camera. I told him he needed both hands on the wheel today. His horse isn't going to steer itself."

Trace laughed. "I'm glad he's out. It doesn't look like we'll get a viewing today but he's had plenty of those. Still, it would have been nice for your girls."

Annie looked back again. Emily had dropped back to ride with Bella. They were talking and laughing. "I think they're enjoying themselves."

As they came down on the other side of the hill, they heard Gray's mournful call on the horn. "That's it then," Trace said. "Time to go in."

Annie frowned. "I just realized I was in the field with your dad on Boxing Day last year."

"I thought this was your first year hunting."

"It is. He called and asked to come with us in the Jeep. No one knew he was sick yet. He just said his knee hurt."

Trace smiled. "And now you and Warrior are carrying on his tradition."

"And you," Annie said, smiling.

"And her," he said, nodding to Daisy and Blondie, who were trudging down the hill with Lindsay at the lead. Daisy was grinning from ear to ear. Lindsay just looked tired. "You got the raw end of the deal, sis," he called.

"I'll say," she said.

Trace swung off his horse. "Go ahead and freshen up for the breakfast. I'll take her from here."

"You sure?" Lindsay said.

"Yep, off you go. The rest of us are pretty fresh. You can check on mom too."

"Well, okay…"

"Yes! Uncle Trace! I want to be with Uncle Trace."

"Okay kiddo, let's go." Blondie followed along placidly next to Bedrock. Annie held back and got out her phone to snap a picture of the big horse and the tiny horse walking side by side down the hill. Elliot would be sorry to have missed that shot.

CHAPTER 54

———

THE RIDERS DISMOUNTED AND WERE greeted by children carrying baskets of carrots. They went from trailer to trailer handing out the Christmas gifts for the horses. Everyone dismounted and put up their horses as quickly as they could, anxious to get out of the snow that was starting to cling to their wool coats. They poured into the house, forgoing the food tables in search of the bar. Dorothy had wisely set up three different bars so the wait would not get too deep. Bartenders were at each station, pouring beer, wine, Bloody Mary's and anything else that was called for.

Dorothy bustled around, greeting everyone with kisses and handshakes. Annie was astonished. Dorothy looked like a new person, and certainly not one who had held the members of the hunt in such disdain over the years. Now she played the perfect hostess. Annie saw her lean in and whisper to Lindsay to ask for another tray of deviled eggs, rush to re-fill Barrett's glass, and cluck solicitously over one of the elderly landowners in attendance.

Trace, too, wore a frenzied kind of cheer on his handsome face. The exertion of the day and the warmth of the room gave his complexion a ruddy glow. He rushed around the room, lighting candles and setting flower arrangements in place. Annie noticed him moving a tray from one table to another. What was he doing? She thought. It's almost like he's arranging something.

"Where on earth is Sara?" she whispered to Trace as he walked by with a tray of freshly sliced ham. He walked past her and set the tray on the already groaning dining table.

"She's not here?" He appeared to study the crowd of faces. "I have no idea. I think she said she had some shopping to do."

Annie's eyebrow shot up. "On Boxing Day?"

"Don't look at me," he said abruptly. "I haven't seen her since last night when she dropped off the horses."

"Humph…" Annie muttered. "This doesn't make sense. Has anyone called her?"

She saw a flicker of relief cross Trace's face. "Good idea. I'll give her a call." He reached into his pocket for his phone and turned away to dial. The doorbell rang. Trace looked at Annie over his phone. "Could you?" he asked, gesturing to the door. "I can't imagine who wouldn't just walk in."

Annie nodded and turned toward the door, making her way past the people who were oblivious to the sound of the doorbell. She opened it to find Grace Leighton, carrying a large basket.

"Reverend Leighton! How nice of you to join us!" Annie embraced the young woman. She tried to take her basket, but Grace kept a firm hold on it.

"Gracious, look at all the people!" she exclaimed. "I knew you folks did this up right but I had no idea! My, my!"

Annie turned and called out to Dorothy. "Dorothy, look who's here!"

"Grace! I'm so glad you came. Of course, you are always invited. But I didn't think you ever accepted."

Grace smiled, setting the basket next to her feet and shrugging off her coat to reveal a pale pink collar under her neat black cashmere sweater. "I thought it was high time I stopped by," she said. "I'm usually exhausted after all the Christmas services, but it seemed the perfect morning…" She looked around the room. Annie saw her catch Trace's eye. She nodded to him. He nodded back but continued his conversation with Barrett.

"Let me get you something to drink," Dorothy said. "Perhaps a glass of wine? Or would you prefer something tamer. Hot tea?"

"Not just now," she demurred. "I can't stay long. I just wanted to share in the day..." Annie saw her hesitate. Then she took Dorothy's hand. "Um, Dorothy, if you could just come this way..."

Annie saw Dorothy's confusion, but she was too polite to resist the minister's request. Grace turned her head to Annie. "You too, Annie."

Grace led them to the center of the great room. She whispered to one of the men seated on the sofa. He immediately stood up and moved off.

"Very nice, thanks so much," Grace said. "Now, Dorothy. If you would just sit here." She gestured to the empty seat. Dorothy looked at her quizzically but did as she was told. Grace turned to Annie. "And Annie, here, if you would." Annie sat in the chair opposite Dorothy.

"I have gifts for each of you," Grace smiled. She produced two small packets. Then she cleared her throat and addressed the guests, most of whom had not even noticed her entrance. "Ladies and gentlemen," she said. She waited for the chattering to die down, and then, as was her custom in church, waited a few more moments as elbows were nudged, and lingering whispers melted into the air.

"I'm here today to present gifts to two lovely ladies," she said. She handed one package to each of the woman who looked at her in astonishment. "Go ahead, open them now," she urged.

Annie looked around for Elliot, but he was nowhere to be seen. She caught the girls' eyes, but they were as bemused as she was. She undid the ribbon and tore off the paper, glancing to make sure Dorothy was doing the same.

"What is it? What is it?" whispered some of the youngsters who peered on tiptoes to see into the packages. Dorothy lifted a sterling silver fox head from the box and held it up for everyone to see.

"It's lovely," she said. "Thank you, Grace."

Annie was examining her ornament too, a twin to Dorothy's. "There's engraving on it," she said. "Can you make it out?"

Dorothy squinted more closely at it. "Oh dear, I think I need my glasses."

"I think it says "Trace and…""

She was interrupted by the opening of a door and the squeal of a small child. Annie heard the Daisy's astonished "oh golly!'

As one, the crowd turned to the door. There stood Sara, resplendent in a sleek gown of white, her arms filled with a bouquet of calla lilies tied with a large red bow. Everyone was silent for a split second, all taking in the astonishing moment. Annie's eyes stung with tears. She looked at Dorothy, whose hand had gone to her chest. Annie stood up and took a place next to her, reaching out to hold her hand. The crowd erupted in shouts and applause. Sara smiled and blushed but held her head high.

Trace stepped forward and smiled down at Sara, resplendent too in his scarlet coat. She untied the large bow, releasing the individual calla lilies. She stooped down and handed each of the young girls clustered around her a flower. "You are all my flower girls," she whispered to them.

Then she called Daisy to her. "And you are my Maid of Honor." Daisy accepted her flower, looking up at her uncle for re-assurance.

Trace kneeled down too and straightened her stock tie. "Ready?" He whispered. Daisy nodded solemnly.

Trace reached out his hand, and Sara accepted it. They walked to the center of the room, pausing to kiss both Dorothy and Annie. Through Annie's tears, she saw that Elliot had entered the back door too, and was snapping away with his camera.

The couple stopped in front of Grace. She smiled and held up her hand to quiet the whispers, shouts and gasps that continued to ripple through the crowd.

"Trace and Sara have come here today," Grace began, looking down at the small leather-bound book she held. She paused and looked around the crowd. "To be with you, their dear friends and family, to share in the joy of a union that…."

Trace interrupted her. "A union that should have happened a long time ago." He gave Sara a humble smile and raised her hand to his lips. Annie's heart skipped a beat.

Grace smiled. "Trace and Sara have been talking with me for a while now," she said. "Many of you may be very surprised to see them here today." She gestured to Sara's gown. "Especially dressed like this."

The crowd laughed appreciatively. "But they decided there was no better place, and no better day, and no better people, than those in this room to share their joy." She nodded to the couple. "Ready?" They nodded in unison.

"Jacob Traxman Grainger Junior," Grace began. "Trace..." she smiled. Annie watched as Trace valiantly attempted to keep his emotions in check, nodding manfully at her as he quickly brushed away the tear that formed in the corner of his eye. "Do you take Sara Katherine Daley to be your lawfully wedded wife..."

The words died away as Annie looked around the room. Emily and Bella were there, holding each other's hands. Elliot was still recording the event, and Annie realized he had known all along. She scanned the faces in the crowd. Was it possible that this was a surprise to them all? She looked at Dorothy. Is this why she had hosted the breakfast? But no, Annie could see that she was as surprised as anyone.

"And so by the power vested in me by the Holy Church and the Commonwealth of Virginia, I now pronounce you man and wife." Grace gave Trace a meaningful look. "You may now kiss the bride."

Applause rang out, along with shouts of congratulations. Trace and Sara were nearly stampeded by well-wishers. The kitchen door swung open and wait staff appeared carrying trays of champagne. A perfect white wedding cake, adorned with a silver horseshoe appeared too, pushed into the room by another waiter. Annie turned to Dorothy. "So you knew!" She exclaimed.

"I had no idea." Dorothy shook her head in wonderment. "The caterers delivered this morning, but the champagne and cake, those must have just arrived." She looked up at Trace and her new daughter-in-law, tears springing fresh to her eyes.

Sara caught Annie's eye. Annie stood and embraced the young woman. "I hope you don't mind," she said. "With my mom and dad gone, I just wanted someone to be with Dorothy for me."

"I am more honored than I can say," Annie said. "You are a beautiful bride."

"Thank you."

Elliot walked up and gave the bride a kiss. "Good pictures?" she asked.

Elliot smiled. "The best. We'll have a heck of an album."

Annie eyed him suspiciously. "You knew?"

Elliot chuckled. "Trace needed a photographer, and someone to confide in. And he wanted to make sure the girls were here."

Sara nodded. "Elliot was the only one who knew. Other than Grace and the caterers, that is. And they were sworn to secrecy."

Annie shook her head. "So you planned this whole thing yourself?"

Sara smiled and looked at her new bridegroom who was busy accepting congratulations from the contingent of Cobie's old cronies. "Nope," she said. "It was all him. He did it all." She tilted her head at Dorothy. "Didn't it seem funny to you that he wanted to host the hunt breakfast?"

Dorothy's mouth gaped open. "He said we should thank everyone for their support this year…. Oh my, I was bamboozled."

Annie laughed. "That was Trace's idea?"

Sara laughed too. "Yep. He suggested the caterer, and then he went and let Lila over there in on the secret. She even sent separate wait staff for the champagne and cake so the others wouldn't spill the beans." Dorothy shook her head in wonder.

"That's quite a boy you have there," Sara continued. "He told me my only job was the dress."

"Where were you this morning?" Annie said in wonderment. "Rebecca hadn't seen you, and got worried when you sent that text. I was suspicious, but I could never have thought of this!"

"Oh gosh, you're right. I have to find her and apologize." She looked around the room but didn't see her assistant. "Trace put me up at the inn overnight. I dropped the girls' horses off here and then went there to chill out. He sent Tracy from the spa to do my nails and everything." She held out her hand and displayed the simple diamond wedding band. "Pretty, isn't it? He picked this out too. It goes with the engagement ring I got all those years ago."

"Oh, sweetheart," Dorothy exclaimed. "I can't believe this. If only Cobie were here...."

Sara squeezed Dorothy's hand. "He is," she said. "I feel it."

Trace walked up and put his arm around Sara's waist. He leaned in for a kiss from his mother. "Have you met my wife?" he teased.

"Oh Trace!" Dorothy threw her arms around him.

"Merry Christmas, Mom," he whispered.

"But why? You could have told me," she protested.

Trace rolled his eyes. "Lindsay has been giving me an earful too," he said. He squeezed Sara's hand. "We wanted to do it our way. We wanted our friends. We wanted the hunt. We wanted the party." He looked down at his wife meaningfully. "But we didn't want the build-up or the gossip. Sara didn't deserve that this time around. I wanted to find a way to give it all to her." He looked around with satisfaction. Music had begun to play.

"Is that a band?" Dorothy looked around, now ready for almost anything.

Trace laughed. "No, mom. I'm not that good. It's just a mixed tape I made." He turned to Sara. "May I have this dance?"

"With pleasure, sir," she curtsied. She paused to hear the opening bars of the song. "Really?" she said.

Trace nodded. "No other song would do," he said, taking her into his arms.

The two started dancing as the strains of "Baby I'm Yours" played. The crowd gradually stepped back, creating a dance floor for them.

Elliot came over and squeezed Annie's hand. "I can't believe you knew," she whispered.

"Sorry," he said smugly. "But I was sworn to secrecy." Emily and Bella came over to join them. Emily leaned on her dad's arm while Bella wrapped her arm around her mom's waist.

"I'm so glad we were here," whispered Emily.

"Sara didn't want you to miss it," Elliot whispered back. "You were the only one outside the club that she was worried about."

"It's perfect," she sighed.

The song ended to the requisite applause. The music continued, now with upbeat tunes to get the party started. Lindsay and John took to the floor, and soon others joined them.

Sara and Trace exited the floor and looked at the empty space quickly filling with dancers. "Never let it be said that foxhunters don't know how to party," she smiled.

"Ready to cut the cake?" Elliot said. "After I get that shot, my official duties are over." He looked over at Annie. "And then we can hit the dance floor too."

"Well, then let's get on with it!" Trace said.

The party continued on into the afternoon. Darkness had fallen in earnest when the last guest finally left.

Emily poured another glass of champagne, tipping the last of the bottle into Sara's glass. "Lucky you don't have to drive," she said to Sara. "Hey, where are you going on your honeymoon anyway?"

Sara looked up at Trace. "I have no idea," she said.

"Seriously?" said Bella. "What did you pack?"

"I didn't. Apparently that's been done for me too."

Trace smiled. "I didn't figure she'd need much."

The girls looked at him, waiting. "Well, where?"

Trace smiled. "Up the hill," he said, gesturing to the backyard.

"What?"

"I think it's a custom, somewhere, for the bride to be accompanied to her bedchamber by her maids."

He looked around at the perplexed faces of the five women. He blushed under their scrutiny. "Well, there should be." He waited again but was met with icy stares. "Tough crowd," he whispered to Elliot.

"You're on your own," he chuckled.

"Okay, come on," he finally said. "I'll show you."

CHAPTER 55

———

Trace produced lanterns from the back porch and handed one to each person. Lindsay joined the group, John having gone home to tuck the sleepy Daisy into bed.

"Where on earth are we going?" Lindsay asked.

"A short hike. Glad you all have boots on. Mom, are your shoes okay?"

"I just slipped on my boots. There's still a little snow on the ground."

Sara paused at the door. "I have these little ballet flats on. I'm not going out there."

"No need," Trace smiled. "You have a ride."

Warrior stood next to the porch, tacked up with a side saddle that Annie had never seen. Trace tipped his head to her. "Sorry I didn't ask you if I could use him. But he was the right color. Elliot said it would be okay."

"Don't be silly," Annie said. "Warrior seems to be destined to perform all ceremonial duties around here."

Trace nodded. He produced a fleecy white blanket from the porch and draped it over Sara's shoulders, then lifted her to the saddle. She was speechless but smiling, now ready for anything.

Trace led the way, leading the horse and his bride through the moonlight on the brilliant white horse. The moon had come out now, lighting their way.

"We're going to Lost Legend," Annie whispered to Elliot. He nodded.

The group proceeded in silence up the hill. Sara, who had the best view, suddenly exclaimed. "Oh!"

Trace stopped and smiled at the sight of the tipi standing on the edge of the darkening horizon, illuminated from inside by lanterns. Outside, a small campfire was already lit. He looked up at her.

"Surprised?"

She clapped her hands. "When did you do this?"

"The last couple of days. Had to hire some guys, I didn't know how it went up exactly." He chuckled. "That's why I couldn't let you hunt today," he told Sara. "I knew you'd figure out a way to go out if I let you, but I couldn't risk you seeing this."

The group stood in awe at the gorgeous tipi. The paintings that decorated it depicted horses and riders hunting across its side.

Dorothy said, "I'd almost forgotten…"

Trace nodded and placed his hand on her shoulder. "I know; it always took my breath away. Glad I found it." He turned to the assembled group. "Ready to see the bridal chamber?"

He led Warrior right to the flap of the tipi. Sara slipped down into his arms. He carried her over the threshold. She squealed in delight when she saw the inside, and the others quickly peeked in to see too.

Trace had placed a four-poster brass bed in the center of the tipi. It was made up with fresh white sheets and a small mountain of down comforters. White sheepskins lined the floor. He had thought of everything, Annie thought, right down to the ice bucket with champagne and a platter of cheese and fresh fruit. A white nightgown and robe lay on Sara's side of the bed.

Emily and Bella peeked in. "Oh my," the girls said in awe.

"Come in, come in," said Trace, clearly proud of his handiwork. "I want you to see it."

Dorothy turned in a circle to take it all in. A patch of starry sky showed through the top of the tipi, and the painted sides flickered in the glow of the lantern light.

Sara sat on the bed, mesmerized by the room.

Emily nodded with satisfaction. "I think you should keep him," she said.

Sara nodded. "I think I will," she said.

"I did good?" Trace asked, fishing for compliments now.

"You did good," she said, kneeling to reach up and give him a kiss.

The small group looked away awkwardly. "Uh, well, I think we should go," Bella said, backing out of the tipi.

"No!" said Sara, jumping to her feet. She looked guiltily at Trace. "Can they stay, just a little longer? I don't want the party to end."

Trace nodded indulgently. "I have plenty of champagne." He turned to open a cooler that was hidden behind a small table. "One more toast? Maybe around the fire?"

Everyone quickly agreed. Elliot carried glasses outside, noting that with so many glasses on hand, Trace had surely planned on this nightcap too.

"I have jeans for you, if you'd like to change," Trace said to Sara.

Sara shook her head. "I don't want to take off my dress…just yet." She smiled at him meaningfully. She pulled the plush blanket tightly around her shoulders. "But maybe a pair of boots?"

Trace nodded and reached down and produced a fluffy pair of Uggs. She sat on the side of the bed, and he kneeled down to slip them on her feet.

They assembled around the fire, which was outfitted with folding chairs and a big log. The moon hung low over the mountain and the stars had come out on full display.

"Here's to Sara and Trace!" Emily said, raising her glass.

"Hear, hear!' Everyone echoed in unison, raising their glasses to toast the couple.

"And here's to a truly remarkable job of wedding planning," Anna said. "I don't think anyone could have done it better. And all in secret too!"

Trace lifted Sara's hand to his lips. "It was all for her. I figured after all these years, I'd better get it right this time." Sara smiled at her new husband.

"Look at that constellation," Bella said, pointing to the northern sky. "It looks like a horse."

Trace followed her finger. "Pegasus," he nodded. He looked to his mom. "Remember the story, mom?"

Dorothy gazed at the collection of stars, seeming lost in thought. Then she remembered herself. "Indeed I do," she said. "It's the story of Lost Legend."

"Lost Legend?" Emily asked eagerly. "You mean, like the hill we're on? There's a story?" She looked eagerly for Dorothy to continue.

"You tell it, Trace."

"Ok, I hope I can do it justice." He took in a deep breath and began. "Well, it seems there was once a mighty warrior...can't remember his name." He looked to his mother.

"Bellerophon," she said.

"That's it, Bellerophon." Trace nodded and continued. "Anyway, seems this warrior was the greatest equestrian of all time. He saw the magnificent horse known as Pegasus, and he wanted that horse more than anything in the world, but it seemed too magnificent a creature for even him to tame."

"So what did he do?" Bella asked, her eyes wide.

Dorothy interjected. "He prayed," she said.

Trace laughed. "That's right," he continued. "He prayed to Athena to help him, and she gave him a golden bridle that allowed him to capture the horse.

"After that, the two of them were inseparable. They spent all their time saving maidens and killing monsters." He paused and looked at the sky again. "But then Bellerophon got too big for his breeches." Trace hesitated here, seeming lost in thought.

All eyes were on him when he spoke again. "See, Bellerophon was quite a rider. Together, there was nothing he and Pegasus couldn't jump, nothing they couldn't hunt." His voice faltered. "He began to think he was invincible." Sara squeezed his hand.

"But sometimes the gods don't take kindly to that kind of success. Zeus got a little pissed off when Bellerophon decided that he and Pegasus would ride all the way to Mount Olympus so that he could take his place among the gods. Some say that Pegasus knew he shouldn't do this and threw him off. Others say that Zeus sent a fly to bite Pegasus."

Trace looked at the assembled faces and held up his hands. "Me, I always thought Pegasus had more sense than to buck someone off over a fly. I think he understood that Bellerophon couldn't handle being a god, and thought he should teach him a lesson." He smiled and pointed back to the stars. "See? Pegasus is upside down. Dumped Bellerophon right off.

"Anyway, you probably know the rest. Pegasus got to Mount Olympus by himself, and now he helps the gods bring in the morning sun." He stopped talking for a moment. Everyone looked at him expectantly.

"But what's the Lost Legend?" Bella said. "That can't be the whole thing."

"Oh yeah," Trace smiled. "Well, you know the story supposedly ends with Pegasus. No one says much of what became of Bellerophon." He chuckled. "Folks figure the farm is named after the horse. In fact, it's his rider who was the inspiration."

Trace stood up and looked at the sky. "Some folks figure he died in the fall. Others say he fell into a thorn bush and ran away, living the rest of his life as a hermit. But according to Daddy, and his daddy too, Bellerophon fell back to earth right here in this meadow."

The girls let out a little gasp.

"Bellerophon had enough sense to know he couldn't get his horse back. So he turned his attention to the horses here on earth. He caught and tamed the horses he found here, and imbued them with a love of freedom, of hunting and of speed. It's he who helps them jump tall fences and race up mountainsides. It's he who teaches riders to be fearless.

And most of all, it is he who makes sure that the riders always get back on their horse, even after a bad fall."

Trace folded his arms and observed the night sky. "Bellerophon married a pretty girl and they settled right here on this land. Every morning, when Pegasus pulled the sun across the sky, there was old Bellerophon up here on the hillside, cheering him on and calling all the horses to the field."

Everyone looked up at the night sky, each lost in thought.

"Anyway," Trace said, finishing his story. "There you have it. The patron saint of Pegasus Farm. A legendary horseman who fell off his horse and crashed to earth."

Sara reached over and put her hand on his arm. He took her hand in his and together they gazed up at the stars.

"The man who landed on his feet," she reminded him with a smile.

CHAPTER 56

———————

ANNIE WAS GLAD TO SAY goodbye to the old year. It seemed that almost every molecule of her being had been transformed over the course of the past several months. Without knowing it, she had examined every part of herself, choosing what to keep and what to discard. The white horse still came to her in dreams now and then, but rather than staring at her from a distance, now they galloped together in perfect synchronicity. After hearing the story of Lost Legend, Annie almost imagined one night that the horse had sprouted wings. But when she woke again, she knew that it was Warrior, and that he would be waiting for her at the barn.

Trace and Sara were busy making plans to expand her school and to establish an advanced jumpers' program with Trace at the helm. For now, they were making an extended honeymoon of the foxhunting season. After the wedding, Trace surprised Sara with a visit to the annual foxhunting weekend at the Low Country Hunt in South Carolina. They spent several days riding at a leisurely place through historic plantations and gorging themselves on roasted oysters and shrimp.

As for Annie, she had never looked forward to winter so much. For her, winter had always been a time to be indoors. Now she found great delight in the wool coats and the chill winds of January. With the coming of winter, the young dog foxes were on the move. This was when foxhunting really came into its own. Young foxes leave their birth homes to search for territory, and mates, to call their own. They enter new ground tentatively, hoping for unclaimed land. Adult foxes will tolerate these interlopers, at least for a short time, before challenging them and chasing them off. With hormones and adrenaline running high, foxes are prepared to run miles to find a new home or defend their own.

The territory around Gladys' place was largely undeveloped, and the meet today hoped for at least one good run. Gray cast the hounds in the direction of the river, and the hounds opened immediately. Soon they were in full cry. The riders galloped to keep pace as the hounds surged through the woods and across the marsh. A few hounds hesitated at the far bank, uncertain, but the older hounds quickly picked up the scent and galloped into the muck and across the ridge line, making a wide arch and cutting tightly back into forest. Gray saw the hounds change course and plunge up the hill and into a thick wall of brush, still hot on the scent.

"I can't follow there," he called to Davis. "I'll take the tree line and catch up with them on the far side." He pressed his horse into a gallop. Monty led the field around too, doubling back to where the hill toppers rode. He held up his hand to Rebecca. Now the whole field stood together on the hillside, giving Gray plenty of room to maneuver when the fox emerged. They watched as the huntsman paused near the marsh, listening to the hounds speak. Annie felt a ripple of anticipation coursed through Warrior. She wasn't sure where to look, so she did what Trace had taught her. Watch her horse. Wherever he is looking, that's where the action would be. Warrior's ears flicked forward and set his gaze on the center of the woods, just past the head of the marsh.

Suddenly, Davis burst from the woods, heading off the fox and keeping him in the open. The pack surged forward as the fox galloped across the full length of the field. Gray's horn sent thrills through Annie's body. Da-dahhhhhhh. Da-dahhhh. Blowing away—the call for the chase to begin. The fox was out of its refuge, and the chase was on. This was the moment they all lived for.

Annie squeezed her legs lightly, and Warrior leapt into action. Annie followed close behind Sara and Deborah, laughing out loud as clods of mud splattered her face. She reached up to wipe off her cheek, regaining her reins just in time to follow Sara over a coop. Annie leaned in and took the jump. The chase continued through the corn field and back into the woods. In high spirits now, the field took jump after jump, thrilling to the cry of the hounds. Suddenly the hounds checked; the line had run cold. Gray pulled up and stood still, waiting to see if the hounds would cast themselves. Annie saw Davis point to the field they had just come from, and she realized that the fox had outsmarted them, stopping and turning while they all followed in hot pursuit of the jumps.

Gray picked up the pack and turned back where they had come from, hoping that the field had not fouled the line completely. Soon, however, the hounds opened on a new line, and the chase was on again. This time the hounds plunged into the woods, singing frantically as they honed in on their target.

Annie wrapped her fingers around Warrior's mane as he galloped up a steep hill, around a sharp bend and back into open field. She saw that the hounds had swarmed around a den. Some sat and bayed mournfully. Others whined and made half-hearted attempts to dig at the entrance. Gray jumped from his horse and blew the sound for gone to ground. Then he praised the hounds lavishly.

Annie leaned in to Warrior, catching her breath and wiping sweat from her brow. In spite of the cold weather, both she and the horse were thoroughly heated. She looked around and realized where they were. Just beyond the ridge sat Pegasus Farm. They had come all the way across the mountain and this was the vixen's den that she and Cobie had visited the previous spring. She wondered if it was the female herself that they had chased. More likely it was the dog fox that owned this territory. Either way, it was safely home after a merry chase.

People who did not understand fox hunting often asked Annie why the fox allowed himself to be chased. Annie honestly wasn't sure what to say to them. The reality was that hiding places were in abundance and a fox could pop into a hole any time he wanted to get away from the hounds. It certainly seemed to her that if the fox ran, it was because it was confident in its own ability to read the scent in the air and to out-smart the pack. Why else would he sit and wait for the pack to draw near, or turn around and backtrack into the line of the hounds?

Was it too much to say that he enjoyed the chase? Annie knew that some would call that wishful thinking. But it was hard to see it any other way.

CHAPTER 57

―――――――

CHILI BUBBLED ON TOP OF the stove as Annie scrambled into her hunting kit. She glanced at her watch, an old-fashioned face style that she wore on her wrist. She had dropped the habit of carrying her IPhone everywhere.

"We're late!" Elliot called, pulling off his stock tie to attempt a smooth knot.

"Leave it! I'll tie it when we get there." Annie poured the hot chili into the crock pot. "We have to drop this off at the house before the hunt." She gave it a quick taste. "I'm determined to win the cook-off this year."

Elliot clamped down the locks on the lid and scooped the pot off the counter. "I'll get this in the car. Come on now."

They rounded the corner near Dennison's Mill to see that most of the trailers had already arrived. Sara's trailer was there with six junior riders. Rebecca, who had graduated in December, was fussing among them, straightening out reins and tightening girths.

Annie saw Sara and Trace pulling their horses from his trailer. Annie knew that Palmer and Warrior were in there too, probably antsy to get out and going.

"Sorry we're late!" Annie jumped out of the car. "Fred called about the exhibit we're putting on at the museum in Richmond, and Dodie needs my calendar for April so she can book some events. I had to heat up the chili I made last night. And I had to place my seed order. It's already almost time to put in peas."

Trace glanced at his watch. "It's only 9:45. You did all that?"

"She's back to her old self," Elliot said, smiling.

"What was that?' Annie called over her shoulder as she pulled Warrior off the trailer.

"Nothing," Elliot said mildly as he accepted Warrior's reins. "I was just saying that…"

"What? Hang on, let me just back Palmer out." By the time Annie came out with the second horse, the three of them were all laughing.

"What's so funny?" She looked from one face to another.

Sara hit Trace's arm. He put his hand over his face to stifle the laugh. "Was she always like this?" he asked.

Elliot raised his eyebrows. "Oh, much worse. This is relaxed Annie."

"That's not true," Annie said, pouting. "I was much more of a control freak…wait!" She grabbed his collar and gave it a tug to smooth it. She stepped back to admire her handiwork. She looked up at Sara, who had already mounted her horse. "Right?"

"Oh, definitely. Right." Sara nodded sincerely.

"By the way," Annie reminded her. "The first board meeting for the scholarship fund is Tuesday night. We're considering candidates."

Sara nodded. "It's on my calendar. I'll be there."

"Have you looked at the applications yet?"

Sara smiled. "Not yet, but I saw your email. Don't worry. I'll be ready by Tuesday." Sara turned back to Trace. "Anyway, as I was saying, when she was actually working for a living, she could multi-task like nobody's business."

"Hey!" Annie yelled, looking over Trace's shoulder. "Isn't that a fox?" She swung onto Warrior and shouted for Gray. "Tally Ho!" she called, lifting her cap from her head and pointing it toward the covert at the base of the hill.

"What the heck?" Gray said, turning.

"She's right," Trace called. "There's a big red sitting right there by that big log waiting for us. Best be off."

Gray quickly called for the hounds and everyone hurried to mount. Monty skipped the announcements, and the field was off and running, the hounds in full cry, horses bounding across the field after the accommodating fox.

As Annie galloped with the field, her cares fell from her shoulders and shattered to the ground beneath the horse's hooves. She was momentarily aware of them slipping, and a part of her brain tried in vain to cling to them. But this sensation lasted for only for a moment. By the first jump, there was no room in her head for anything but the chase. She gave herself to it, body and soul. Like so many foxhunters before her, her heart sang with that of the hounds' voices, and her heart beat to the rhythm of her horse's feet. Away, away, it called. And she followed.

Everything else could wait for tomorrow. And tomorrow, Annie knew, would take care of itself.

The End

ACKNOWLEDGMENTS

THIS BOOK IS THE PRODUCT of many people's knowledge and experience. Although the characters are fictitious, many real people in the Charlottesville community contributed to it by sharing the spirit of the hunt, the deep-seated love of the hounds, and the dedication to the land that are reflected in these pages. Many thanks for the stories provided by members of the Keswick Hunt Club and their intrepid huntsman Tony Gammell. Although the salesperson at the Horse Country store is fictional, the beautiful shop in Warrenton, Virginia, is in fact very real and very much worth a visit.

My team of advance readers provided invaluable insight and helpful critique. Cissie Meehan, Roberta Jalbert, Marcie Siegel, Laurel Moore and Patty Ames each generously provided unique and useful perspectives. And of course, my thanks to The Anonymous Foxhunter—you know who you are.

Special thanks to my daughter Jennifer Lovejoy for encouraging me to get back in the saddle, and sharing the joy I felt in the telling of the story. I would not have been able to write this book without the support of my wonderful husband Jim Rowinski, who gave me the space and the freedom to create it. In spite of all this support, if there are errors in these pages, they are mine, and mine alone.

My ever-lasting gratitude goes to Hannah and Ben May. Without your joyous love and your clever planning, Trace and Sara might not have had their happy ending.

ABOUT THE AUTHOR

KATE ANDRUS IS THE SUCCESSFUL author of several books about nature and the outdoors. Her books' topics include cooking, photography, fishing, and bird watching. Kate's knowledge and love of nature shine throughout her vivid descriptions in *Sky Horse.*

Kate currently resides in Charlottesville, Virginia, with her husband, Jim, and their many animals.

To learn more, visit www.kateandrus.com or write to her at kate@kateandrus.com.

www.ingramcontent.com/pod-product-compliance
Lightning Source LLC
Chambersburg PA
CBHW070653180626
46817CB00006B/2354